IMAGINE WAGONS
CARAVAN OF BLADES
VOLUME ONE

by JP Weaver

Riverfolk Books

Imagine Wagons: Caravan of Blades Volume One

©2024 JP Weaver

All rights reserved

Cover Artwork by Dino

First published in 2025 by Riverfolk Books.
First Edition

Riverfolk Books
http://riverfolkbooks.com

This novel is a work of fiction. The names, characters and incidents portrayed in it are the work of the author's imagination. Any resemblance to actual events, locations, or persons, living or dead is purely coincidental.

For all the baby eggs. May you never have to face a zombie apocalypse alone.

PROLOGUE

It was a perfect day for meditation when the silent retreat ended.

A cool, crisp breeze rolled in over the participants as the afternoon sun warmed them up. For thirteen days, the distinctive taste of the salt mountain had been a constant presence for all involved.

A mix of people all sat together in calm silence for the entire time, attended to by the dwarven clan that sponsored the event. It was made to be something that brought all of the races together.

Finley, the traveling wood elf trader, had used it as an excuse to reset himself after two years of traversing the four kingdoms. Tall and thin, his wood elf heritage made his skin slightly green hued. He felt eyes following him as he returned outside to the storage area where everyone had changed. They had spent most of their time in fellowship in that courtyard. The garish garb conflicted with his skin tone as he swapped the tan robes of the faithful of Yil for his tinker clothes.

Reds, purples, and pastel colors joined ribbons that were meant to catch the eye of an observer and then keep it. He wrestled with his belt as the few dozen who had attended the event with him got their own clothing on. It wasn't hard for Finley to see the stares, but as usual, he ignored them. While he had been in the silent retreat, the Yil-aligned dwarven clan had been hard at work on his caravan and he was ready to see the result.

"Heading anywhere good, Tinker?" a weak voice spoke.

The speaker, a dwarf, was still in his robes. Finley nodded to the dwarf, clearing his own throat.

"Back to the Irumian Kingdom, I imagine," he replied, his voice low. Neither of them had spoken for any reason for their entire time; Finley had expected the dwarf's voice to be a bit deeper, but his salt-and-pepper hair looked to be more of a stylistic choice than a product of aging.

"Ah. Perhaps I might send a package to one of my cousins there. Would you have space in your caravan?"

Finley took a moment to take stock of the current situation. He shifted into his tried-and-true customer service persona. Then he pushed on his storage skill to see exactly how much he could store. There was room in the back somewhere. That skill that he got from his tinker job was paying dividends.

"I absolutely have the space. And since you helped during the retreat, this one is on the house. Of course, if you want to sell me anything else, I had my eye on some of the salt here. I would give you the family price."

"Ah, you tinkers and your family. As a matter of fact, I might just take you up on that. There's a lot more food here that we made for the other races, but it was mostly dwarves for this retreat so..."

"You salted any of the meat and kept the rest cold?"

"It's why we keep a cryomancer on staff."

"I'll be just down by the Yil's Mount stables checking my pack horses. Bring whatever you have to sell down there and I'll sort it out."

The dwarf nodded and then turned on his heels and moved back towards the common area and the kitchens.

Finley stretched his jaw. It had been quite some time since he had talked to anyone. He grabbed his water skin and drained it before filling up. There would be time before he checked everything, and he wasn't in any rush. Before long, Finley was walking down from the assembly area towards the little village that housed the families that ran the retreat. The dwarven huts all had a combination of stone masonry and thatched roofs. That gave them a uniform look and a generally planned aesthetic.

In the center of the town on the south side was the Yil's Mount tavern. Several dwarves and gnomes fussed over animals in the stables. Finley went directly to his two bay mares, the large beasts stirring at his touch. He rubbed the two animals down, tapping into his druidic animal handling skills.

They were instantly alert and ready to go, having spent the time in the small pasture that fed all of the goats and cows that the dwarves kept. He checked their coats and their hooves, going over each beast thoroughly. A dwarf attendant dropped off two water buckets for them. The only problem with the elevation was that there were not enough lakes and streams, making water less available. Finley would run out, but he could fill up when he reached the lower lands at around midday. All of his travels through the four kingdoms were never too far from a place where he could bring his horses to drink.

A gnome with a riding crop and coveralls approached Finley.

"Ah Master Tinker, what a good morning. Your horses have both been such wonderful tenants. They are always welcome whenever you wish to return," the gnome in charge of the stables said, "and the lacquered paint has been redone on your caravan, none too soon. We replaced one wheel that was set to go within the short term and your whole fee for everything is ten gold pieces. Let me check my records; it says here that you've paid in advance?"

"A tinker is nothing without his wagon or horses."

"Or family," the gnome said. "Shame that I cannae join you. But I—"

Finley clasped his arm. The gnome clasped back.

"Family forever. No matter if we stop for good."

"Tis good to hear, lad."

The gnome choked up, taking one look at the wagon and then attending to other matters.

His standard tinker wagon had badly needed repairs. With a potential war on the horizon, Finley had done the prudent thing and found a place to lay low and do repairs. He had been happy to find a tavern bearing the marks of the family—one that a tinker would always recognize.

When he asked if they could fix his wagon, he hadn't expected much. They had far exceeded his expectations. It was the standard tinker covered wagon, but it had badly needed someone to look at its axles.

Finley checked the doors on the back. They had even changed one of the hinges that had been a problem. He was a bit light on goods now since he had intended to unload a lot on his way, but the ratio of gold pieces to saleable merchandise had been off-kilter towards the working capital side for his entire trip to the mountains. Not that he minded, as he could fend for himself, but it was difficult to eat gold pieces, if not impossible.

"They got the rear door to stop squeaking when opened?" he muttered to himself.

He then checked the wheels. The proper tinker procedure was to kick them once and see if they moved. His were solid. The replacement wheel was painted the same color as the other ones.

The rear right corner of the wagon held the secret markings that gave other tinkers notice. They had, of course, not disturbed it. He felt the sides over with his hands, making sure that all the runes were in place. When he touched them, they sang to his inner spirit.

Only family could hear that sound. Only family could make more family. When you heard the noise, you knew that wherever you were, it was home.

With the wheels done, he inspected the undercarriage. All of his axles looked in order. On the front of the caravan, his seat had been freshly lacquered. The wood looked like it had just been done up but he knew better. That was an effect made by a master artisan. He had seen the kind of effect before, and even sold a few masterwork pieces. They all came with certificates of validity and a story.

Sometimes you only had the story to go off. They still sold. High-end knick-knacks were the candy of the cousins of royalty and members of the court.

Finley had played the role of candy man more than once. He briefly considered tracking down whoever had done that particular portion and seeing if they had anything that he could buy. He started to spin up a story in his mind of a dwarven outcast who had left to seek redemption up in the Yil Foothills. The dwarf would then have lots of drama surrounding leaving a dwarf hold that had supported him into becoming a master worker, and then as is custom, he would have left to seek his fortune. There would also be a bit there about how he turned down a princess, after something valorous happened. Finley was confident that he could workshop that piece on his long ride.

The dwarf from the retreat showed up when he was done working with his axles. He had brought two wheelbarrows and an assistant. Both dwarves sat down to watch as Finley inspected the contents of the first wheelbarrow.

"This is the package for my cousin. You'll see his address right there. I greatly appreciate the assist. I brought some other goods that I think you might be able to sell down there. Salt, salted meats, an ice block that my cryomancer swears will last for at least two weeks. That part is on the house, mind you, because I've also brought some deer and goat that you should be able to pass off as well. We had a good season as of recently, and since we haven't had a lot of guests, we're fully stocked. Honestly, you're helping us out a bit here just by taking this off our hands. We really expected more people in the tourist season, but it's been quiet."

"I'll buy the lot of it."

Finley inspected the two wheelbarrows that have been brought down. All the meat looked good, and the salt, though heavy, would not spoil. There was enough meat there to last Finley six to ten months on his own.

"Do you need any help loading up, elf?"

"No, just unload there and I'll have at it. Thirty gold pieces good for the lot?"

"How about thirty-five? Since you're already loading it up and all."

"Everybody wants the discount. Thirty-two?"

"You've got a deal."

Finley pulled out his purse and began counting coins. He was hoping to get a rank up for his tinker job sometime soon, but this wasn't enough to cover it. It was so close that he could almost touch it.

They quickly and methodically put everything into the back of the caravan. The dwarf and his assistant placed everything in neat piles. Finley checked that the piles wouldn't collapse under normal wear, then checked that they were there in his storage skill. He could see all the items there. Everything seemed to be in order.

"Thank you for your business. I appreciate it."

"This gold will go a long way towards helping the upkeep of the retreat."

The two clasped hands, the taller, lanky elf having to reach down to do so.

"May you find safety upon your route," the dwarf said.

"May you find happiness in your time," Finley replied.

Once again Finley found himself alone. He pulled himself into the driver's seat and found it to be as comfortable as he had expected. His elvish throw pillow was underneath the bench that made up his seat. He packed some water and unloaded all of his personal effects save his coin purse into the ornate storage unit.

He grabbed the harnesses for the horses and went over them, looking for any problem areas. Then he turned them around and grabbed the first of his two horses.

The first mare accepted the harness readily and he walked the horse over to hook her up. The harness attached to her chest and looped up and around. The network of straps connecting the horse with its many buckles of loops and lines fit the mare perfectly and he took care in its placement. Then he grabbed the second mare and did the same.

"Ready, girls?" he said, upon connecting the last loop.

Both horses snorted approval. The caravan was out of the stables, his repairs were paid for, and he was ready to go.

With a gentle pull on the reins, he spurred the mares into movement, steering them towards the gently sloping downhill that led out of town.

The dwarves and gnomes in the village waved as he passed them, his horses going at a steady clip. With the downward slope he would be able to move a lot faster towards the dwarven kingdom.

The retreat leader's words sounded in his head. *Let this small moment of peace ripple forward in your life.*

***

Five hours after he had left the town, it became one of the final outposts of the enlightened to be taken by the zombie horde.

1

A voice flitted through Finley's head.

"You have been granted the title Tinker King. Your tinker card has upgraded to epic rarity."

Finley continued down the road. The messages from his soul deck were a distraction at best. It wasn't that he didn't care. It was just that he hadn't been on the road in so long. He wanted to savor the ride.

Staying put felt odd to him.

But this? The open road? This was familiar. This was home.

It kept him from checking his deck at least. What kind of message was that?

It was a bit quieter than he thought it would be, but it would probably pick up. He hadn't seen hide nor hair of any travelers approaching the mountains, but he had left early in the morning and the closest village was a day's travel away.

He breathed in and then checked his active deck. He always kept two cards in. He had to. Those two had bonded to his spirit and his body for so long that to take them out would mean death. Other cards he swapped around as needed.

Epic Class Card: Tinker Level 3

Skills:

Appraisal Level 3

Identify Level 3

Animal Handling Level 3

Storage Level 3

King Level 1

As the last remaining Tinker, you have the ability to induct new people into the family.

This is a soul card and cannot be removed.

Rare Class Card: Spore Druid Level 5

Skills:

Wild Shape Level 2

Plant and Fungal Control Level 5

Elemental Magic Level 1

Survival Level 4

Medicine Level 3

This card grants mana.

As a spore druid you have enhanced control over plants and fungi.

This is a soul card and cannot be removed.

His tinker card showed the classic design of a tinker's covered wagon camping. With the upgrade to Tinker King a little crown now adorned the wagon. He was confused by the message as he didn't understand the prompt. The card displayed in front of him showed a three-dimensional representation of the actual magical artifact inside of his body.

Getting an epic card was a dream come true as those were quite few and far between. How his tinker card had upgraded, and the message, were troubling but there was nothing that we could do about it.

What did it mean that he was the last remaining?

For him to receive the Tinker King title meant that every other suitable tinker had to have died. That was a chilling number of deaths if the last tinker summit was correct on the census of living tinkers.

He couldn't… it was too much to think about.

The title passed on between members of the family through some arcane method that had never been adequately explained to him. That it wasn't his original soul card made him even more concerned.

If his whole family was dead, then—he couldn't even fathom it. He needed some time to process that. It couldn't be true. The change had to be a lie.

He had traded several of his cards recently and realized that he only had a few in his stock that were all common or uncommon skills or abilities. He had plenty of card pieces that he could use to make a new card if he wanted to spend the five minutes to make another, but he didn't feel the need. With forty-two pieces he could make up to six or seven common or uncommon cards, or perhaps a rare if he spent some mana.

His druid powers would defend him, and he didn't fear anything wild. The mares trotted on as he stewed in his thoughts, desperate to think about anything else for the moment.

He began to count trees. One, two three… he kept it up until he got to one hundred and then the thoughts returned.

There was nothing to it, except to continue.

Two hours after he departed, he decided that it would be time to stretch his legs. The pine forests had continued unerringly, a slap in the face as he tried to not think about anything.

Down the road, a shape emerged, walking along the side of the road.

A stout human with a beard and a top knot was walking down the cleared path. When they saw each other, he gave the normal wave.

Having not spoken to anyone by choice for days, Finley relished the opportunity to talk to someone and perhaps take on a passenger for the price of his fare.

He slowed. Any excuse to not think about his problems would work.

"Whoa there, human, you are far from home and hearth stone. Are you headed to the Irumian Kingdom on foot? You're three days by riding away."

The man held up a hand, his expression uncertain. Finley reminded himself that humans were a generally fast-talking bunch that lived on a timescale that elves didn't understand.

"Irumian? I'm sorry, are you an elf?"

The cleared dirt road between the pine trees was as good a space to stop as any. Finley bade his mares to slow down further. He pulled next to the human.

Seeing a human so far into dwarven lands was odd on its own. Seeing one so far from a town was a shock.

"I am, indeed, good sir. Tree elf and tinker by trade at your service. Should you need rations or a ride to the city, all can be bought for a price."

"Ah you see. I don't have any money on me."

The hair on Finley's neck stood up.

Finley immediately suspected a trap and looked around for a pack of hiding bandits. He called upon his natural affinity skills to search the trees and grass for intruders but found none.

All this happened in a short time while he kept his eyes locked on the man.

"No money? How did you end up here, then?"

"I'm not actually sure. I was doing a case report on my latest patient and suddenly, a goddess yanked me into wherever here is and gave me this magical card and asked me to kill some zombies? Does that sound familiar?"

Finley gave the man—the lunatic—a moment to compose himself. He had to be lying. "What city are you from?"

"Brooklyn?"

The man seemed uncertain. Finley wavered. Something told him to move on, but a bigger part of him wanted to see if it could be true.

"She said I was chosen," the man said flatly. "Honestly, where the fuck am I? I have a delivery scheduled for tomorrow and… I'm not going to make it am I?"

Finley considered the words carefully. "It's doubtful."

The man looked down, dejected. Finley took in his clothing, a rich blue textile that had the finest stitching he had ever seen.

A strange man in a strange place? He could be a chosen. Was he?

"When the world needs heroes, sometimes the gods summon a hero to do the job. Usually, they summon one or two. I know several stories about those types of events. I don't run a charity though, so I presume she gave you a class card of some kind?" he said.

The man wavered. His odd clothes with their somber blue color looked regal.

"This is normal? I guess that makes sense. She gave me a choice and I picked the cleric of Yil class. Do you know anything about it?"

"It's got several skills on it?"

"Yes?"

Finley sighed audibly. If he was a chosen, he couldn't afford to leave the man to his own devices. His indecision warred with his need to make a quick copper.

"A tinker can't turn down a hero. Get on. Next to me here," he said, patting the bench, "And tell me all about exactly what she said to you. If a god is going to show up with a hero on my doorstep this must be a good story for me to tell the family. I'm Finley."

"Anthony."

He placed a hand on the man's arm and levered him up.

"Welcome to my wagon."

Finley spurred the horses onwards. Anthony sat down next to him.

"Where are we going?" Anthony asked.

"I'm heading to the capital. It'll be a while though. We'll be able to find a spot for you soon. You said that you're a cleric of Yil?"

"The card said Cleric."

"Why did you pick that? That's a rare skill but…"

Anthony shrugged. "So back in Brooklyn where I was a midwife with my son, I delivered babies for mothers."

"Human mothers?"

"Yes. There were no other enlightened races there so…anyway we had a catchy name. Father and Son Midwives. You wouldn't think of a man as a midwife, but I am a nurturer. Had to go back to school to get my master's degree in midwifery, that was a trip but worth it. There's just something about helping deliver life into the world. Plus, babies are cute."

"I imagine they are," Finley said. He didn't really have an opinion on human babies.

"Not a fan?"

"Not particularly." Finley chewed on that for a bit.

The evergreen pines were thinning out. Finley saw someone in a woodsman's outfit walking down the road. The man was shambling ahead of them, facing away.

"He looks like the walking dead; I should try to heal him," Anthony said.

Finley held up a hand. The two bay mares whinnied giving off a sense that they wanted to be anywhere but here. "Something is wrong. This might be a bandit attack. Stay vigilant."

"Oh crap," Anthony said, "I never even got a weapon."

"There's a club. On your left." Finley cringed at how the man was holding the weapon. It was like he had never held anything like it. And he was supposed to be a chosen hero? "Anthony you're brandishing the club all wrong. Two hands. Strong hand on top. I'm going to try to steer wide. Hold on."

"To what?"

Finley moved the reins pushing his horses to go right around the shambling man. On his left, the man began to turn. His skin looked off, but not far from what Finley considered the normal hues for humans.

"Those eyes," Anthony hissed. "That's not human."

"If you have any offensive spells, this is the time to use them," Finley said, his voice cracking, "Yah!"

He let his animal handling skill take the forefront as he spurred the beasts into motion. The trot became a fast gallop as the man lunged towards them.

"Take this!" Anthony said, whipping the club at the man's head.

The club and the man both went down, much to Finley's consternation. That had been a nice club and he wasn't likely to turn around for a lost item. He gripped the reins harder.

The caravan passed the man, picking up speed as the horses drew themselves towards the center of the road.

"Head through the wagon—don't touch anything—and see if you can get a shot at him," Finley yelled over the sound of the hooves.

"Got it! Shit shit shit…"

Anthony clambered back through the neatly stacked rows of general goods before opening the flap that led to the back.

"Finley! He's running after us!"

The hair on the back of Finley's neck stood straight up again. "What do you mean, he's running after us? YAH!" Finley pushed the horses, mentally wishing for them to head forward.

"I mean—HE IS RUNNING AFTER US!"

"SO, USE A SPELL, HERO!"

"I'M TRYING! Holy bolt!"

The already bright day turned to half shadow, half blindingly bright as Anthony's spell rocked the path. Both bay mares whinnied but continued.

"Holy fuck that worked!"

Finley waited a tense five seconds before turning to look through the caravan. Anthony was standing there, blinking as he turned away from the light. It had died down by that point. Finley suspected that the aftereffects were going to last far longer than intended.

That a chosen started with a strong class card when the gods called them up was a boon that couldn't be denied. Finley felt a twinge of jealousy, before a hand touched his shoulder.

Anthony's head dipped out as he too looked towards the crater they had left in their wake.

"That was a little bit much don't you think?"

"Now I can't see anything. Did I get him?"

A puff of smoke from the blast obscured their view.

"I can't tell from here."

"Well, I can't see," Anthony said. "That was intense."

Finley turned his head to look at the road. Whatever was behind him wouldn't immediately kill them. What was in front of him, could. "There's more of them!"

Four more men shambled along the pines, limping like they had broken ankles. The telltale sign of a drunken student or toddler, Finley found out at that moment, also applied to zombies.

The human was still covering his eyes.

"I hope you have some mana left!"

"What?" Anthony said.

"Try to heal your eyes! There's more of them!" Holy light seeped out of the caravan as Anthony cast something. Finley hoped that it was a heal spell, but he had known humans to be a bit stupid.

Humans were the only enlightened race that were not born with a card in their core. As such they had to acquire or make their own.

This made them a hungry enemy, but nothing near the rapidly approaching zombies.

"This is insane. I'm going to die here," he whispered.

"Oh, come on. It's not all bad. Those four are out of our path on the road. They probably won't get in…"

The lead zombie lunged, stepping into a run.

"Shit!" Anthony's head ducked back into the caravan.

"Oh no you don't, you come back here with your healing spells!"

The three behind it were still behind the tree line as the lead zombie went to intercept the horses. Finley wondered if his mares tasted good briefly before tugging on the reins to alter their course. Horse meat wouldn't taste right no matter what he did to it.

The road which had been clear-cut to be wide enough for three horse-drawn wagons at a time, wasn't big enough for the two of them.

Finley sighed and began casting a spell to entangle the zombie. Mushrooms grew rapidly in front of it to trip the monster. Then the fungi held onto it, not letting it move forward. It fell, still ahead of them. The horses ran straight over the body and a loud crack sounded.

They passed by the other three, who had finally broken through the trees. Finley stole a glance behind him to see Anthony retching out of the back of the caravan. At least he had the decency to relieve his stomach pressure outside of his method of conveyance.

If there was one thing that Finley detested, it was an unclean caravan. It made him itch.

"Uh, Finley? Problem."

"Yes?"

"Do people usually rise up after their bodies have been crushed by a horse and cart in your world?"

"Not really. Why?"

"Also do you remember the first guy I hit with my magic?"

"That guy I remember."

Finley snuck a look back after making sure that the road was clear ahead. Four undead men were running after them. A fifth that was missing a third of his torso was behind them.

"Shit."

"Shit."

"Hold the reins," Finley said, pulling the man out to take his place.

Finley pulled on his mana reserves to grow a wall of vines behind the caravan. He focused on a spot that was moving and… there.

A four-foot-tall plant wall popped up, growing with incredible speed. It wouldn't last long. He just needed to slow them down so they could make their escape.

The zombies slammed into the wall as it entangled them, pulling their bodies to the ground. It wouldn't kill them, just incapacitate them for long enough that they would be out of range.

Finley slumped in the back of the caravan. He hadn't even had the time to give the stranger instructions on how to handle the horses, though the man seemed to be doing just fine.

He counted to three and then made his way back to the front. If the human couldn't see, then he was probably driving blind, and they were too far from the next town to have a breakdown.

Anthony was still breathing heavily when he arrived. Finley almost reached for his animal handling skill to calm the man before realizing it wouldn't do nearly as much as he wanted it to do. Or really anything; unless the man saw himself as an animal it wouldn't work. That was a question that he hadn't gotten around to asking in the half hour they had known each other.

"I'll take it from here, human," he said, slipping back into his comfortable seat.

"Yeah. Please do."

2

Finley flexed his storage power, trying to push it to the limit. It was about all he could do to keep from thinking about how such a brazen monster attack could occur on well-traveled lands inside of the dwarven kingdom.

The Irumian guard was well known for being fastidious about their work to a fault. On his way to the Yilish mountains, Finley had seen patrols nearly twice a day.

It all depended on how close they had been to the local towns. Many of the roads he traveled were next to a rail line with the Yilish line being under construction due to its far away nature.

They would see it at the end of the day when they reached the first town at the pace they kept. Finley had been spending all his energy looking for more zombies, who though rare, were known to not harm a tinker.

It was well known that tinkers weren't violent so long as people obeyed their customs and courtesies. It had been one of the reasons that Finley had joined the family. You see, the tinkers accepted not just the enlightened races into their family, but any monsters that swore an oath of nonviolence against all tinkers. There was a second path that many tinkers took to be nonviolent against all, but that was a step too far for Finley.

His upbringing made him uncomfortable around strangers and made it hard to trust anyone. That they had grown to trust him was a point of pride for the spore druid.

"We're about an hour's ride from the next village. If you hadn't been summoned exactly where I had been, you probably would have died out there. As is, I can probably hand you off to the local government there to aid you in your quest or you can pay for your passage further by helping me with those kinds of incidents," he said. "What do you say?"

Anthony stared out into the distance. He was still in shock. Was it the new world? Was it the summoning? Either way, he looked like he wasn't going to protest.

"You don't have to talk now. Monsters here—I've heard that heroes sometimes come from lands where there are no such things. I couldn't imagine it."

Anthony continued his vacant stare. Finley activated his animal handling skill to check on his animals. They felt fresh still. Good enough to trot all the way till nightfall.

They went on that way for a long time as the evergreen forests finally gave way to rolling hills. The breadbasket of the kingdom, field after field of grain provided food for the millions that lived in the kingdom. The first farmhouses started up, those still a long walk from the center of the next town.

Normally, Finley would feel safer, but today he felt nothing upon passing the dividing line between all forest and mostly farmland.

"I expected to find another traveler but today must be cursed. Found myself a hero and now—oh wait what is that?"

Up ahead, a plume of smoke carried up from close enough to the road that it was concerning. Then as they approached Finley draw upon his natural affinity to try and see if the plants could tell him anything that his eyes could not. A wagon loaded down with what looked like it had been a bale of hay was on its side. His natural affinity told him that aside from the surprising wagon, nothing was out of place.

Except for the suspicious lack of farmhands in the fields.

This put him even more on edge, as he looked for pack animals. The direction of travel had been the same as his and the cart. Any horses would have been on the far side, if they were still tied up.

Then, he felt it.

The wheat was all crushed under something the size of a horse. Seeing no one moving, Finley decided to risk it and rolled to a stop. It would be a good distance away. Now he just needed Anthony to watch his back.

"Watch my back. I'm checking this out," he said. "There might be someone there."

Anthony nodded, taking a few deep breaths.

Finley slowly dismounted and approached the cart. If the rider had been thrown off, he would be able to see it. He could see the legs of the horse, still and unmoving. Whatever had tipped it over could still be there. That might have been the horse. Giant claw marks along the side of the horse indicated the reason that it had bled out on the side of the road.

Finley searched for a rider.

He came up on the side of the cart next to the horse. It was clearly dead but hadn't been for long. The cart was clearly just for hauling grain over short distances. There were no side compartments or secondary storage anywhere.

The grey body of a dwarf was stuck halfway under the horse. The eyes were vacant as dead arms reached out away from him. Even in his death, the dwarf looked strong.

When he got to within a short distance of the dead dwarf, it started moving. Its arms reached out for him and were it not for being trapped underneath a horse he might have been in danger. He narrowly missed being grabbed as he stepped backwards. His ankle flared up, nearly rolling on an unexpected lump. That lump that just happened to be a severed leg.

Finley jumped back in alarm as the dwarf swung its arms at him ineffectually. Then he realized that he could become the zombie dwarf's next meal. He ran back to the wagon at a slow jog. It was time to see if the hero was able to earn his passage.

"Hey! Anthony! I'm going to need your help. Earn your keep. Can you help me kill this zombie I found?"

Anthony nodded.

"Just use a weaker version of your spell while it's pinned down. Don't hit the horse."

"I can do that," he said weakly.

Humans were not Finley's forte or even his flavor of the week but even he thought that Anthony looked a bit pale.

"Why should I do that?" Anthony asked.

"For the card pieces?"

"Oh right. Uh what are those?"

"I'll explain in a minute. Just kill it, please. Aim for the head."

"Uh, okay."

Anthony walked around the horse, blanched and then cast his spell. A bright light where his holy light appeared flashed and then disappeared just as quick.

A bright golden light flashed over the corpse of the zombie.

"This may be a bit gruesome. I need to tend to this briefly," Finley said. The elf took out a long sharp knife and began to cut into the corpse.

"Hey! What the hell are you doing?" Anthony said.

"I'm getting… this."

Three inches into the chest of the corpse, Finley stuck a now bloody hand in. He pulled out a card and several square pieces. Each had a dull golden glow.

"So, uh what is going on?" Anthony said. "Is that what I think it is?"

Finley nodded, plucking the card up and then placing it in his hand. He turned the card over and examined it, getting a bit of blood on his hand.

Finley would have to show the man how to put a card into his body later. Then Finley grabbed the fragments off the corpse and slowly walked backwards.

Finley attempted to commune with his patron deity, dropping to his knees. He closed his eyes, reaching out for the familiar warmth of his goatish self. Then he tapped into his natural affinity, pulling nutrients from the dense farmland around to grow a circle of yellow flowers around the horse's body.

"In his name—" Finley bleated.

"I'm not even going to ask about that," Anthony said, settling beside him, "and this is a card? Like the one I have in my soul?"

"It's how we harness magic here. May I see the fragments?"

"Here," Anthony said, dumping the fragments unceremoniously into the waiting hands.

The little pieces appeared like glass. The fragments gave off a bit of natural shine as he held them out.

"Five fragments. That's nearly enough for a card. And they're all rare. This is quite curious. You may be truly blessed by the gods however cruel they must have been to send you here."

"Fragments? As in I can make a card with these?"

"I have another rare fragment somewhere in my caravan," Finley said, feeling the space with his storage skill. "Once we make camp for the night, I can help you forge a card."

"You know what, I was about to say that I'm too old for this shit, but then you go and slice up a corpse," Anthony said. "The card I have has helped so much, but this?"

"It's the only way to get a card out of someone's soul deck. How old are you, then?"

"I'm…old enough to have adult sons," Anthony said. "Fuck. My boys. They're not going to know about this. I cannot imagine the— hold on, what's that?"

Anthony pointed down the road back towards where they had come. One of the first farmhouses that they had passed stood out against the rolling fields of grains and grasses. Had it been the first? Finley hadn't remembered a second one yet.

Anthony wasn't pointing to that, however. His gaze was locked on a group of about five stout figures who were walking with a now-familiar gait.

Finley shook the man by the shoulder.

Whatever was in the field advanced upon them.

"Into the caravan, hero. I said, into the caravan hero!"

Finley nearly had to pull the man onto the seat as he gave the horses the command to stop eating grains and to start to move.

Every step that the horses took away from whatever was happening in the fields would be another step closer to safety.

Every minute they stayed was another minute that they could end up as a zombie's next meal.

"What the hell is going on?" Anthony said once the horses finally agreed to move.

"Whatever is happening, keeps happening. If I didn't know better, I would say that we're being tracked or followed."

He stole a glance behind himself to see the shapes moving towards the road.

"I can't believe that I left my son and wife back home and came here to this. I would throw up more, but I don't have any food left," Anthony said, leaning back against the caravan.

Finley concentrated on pushing the bay mares to a trot. All he wanted to see was horsepower.

"I purchased some jerky today from the dwarves," Finley said. "Hold on to the reins and I'll grab you something to eat. I have water too."

"Thanks," Anthony said, switching seats with him. "You're quite kind for an elf who just had me kill an undead monster."

"You've got to level your class skills otherwise you won't make it far here fighting monsters."

"Oh? How do I do that?"

"You probably kill monsters. Look I have a merchant class and a druid class, I'm not a card expert."

The sounds of the mares' hooves trotting were a loud respite for their talk.

"Who was it that you prayed to back there? For a moment it felt like I was a kid back in mass. Back before I was a midwife with a packed schedule. Back before the back pain and the hernia… hey are you listening?"

Finley wasn't listening. The stress had made him hungry, and he had packed a good number of snacks. He slipped a hand into his secret storage compartment.

A green tinged forearm held out a thin salted cut of meat, offering it to the human.

"It will have to do," Finley said. "I can teach you about the Goat Lord later. Right now, I'm worried about our safety."

Finley looked out the back. The undead hadn't stopped running in their direction and the open road let him see far up the slow slope. They weren't the only group behind the caravan.

Another group of five followed along behind them.

Finley needed a good trip over a bridge where they could all fall to a glorious death. Not him of course, as he valued his new life, and not Anthony, but the growing mass behind them. It would be nice to burn a bridge or two so long as they were behind him.

He considered if making another wall with the grain around them would be beneficial. Their pursuers seemed to have a single-minded interest in them and probably wouldn't be deterred for long. What he didn't know was what kind of card the man had received.

"Hey, hero, what was the card you got from killing the zombie?"

Anthony held the card up.

Finley squinted. It did look familiar. He should probably have asked more questions, unfortunately they kept getting interrupted.

The silvered design of the card displayed an axe. It was either a class card for a lumberjack or an axe skill. Either way he couldn't see much worth in it. Unless it was a woodworking skill, then he could really use it.

"Alright I would normally not attempt to form a card in a moving caravan, but do you consent to—"

"Will it increase my chances of not dying on my first day here?"

"Yes—"

"Then do it."

Finley grunted. He had expected that type of answer. When forging a card, the situation one was in affected the card produced. All he could think of was that he would need some of his tools to complete the job.

He grabbed his slate and then pulled out his bag of card fragments.

Dozens of common and uncommon fragments in a uniform size filled a small bag. He'd been saving them for a rainy day or a day like today.

First was the slate. He placed five of the rare fragments from the human together. Then he placed the last fragment that he found at the bottom of his common and uncommon pieces. The slate was designed to house exactly six pieces.

When creating a card, he joined six pieces of the same rarity together: common, uncommon, or rare. He'd never seen an epic or higher piece.

Cards with a higher rarity like epic level cards and higher could only be found by taking them from others' soul decks, or by merging cards of lower level. Merging lower-level cards in a set of five created a class card, so long as the abilities worked together.

Upon placement of all six of the pieces, the slate began to glow and then the pieces turned into one card the size of his palm.

In a flash of light, a new card appeared. "Excellent," Finley said.

3

"What does it do?" Finley said.

Anthony examined the card.

Rare Skill Card: Refresh

The user of this card can push someone far beyond their limit. People can run farther and longer. Animals feel rejuvenated. Effect lasts for four hours. There is a corresponding time period after where subjects of the ability will be at reduced endurance.

Cooldown: Thirty Minutes

"This is the kind of card that is going to keep us alive," Finley said, briefly explaining the skill card.

"Now that is something," Anthony said, after getting the explanation of the skill. "Right?"

"It should be helpful. My horses have been at it all morning, so they're going to need a break eventually, but…"

Behind them the small group of zombies hadn't slowed down. If anything, they had picked up more speed on the way.

"We're probably going to have to deal with that. If we ever want to rest that is," Finley said, patting the human on the shoulder. "You humans are good at killing things, right?"

Anthony shrugged. "I guess that is something we're good at. If the humans in this world are the same as the ones in mine."

Without a basis for comparison, Finley didn't know whether to agree or not. Either way, he was stuck out here with a human while the dwarven zombies behind them continued to mass. There were about twelve zombies behind them, and they were two spans away. The bay mares had continued to increase the gap between them the longer they had gone on but neither group had stopped. Finley had estimated that it would be ten more spans before they arrived at the next town.

"Got any bright ideas?" Finley said.

"Are there any guns here? Not that I know how to shoot any but…"

"I'm not carrying any. You're talking about muskets, right?"

"That answers that question. Thank you. Do you have any arrows? A bow?"

"I have a ceremonial spear on top of the caravan, it's only used to pick fruit from high branches though. We're going to have to rely on magic. Especially if you have a class that lets you cast a spell like that. Do you know how far your range is?" Finley pointed to the top of the painted wagon.

"How would I know that?"

"In some skills it's listed. And others you have to kind of play around with it. It sounds like this is the kind of skill you have to play around with. And good thing we have so many targets for you to do so with."

"My dear caravan driver, what exactly are you suggesting?"

Finley turned on his customer service voice and smiled before he decided to answer the human. "Have you ever speared fish in a barrel?"

***

Ten minutes later, and all of Anthony's youth playing at the arcade down the street finally paid off. Finley had slowed the caravan down enough to allow their pursuers to close the distance. He was giving the horses a chance to rest while at the same time giving Anthony some target practice.

As a young lad, the games that had interested Anthony had involved using a plastic gun to shoot at fake zombies. A careful application of his finger with magic from his holy bolt spell, let him do nearly the same thing.

He took shot after shot as they closed in, trying to get a handle on how accurate he could be. As they got to within half a league, he was hitting a target every five shots.

When the horses started noticing that the zombies were closing in, that was when he was hitting one every other shot. Then he made the unfortunate discovery that they kept getting up unless he hit them in the head.

That was when he got tired.

"Finley, it's getting harder to hit them now," the human said.

"You're probably getting tired. If you overdo it with magic, you're going to get a headache. I think the goddess gave you that card on purpose. If you need me to use it on you, I can. I have a side deck that I can stow it in. If you put it in your soul deck then you'll be in withdrawal if you ever take it out, in fact, just give me that card so I can use it on you."

Anthony debated for a second if he could trust the single elvenoid being that he had met since arriving in this strange forsaken world before taking it out of his pocket and giving it over.

A glow covered Finley as he used an ability on Anthony.

Suddenly, it felt like he had taken pre-workout and Viagra. His neck itched. "These side effects are… Have you tried this card out before because—"

Anthony trailed off as he focused on the lead one. One of the zombies had broken from the pack and he fired off a holy bolt right at the man's head, finally bringing his second down.

Two of the ones behind it stumbled, much to his amusement. That short amount of time almost immediately went away as he realized that he had to headshot ten more to stop them. At least his headache had gone away.

"Finley! They're dropping cards when they die!"

"Shit."

Some of the magic here had seemed odd, like having class powers tied to a card that had bonded to his soul, but he was rolling with the punches so far.

He remembered what Yil had offered him. His soul card felt like so much of a part of him that it was like it had always been there. It had a picture of a man holding up a hand against a horde of zombies. He checked it quickly to see if anything had changed.

Rare Class Card: Cleric Level 1

Skills:

Divine Spellcasting Level 2

Divine Rituals Level 1

Heal Level 1

Survival Level 1

Medicine Level 1

This card grants mana.

As a cleric you must have a patron deity.

This is a soul card and cannot be removed.

"Ah yes! I leveled up one of my skills!"

To celebrate he hit a zombie in the knee, making it stumble and slow half of the horde. Then with the acuity and hardness he had gotten from the refresh skill, he hit two more in the head.

Then he felt a little tug, a gentle pull towards the zombies and to jump out the back of the caravan to go grab the gorgeous shiny cards.

"Finley! I think the goddess wants us to gather up these cards!"

"Shit. My deity is telling me nothing of the sort, so just let me know when you're done with target practice so we can turn around," Finley said from the front. "The Goat Lord isn't known for being particularly verbose."

It took four more minutes, but Anthony finally got the last of the zombies down and it felt like a minor miracle. They weren't getting chased anymore. He breathed a sigh of relief.

"We need to go back for all those… Look, it's a short jog, do you mind it if I?"

Finley looked around, then closed his eyes. His pained expression spoke to their situation. "The trees and the grass here tell me that we are relatively safe so, go. Be quick. I'm going to give the horses some rest."

Anthony started running back down the road; the closest one was just fifty meters behind them. He kept jogging until he was close enough to carve out the cards and card pieces. The furthest downed zombie was almost half a mile away. He realized that he would have to carry the pieces in something, and he hadn't brought a backpack or a sack to carry anything. He cursed the lack of pockets in his scrubs.

The first bloated corpse gave him an idea as its former owner had worn what he assumed passed for a backpack. Anthony rolled the dwarf's arms out of it and then tested its integrity. It held up well and he thought it could hold the pieces he would need.

He looked up, checking around him, quickly ascertaining that the caravan hadn't moved. If anything, Finley was doing some magic in the back that gave off a golden glow.

Now was the difficult part. He had grabbed a large knife and with it he meant to do the opposite of healing.

"Keep it together Anthony. It's a strange new world and you're opening corpses to get the magical cards inside of them. This will totally be fine."

He made quick work of it.

"This must be how surgeons feel. God this is awful."

The smell made him gag, but he kept working.

Rather than leave the cards there and return, Anthony scooped them up and put them into the bag and then added the pieces.

Then he jogged to the furthest one, making it in record time. The reduced endurance of the refresh skill had worn off by that time and he was able to jog normally.

"This is just another day in the office," he whispered cutting into the next. His hands were bloody, despite his careful touch. "Someday I'll wake up and this will all be a dream."

He gagged at the smell.

"Or I'll just be in this nightmare."

He grabbed the card without checking it, stuffing it in, then grabbing the pieces as well. Then he went down the line, gathering up twelve cards and enough pieces to make his pack feel heavy.

The weight of the corpses was heavier than his bag as he walked back to the wagon. He wished that there was a stream nearby. Something, anything to clean off the blood. He would even go so far as to use his scrub top if he had to. He didn't want to, but the Goat Lord, he missed running water.

***

Finley finished pushing his mana into the six pieces, making another uncommon card. He put it on the pile. The horses were getting a bit restless. It was well into the afternoon, but despite seeing the last couple of hills before the next tavern, a little voice in the back of his head was telling him that he should probably stay.

If the new reality they lived in was going to continue like this then he would need to do something to increase his mana pool. There were enough options now that both could choose something to augment their current decks. Finley had sorted them into piles and was prepared to give a little lecture on what the cards all were and meant when Anthony woke up.

Of course, the first thing the human did after waking up was to go relieve himself on the side of the road. Then he scanned the horizon. Then and only then did he sit down next to the elf.

He held out his forearms. They still had some dried blood on them. The once-red color had turned brown.

"No immediate threat?" Anthony asked.

"No. I wanted to talk to you about adding some of these to your deck. Especially if you're going to try to pull a move like what you did with our followers again. That was reckless. And since we're close to town, I wanted to give you the best shot I could. I don't know what's ahead of us, but I don't—I don't have a good feeling about this."

"I don't have a good feeling about anything. This whole experience has made me rethink a lot of how I just don't want to kill things. So, I would greatly appreciate it if we could fix that little issue. This whole experience of carving up the dead to get stronger…" His eyes pleaded with Finley.

"Well," Finley's customer service voice said, "you came to the right tinker. Because I have a vested interest in fixing this issue. I would like to level my merchant class skill. And if I don't have customers, that's going to prove to be difficult."

"That's rather pragmatic."

"I got a message that I had been elevated to Tinker King because I was the last remaining tinker. At the very least, I would like to continue the traditions of the tinker family and pass on our customs and courtesies to the next generation no matter what. The next generation is yet to be found."

"Tinker King?"

"It's the title for the head of the tinkers. He who sets down the law and administers justice. Tinkers roam this continent. I have never known a card's power to lie."

He left out that they were probably all dead and if lucky not zombies.

He knew people that lied about their powers. He had never known a card to lie.

"Alright. You're like merchant royalty, then?"

"Yes. I guess I can now add people to the family. It's something that a caravan chief can do. I was never a caravan chief."

Anthony got up, standing on the back of the caravan. There was a space where he could step up to get more height. He looked around.

"Sun's going down. Or getting lower. I presume that means we only have a few hours to get somewhere safe?"

"If the town is safe. Honestly it might be safer to just hole up here. If I had an earth moving power, I would feel a lot safer. As none of the cards we got have an earth skill, I don't know."

"Do we have anything useful at least?"

"Of the twelve you got, none are class cards, but three skill cards—tracking, survival, and hunting—all could be combined with two other skill cards to make the ranger class card. That would be useful if we got a good bow. I might be able to get one in the next town."

"On to the town? As your duly appointed security detail, at least we'll be able to hole up if there are any walls."

"If."

Anthony brought up a shaking forearm. Finley was looking around for a puddle because the lack of water was beginning to bother him.

"I wasn't ready for that. If there's more zombies in the next town, I don't know what the goddess is doing to us. This situation is so fucked," Anthony said.

"Ah… Speaking of which." The elf held up two arms and a row of yellow flowers popped up around each of the zombies behind them. He couldn't just create water.

"It's the least I can do."

"That's a lot of control. That far out? That's like what half a span?"

"It's not a combat spell unfortunately. More like a death ritual. Which reminds me—" Finley bleated twice. "Gotta let the Goat Lord know he is going to have visitors."

4

Of all the things that Finley had in stock, space was not one of them. He had taken on as much as he could from his last two trading stops. There was one free corridor down the center of the caravan that allowed him to walk from the front to the back.

He generally kept that area pristine. It was just enough room for him to lay down a bedroll at night. At least for him, that was his little slice of heaven.

So long as his bay mares had a nice cover over them, he was happy. He hadn't bought the little horse port that other tinkerers had raved about. At that exact moment he was regretting that decision.

"I can make a tripwire with local flora. It will give us a head start if some zombies decide to attack at night," Finley said.

"Will that be enough?"

"I honestly don't know. You said that you saw the goddess, right? Did she say anything special about how you were supposed to proceed?"

Anthony's blank stare told him all he needed to know. "I honestly don't recall. The last few hours have been traumatic. Can we talk about something else? If I remember something, I'll bring it up. Also, if we see a stream, I'm jumping in."

Finley paused. Knowing that there was a stream by the next town was different from being there. Dunnamore was his next stop, but it would probably be safer out in the open. He just worried about not being able to see zombies in the night. He did not want to be overrun.

"Do you want to take a vote? About what to do next? I assume you want to stay with me. I'm still heading to the kingdom. If anyone is alive and holding the line, that's where they will be."

Anthony sat in a reclined position against the caravan, propping himself against the wheel. The sky was a gorgeous blue and the fields were so pastoral that he couldn't help but wish he had time for a nap.

"What are the options? Hole up in the middle of nowhere, or head down to the nearest village? Are we going to sleep in shifts?"

"I don't need as much sleep as a human so I can do most of the watch. The darkness though, I'm not sure I can ease the horses in the full dark that it will be. We can make our way back to one of those farmhouses and clear it out. If the zombies can't see us, then we should be safe… If there are any more of them."

***

The chosen ranger snuck past the patrols outside Dunnamore. The walls were fortified and there were bonfires raging inside. He was uncertain how the undead had arranged patrols and kept fires going, but it was just his luck to be stuck with such an assignment.

He popped his head out over a gaping crack in the wall to see a group of them sitting around the fire. Next to them he saw about a dozen men and women in a large cage.

Beyond that was a cluster of three buildings. One of them must hold the controller of the undead around the area, and if he took that one down then the rest would be more mindless, easier to kill, and perhaps help him to get the second class that his deity promised him.

There was only one guard on top of the wall. Of course, he did his job with the patience only the dead possess.

He would be the first one.

Tucking his crossbow into a sling, he pushed it up his back, thanking whomever that dead shop owner was that had left his door open when he became undead.

The ranger said a silent prayer to Mork. He had no specific words, just sending a feeling up.

Hand by hand, he climbed, getting to where he could take a shot. He lined up a shot on his favored enemy and then loosed the bolt from his crossbow.

He had twelve bolts left. They were going to need to count.

The undead knight fell, silently slipping forward over the wall. The flash of the cards coming out of the undead was nothing against the bonfire behind the wall. The ranger gathered the card and card pieces efficiently. Cutting into the corpse to get the cards was an unfortunate part of the job.

He examined it quickly. Fortuitously, it was another bow ability. Excellent.

He didn't have time to read the card right now, but it was going to be the next thing he did in his downtime. He shoved it into his soul deck.

A sound from horses kept inside the walls alerted him of their direction. If he had known that they were keeping horses, then he might have brought one. It would be how he left, either way. A quick glance told him there were about twenty horses.

He saw a chance to cause some mischief and pulled out a vial of grease.

The horses would provide a good distraction.

He spread some of the grease evenly across the rope connecting to the stables. He pulled out a prepared snare trap. It wouldn't last long.

It only had to work once, and then badly. Using his woodsman skill, he primed a torch attached to the snare. Then he added the one thing he hadn't thought he would get some use out of—candle wire. Having not found any dynamite, he would have to content himself with homemade explosives.

Then he looked down, discerning which of the three targets to go for. The three tents looked similar in size and shape. Any one of them could hold an intelligent undead. If he was able to think like them, he might hazard a guess, but with all that he knew, any one of them was good enough.

It was the old Monty Hall problem that his granddad had explained quickly to him as a youth. Now if only he could remove one of the options.

He had to think that Mork had chosen him because he knew about the Monty Hall problem, as the rest of his life dealt little with the things that the god of death and mathematics cared for. It stung.

He picked the center tent at random after deciding which would be the hardest to sneak up on. There was no reason to hide. He would sneak in, decapitate the head of the undead here and then make off with one or more of their horses.

Probably.

The middle tent looked to be the hardest to reach, but would top brass want a longer walk to the exit? Either way, he found his way to the interior of the wall's edge.

He leaned into his ranger stealth skill, which had already reached fifth level. It helped him to find a pathway in the dark, avoiding the bright light of the two bonfires. He briefly wondered what they were burning before he saw a bony protrusion and his curiosity went away.

If he'd had a team for backup, he probably wouldn't be so nervous. But then again, if he had a team, he probably wouldn't be on a suicide mission from Mork to complete this damn quest. If Mork had given him more details than that he would be rewarded once he killed the death knight, then he would be happier, but then again?

He was at the rear of the tent, where the shadows were the darkest. The courtyard of Dunnamore had a lot of nooks and crannies around its single-story shops.

He felt the cover of darkness come over him. His stealth skill was paying dividends.

It was jarring that he got confirmation that he was doing what he was supposed to be doing. He paused before gently opening the flap with a bolt. If he had more bolts, then he could slowly whittle the zombies down. But he needed a good blade, and the death knight would have one of those on top of whatever card was in its soul.

Mork hated the corruption of the zombie rot that turned the living into mindless beasts. If he could get an unlimited ammunition skill, he would be laying waste to the zombies with hit and run tactics. But he wasn't there yet.

The flap opened to a half-naked knight.

"Who are you and why are you here?" the gravelly voice said.

"Paulie, here with a special delivery, bada bing, bada—"

Thwip!

He loosed a bolt into the knight's face, blowing the head clean off at that range.

"—boom."

On the side of the tent, a large sword in a special stand leaked dark power. He hesitated for a second before grabbing it and then thrusting it through the death knight's chest. The glow of a card popped up.

Epic Skill Card: Pathfinder Level 1

Find a friend or foe within five miles unerringly. As this card advances, the range advances.

He looked at it briefly before putting it directly into his soul deck. This would complement his existing skills immensely and Mork had intended for him to take this card. He had just met the deity, but he hadn't been steered wrong yet.

It was about this time that the rope he had greased up finally lit on fire. As he ventured out behind the tent to look for any guards, one of the other tents caught fire. Every single undead head in the place had turned to look directly at him.

This time it was the mindless look of zombies that only cared for flesh.

Perfect.

At least they weren't looking at the poor prisoners.

***

"The next town over—" Anthony said.

"Dunnamore. It's a dwarven holding. Very rural. It supports the Irumian Kingdom by providing them with all their food needs. Even farms this far out."

"Dunnamore. Ah. And you say that there's a walled courtyard we could use if we need to hole ourselves in there?"

"This is where the earth skills would come in handy."

"Interesting," Anthony said. "Like shaping the earth to form a part of the wall?"

"To patch it up, yes. I could do so with plants, but that would be difficult. And I wouldn't want to spend all that effort for them to just gnaw through the vines anyway."

"Ah. I see."

"If we wait for dark, at least we'll have some advantage. I'm sure that they're more dormant at night," Finley said, gulping.

"Are you sure about that?"

Darkness approached and then they could see two bonfires poking over a large wall.

"I'm certain that those were made on purpose. There must be dwarves there. They're probably using them to incinerate the undead," Finley said.

"That makes sense," Anthony said. "Is this a common thing?"

"I have never heard of it happening in my lifetime."

They continued in silence for a bit.

"We can still turn around, you know. This close to the town, there are more roads than just the one that leads in. We can just go around it," Finley said.

Finley's sense of the place did not extend inside of the city. He had expected some plant life to give him an idea of what was going on, but he could barely see the town with his eyes from a span away. The sun dipped below one of the western mountains and the bonfires became even more pronounced.

"Hey, hero—Is that light getting brighter?"

"That… can't be possible. Two bonfires and it's getting brighter?"

Finley reached for the horses, readying them to move.

"There's a road that goes around the town in a circle. We'll take that one," the elf said, getting up. "It's going to be a hot night."

***

As soon as he activated the pathfinder card, he could feel it. Mork was pushing him to follow, in a very specific way. It wasn't just taking him to the right horse, it was pushing him away from the now-mindless horde.

Next time, he would plan more ahead. Mork had promised him that there were more people that would fight against the undead. He needed to lead them away from the twelve that had thankfully been put into a cage, even as some of the mindless undead scraped at the bars.

The horses would need to go first.

His pathfinder skill was telling him to pick one of the closest steeds, a white horse. Had he been a ranger for any longer, he might know the first thing about horses. His animal handling skill assured him that he would at the very least not fall off his horse.

He ran along the side of the wall as the zombies charged him. With no one directing their actions, they were far less effective. There was no teamwork between them.

The half door to the stable was easily dealt with. Then all the doorways were quickly opened. He ran up to the white steed, pulling on his animal handling skill. If nothing else, he was going to ride out of here like a hero with a sword and a horse.

After making sure every horse was free to go, he pushed open the barn doors. The undead behind him hammered the entrance.

"They can't get all of us, can they?"

He could hear a familiar laugh as the barn doors opened and the horses made their way out. For a moment the chosen ranger felt like they were doing what he wanted, as they attempted to trample the first line of zombies.

"Quit horsing around guys," he said, spurring his steed onwards, "I have someone to meet."

5

He could feel Mork's hand, empowering his skill in animal handling. These odd card powers combined with the holy card he had been given worked in so many strange ways.

The caravan's front axle had turned enough that they could see the area clearly.

"Is that a man riding a horse in our direction, followed by a herd of horses and"—Finley squinted—"a horde of zombies?"

"As I have never seen such a thing and I don't think that zombies ride horses, or that horse zombies exist in this world, I'll accept your assessment. Now, what are we going to do about it?"

Finley pushed the bay mares to turn onto the beltway around Dunnamore. Without any rivers, it was simple to ride around the bluff that the city occupied.

"We ride. Can you get some of those zombies from here with your holy bolt skill?"

"We can—whoever that is, is coming towards us. If he changes course, then…"

"If he can ride a horse then he is among the living. If zombies are chasing him out of Dunnamore, then it's overrun."

Finley left his thoughts about how the town had to have been before they had arrived. He had to live in the here and now if he was going to survive, and the cloaked rider was approaching. As they moved towards the beltway, the rider changed to an intercept direction, looking to cut them off or join them ahead. That at least made him intelligent.

"Finley! He's waving! Maybe he's not undead!"

"Well, save him for last, then. Do what you can with the horde behind him."

The horses had clearly changed direction as well as the horde behind them, who moved at a noticeably slower pace.

"Do they have any weapons?" Finley said, eyes glued to the dirt. "That seems relevant right now."

"What? Who? The horses? The zombies?"

"The lone rider."

"He is slinging a crossbow and—Oh! He is a good shot! Get them!"

***

The chosen ranger closed in on the caravan. One elf and one human sat in front of it. He could see the elf, spurring their horses on.

Three horses had paid the ultimate sacrifice to get him out there.

It was a very light push to his skill that had allowed him to pull off that maneuver. It had driven the horses to become shields against the zombies and he would find a way to honor their sacrifice later.

Using the horses to push off the zombies and trample them, he was able to ride to the north of Dunnamore. That was when he realized it had finally become twilight, and that he wasn't alone. The bonfires lit up the area for nearly half a mile away, much of it a flat grassland.

His pathfinding skill was paying hard dividends as it showed a beeline towards the approaching caravan. He could feel the caravan move and he felt a strong prediction for which direction it was going and how far it could go.

Shortly after he emerged from the interior, the caravan changed direction; he followed suit. He pushed his horse to catch up. Instead of coming straight at him, the horde had turned, away from the last remnants of light from the sun.

They waved at him; he waved back. He wasn't sure exactly what they knew but when one of them started firing light bolts into the horde, he knew he had made the right decision.

He finally pulled up his horse alongside them. He kept pace with the caravan, slowing slightly. With two mares pulling, they kept good speed, but he did not know for how long. Once again, he wished that he had leveled some of his ranger skills, rather than having to lean on a temporary boost.

"Are you boys looking for some help? Because I could use some right about now. I'll even make it worth your while."

"What do you need, stranger?" a man with a Bronx accent said.

"Just a bit of help. I think the thing they need to understand is that I'm working here. I have things to do, and these guys are just raining on my parade."

"We're trying to avoid being eaten by that horde over there. So long as you're not on their side, what do you need?"

"I'm planning on leading the horde around the city a few times in order to give me a chance to whittle them down. Without a death knight to control their movements, they're all mindless. They'll seek out the closest form of sustenance in front of them. Or at least the closest one available to them. That would be you guys, me, and all of our horses."

He hadn't failed to notice that the horses were now congregating around the caravan in a pack. All the horses and he hadn't known what to do with them. The horses, it seemed, had the right idea already. They ran behind the path that the caravan was taking with a single-minded focus.

The beltway around the city had been built to carry large loads of rock around. Able to afford a clear berth to dozens of travelers at a time, it was wide. The ranger found that the caravan was now pushing to keep up with the horse he was riding bareback.

"I see you have a crossbow," the man with the Bronx accent said. "Are you any good with it?"

The ranger smiled. "I only have so many bolts, but I have not missed a shot all day." He left out the part where he'd only shot once.

"Impressive. My friend here is whispering that he has more bolts for you. Would you like to be part of a friendly wager?"

"Why my good sir, what are your terms?"

"Let's see who can take down more of the horde."

"You're on."

***

If there was any question in the ranger's mind if there was another death knight in the area, it was put to ease when the zombies did not react to being shot in the face.

Oh sure, the ones that got shot fell.

They were gone.

There was no return policy in the world that was going to account for this kind of normal everyday wear. No shopkeeper would accept a facsimile of a dwarf, except maybe an undertaker, and return any amount of money.

Zombies gave you store credit.

The chosen ranger had decided that he was going to get as much zombie cash as he could. And to do so, he would need to use all the bolts that his new friends had just given him.

There had to be at least thirty zombies in a horde behind them. Feeling the quiver, he had at least that many bolts.

It was too bad that he didn't have a mounted archery skill to work on. That would have come in clutch just about now. Then he saw one of the humanoids go to the back of the caravan and begin to shoot holy bolts out of a finger gun.

"Is he slaying zombies with the power of finger guns? Mork, why didn't you give me that power? Don't answer that."

He could hear chuckling from the ether. At least his God had a sense of humor.

He strung the first bolt. Time to work on his archery skill.

He pulled away from the caravan trying to get the zombies. If nothing else, to split their attention. The bonfire on the other side gave him enough light to see.

He could see the faint glow that marked a card appearing from a corpse. It was enough to give him a clear picture of a zombie he was tracking, and he made his first shot. The glow made him smile as he nudged the horse back in the direction of the caravan.

This horse was used to mounted combat, or at least archery.

Three corpses dotted the ground.

Did he have enough time to swoop in and grab their cards?

No. He cursed.

If they were going to lead the zombies around the town, he would have a chance to reclaim those cards. That was a big if. He wouldn't have the glow to mark their location.

His horse picked up speed as it trotted towards the herd.

The mage in the back of the caravan kept firing, hitting something every third or fourth attack.

He was going to have to pick up the pace if he wanted bragging rights.

****

Finley kept to the well-lit path. The moon rose over them with its green glow, the red of the bonfires mixing with it.

The rider that had appeared with a herd of horses seemed impressive enough initially. Then he saw how the man had to load each crossbow shot and it looked like he was getting more and more tired. He was also missing two out of three shots.

By that time, they had circled the city once. Finley kept checking in on Anthony as he scored hit after hit, but he too was getting tired. He was missing more and more and there were still more zombies. About a dozen or so still chased them, their movements slower in the dark.

***

If one of the two had some sort of skill that could give him energy, the ranger might be able to pull it together. Or if the city boy had any skills in riding horses, he might do so.

They clearly didn't want to leave the safety of the caravan come hell or high water.

Their help was the only thing between him and certain death in the dark.

He aimed to keep it that way and rode within talking distance.

"I might be able to start grabbing some of the cards. I can go ahead and grab some."

"There's still too many of them. I can hit them for sure, but they need to be close now. And without the fire we would be out of luck," the man with the Bronx accent said. "Why don't you go to the front and ask the elf if he has any bright ideas?"

"Will do."

Then he was gone once again, spurring his horse forward. Swinging around the front of the caravan, the rider got close enough to the elf to talk.

"There's only about a dozen of them left. I'm out of crossbow bolts but if we go around Dunnamore once again we should get all of them. Then we can harvest their cards. Oh, and the guy in the back asked if you had any bright ideas."

"I have a few ideas. Once I don't have to hold to the horses so tightly, I can make a mage light to help us see."

"I'm less worried about finding these things. I have a skill that points me in the direction of things that I'm trying to find. Mork actually helped me find that card as part of a quest."

"First Yil, now Mork? I suppose you've just been summoned here recently then. Hmmm."

Behind them, the other man hooted and yelled. "Eight more!"

"Also, seriously I am out of crossbow bolts. I don't have any other ranged skills so I don't know what I can do to help you out here."

"Can you be the bait?"

"I'm not sure if they'll follow me instead of you and the horses. They're just looking for something warm that they can gnaw on. Let's try to avoid that being you."

6

In his role as the bait, the chosen ranger did not feel like he was being utilized to his full capacity. It was like he was an espresso machine with all these fine knobs that had only been used once. It was hit or miss if he got the zombies to follow him or not. He would look out to see the mage light, judge the distance and then try to pull them in.

He wanted to give what had to be a cleric the best shot he could. This meant he had to pull them away from the direction of travel more than once. While the caravan continued, he steered in a line then zigged and zagged back and forth.

Their numbers dwindled, until only one was left. He wasn't mad that he had lost a wager about the number of kills. There would be time to get that back.

He was mad that he would have to go back and pick up all his bolts if he wanted to shoot again. It was just that they had proven so useful in the past couple hours, and he was very reluctant to part with them.

That was when he remembered that there still might be living humanoids stuck in a cage. If the zombies hadn't gotten to them.

***

The herd around the caravan were moving in a very slow trot. The two bay mares that had been constant companions to Finley looked like they were about to quit.

Finley himself wanted to quit. When Anthony killed the last of the zombies, he didn't have enough energy for a cheer. He allowed the horses to slow down. Pretty soon they were going to have to rest. Or they would all be the walking dead.

He released his hold on the herd of horses. Though they were free, they didn't begin to run. He looked for two fresh horses to swap in for his bay mares. If they were going to move again tonight, he wanted to be ready.

Tinkers always took care of their horses. When one spent their time moving from place to place, they could easily be sold a bad horse. Thus, they had to learn animal husbandry from an early age. Elder tinkers took pride in the care of the animals, passing on their knowledge to the youths in their caravans.

He cast another mage light, letting it float up. He tied it off to the center of the caravan so it would show everything around.

"Anthony, do you want to come up here?"

"On my way, boss. If I could get another one of those…" Anthony scrambled to the front.

"You're good."

Finley did not want to spend any more mana casting refresh. He had heard horror stories about people being addicted to card effects. They had, he judged, more important things to do right now.

"We'll do one more loop with my mage light on. I need you to gather up the cards. Either that or you can handle the reins while I do that. Your choice. Then I want to teach you that." He pointed his hand up to show the mage light spell. "It's something that you should be able to cast."

"That would be very convenient. Are you sure that I can't have one more for old times' sake?"

"No."

He was too tired. Not to mention it would take all his mana to use the spell. Finley was going to need some sleep even if it wasn't that much. Anthony was going to crash very soon. They needed to find a way to get some real rest.

***

The wagon slowed. One of the riders dropped down to pick up cards but stayed very close. He would walk ahead, staying within the brightest part of the mage light.

The chosen ranger did the same. That spell was hopefully something that he could learn. The herd loosened, moving around the caravan towards green fields north of the town. He considered letting his horse loose, but they had already been through so much and it still felt restless. His animal handling skill had leveled up. It had felt useless before, but now it was doing a lot of heavy lifting for him.

He patted the horse's mane. Did it have a name before him? It didn't matter.

"I think you need a new name after that baptism by fire. What do you think?"

It neighed, leading him towards the caravan. The elf with the pointed ears looked back at him.

"Human, thank you for your help," he intoned, brushing a hand against the horse's side. "This one too is grateful for your help. It saw some of its siblings die. That can't be good. I am Finley, tinker and traveling trader elf."

"My name is Bob," he said, pulling back his hood to reveal a half-bald head. "It's a pleasure to meet you. I'm a bit new to the area and would appreciate a map or some direction."

"Maps I have… The times are a bit too uncertain. I would trade for some uncommon card pieces."

"Is that what these are? They seemed valuable." Bob patted a pack on the side of his belt. They jingled briefly, the metallic card pieces sounding a familiar tone.

Mork had told him to keep them.

"They're less useful without the tools to make a card, unless you picked up a card-making skill."

Something told Bob to trust the elf. Perhaps it was the blood on the ground that they had shed together. It could be his smile or some charisma skill.

It could be that he was among the living and had a cool ride. A covered wagon with runes all along the sides?

"I have not. Is that a thing?" Bob asked.

"It's a thing."

"If you had a card like that, would you trade for it?"

The elf couldn't hide his grimace.

"Oh, they're valuable then, I see."

"The guilds… it's reserved for trained craftsmen. But you can kind of see what's going on right now. Luckily for you I have just the thing to turn those card pieces into cards, if we have some time. You could do it without a frame, but it would be a lot easier with one."

The horses in front of the wagon both bent down to eat grass.

Bob, the chosen ranger of Mork, dismounted. "Shit." The ground was far squishier than he had expected, and his boots sank in an inch.

"What?"

"I forgot about the people in the cage in this rush."

The elf sucked in a breath. "People in a cage. Where?"

***

Twelve people sat in a wrought iron cage. Their only saving grace from the two zombies that remained was two inches of iron. That was enough to keep the zombies out. They struggled against it. The same undead who had been their jailers before had suddenly turned mindless. The pounding became increasingly incessant as their maws drooled more and more.

Julie huddled in the back. Ever since being summoned to this world two days prior she had been in a living hell. She cursed the trickster god which had given her the cursed card she got her powers from. It was all useless in the cage.

How was she supposed to know that picking the warlock class would make her powerless?

There was only one bright spot in her life.

That stranger had cut off the head of the snake.

Julie lifted her hands up. There was a trickle of mana. She had rested enough to try another eldritch beam.

She didn't have a choice. She needed to survive.

The short zombies clawed at the iron.

It had taken everything she had to just wriggle out of the magic sapping cuffs. It helped that her hyperhidrosis had made it to this new world. Another curse from her old life, now a blessing.

She had just gotten the cuffs off when the two zombies changed their behavior. She wasn't looking at them when the scraping stopped.

"Holy bolt!"

Then a flood light lit up the entire cage and the rest of the humans and one dwarf that had been thrown in with her.

For a moment, hope welled up inside of her.

She might get out of this place intact.

She quashed that feeling. There had been too much hope, and she needed that part to die.

Cara, god of drug deals and overland transportation, was probably smiling at her indecision. There was a chance that the stranger had returned, whether to kill them or not, she didn't know.

She was prepared to die again. She didn't want to, but the thought no longer bothered her.

"Hey! Dwarves of Dunnamore are you okay in there? Oh, a human! Wait, you're all human?" The cloak hid the man's face, but the voice was distinctly an accent she knew, but just couldn't place.

"Not just humans," she said weakly, her lips cracking with the exertion to talk. She felt so dry.

How she thought that she would be able to pull off some more magic was beyond her. She settled back down as the man fiddled with the lock.

"The guard over there has the key. The one you just decapitated," the dwarf next to her said. "Free us and we shall thank you, stranger."

The dwarf put a hand on her shoulder; she could feel that he needed a push to get up. She might have been tossed into the large cage, but she was sure as Cara going to walk out.

He probably felt the same.

The man had the keys out and they could hear him fiddling with the lock.

Salvation at last looked close at hand.

"Hey, can you shine that light a little closer? The locks are not on the side that the bonfire would help." The cloaked figure dropped his hood to show off a sweaty half-bald pate.

Behind him a second figure appeared. This one, a tall green-tinted elf, was clearly casting the magic light.

Julie was jealous.

That would have been a nice talent. The bonfire's heat and light had been the only thing keeping her from shivering in the cool breeze wherever they were.

"There it is. You're all welcome to come out now. We have a healer outside that can help you. He is on guard duty right now or we would all be here," the elf said. "Does anyone need immediate healing? If not, is anyone here from Dunnamore?"

"We're thirsty and hungry," Julie said. "If anything. I'm not from here."

"Ah. Another human. And so far into Irumian territory as well," the elf said, glancing at the balding man in the cloak. "Bob, can you lead them out? Can everyone walk?"

Julie stood up and held the dwarf's hand. She stepped through, then pulled him through.

"I thought we would die there," she said.

"Aye lass, that's what we all thought."

They followed Bob out. Julie idly wondered how many heroes were named Bob. Every step away from the cage felt like a step towards freedom. That combined with the feeling of her magic returning to her made her feel nigh invincible.

They left the walls full of energy but then it all caught up to her. Seeing that she had made it, her legs gave out.

***

"She's just exhausted," Anthony said. "She needs rest. Now we have enough horses for everyone, if they are all able to ride, but we can only fit what, four people in the back? And even then, they're packed in."

It was hours later after all the former prisoners had collapsed in the relative safety of the caravan. Six slept underneath the caravan, three were in it and the final three just couldn't sleep and had joined the sleepy council.

They sat around a small bonfire. This one was outside of the town. Julie, one of the former prisoners, had an earth power which let them shape a sitting structure around the circle. Combined with the druid's powers, they were able to stoke a good flame.

"Bob, you went through and ransacked the interior? Besides the houses outside of the inner courtyard, do you think that we might find anything in any of the houses? I can't believe that none of these people are from here. I've heard of one or two heroes summoned from beyond, but fourteen in two days…What the hell happened, exactly?" Anthony said.

"Mork summoned me. He gave me a class card. Told me that I was his chosen ranger. This is of course after I selected ranger from the options he gave me. He said that I was needed."

"Mork? As in the god of death? The one who hates necromancy with a passion?"

"Mork said that they're also the god of fertility, mathematics and scouting? That just seems to be a lot."

"How many things are the gods in your world responsible for?"

"That's a bit of a loaded question."

Finley, one of the people around the camp that hadn't spoken yet, looked up.

"Everything and anything. But there aren't so many," the elf said.

"I think we can talk about this while we set out what our next steps are. We still have all the cards from our raid. And I'll go through the town when the sun goes up again." Bob held up a stack of cards, passing a few to Anthony and a few to Finley.

"Were there by chance, any class cards in that pile?" Finley said, leaning in.

"I see several artisan class cards. There were a lot of skill cards as well," Bob said.

"I think we're going to need to use them all. As much as I want to hold up here, I don't think this is going to be good for the long-term. We need to get as much food as possible into the caravan," Anthony said.

"What are we going to do about the people?" Bob said.

"I honestly don't know. If we have enough animal handling cards, we can get those out. It's a good skill—" Finley steepled his palms together.

"I love that skill," Bob said enthusiastically. "I thought it would be a dud, but it saved my life back there. It's one of the reasons I chose ranger."

"Alright let's make a plan then. We're helping them, I take it?" Finley said.

"As much as we can," Bob said.

7

"Before we can even ask them if they can come with us, we need to see if we can support them. We can't slow down if there are zombies all over like there were tonight. They would have to be fast or mounted. We could—"

"We could do what? Find another cart? A caravan? Hitch up some more horses? My girls are already half dead, and it has been a day since this started." Finley reached out to feel them contentedly sleeping next to the herd. They needed this. This downtime was a boon for them all.

"If only we had somebody with a skill that could make more wagons," Finley said. "Unless there's another caravan around?"

"I haven't seen one, but if the undead here were intelligent, they probably had a few. Otherwise…"

"That still shocks me to the core. I've never heard of undead being intelligent unless they're a wraith or a lich or—"

"Or a death knight."

It was the first time that Bob had spoken in a while. Anthony was almost certain that the ranger had been sleeping.

"A death knight?" Finley said, his tone quiet.

"I killed a death knight. The quest that Mork gave me here was to kill the knight and if possible, to save these people," Bob said. "And I did it."

"If there's a death knight, then something has gone terribly wrong. They're like heroes of the undead. There are fables that talk about one taking down a city and…"

The flames flickered.

"And what?" Anthony said.

"And I just realized that none of you would know any of the stories. None of you are from here," Finley said, slumping down against the rucksack he had prepared for his back support.

"That's… something," Anthony muttered.

"I'm going to have to tell you all the stories one day. This will not stand."

"I'd be down for that especially if there's a brew involved," Anthony said.

"Mork, what I wouldn't do for a good stout right now. And some eggs," Bob said. "There's eggs here, right?"

"There are eggs. I saw some in the caravan. Finley, with dawn approaching, do you mind if I make some breakfast for the crew? Then we can decide what to do on a full stomach?" Anthony asked.

"I've got pans next to the cryomancer-enhanced chest in the back. It's the one that looks like it's leaking vapor. I can't think of a better time than now to use what I have."

Anthony got up to rummage around the back of the caravan, returning shortly with a pan and some supplies.

"Was anyone a cook before this?" he asked the crowd.

"I was a chef," Bob said. "Allow me."

Together the two men were able to slowly work out a system using the fire and pan to cook for the ravenous crowd. They had all woken up to the smell just as the sun peeked over the horizon. Finley passed out plates and wooden forks to them as they waited.

"Don't eat too quickly," Bob said. "I know you were here, but take your time."

Anthony felt warm from sitting next to the fire. He'd broken out a mitt to handle the cast iron pan. If only there were running water he could use to clean it, then he would be happy. But there was more work to do.

He had slept in shifts with Bob in fits and starts but hadn't felt at ease. Maybe getting started on something, anything would help.

"You're a local, Finley. What do you think of this situation?" Bob said.

The elf shrugged. "I don't know. I generally ride about trading at various posts along the Irumian line to the Ice Cloak Mountains, all the way down to the human lands in the south. Sometimes I venture east. I haven't been to the elven kingdom recently."

"There's this kingdom, the Irumian one, correct? And south is some human kingdom?"

"They call it the Alliance. It's not exactly the way that the gnomes and dwarves run their business either, though they are the largest kingdom. You humans have a lot of children. It's south and east."

"No offense taken," Anthony said. "Well with all of that, can you think of a place where we could hole up for a while?"

"Better than here?" Finley pursed his lips, "That's difficult because so much of this land is farmland and with so many mouths to feed… I would need to know what's going on in the rest of the kingdom. Because there's only so much farming we can do here before winter sets in. I would want to be south of the capital then. Did I mention the Ice Cloak Mountains? They're just north of here."

Finley waved behind himself, northward as if the mountains would just make themselves known. Their height reached some of the lower clouds.

The human sighed. "We can't stay here long term. But we… We probably should talk to everyone here and ask if they would be okay on their own here."

"Or if we want to even head out with you strangers," a woman's voice said.

Julie stood behind Anthony.

"That's also a consideration," he squeaked. He hadn't seen her show up, and how she immediately had him gulping at the sight of her gave him pause. Why was he afraid of her?

"We can help you saddle up a horse and you can take your chances out in the wild but if what our traveling tinker here is saying is true, then we need to consider that staying here long term won't work out too well. How long is it until winter hits?" Julie asked.

Finley stirred from his thoughts. "Three weeks. It'll take most of one week to make our way down to the center of the kingdom. I don't know how I'll feed everybody."

"Does anybody have a card that lets them create food?" Anthony asked, looking around. The former prisoners were now all sitting around the embers of the cook fire. It looked like he had a quorum.

There was some grumbling, but no one raised a hand or said anything.

"I thought so. I only have so many provisions though what I have is yours. I would appreciate getting paid but what use do I have for gold? I can't eat gold. Card pieces and cards I could use but they would probably be better off in the hands of somebody who could use them to fight the zombie horde." Finley said.

"I propose," Bob said, "that we band together. We all have strength in numbers. We should be able to work something out with all those horses. If we find a cart or wagon, then it would be a lot simpler. There's no telling when or if another group of zombies comes down on us. I would feel safer with a group of you watching my back. Who else feels the same?"

There were a few more positive grumblings from the crowd.

"Are you trying to conscript us into a small army?" Julie asked.

"I wouldn't call it an army. Maybe like a cartel?" Bob said.

"What did you say you did back on Earth? What exactly?"

"I ran a successful cake shop in Hoboken. You probably saw it. It was featured on Cake and Bake."

"Oh! I saw that one!" one of the younger humans said. Anthony hadn't gotten the boy's name. "Wasn't yours the one shut down for all of the health code violations?"

"No, uh and this is not about me. We should all probably do introductions as well."

"Hi, I'm Anthony. I am originally from the Bronx. I used to be a midwife back on Earth. I ran a small company called Father and Son Midwives. Yes, it's real. No, don't laugh. Julie. Come on."

"Did you want to mention what card or card powers you have?" Julie asked.

"I chose a class card. I'm a cleric. I have skills that involve healing and yeah brand new," Anthony replied, waving his hands and throwing up a weak mage light.

Bob stood up with the swagger of a mean girl. "I am Bob, the chosen ranger of Mork. Mork gave me the ranger class card that has saved my ass so many times already." He held up a tankard of water.

"I'm Julie. I was a social worker on earth. I can cast eldritch beam as well as other spells, though they are mostly offensive. I fully intend to tag along with you boys." Julie flipped her curly blonde highlighted hair.

Of the eleven saved, all had a class card. One was a dwarf with the artificer class who had chosen it because it looked cool. Three other humans had chosen to be fighters. Three had chosen to be monks. Two were rogues. One was a wizard and the last a different type of druid than Finley. All in all, there were six women, five men and one dwarf.

None of them had any skills that Anthony was looking for. He was really looking for a card to help create a second wagon. Or at the very least, fix the one they had.

They had, of course, all been summoned as heroes to this world. Anthony was speechless. He hadn't expected to be brought into a fantasy world. He hadn't expected to be only one of a few that were brought to this world.

"All right, with introductions out of the way, let's see if we can find some common ground. Is everyone looking to help us survive the zombie apocalypse?" Anthony asked.

"A better question might be," Julie said, "does anyone else have a quest from their god to get through this problem?"

Bob raised his hand. Julie put hers up as well.

"What's with the raised hands?" Finley said.

"Oh! Sorry Finley. Back on Earth when we have big meetings like this, sometimes we raise our hand to indicate that we want to speak or that we agree with the speaker or something very contextual. Like for example, who here likes Star Wars?"

Every hand except for Finley's went up.

"Oh good! At least I'm in good company, then," Bob said.

"I have never heard of the Star War. Is it something that is common in your culture?"

There was light chuckle. A little something to take the edge off. Anthony let himself laugh a little bit. There had been so much killing and he just needed to release a little steam. He could feel his mana returning to him.

"It's a pretty common cultural touch point. I wouldn't worry about it too much though. You're going to tell us stories about this world? That should be enough." Anthony said.

"Well now that the introductions are over," Bob said, "let's talk about next steps. It's just dawning on us now. I think we're relatively safe if we take some prudent measures to ransack this town. Safe to say the former residents will not fight us for any of their old belongings. This is assuming that everyone wants in. If you want to do your own thing we understand. We will take stock of what we have and try to…"

Bob nodded to Finley.

"I'll do my best to give you a good chance to survive out there. I can't guarantee you anything," Finley said, playing with his hair.

"So having said that, and understanding that my guess is a lot of you got caught and shoved into that cage because you were on your own, do all of you want to form a party?" Bob said, trying his best to look heroic. But there was only so much heroism that one could exude without a full beard.

"And if so," Anthony said, "do we need to elect a leader?"

"I think that there is a clear and obvious choice," Bob said, puffing up his chest.

"There clearly is," Julie said, standing behind Anthony and patting him on the shoulders. "And I vote for this guy."

Bob shook his head and Anthony turned to see that Julie had impressive full-sleeve tattoos. How had he not noticed that before? They looked amazing and he chalked it up to the darkness of the night prior as to why he hadn't appreciated those beautiful drawings yet.

"Clearly you're mistaken—" Anthony said, shocked.

"Uh, what?" Bob said, reeling.

"What? Just because you saved our lives doesn't mean that we're going to follow you blindly. You're both smart, but you're an idiot if you think we're going to jump into certain danger like you did last night. What you did was reckless. You could have died. This guy? And this guy?" Julie pointed to Anthony, then Finley. "They had the right idea. Now, is anybody else voting for midwife Anthony?"

Anthony covered his eyes with his hands. He did not want to be in charge. He hated being in charge. He hated paperwork. He hated filling out forms.

Heck, the only good thing about delivering babies was the practical work itself and the golden hour.

But he damn well would do it to the utmost if these people wanted him in charge.

"You're serious? Julie?" Anthony said, "I mean I'll do it but…"

"Then do it."

Anthony opened his eyes to see all but one person had a hand in the air. Even the elf had one there. And he was waving it like he just didn't care.

"Alright."

8

"What we should do is see what we can get from the town and then go from there. Salvage what we can, trying to get as much food as possible. Cards would be good, but we'll need food more," Anthony said. "Before we start, we'll probably need to pair up, or move in groups of three—for safety—and then someone will need to stay with the caravan, to keep that safe."

"I'll stay with the caravan. The horses will follow us to the south as well. We can get a good look at the road to the next town and since we camped out here on the north side. It would be a good chance to work out the kinks," Finley said. "Do you rogues want to come with me?"

The two female rogues nodded.

"Good. Is anyone wounded? Well, if you get injured head to the caravan. It'll be by the horses. Julie, do you want to go inside the courtyard walls or head to the houses east of the town?"

Finley could see that Anthony was looking to delegate everything he could. He gathered up the supplies, using a cold spell to ensure that the cast iron pan wouldn't burn his hand as he placed it in the back of the caravan.

The two rogues followed him a few steps away. One had introduced herself as Bella, and she had beautiful brown curls that made it appear as if she'd just gotten out of a shower. The other, Sophie, had been through the wringer, though she had a faint smile underneath her wrinkled face. Sophie was a bit older than Bella.

Finley pulled out two double-length daggers and passed them to the women as he waited for Anthony to finish giving out assignments.

Of course, he would give himself the cooking job once he'd surveyed the interior of the courtyard with Bob.

Bob was going to do a sweep of the perimeter first before they delved into the walled off part of the city. He was taking the monks as they had an unnatural speed ability that made them an excellent go-between.

Their unarmed abilities meant that they didn't need any weapons, something that Finley thought he would find more of. Two of the monks were with him, and the other one had volunteered to be a runner and stick by the caravan, in case something happened.

Finley walked his bay mares behind Bob's group. They went counterclockwise around the city, taking the western courtyard wall. A few houses had sprung up on the south side, but it was clear that most of the people that lived in the town had lived on the eastern side. The wall did not cover the entire town as it had been a strategic trade post, not a regular garrison. Over time, more people had moved in and expanded outwards.

Finley paused next to the southernmost building that could still be called part of the town. A two-story inn with a broken sign looked like it had been in constant use for years.

Bob held up a hand while Finley calmed the horses. The ranger briefly talked to the monks with him and then both took off, running to the door of the inn.

Finley motioned for one of the rogues to follow. Bella took his cue. Her hair bobbed as she ran after them.

When Bob opened the door, one of the monks rushed in. Finley took the opportunity to position the caravan towards the road leading away from Dunnamore.

After two tense minutes, Bob re-emerged from the inn. A smile lit up his face. He ran over to where Finley had stopped the caravan.

"It's fully stocked! Or at least I think," he said. "But no zombies are inside and there are real beds! Oh, and there's a stable on the side!"

"Anything else of note? Sophie, do you want to see the stables with me? We might be able to find something useful."

She nodded, brushing back her hair. It immediately went right back to in front of her. She huffed, following behind Finley.

There wasn't a full wagon in the stables, but there were enough parts that Finley thought he might be able to assemble one. Bella arrived, fist-bumping Sophie.

"Oh. This is good," he said. "Bella? We're going to need that artificer. I think we can make a second wagon with what we have here. I see two axles and six wheels."

"I can get him, or swap places with him. He was… I forget what he was doing but do you want me to go grab him?"

Finley rolled his shoulders. "Let's take stock of what we have here and now. Bob and his monks can get him if they see him. We should look around for a workshop and then I'm going to craft a few cards with the pieces I have. Hopefully I'll get a woodworking card."

"You sure we shouldn't get him now?" Sophie said.

"Let's stick together. They're going to be clearing the town house by house and it would only take one zombie to kill and potentially turn one of us. I for one would not like to die in a brave but fruitless endeavor. That's not for me."

Bob walked around the stable area to join them. "I'm going to mark the doors of the houses we have searched. Is there anything I could use to do so?"

Bella grabbed a large flat rock from the ground and hefted it. "You could put a rock in front of the door? Plenty of rocks here. You can put a bigger one if there's stuff for us to salvage? Or work out some system."

"That's a great idea!" Bob said, grabbing the rock. "Well you all know that this one is zombie free so long as they don't sneak in when we're not looking."

"I'll pasture the horses around here so if they are scared then we'll be alerted," Finley said, reaching out to handle their emotions and pull them towards the inn.

"Did he used to be so green?" Bella said.

"I'm sure that's just some of the magic of his card powers. I mean it's just his forearms," Bob said, before checking the corner. He wandered around the back of the house, probably doing some human business.

Finley's forearms indeed were turning green, giving away something that he hadn't wanted to admit to all the people around him. Underneath that beating heart, lay something that wasn't entirely an elf. However, Finley wasn't ready to explain his past to the women in front of him just at that moment, so he just gave them the shopkeeper look. Then he growled a bit.

Bella stepped back, keeping her eyes on the ranger as he moved. "Should I lead the caravan over here? What do you need to do to set up? And I'm going to need you to not do that. Sophie might get the wrong idea."

Sophie indeed had probably gotten the wrong idea as the smile plastered on her face was unmistakable. She was looking for elf in all the wrong places.

"Ah. Sophie. Sorry about that, uh let's just say that using so much of my card powers taps me into my druidic nature. I'm using it to move the horses around, but now I need to save some to put these card pieces together."

"Let's check out the inn, then," Bella said. "If the horses are an early warning for us, then we can look for some tools and food. Any maybe start on lunch if there is a kitchen."

"Gods, I would love a kitchen," Sophie moaned as the two left Finley.

With the two humans out of his hair, Finley grabbed his sack of card pieces out of the caravan and his frame. With great care, he assembled the six parts of the frame at the workbench in the stables.

Each piece clicked into place as the runes inside itched with power. Finley pulled back from the urge to push power into it as he grabbed six common pieces, putting them down one by one.

He breathed in his intent to make a new card.

He breathed out his mana.

Drips of mana fell from his hands, joining the seams along the edges.

It didn't have to be perfectly aligned. His mana would bridge any gaps, as it pulled the pieces together to form a full card. As the final piece connected fully, the frame flashed. The shine of a new card lit up his smile. An image of a camper sitting by a fire dominated the silvered copper surface.

Common Skill Card: Survival Level 1

Survive harsh conditions instinctively.

Improves field craft and related abilities.

As this card advances, the wielder will become heartier.

Bella poked her head out of the inn just then. There was a servant's door that led to the stables.

"Oh hey, you did it boss! Good work! What kind of card is it?"

"I made a survival skill card."

"I'm kind of scratching my head here, is that good?"

"We could use it and four others like it to make a class card, so this is very good."

Bella checked something, and Finley knew that she was looking into her soul deck.

"That's not one of my rogue skills. If I equip it, will it make me stronger? Wait, let me see. I have…. expertise, sneak attack, dodge, use magic relic, and perception?"

"We should probably wait but you would have room in your soul deck for this. It would be rough to take it back out, but you wouldn't have much of a problem. So long as your soul card is uncommon or rarer, taking this out and putting it back in won't be a problem. But uh…we should probably wait for a bit," Finley said.

"Alright," she said, strongly and slowly winking in his direction, "I'm a girl who can wait for a good thing."

"Also," he said shaking his bag, "I'll be making a bunch more cards so we can see how this shakes out. Not like any of the gold pieces that I have been saving up are worth anything now. Damn zombies."

***

Anthony passed by the inn after he saw the horses there. The two-story structure sat behind a large town sign. He had thought that it was a quaint little bed and breakfast that he would have gone to in another life. Here, it just looked like another place without a good shower. He was beginning to stink, and the fact that Dunnamore had to rely on rainwater and melting snow to keep its easterly river in business meant that the water was frigid.

He found out almost by accident as the river had been close enough to warrant checking it. He didn't regret the cold. No, even as his shivered in what had to be a late fall gust of wind, he was glad to be able to wash himself. He had gone over in scrubs and his dadliest New Balance shoes. Those items did not agree with the muddying roads and walkways that this world loved. The muck remained a constant reminder that he wasn't back home. It stuck to everything.

The houses were generally four or five rooms and single-floor. All were made from a combination of masonry and wood that he hoped would keep the heat in. What little heat there was.

Every time they cleared a house, they placed a stone in front of the door. It was a reminder that they had finished it as well as something close to a grave marker. They didn't encounter anyone living, making him think that either they had run away when this all happened, or been turned. He didn't know which outcome would be good for them. It all stunk.

In his second house, at least, he found a set of cards that looked like some sort of heirloom inheritance. He pocketed them for later. The metallic copper cards clinked in his pocket. They were all skill cards. One was a magical skill, the only iron card of the bunch. It granted the user Divine Magic.

Uncommon Skill Card: Divine Spellcasting Level 1

This card grants mana.

This card allows the user to learn and cast divine spells.

He checked his own soul card and found that this mirrored the same skill he already possessed. This could be useful, but as he already had one, it wasn't going to be useful for him.

That didn't mean that he was going to give it up though.

He wondered what Finley would trade for this? Probably something good. A better question was if the elf would trade anything. He would do something for food.

It was about that time when he realized the search was making him both hungry and thirsty. Was it the situation that was making him feel this way?

He found a clean bucket that had clearly been used for water and waved to one of the warriors with him, pointing to the bucket and then the stream.

It was time for a break.

9

"You know what. We all need to drink water," Anthony said, carrying another full load of two buckets on the yoke he found scavenging.

"Yes. But you can let some of us help you bring water to the inn," Bella said. "You're a strong guy, but you don't need to go it alone. And this isn't me yelling at you because Julie said to."

"Right," Anthony said, draining the second bucket into the clean glass pitchers.

"You have magic," Finley said, "Why don't you use it?" He took the pitcher out from the inn's common room, where he set it by the door, returning with a rag. He passed a clean rag to Bella. His arm was fully green, and he moved to hide it. Anthony noticed the change but didn't say anything.

"As I said before to someone, who won't dignify me with showing her face right now," Anthony said, "I want to carry it."

"I heard that," Julie's muffled voice came from outside of the kitchen.

"I'm not an old fart. I'm barely forty. Forty-ish."

"Says the man who has a father-son business," the muffled voice said.

Bella and Finley amped up their cleaning.

"Her snark knows no bounds," Anthony muttered. "I like it."

Humans were strange. Especially these chosen heroes. Finley wanted to be content to let them pass arguments back and forth. But while he worked he needed to make sure that they were making some progress. He didn't want to be in charge, but he did want a say.

The tables were all done, so Finley stretched a bit. The benches and chairs would be next. He grabbed one of the many chairs and began to clean off the dust and dirt.

"Is this a common mating thing among humans?" Finley said to Bella.

"No," Bella said, "they're both on edge because of last night. When you get that close to death, your priorities change. I could die tomorrow. Heck, I could have already died. Julie was talking about how that made her feel and then she saw him brooding and also working and well here we are."

"Ah. I see. Then they'll do some customary mating dance, correct?"

"Gods no. Whatever would give you that—oh you're really funny," Bella said.

"It's totally what I hear humans do here. They have these big balls and for some reason they all need to dance with them. It has never made sense to me."

Anthony loaded up his equipment to return to the river. Finley and Bella placed a bucket on each side of the yoke, making it easier for him to carry.

Anthony began his march. "Anyway, with Julie and Sophie started on lunch have you got any idea if we can make something out of that pile of wood? There's two good axles and enough wheels if we can figure it out."

Finley shuffled in his pockets. He pulled out an iron card, passing it to her. "I'll do you one better. This one? It's uncommon, making it slightly stronger, though it would be strong as a common. But see the effect."

Bella investigated the card. "Wood crafting? Oh, this is great! And what does level one mean? I mean all my skills are level one right now but… How high does it go?"

"This one can go up to level ten. But since it's uncommon, we can find four other skills and turn it into a class card, giving it extra bonuses. I haven't merged a card in a while but if we get this to the artificer, maybe he'll be able to use both sets of skills together."

"What kind of class would have a woodworking skill?"

Finley paused his work on one of the better chairs. "An artisan class? Martial class cards like yours are rare. It's far more common for someone to have an heirloom class card that their parent passes down. Something like a farmer or a laborer that works with their hands. Try not to think so much about combat classes. They're a rarity, or at least they were."

"I didn't think about that. It's good to know that we can do more than just stab things here. Although the current situation kind of makes it necessary," Bella said, holding up the cleaning bucket. "Do you think that our friend would mind taking this back with him and cleaning it out?"

She tossed the dirty water out the front of the inn, narrowly missing Bob.

"Oh, hey Bob! I almost sneak attacked you there. You should probably watch out."

"Sorry, Bella. I could announce myself. It just sounds like a lot of work, when I could just dodge."

"I'll aim better next time because my sneak attack leveled up from that."

"Bella!" Bob said, taking off his cloak to make certain that it was dry.

"What? I wanted to see if it would work, and it does!"

Finley chuckled. He had heard of skills leveling unintentionally. He hadn't heard of someone leveling a combat skill through tomfoolery. Not that it was impossible.

"If you can do that with him," Finley said. "And it has to be a sneak attack, there's a few more people coming. What level is your skill?"

"Level two."

"Let's see if we can get it to level three."

***

Bob, former chef and current chosen ranger of Mork, apparently did have time for tomfoolery. As people arrived for lunch, he waved them over to come in through the exact doorway that would provide for an ambush. Bella for her part got almost half of the people that returned, though she used an empty bucket.

It wasn't until the artificer threatened violence that she stopped. The part about him ending her line hit particularly close.

"Why is it that you think I'm even going to have a line? My mom is back on another planet. Also, we're no contact because fuck that bitch."

"Bella!" Bob said. "Language!"

"And you are not my dad."

"You both probably need to go blow some steam off," Finley said, eyeing Bob and Bella

Bob had never experienced what Bella had gone through and was having difficulty relating to her experience. Mork only knew that he would never let himself be captured alive. At least after seeing all the people in the cage, he knew that he would rather die fighting.

"Yeah probably," Bob conceded. "This has been a wild two days."

The meal that Bella had prepared was about the tastiest thing that she had eaten in what felt like ages.

"Hey guys. Not to get too existential on you, but are these the same bodies that we had on Earth? Because, like, I died. I was just thinking about how good this meal was," Bob said.

"That's a little heavy for lunch, Bob. We can trade death stories when we get to know each other a bit better."

"Sorry Bella. Maybe after a brew. If we ever find a brewery."

Bella patted him on the shoulder after she got up. "Hey, so since I cooked… you guys got the cleanup right?"

The group grumbled but eventually when they finish eating started cleaning up. Then a few of them picked rooms upstairs. Bob didn't feel like he was ready for that kind of commitment. They still had half the town to search. With a full stomach they might even get it done by night. Especially if they pushed it.

***

It was late afternoon by the time they had gone through all the houses. Finley hadn't expected much, but to find nothing? It was as if the families had gotten notice—that stood out the most. Things were missing, most notably people. If any of the families had a card library, those were gone as well, though shelving was still there.

They had decided to stay the night. It was about that time that Finley found that there was another wagon. It was serviceable though not covered. It even had all the important pieces to harness up a horse or two. He slotted the woodworking card into his side deck. The artificer had been working on all the moving pieces while he made more benches.

Once the benches were done, he would move on to some sort of covering. There was enough tarp material to do so, and he would make a fully enclosed space for sleeping and storage. His storage skill pinged, letting him know that it would be easy to add some storage under the bench.

If only he had a cryomancer skill or a spatial storage skill. He'd heard about wizards that kept items in containers that were larger on the inside than the outside, and he wanted that for himself. He wasn't sure if it was a card power or skill, but he had been dreaming of the idea when he made all of the cards he could.

The cards he had made that morning had been useful up to a point, but there was only so much that he could get out of a group of commons and uncommons. He had about half of the pieces needed to make a rare card.

Making a rare or epic card would do a lot to help his situation. Whatever he needed to survive, he wanted to do. Even if it meant listening to Bella and Bob talk back and forth about the right way to wash the dishes. As if there was a wrong way.

"Hey, Finley, was it?"

The dwarf came up to Finley's chest. Finley didn't consider himself tall; his thin elvenoid body was taller than most humans but still, only by a little bit. This dwarf, for some reason, didn't have a long beard. Finley reminded himself that it took all types. He also had lighter skin and straight black hair. It reminded Finley of the mane of a horse with how straight it was.

"Yes. Andrew, wasn't it?"

"Yeah. Bella gave me some stuff to work on with you and said that you were turning the stables into your workshop…"

He walked in, standing next to the wheel that just needed some tender love and care.

"Oh, this one is good. Just looking at it makes me itch to give it an enhancement. Hey, since I know you have a druid class card, I was wondering if I could lean on your mana."

"Ah, yeah that would be fine. Just don't take too much."

The dwarf walked over, holding out one hand, palm up. Finley had worked with an artificer once and they had particular practices about mana. He'd only seen it done though.

Andrew closed his eyes briefly. "I haven't done this before so uh please bear with me."

Finley held a hand over the dwarf's, concentrating mana in that area. It took a few seconds, but a small green crystal formed between the two of their hands.

"Oh! That's neat! I wonder what I can do with it?"

"Well, try and use it on one of the hinges maybe?" Finley said. "Isn't experimentation one of your skills?"

The dwarf frowned. "It isn't. But I'll do just that and see what happens."

"Hey, uh did you get a woodworking skill?" Finley asked, "Because I made a card with it. I can give it to you. I got it to level two already. That should help you out."

"If you're leveling it now, then keep it. I can take it later. Maybe you'll make another?"

"I'll try. I'm out of pieces, though Bob has some that he is holding back."

"Yeah. He's a funny guy, that Bob."

"So, all the humans were talking about some place called Earth. I uh… noticed that you've been quiet especially at lunch. I thought I was the only one from here. I was just up at the Yil Foothills, and I didn't see you there. Are you from… here?"

The word "here" carried a lot of weight in Finley's view. If the artificer was from this world, then he might know more about Dunnamore and the Irumian Kingdom. So far, he had been quiet, and his lack of words said a lot. It was indeed a plethora of information that Finley had gathered from his being withdrawn from the conversation, though that could easily be explained by his being from another world.

"I—uh… Finley you're not going to say anything to anyone are you?"

"Of course not. If you want to keep a secret, well the tinker code prevents me from spilling it."

The tinker code prevented no such thing. What it did was outline how tinkers were never to lie to each other or kill each other, and how to greet another member of the family when out and about.

There was a second set of codes that prevented tinkers from killing enlightened beings to include all races they traded with, which was part of the reason that they didn't tread to the orcish lands far to the south. This second set gave the tinker a bonus to their charisma at the expense of defending themselves, and a skill that helped with money laundering. Only those that swore the second set of oaths knew about the specifics.

"I'm not from Earth. I'm also not from here," Andrew said. "Surprise, surprise."
     "Oh. OH!"

10

Rare Class Card: Artificer Level 2

Skills:

Simple Crafting and Forging Level 2

Enchantment Level 1

Blueprinting Level 1

Tinkering Level 1

Alchemy Level 1

As an Artificer, you may use others' mana for enchantments, and while in range, casters with mana can turn mana into crystals for your use in artificer works.

This card allows the user to imbue spells known by nearby casters.

This is a soul card and cannot be removed.

This strange world held many mysteries for Andrew. The first of which was the magical card system. As with everything he had seen, all the horrors, he had just accepted it. It was the way.

His way.

He worked on the carriage assembly, checking out the differences between the tinker caravan that Finley traveled in and the spare parts that they'd found around town. In the process, his simple crafting and forging skill had continually led him in the right direction. That had given him the first skill leveling notification and increased his artificer class level. Now with two similarly shaped wagons, he looked to make a blueprint from the working wagon.

There were a lot of similarities between the two. He'd readily accepted that there was a right way and a wrong way. The two wagons differed more than different shades of gray. Barring the covering that was part canvas, part load-bearing wooden cross beams, they could have been made from the same place at different times.

The main problem he needed to solve was how to attach the load bearing portion that connected to the wheels to the wagon frame itself. This was a worthy problem in a test of mostly easy questions. He tackled it with a smile.

The wagon was helpful in keeping him from thinking about how he'd been ripped from home and taken here. Before, he'd lived a quiet life, keeping to himself and tending his clockwork shop.

His world hadn't been too different from this one, though it lacked so many things that he had really thought he would see.

He had asked Finley to keep his heritage a secret. Though how far that would go, he could only guess. He didn't feel close to the humans yet and that they were both non-humans helped a bit. It meant that they were both outsiders for a different reason. He saw something in the elf.

***

It was getting close to dinnertime. The sun, as it does, of course threatened that time was about up. That was the first time that Bob's quest card pinged since the night prior.

Rare Meta Card: Quest Level 1

This card creates quests for the wielder and generates rewards for quest completion. Quests may also be given by a patron deity. The more this card levels, the more information about the quest and quest rewards you will receive.

A voice clearly spoke to Bob.

> New Quest: Survive.
>
> Reward: Five common cards.

"Fuck," said Bob, chosen ranger of Mork. "Hey guys look alive. I got a quest."

"Finley," Bella said. "Wake up."

The elf had been sleeping, trying to get a short nap in before dinner. After a full day of work, Bob could understand the impulse. No one knew when another attack would come and there was little that they could do in the meantime except rest and prepare. It was one thing to fight zombies; it was another to do it on an empty stomach.

Bob walked outside to check the horizon and see what exactly was happening.

"What's the quest say?" Bella asked.

Bob pushed a window open.

"All it says is, 'survive.' If I survive then I get five common cards," he said, scanning the outskirts of the town. "Now where the heck would they be coming from? Does anyone see Anthony anywhere?"

"I'll get him," Sophie said, heading to the stables.

"Wait! Bring a friend. I don't like this," Bob said.

"Alright. Bella?"

Bella and Sophie slipped out the side entrance.

Bob turned back to see who else was there. Finley was getting up. Julie was snoring loudly. Bob gently nudged her. The snoring stopped as she slumped off her bench seating onto the floor.

"Hey, you asshole, what the heck?" she said.

The rest of the survivors all started moving around, getting up.

Bob still didn't see anything, and he wanted more than anything to go do a sweep of the perimeter. He would need Anthony to help. The monks split to opposite corners, checking every direction. None of the horses had moved yet or done anything but graze next to the inn.

Bob regretted not saddling every horse. There were more horses than people to ride them.

"Finley, we might need to move quickly," he said once the elf joined him by the window. "Can you make the horses ready?"

"They're in a state of rest but… alright, now they're all looking at us. They don't see anything either."

Bob and Finley shifted to the side of the inn with the stables. The dwarf was still working hard on what appeared to be a half-done third wagon. The second was set up next to the bay mares, just lacking horses hitched up to pull it.

Anthony ran in. "What did I miss?"

"Ranger Bob's Quest skill? It pinged. Something about survival. We're checking out if there are any zombies on the way," Bella said. "I'm going to load up what I have been prepping into the second wagon. Thanks to that one cryomancer card we should be good if we can make a fire."

"I'll get two of the horses hitched up," Finley said. "Can I get some help loading? And if anyone has a saddle this will be a hell of a lot easier. I made three animal handling skill cards so I can pass those out. I can't get any benefit from multiples of the same card skill."

He handed the cards to Anthony to deal out before leaving. Bob wished that they had more time to construct their decks and learn a bit more about the cards, but the elf was both overstimulated and overtired by the time it reached afternoon. So what if he only had to take a power nap every day; if he needed to do it every time his mana went low that would be a big blow.

"Thanks. Warriors?" Anthony asked, "Help the elf and dwarf load up everything. Monks? Make sure everyone is up. If we must move, we will. We'll decide where we're going next on the road if needed."

"Yes boss!" the monks said, sprinting ahead of the warriors.

The warriors followed along. The group's wizard, still sleeping, was being carried by the only male rogue in the group. It was as if they had all made terrible decisions based on their own choices, and Bob had to pay the bill. Each one had to pick a class when they had been summoned, if the other gods were like Mork, so having all of them as melee focused classes was suboptimal.

Bob rotated to the western-facing wall, looking for anything and hoping for nothing. Then he could see plants moving in the grasslands west of the town.

"From the west! There's a lot of them!"

Behind him, Anthony crowded the window. Bob showed him the figures emerging from the grass.

"Mount up!" Anthony said. "We can't stay here right now. I know we were going to practice this, but we don't have time. Grab whatever you can carry. Stack it all in the open wagon. Is everyone here?"

"What's going on? One second, I was talking to my patron and the next…" Julie said, her voice groggy and low to the ground.

"Can somebody get the warlock? We're going to need her ranged attacks. Julie, can you fire from here?"

"Anthony? Why are you yelling?"

"Because—fuck these zombies—I don't want to die, Julie. And I don't want any of you to die."

Bob put a hand underneath her armpit and helped her up. She had a lot of firepower. The reason that she was sleeping was her practice. Bella had given her some of the glasses to use as target practice. She shot blast after blast until she tapped herself out. Bob wasn't sure yet how much range she had. Not needing to have arrows was a big boon.

Bob was jealous. He didn't have time for it, though. With Anthony and Julie as their ranged support, it fell to him to get the horses set up on the second wagon. When he left the confines of the inn he had expected to spend the night at, he paused, checking to see if he had left anything.

He felt his bow around his cloak, and with his full waterskin at his side, he moved to calm the horses.

He'd retrieved several of his used bolts, much to the dismay of the monks with him. Those bloodied bolts all sat on the back of the wagon, next to the pile of wagon parts.

Finley's tips had helped advance his animal handling skill. He was grateful for the new ability to push the horses in a direction. It felt like pushing rope a bit, but it didn't take mana.

Another voice popped into his mind.

Quest Updated: Survive: Survive for the next twenty minutes.

Quest Reward: Five Common Cards, one Uncommon Card, ten Rare Card pieces.

"Fuck. Guys!"

***

The caravan was ready to go. Both their second wagon and the incomplete, open-topped third one Andrew had been working on finally had horses tied up and in position. Anthony scrambled to get people inside. The four people that had animal handling as a skill card had coaxed some of the horses into letting them ride along. They had saddles, salvaged from the interior courtyard.

What use zombies would have for saddles, Anthony would never know. He never wanted to know.

The idea of intelligent undead using animals to further their own interests scared him.

"Is everybody here?" Anthony said, testing the reins of the wagon. "We don't have time to sit here."

It hadn't been a minute since the dwarven zombies all came out of the grassy plains on the western side of the city. Now they were crossing the open area that marked the southern half of the city.

Ahead of him, Finley had his caravan pointed south toward the direct route to the Capital. According to the tinker, there was another town only a day away. That town would have a fully-fledged card shop, as well as a few other things that would help them on their journey. He didn't want to leave Dunnamore. The grass was shaking, they didn't have a choice.

Finley's wagon and the herd of horses around them began moving with a jolt as the screaming started. It wasn't the zombies that chased them, as their vocal cords had stopped working some time ago. Neither was it Bella and Sophie, who sat on the back of his wagon, guarding the wizard. The screaming came from Bob himself.

"Get him down!" Anthony yelled. "He's losing his cool!"

"I'm trying," Bella said. She slapped Bob several times before he snapped out of it.

"Bob! Was that another quest update? Or did something else happen?"

"Their gaze. I wasn't paying attention. Those red eyes…" he said.

Anthony turned his attention towards the horses that were just now getting up to speed, keeping pace with the riders next to him. The three on horseback were riding ahead, though without weapons all they could do would be to be a distraction.

All they needed to do was to stay ahead of the horde. And if they survived for twenty minutes, then maybe Bob would get a good card? Anthony wasn't entirely sure how it worked. He just knew that if the gods were going to give them something then it better be damn good.

***

Bella's perception skill leveled up and she cursed.

"There's got to be at least two hundred of them. That explains where all the townspeople went. Do you think we could take down all of them?"

"I honestly don't know," Sophie said. "But you got an ice spell, right? Is that going to help us out?"

"It kind of feels like I can do a bunch of things, but I have to, like, focus on it. Besides making the ice chest for all the meat and food. The power wants to be called. I don't know how well this will go. I'm really hoping that we can just outrun them."

The wagon rattled as they moved. Bella instinctively reached out for Bob. In between them, she found herself holding his hand, their arms pressed together.

"All the things I said earlier," she whispered. "I'm really sorry."

"I know how it is."

"What, you're not going to apologize too? We could die!"

"I'm really sorry. And we can continue this discussion later when we live," Bob said, winking at her.

"You're damn right."

"Ahem," Sophie said from the far side of the wagon as it jolted. She held onto one of the spare wheels with one hand.

"Sorry, Sophie!" Bella said.

From the front of the wagon, Andrew briefly flew several feet into the air as they hit another bump. Anthony stayed on the seat. Everyone else but the five of them was either riding a horse or in the caravan.

"They're speeding up!" Bob yelled.

"Well shit. The warlock and the wizard are in the next wagon," Bella said. "Let's see what we can do."

Bella tapped into her ice magic. If the zombies were moving, what would they do if all of a sudden, the area was impassable? The road they were on had a gentle downward slope. It was so gentle that you wouldn't notice it unless you looked far to the south.

Bella tapped into her mana, drawing on the water that was loose in the air.

"How much time do we have? Bob?" Sophie said.

"The quest is giving me ten minutes."

"If you see a rider, tell them to get ahead of us. Don't let them drop back."

Bella concentrated on the ambient magic and humidity, it would do nicely. Blue sparks flew out of her hands as she spread them to the side. The thick packed dirt gave way suddenly to a thin sheet of ice as the spell drank up her mana.

As they moved, the road behind them turned into ice more and more.

"Don't burn yourself out," Anthony yelled.

"What?" Sophie yelled back.

"He said don't burn yourself out," Bob said.

"I can handle myself. Don't tell me what I can and can't do," Bella yelled back as the mana dropped out of her and into the air behind the wagon.

As they moved, the wagon looked like it was grading the ground and covering it with a clear glaze. The now-flat ground was about to meet with its first and probably last enemy.

***

There's not a lot said about zombie foot care. There are no zombie podiatrists. In fact, there's no zombie primary care and definitely no zombie orthopedists.

That said, the compulsion to eat the flesh of the living drives one to do silly things.

Silly things like not wearing shoes or boots when one is searching for a warm body to eat.

Such is the case for many of the zombies that found themselves starving and chasing down two caravans full of tasty morsels.

For those zombies, none of them had thought to bring winter boots on this occasion. To be fair, most zombies don't think much at all.

These ecologically friendly zombies who did not build fires or contribute towards society in any way good or bad only wanted to satisfy their base instincts. So, one could imagine that the gibberish that they screamed while they chased down their prey could come out as garbled screams, even when the zombish phrase "Welcome to Dunnamore, please stay forever and ever" didn't penetrate any thick skulls.

It was rather unfortunate when the first barefoot undead dwarf met with a very elaborate icy slide. Unfortunate in a sense that they didn't have a natural inclination of how to deal with such a problem. Fortunate for them in that several were able to propel themselves on the slight decline just by virtue of slipping on the zombies in front of them.

Said zombies turned into a one dwarf bobsled team almost by accident. It wasn't every day that zombies worked together. And today wasn't going to change that fact. But if all the zombies cared about was getting closer to dinner, and in doing so they didn't have to move, then they were happy.

Really it was just thanks to one person who had misjudged a card ability. If the zombies could have prayed to their god, they would have thanked them profusely at that time. And so it was that most of the horde of zombies got caught up on the ice. About a dozen were able to continue down unhindered, no thanks to their foot hygiene.

Of those, several were using other zombies as makeshift sleds.

Were they doing this intentionally? No.

Were they picking up speed? Yes.

"Bella?"

"Yes, Sophie"

"Are those fucking zombies bobsledding?"

"It would appear so, Sophie."

"And are they going faster now than they were before?"

"It would appear so, Sophie."

"Bella?"

"Yes, Sophie?"

"How do you kill a bobsledding zombie?"

11

"They've got to slow down sometime, right?" Bella said. "Friction is a thing here. I'm running out of mana!"

"Don't burn yourself out trying to save us now. You're not the only one with card powers," Bob said. "And five minutes, by the way. I hope that this works."

"Five minutes? What a girl wouldn't give for a Molotov cocktail right about now," Sophie said. "What? I'm just saying what we're all thinking."

The looks that she was getting made Sophie melt like a zombie luge.

"No, no, you're right. She has a point," Bob said. "Hey uh, what about like the opposite of a Molotov cocktail?"

Bella gave the cute balding ranger a pat on the shoulder.

"Opposite as in, not fire? Like it sucks the air out of the area? Or like water or…. Oh!" Bella said. "Where's that barrel of water?"

The barrel in question had been strapped down exactly in the middle of the wagon. It was the place deemed most likely to be the least problematic. They weren't playing Fast and the Furious, but the wagon did pick up a lot of speed. The ropes that held the barrel in place were all but glued in, and it would be hard to undo all of the hard work. Also, as it was their entire water supply, it would be bad for the long term. None of the motley crew had any idea where they would be able to find water next. Bella realized that she was stalling. A guttural squeal from a zombie brought her back to the present.

"What are you thinking about, Bella?" Bob said.

"Well those guys are still chasing us. If I had a bottle of water I could—now hear me out and don't laugh—I feel like I could make it detonate on a short timer. Like an ice grenade. That barrel would be perfect for it, but we would be shooting ourselves in the foot."

Of the dozens, if not hundreds, that had been chasing them, most had fallen to the wayside. The wagons kept moving, the horses kept moving, and the zombies couldn't keep up. Except for the ones that had slid just right. All counted. It was just under a dozen of those. They weren't close, as Bob kept telling them. He was tracking how fast they were relatively by landmarks on the side of the road. A rock they passed would be passed by the zombies about ten seconds later.

This was an improvement from the five seconds it had been when Bella stopped making a zombie slide.

"We probably should have made the ice vary. Like rumble strips. But why don't you use a waterskin for this?" Bob said holding up his Mork-branded waterskin. "I can think of no better way to honor Mork, than to use his implement as a fragmentary grenade against his hated foes."

"You want to charge my water skin, toss it into the crowd behind us and try to do some damage with it?" Bella asked.

"Exactly." Bob grinned. "You know what? Go right ahead. Here it is. Ice it up, girl."

Bob handed her his water skin. With the time they had used to recover, Bella could feel a pool of mana just below the surface. She concentrated on what she was trying to do, feeling the skill working. It wanted to obey her commands, but this particular task seemed to be more than the norm.

She could feel it would just need a little push. She thought about the satisfaction she would get from this working, but that felt wrong. The skill wanted her to think about how water worked, there was some word she remembered from chemistry class about a solid turning into a gas rapidly.

"Sublimation."

She chanted it and the spell clicked in her mind. It was the opposite of freezing something. She tied it off with a four second countdown, something that felt natural and she got it. She placed the trigger as a trickle of mana.

A quick check of her card showed that her ice magic had already reached level three.

"Two levels? What the heck," she said. "Bob, do you want to do the honors?"

"No, this is all you. Make us proud."

Bella aimed. The one semester of college where she played softball ran through her mind as she underhand lobbed the sublimation grenade. As it left, she triggered the internal countdown.

There are certain times in a woman's life where everything peels away and the raw emotion takes the front stage. Times like the day she gets married, the first time she has to file her taxes or bury a loved one. Such a day would stick in one's memory and loom large in the consciousness.

The moment that Bella froze a dozen zombies solid was one such moment.

All movements from the lead zombies ceased as the night finally fell.

"You did it! Great work babe!" Bob said.

"Babe?" Bella said, leaning on him "How about something more suitable like Ice Queen?"

"My liege," Sophie said. "Us peasants are unworthy of your grace. You bless us with your actions."

"You're both too kind. Now I'm going to go curl up for a bit. Wake me if they catch up."

Bella yawned and leaned into Bob, the warmth of his body a creature comfort that she needed.

***

The god of death could have been mean to Bob, his chosen ranger. He could have done something like making all of the quest rewards be stuck inside the chests of the zombies that were frozen solid. Or he could have let the quest rewards be unattainable. But over the few short days that Bob had been on Noveria, he had found the quests to be fair.

So, when several shiny objects found their way into a Mork-themed tote bag by his feet, he was more than a little surprised. Inside the bag were two Mork-branded waterskins, if nothing else the god had his messaging on point, and the entirety of the quest rewards he had been promised.

"Will require… head pats? Oh holy shit!" Bob forcibly shoved the rare card into his chest and then activated it. A black cat appeared and then after a brief glance sauntered off.

"Bob, mind explaining about this secret cat power?" Bella said.

"It's a quest reward."

A yowl behind them made them turn. Bob saw the tiny black cat moving incredibly fast to the ice-cold zombies, then he watched as the cat sliced through reality to grab a shiny card in its teeth. The card pieces all disappeared from the first zombie.

"Really, Bob."

Bob projected the card in his hand, a little trick that his god had keyed him into. The golden card had a three-dimensional image of a black house cat rubbing itself around someone's leg.

Rare Summon Card: Ca'at

This card allows the user to summon Ca'at, a greater feline thief. Ca'at has claws that will pierce any defeated foe and draw out all cards in their soul deck. Ca'at can be directed to steal cards from downed foes and will carry and return all such cards to the wielder, but will require head pats.

Ca'at has a range of three leagues and a cooldown time of four hours.

"You summoned a cat?" Bella said.

"Ca'at, but yes," Bob said. "I have the other rewards here, but they all look like they're all common skill cards? Huh. Ten skill cards, some rare pieces and an uncommon card that Mork upgraded to a rare? Plus whatever the cat brings."

"That cat is eating the card pieces," Sophie said.

"What?" Bob said.

"Yes, what?" Bella said.

They watched in horror as Ca'at sliced the frozen zombies one by one, each time pulling out their soul cards and then somehow eating all of the glowing card pieces underneath.

"I'm sure it's fine. This has to be a good kitty, right?" Bob said.

Its business concluded, the summoned creature turned to the wagon and began to run. Bob's eyes raised in feigned alarm.

"How is it moving so fast?" he said.

Before he finished his sentence, Ca'at had arrived in the wagon. Bob nervously gave it head pats. The cat horked several times, trying to get out the world's worst hairball, finally lowering a dozen copper and iron cards onto the wagon bed.

"Good girl? Boy?" he said, his voice wavering.

Bob grabbed the cards with one hand, putting them away.

For its part, the cat began to hack and cough. Sophie and Bella moved away as fast as they could. It raised its hackles and coughed up a shiny hairball.

"Did that thing just cough up card pieces?" Sophie said.

"Yes. Fuck yes," Bob said.

Bob stuffed the pieces into his designer Mork purse. He dearly hoped that the cat wouldn't be doing that every time. That would begin to be problematic. And he didn't want the Mork purse to smell. That would be really terrible.

Satisfied by its work, Ca'at curled up in the middle of the wagon bed.

***

"They've successfully stopped the zombies," Julie said. "We can outrun the rest."

"You hope we can outrun the rest," Finley said, spurring the horses on. "I don't think that we'll be so lucky."

Julie sat next to Finley. Her warlock ability was the reason he had asked her to pop up to the front. He'd known warlocks before, and knew that she had real power behind her card skills. The groans of the zombies had long ago ceased behind them.

"Oh wait, that means that Bob probably got his quest reward. I wonder what it was?" Finley said.

"I heard something about a cat. It feels like I'm playing telephone here with the wizard girl in the back of the caravan."

Zan, the wizard, was the final person in the caravan and had gotten word from the uncovered wagon crew. She was joined by two of the female warriors, the only male rogue and the one male warrior that had been isekaied, as well as the three monks; the entire group had been changing who was riding horses as there was only enough room to stand.

"Telephone?" Finley said.

"It's some earth thing. I swear that the message might have changed along the way from the back to the front. We can ask a rider to pass a message, though. They're not doing much."

"They need spears."

"Spears would be good. Do you know where we could get any?"

"There should be a shop in the next town. If we make it that far."

"You really think it's that bad?" she said, waving a rider over.

"I got an unusual skill right before all you chosen started arriving. Unusual as in unique."

"Ah."

The monk on horseback got within speaking range.

"Hey, can you find out what's going on back there?" Julie asked.

"On it. They're all good though? And somehow they acquired a cat?"

"Ask them what happened. Finley and I want to know," she said waving him off. "Honestly if anyone is able to find a cat in this world, then good on them. Crazy cat ladies are a sign of a good social support network."

"Those are all words that I understand," Finley said. "But that order is troubling."

"This is a good thing. Maybe it's a crazy card power?"

"There are often powers that make no sense, especially some of the common or uncommon ones. I once heard of a common card that just changed someone's hair into a random haircut once per day. Really useful at a party, but not anywhere else."

"I could see how that might be a problem."

Julie watched as the rider returned.

"All is good. Bob said that he found a way to harvest cards from the zombies chasing us. Something about feline grace and agility. He wonders if we're going to have a chance to stop soon. He got a bunch of card pieces that he wants you to see if you can make them into something. Also, a set of five class skills that he has questions about," the monk said. "He said something about you telling him a trick to combine them?"

"Ah. Tell him to hold off doing anything with them for now. There's a small hill up in a few spans where we can set up camp for the night. We'll need to keep a watch though. The last time, the zombies kept coming. It's a special spot for tinkers—I know it well."

"They're more than a span behind us now." A slight jolt caused Julie to make contact with Finley's arm. "Sorry!"

"If the warlock could ride and you all had ranged attacks you could lead them away, but," Finley said, "she needs to keep the rest of us safe. Her and that wizard will need all of their strength if we're going to stop tonight."

"I'll relay the message sir," the monk said, before trotting a bit outside of the caravan's speaking range and then slowing to meet the wagon behind them.

"Now, please tell me what magic your warlock class card lets you know, because it could save our lives."

12

The caravan kept moving through the night. It was about then that Finley realized another flaw in the design of humans. They didn't have night vision. Not that they needed it with the full moon in the sky, but it could have easily been overcast. He didn't know if the dwarf could see in the dark and he would have to find out. The night could turn as deadly as the zombies.

He could only hope that the zombies had a period where they were less active. The horses might run themselves into the ground.

"I think I have it now," Julie said next to him. "Eldritch light!"

She lobbed a ball of dark light up ahead of them. The ball kept a steady pace, anchored above their horses. Her previous attempts had continually fallen behind.

"Oooh! A skill level!"

Finley groaned. They seemed to be getting levels far faster than he did. Of course, **they** were the chosen of their gods, but well he had hoped that being the Tinker King would give him something.

"That's great. I guess keep practicing it, but let's keep this one going. Your previous attempts were good but your control has really shown marked improvement."

"You gotta teach me some tricks," Zan said from behind them. "I can learn just about any spell according to my class. That eldritch light looks useful. Oh, and bossman, I think I have a better way to store your stock. Especially if we're going to use two or more wagons."

The meek woman had come up with a system for shuffling around Finley's stock without asking him for input. That she had stopped before doing a random reshuffle, he was glad for. He had heard of couples getting into arguments about this kind of thing, one of many reasons that he traveled solo.

"Thank you, Zan. We can discuss this matter at greater length when the horde isn't a threat. Since we changed roads several times, they're unlikely to continue after us. I hope that you or Julie here can come up with a warding scheme that we can use for early warning. Who knows how long these horses are going to want to stay with us? Though they seem content for now."

"That brings up a question that I really should have asked earlier. What do you know about the zombies here? Do they have some elemental weakness of some kind? Back home we have these games where some sort of holy magic is the way to kill zombies and—" Julie said.

"You kill zombies for sport back home? How terrifying. No wonder you became a warlock," Finley said.

"Well no. It's more like we pretend to kill zombies. There are no real zombies on earth—" Julie said.

"Unless you count Florida Man high on bath salts," Zan said.

"Fuck Florida."

"You're going to have to explain what a 'Florida Man' is to me," Finley said, edging between the two.

So, the girls did, explaining all the ins and outs of the culture of the southern state. Finley wasn't prepared for the discourse and had to shut it down half an hour later when they arrived at a tinker waypoint.

"The large stone?"

"The flat ground?"

"All of the above. Those are all reasons that we start there. We used to call these way stations here and they—well, I guess it's just me now."

"Zan, do you want to help Bob's team? I think we're going to need some light back there," Julie said.

Zan shivered. She nodded and hurried off to the back of the caravan as Finley came back to bring it to a slow roll. Around them, the herd of horses all found convenient patches of grass to roll around and rest in. Once he was sure that he had found the exact spot that would make it the easiest to leave from, he set the brake and stepped down.

"Hey." Julie held out her hand for him to grab.

"Hey."

"Sorry if that got a little close to home. Losing your entire tribe must be hard on you." She intertwined their fingers squeezing for the briefest moment, "But we're here now."

Finley felt the warmth in her hand. It was nice. He headed over to the stone. It was a large flat stone about half as tall as he was and as large as a dinner table. Tinkers had often used it as such. Finley drew upon a fond memory about another stone. His caravan had stopped at one of the stones, and by sheer coincidence had arrived the same time as another tinker group. They laughed and played and sang songs for two days longer than they had intended.

They had made fun of him because he appeared to be a grown elf still getting used to things, still green. His adopted family had admonished them about his awkwardness. It was the first time that the tinker had felt that warm feeling of family.

He placed a hand on the stone. He wouldn't be able to memorialize all the zombies that were following them. At least not right this moment. The Goat Lord would understand. Instead, he promised the Goat Lord that he would grow sunflowers at this rock. He tapped into his mana, reaching out for growth. He grabbed a seed from his pocket, scooped out some dirt and put it in. He placed the dirt over the seed, bleated, and then covered it up.

Mana dripped into it from his fist. As if he squeezed an orange, the juice dripped down. A little sprout popped up. Finley finally cracked a smile.

The flower would grow in time.

He turned to find Anthony dismounting.

"Anthony, welcome to this tinker way station. If I could, I would make this place more like it was, but this is not the time for merriment. We must find a way to guard against the horde."

"This place feels reverent. I hadn't noticed it before I stepped down. I can't put my finger on it. Do you know?"

Finley had been to many way stations. In the past, tinkers had been reviled and turned away, and due to their nonviolent nature, they often just turned the other cheek. For something to happen at a way station, it would go against the family.

No one went against the family.

"I think you can tell if you look deep enough," Finley said, stretching out his own druidic magic to feel the familiar sign.

Anthony closed his eyes. His face went through a series of contortions that reminded Finley of someone trying to fix the undercarriage of a wagon. Finley knew the familiar feeling. It was something that he wanted to experience for the first time once again, but seeing someone else experiencing it would suffice.

Anthony sat down and began to meditate. Finley left him to it. Moving, he greeted the horses. It was time to address the horses that had drawn the wagon behind him and kept the strange crew alive. One by one, he stood next to the mane of each horse, thanking it in turn. As he worked his way around, he took the two horses that had pulled the wagon out and replaced them. The herd was following them out of a sense of safety, not obligation. They were all trained war horses, with the exception of his bay mares.

When he reached the final two horses, he pushed them to replace his bay mares. There was no telling if any zombies would come upon them at night. They were at most half a day's ride away from the nearest dwarven settlement. He needed the horses to be fresh.

His horses only needed to sleep for a few hours and then would be up again. They treasured those power naps. Once he was certain that they weren't missing any horses, he checked to see if there was enough water close by for the horses to drink.

Finding a small brook, he pulled the horses towards it. It wasn't more than a tree span into the woods. As the horses plodded out to drink, Julie cast and then tied off a dark light above the stream.

"Hey! You found some water. Once the horses are done drinking, I'm sure that some of us will want to take a quick dip. I will—hey your arms are really green," Julie said.

Finley looked down to see that they had indeed become greener.

"Druid stuff?" she asked.

"Druid stuff."

"Ah. That's interesting."

"If you're going to strip down and jump in the water, it's not too deep, but I wouldn't jump in. You know how to swim, yeah?"

But she was already stripping down. Finley sighed. They at least needed to set up a watch before they did all those wacky things that humans were fond of doing. Like, for instance stripping naked in the middle of the night after a zombie attack and jumping into a stream.

"Anthony, you have some sense, right?" Finley said, returning from the edges of the way station.

"I'm not well known for it yet, but sure."

The tall bearded man was checking the way stone. Everyone needed some rest, but if Anthony was in charge, he would be setting up things.

"Would you wait a minute before jumping into a river you just found? Or just jump in?"

"Depends on what my friends are doing."

A loud splash interrupted Finley's thought.

"Ah. I see. I'm going to hold off for a bit. I didn't see too many towels anywhere so they're going to be a bit chilled when they get out. I don't suppose that there's a cleaning skill? Or a cleanse card?" Anthony flexed, stretching out.

"As a matter of fact, I think I have something just like that," Finley said, "Let me check in the back."

Finley rummaged around for a minute. More and more splashes and laughter were heard. Then he held out a copper card for all to see.

"Ah here it is. The copper bucket is just how I remembered it," he said holding a card aloft. "Do you want to…?"

Anthony inspected the card.

Common Skill Card: Cleanse Level 1

This card grants mana.

This card allows the user to cast a basic cleaning spell on any living creature or object within a radius of one arm's length and can be reused while the wielder has mana.

"I'll pass this on to Julie, the first person to jump in."

"I'm sorry, I only have one side deck so she'll have to put it in her soul, but I don't think it will be a bother for her to remove it," Finley said, "Plus how long was she in that cage? Two days? She deserves a wash if she wants."

"Bob is resting in my wagon, but he got a lot of card pieces when uh—so, he got a strange card as part of his survival quest."

"A strange card?" Finley said.

Anthony nodded for the elf to follow him.

There in the wagon bed sat Bob and a creature that was entirely unfamiliar to Finley. Ca'at meowed loudly, its eyes a clear blue against black fur. Finley bristled at seeing the tiny beast. Summons were rare, but not unheard of. Then it growled at him and he stepped back. Satisfied at its show of force the otherworldly eldritch being curled up.

"What tier of card made this summon?" Finley said.

"Oh, hey Finley," Bob said, "Ca'at is a rare card. I got it from a quest reward of all things."

"You got a rare card from a rare card power?" Finley said, crossing his arms.

"Yes I—don't look at me like that!"

Finley bleated a curse. He caught Bob off guard and the human didn't seem to know what to do with himself. It was just like a human to get bullshit card powers, while he had been working on his merchant skills for years to scrape some of them to level three. For these people to have more than one rare card in their soul decks after being in his world for less than a week—he was going to have words with the Goat Lord.

"Can your summon act as a guard? That's what we need right now."

"It has a cooldown time but doesn't specify how long it can be active for? Is that normal?"

"No. Or maybe yes. Summons aren't that common. What are the other cards did you get?"

"Oh, well, I got several common skill cards that kind of look like my class skills. I didn't know what to make of them."

Finley smiled. "Finally, some good news."

On their side, Bella returned from the river, her naked form illuminated in the moonlight. Bob and Finley turned to greet the dripping wet rogue.

"Hey, so don't be weird about this guys, but does anyone happen to have a towel?"

13

"Hey Bob. My eyes are up here. If you're going to take in the show I expect at least a few rare card pieces for my trouble. Also, you have a bit of a smell about you so maybe take a dip as well? I heard that someone has a cleaning power?"

Bella didn't mind Bob looking. She did mind him smelling like he hadn't showered in a long time.

"Bob, go jump in the river. Bella can handle herself," Finley said.

Bella could see that Bob was still locked up and she snapped her fingers in front of him several times. That finally broke him out of it.

"Oh yes, uh sorry. Who had the cleaning powers?"

Bob began to strip down in front of her, a choice that she wanted to avoid. True his muscles were a choice cut—Bella had to remind herself that they were in a life-or-death situation, and she probably shouldn't have jumped into the cool clear water. Her hair was still dripping wet.

"Hey, I really hope that you have a towel or two in the caravan. Some of the canvas material was clean. I wouldn't trust it though," Bella said once Bob was down to his shorts.

Bob stripped off his pants and instead of running to the stream, just casually strolled over without a care in the world. "Cleaning?"

"Oh yeah," Finley said, "I got this card that I meant to give to Julie. I thought she would be the first out but—"

The look that she gave him would have melted an already viscous cheese.

"—or you can take it."

"Or I can take it, yeah," she said.

Bella took the card and held it out.

"Alright. What do I do with this again?"

"Just place it above your heart, then will it into your soul deck. Since you already have cryomancer magic this should be easy."

Bella pressed the card against her bare chest then gave it a little push. She could feel the skill and immediately activated it on herself. Instantly, she felt like she had spent a day at the Korean spa she loved and was now cleaned inside and out. Blue flames tingled her skin as the affected part extended from her in a large cylinder.

"Finley, I could kiss you but—oh hell yes this works on my clothes," she said.

She ran back to where her clothes were, not even noticing the circle of cleanliness that she left behind. The pile of clothing by the river sat all alone as six people splashed around in the water.

"Oh, boys and girls! Who wants to be clean as a whistle?"

"Bella?" Bob asked, as he dipped into the cool water.

"The one and the same. Now everyone come closer to me so I can show you all the best card power I have seen so far."

***

Anthony watched as Bella used her cleaning power over and over. Each time the blue flames washed over her companions she giggled. Then he turned back to look at how the group had set up. They didn't have camping supplies to set up a tent, but they did have enough canvas to finish the top of the last wagon in case it rained that night.

Now he just needed to wrangle all of the cats. Six people were in the river, which left him, the dwarf, and Finley in the center. He felt like he needed to unload, but he didn't have anything to unload. And setting up an elaborate camp wouldn't help them in any way. Their primary needs were, in his eyes, security and safety from the zombies. If the cards and card pieces they got from Bob's quest power could fill in that gap then he wouldn't need to find a way to get bows and swords.

Their next need was food and water, but they had enough for a few days if they kept eating the way that they had. Once everyone was done getting clean then he could refill the water barrel in the wagon, but it didn't need filling now.

Some form of shelter would be their third objective. If they needed to, they could sleep in the wagons. Some of the horses already looked asleep, judging by their stillness. Some stood up to rest, but most lay by the way stone.

He thought back to all those nursing classes where they went over Maslow's hierarchy of needs. Then he remembered his favorite meme where someone had replaced the entire thing with getting railed in a sundress and smiled.

He could start with their basic needs and security first. That meant that he needed to set a watch and begin planning for the short term. He had no idea what Yil or Mork wanted them to do against all the zombies. Some guidance would have been nice. It felt like someone had just given him the keys to an airplane and told him to figure it out. Anthony didn't even know if airplanes needed keys. They probably worked off some ridiculous key fob.

With fifteen people, they could work in shifts. That was when he ran into his first problem. In the dark of this new world, he didn't have a way to know exactly what time it was. He hadn't found any pocket watches, and had not thought to get a clock, so how would they even think about doing shifts?

"Hey Finley," he said, drawing the elf away from his work piecing together more cards for them. "How do we mark time here?"

"Do you mean like a calendar?"

"I mean, like the hours. How can I mark it when several hours have passed?"

"That's a good question. I have one wind up clock in the caravan that nobody would ever buy. So, I just kept it. I never really needed it for much. You want it?"

"We're going to have to set a watch. There are fifteen of us. I need some way for them to track time, especially if they're splitting shifts, and need to wake someone at a particular time. I don't want those zombies to show up as a surprise, even though I think we lost them in the shuffle."

"Let me grab it."

Finley pulled out a clock from the caravan and passed it over to Anthony. It looked straightforward at first glance. A crank on the back made it look like a jack in the box. Anthony handed it back. Finley chuckled and turned the crank a few times and the clock face began to tick.

"Alright, now we need to gather everyone. Not the horses I don't think so. Question about the horses—this is some power you have, right? They're not intelligent and trying to not die to zombies, correct?"

"They're not intelligent the way that you and I are. They're smart enough to know that if they stick with us, they'll survive what's about to happen, but they're tired. My two bay mares are unaccustomed to all this drama as well." Finley pointed over to the river. "You can't see it but they're both sulking."

"Ah. Next question was if they would be able to go in the middle of the night if we got attacked. I need to know if I can count on them."

"You can count on them. I switched the horses leading the wagons and the ones that are there now understand that we might have to leave quickly."

A small crowd began to gather around the way stone. Anthony counted ten with himself and Finley.

"I guess we need to talk as a group. I thought I had more time."

"Well," Andrew said, from off on the right. "Now you have all the time."

Finley cast a dark light and tied it off in the air above them. He made it intentionally dim, bright enough for people nearby to see, but not a flashlight.

"Hey. Gather around, you lot," Anthony said. "As everyone filters in then we can kinda get a sense of what's going on. I guess we should think about what cards we have, but since Bob has most of the loot, we should bring him in."

"Can someone get Bob from the stream?" Sophie said from the front, clearly drying her hair in a blanket.

"I'll get him," one of the monks said, zipping out.

The group heard a splash and then a yell.

"Did that monk just?" Anthony asked.

"Yes, he did. He just jumped in," Sophie said.

"I feel like I should bust out the holy finger guns. I should just call this meeting to order," Anthony said. "Alright… well since all of you elected me the leader of this little caravan through the apocalypse, I should set a few ground rules. First thing. I know we're all tired but I need five people to take up the watch immediately after this. I would prefer volunteers but I'll pick people if I have to."

Five hands went up, including Sophie.

"Great. You guys will be responsible to be on watch tonight. As thanks, I expect unless something strenuous happens you all should be sleeping during the day. Sophie, do you want to be in charge?"

"Got it, boss man."

"Don't call me boss man. Maybe think up a better title?"

"Caravan Commander?" one of the warriors said.

"That might work. Though I am also the medic. I expect Bob will be in charge of acquisitions and intelligence. Finley here, who saved my ass twice already, will be the caravan's quartermaster. Assuming that works for you?"

"Fine with me," Finley said.

"Great," Anthony said, turning around to look at the assembled crew. "Now we have a haul of cards from the past day and I want to make sure that everything gets used. Some cards, like the woodworking card, could be useful for one or two people. Others like the cleanse card, we all really want. Then there's cards that give ice magic like Bella got since she is in charge of food, but the rest I want to split up evenly. I'll remind you all that survival is our number one goal so as fair as I want to be, not everyone is going to get everything they want."

"If you want we can do some sealed bid drafting," Finley said. "If we figure out some way to set up our own economy. All the gold that I have been hoarding is now useless, as well as the bartering skill I had been working tirelessly on."

The elf sighed, slumping against the wheel he had propped himself up against. "Also there's the matter of combining cards to make better rares and uncommons. I have five cards that I think will make a rare class card based on my understanding of how this works— some."

There was a murmur among the crowd.

"What kind of class exactly?" Bob said from the back.

Bob, faithful servant of Mork, stood there in his birthday suit. Anthony sighed inwardly. Of course the cake baker was a nudist.

"Bob, uh I think you can afford the time to put on your clean clothes. Bella can dry you off and clean your clothes with her new card," Anthony said, pinching the bridge of his nose.

"That would be an excellent idea."

Finley tossed him a set of white clothing from out of nowhere. It was stamped with the Irumian crest on the arm, with gold accented black thread showing a hammer and chisel crossed.

"What? It's what we were all thinking, I just had the robes handy."

Bob quickly donned the white trousers and robe, then sat more towards the front.

"So what did I miss?" Bob said, inspecting the crest on his arm.

"Oh you're the acquisitions guy now," Sophie said. "Finley is in charge of quarters, Bella is in charge of food and we have to be on guard in shifts."

"Outstanding. My mother always said that I was good at getting things," Bob said.

"If we could get back on track. I think we need to give out some cards that cannot wait and make a decision or two," Anthony said. "I would prefer a straight up or down vote, and I can be the tie breaker if that comes to it. First thing: do we make another class card and if so who gets it?"

"Not one of the mages or Bella. They all already have magic and mana. I suspect that I'll make a druid card with the specific combination that I have. As such whoever takes this will have to help with the animals." Finley waved to the horses.

"So, animal handling is one of the skills?" Bob asked.

"Yes. And divine magic, though that can change a bit. Combining cards is a well-recognized phenomenon. I think everyone is here now and I can go over what I have to allocate out."

Bob leaned in. "It's as good a time as any, Finley. Tell us what we've got."

14

There were a dozen copper common cards that all had various useful but not strong abilities. Common cards all had a monochrome image of the ability or enhancement. Then there were the five common skill cards that appeared to be the same as his druid class. Perhaps they would become a druid of Mork, given the source.

On top of that there were a dozen iron cards. Uncommon iron cards were pretty good but often had a little drawback. Some had a cooldown period. For others the drawbacks made them unusable except in strange situations, like the tree walking skill.

Then there were all the card pieces from their raid on the town. Finley brought out his frame and put together thirty common pieces, thirteen uncommon, and six rare. Those were enough for it to be worth it for him to take the time to craft more cards.

If anyone had taken a card and kept it while searching, Finley wouldn't have any recourse. He hoped that they all would work together, but the need to get more and better cards was a new itch for some of them. When he proposed that cards go to people that hadn't already gotten something, there seemed to be a consensus.

Finley cleared his throat. "Alright. That's a bit of a summary of the cards we have. Three of the common cards have direct applications to combat—water magic, fire magic, and basic warding. Those would be great for a start. Then there's the arrow creation common which might be useful but is situational. The rest are less applicable. For the uncommon, we have weapon proficiency, tracking which I believe to be related to Bob's pathfinder ability, and this mounted archery card.

With the common card that lets you generate arrows that would be a great combination in the right hands."

Anthony let the words hang in the air. "Hey, Finley, how common are cards?"

"Pretty common. Every race except humans is born with a card, and monsters tend to drop card pieces. More powerful monsters drop more powerful pieces, though epic pieces are almost unheard of. There was a thriving trade between gold and card pieces and now—well I shouldn't have traded it all to gold."

"So, fair to say that there will be more?"

"That's safe to say. There might be some monsters in these woods that we could hunt for their meat and magical properties, but it's doubtful."

"Alright. Now I don't want to be a dictator, but we can't have one person with all of the card powers. If they get incapacitated, then it's game over. I propose that we give the magic skill power cards to anyone willing to ride alongside the caravan as they'll need it most."

There was less grumbling.

"The ones that got the handle animal skill cards? Otherwise, they'll have a tough go of riding a horse," Bob said.

"That seems reasonable," Anthony replied.

Finley watched as Anthony dictated the pace of discourse. He had done his part setting this up and he wanted to make this class card if they were going to do it, sooner rather than later. He brought out his frame and grabbed the five skill cards from the pile.

"Anthony, I'm going to make the class card, alright?"

"Oh, sure, go ahead Finley," Anthony said. "I think we have a consensus on that. One of the monks or warriors can get it."

There was a groan.

"One that hasn't gotten animal handling and another one of the skills, of course."

Anthony's beard and man bun flickered in the dark light as Finley put the cards into the frame. He was going to need another frame eventually as a backup, as this one had gotten far more use than he had expected. In went Weapon Proficiency, Magic Control, Elemental Magic, Survival, and Medicine. Any one of which would be a good card, but the combination of all five would create something much better.

Anthony pulled the frame out, resizing it to fit six cards. He placed them in, leaving a spot in the middle row. If he really wanted to roll the dice, he would add a sixth card to center it around a theme, but he didn't have any to spare. Instead, what he did was again squeeze mana into the cracks between the cards and then fill the empty slot with green mana. Unfortunately, if any of the skills were above level one then the resulting card would favor that skill, but as they were all level one, he didn't need to worry.

In less than a minute he got his answer. A singular shiny gold card replaced the five as the frame resized itself automatically.

Rare Class Card: Wilderness Druid Level 1

Skills:

Animal Handling Level 1

Nature Control Level 1

Elemental Magic Level 1

Survival Level 1

Medicine Level 1

This card grants mana.

As a Wilderness Druid, you have enhanced control over the natural world and can more easily survive in a rough environment.

Weapon Proficiency had turned into Animal Handling, something that had been unexpected. As a druid, Finley was more likely to create a druid class, but he knew that wasn't going to affect it that much. The chance was slight.

Finley was jubilant, showing the card to everyone. "Hey guys. I think we got a winner here. This class is pretty similar to my class. It will be potent in the right hands."

"Do we have any volunteers for the support role? Hey, is there any limit on classes?" Sophie asked.

"There's a limit on how many cards and then it's hard to split your time working on different skills."

That got a few of them talking. Finley just wanted to pass this one off and get some rest at this point. The day had been long, and his energy had now fully worn off. He still needed to make some trip vines before he went to bed.

"Oh, and whoever takes this should follow me. I'll be putting some trip vines around the way station. Enough to back up our watch team."

"That reminds me that we need a second team to relieve them," Anthony said.

Bob raised a hand along with Bella, Andrew, Zan, and one other human.

"We can keep these groups, so I'll be with Finley and the remainder of the people. Julie as well," Anthony said.

"Can I take the wilderness druid card? You said that it has medicine, right?" Sophie said. "I had some medical training on earth."

"What kind of training?" Anthony said.

"I was a psych tech. I worked in a mental hospital."

Everyone turned to look at her. Sophie crossed her arms.

"What! It was putting me through college. And no, I'm not going to diagnose you guys with anything. Plus, I failed at chemistry so med school was straight out."

"I was a midwife, so between the two of us and Finley we should be covered. Anyone have a problem with us putting Sophie as a healer? Especially if she's on the first watch group?"

In the dark, Anthony couldn't make out any dissent.

"If you want to get the next class, talk to me and we can start a wish list, but Sophie why don't you follow our resident elf around and set up some security. I'm not going anywhere if anyone wants to talk, but I think if you're not doing anything, we all need to rest. I'm not saying go to sleep, but for those of us that are, please keep it quiet."

"Hey boss, can we make a fire? It's a bit nippy."

It was one of the monks that had returned from the stream. He hadn't returned with a shirt, and it was evident that he was experiencing a bit of a chill.

"We don't know if the zombies can see smoke or fire. Finley?"

"I'm not a zombie expert. Someone with the light spell will need to stay up, and I don't need to sleep much, so I can relieve them if theirs runs out."

"That's some elvish trick, right?" Andrew asked.

"You could say so," Finley replied, turning to look down at the dwarf. "I wouldn't."

Anthony held out his arms looking for more input. "Anything else before I release everyone to do what they will? No? Okay Sophie and company, you're on watch. Keep us safe."

***

The meeting broke up and Sophie gathered her watch group. They split into two groups, one of two and one of three. The group of three followed Finley around the outskirts of the way station. As they went, the two of them cast the same spell, creating a series of overlapping vines. The walk took only twenty minutes and when they returned, Finley showed her the spell to cast a red light above them.

It was enough for them to see by but wouldn't go far. At first, she could only hold one at a time, but after a half an hour, she got the notification that her skill had advanced to level two, and it felt immeasurably easier. By then, most of the people with them were sleeping. Sophie sighed, sitting around the red light with the watch crew.

She didn't know what to call them. Fellow victims? Comrades? Heroes? Caravan mates? None of the words really stuck.

Before long she was able to summon two red lights at once and she had them orbiting each other. It felt draining and more than one of the lights went out. The darkness didn't feel so unpalatable just then. More to the point, Sophie really wanted to understand some of the changes that her body had gone through.

Coming here, there had been some unexpected changes. She had lost weight and felt a lot more mobile. Other things had changed for her that made her feel like she hadn't just been summoned. But the biggest change was the cards.

She found herself looking at her cards. She had figured out how to use vines to make traps. By combining her rogue skills and druid magic, she made a trip wire that would do more than alert her.

Rare Class Card: Rogue Level 2

Skills:

Sneak Attack Level 2

Skill Mastery Level 2

Weapon Expertise Level 1

Infiltration Level 1

Evasion Level 2

Stealth Level 1

As a rogue, you may learn one extra class skill per level. New skills start at the average of your other class skills.

Bella had leveled her sneak attack skill by catching people unaware. She then reported on her success. Sophie couldn't work on weapon proficiency without some sort of weapon, but she could work on her stealth in the dark. The combination of elemental magic with her skill mastery meant that any class skills would advance faster.

Sophie didn't know where she was going with any further cards. She felt like she had won the jackpot with what she already had. As well the changes to her body had made her internal sense of herself match the outside. It wasn't unpleasant, just something that she'd longed for her entire life.

She stayed up on watch until the morning, when most of the caravan woke and began to prepare for breakfast.

***

The next morning, Bella began to cook. Dwarves tended to like potatoes and meat. According to Finley, they did potatoes every which way but mashed and put into a stew.

Bella only had two pans and was grateful that there was a stream nearby. Cooking for fifteen people would need a larger amount of cookware, especially if it was going to be done in a timely manner. The other problem was the number of plates and utensils. There were enough for two people. Thus, Bella fed two people while she cooked for two more, a process that she probably should have started while they all slept. Having a roaring fire and some sort of grill or grate would have done wonders.

The horses were all grazing, those attached to the wagons being rotated again. Sophie helped move the horses, her touch eliciting a positive response with the animals. Bella couldn't help but smile. Sophie was knee deep in work and enjoyed it. There was something about a woman who was doing what she enjoyed. She looked free, and Bella wanted that for herself.

Bob and Anthony had asked to be served last. It was then she saw Bob referencing several maps that she hadn't known existed. She stayed longer than she strictly needed to try and comprehend the picture of what she was looking at. Then, Bob dropped the bomb on them.

15

"How many quests?"

"Five, actually."

"Well, shit, Bob."

Finley had heard of powers like Bob's. He had even heard of gods favoring their chosen heroes with four or more powerful cards. Bob's ranger card made him exceptional, but it was something that one could attain. Bob's pathfinder card working together with his ranger skills made him a force to be reckoned with.

"The obvious one is the assault on Plainsmount. It's a simple one: get in, grab the supply, and get out. The thing we need to survive long term is supplies that we'll need to find."

"So, your card just told you the name of the city? That's something. Like if I wasn't here, you would know it," Finley said.

As they talked, Finley sketched the local map including Dunnamore and Plainsmount. He pointed to the line between the two. "There's a very well used trade route between the two places. In fact, we took it until we branched off. We went to this way station."

"Tell me about this town, then."

"This one? Far more than Dunnamore, this was a trade hub. If the Irumian capital is the center of the wheel, this is one of the spokes. Caravans would travel back and forth on these roads, regularly moving goods and trading. There are several warehouses full of hay and staples of the dwarven diet. And they're positioned on the outside, which would make this less difficult."

"Could we potentially hole up there? How big is the population?"

Finley began to draw a town map in the dirt. He remembered the two main east to west roads as well as the highway that met them in the middle. He marked a wholesaler that he used frequently on the north side. Then he placed the approximate location of all the card shops in town. Some of the other finer details eluded him.

It was good enough for a start.

"Thousands? Enough that they draw in people from far for their festivals."

"I have to assume that every single person of those thousands is now a zombie," Bob said.

"I-I hadn't even thought about that, but yeah it makes sense. Makes me want to turn back to Dunnamore and improve the fortifications."

"I don't think that would turn out well. Then we would just starve in the cold," Anthony said, from across the way stone. "Because winter will be upon us before too long, correct? Zombies aren't affected by the cold?"

Finley scrunched up his face. He would be cold, but would that effect the dwarves?

"Dwarven zombies aren't affected by it. At least I think so. We could come back after the winter, but winters are long here."

Anthony and Bob sat in silence contemplatively.

"Bob, tell us about these quests," Anthony said.

"Four of them are about killing chosen zombies. The fifth one is about getting supplies."

Finley sputtered. The tea he was drinking was now all over the way stone. He moved to clean it with his arm.

"Now when you say chosen zombies what do you mean?" Finley said.

"They were people like us, summoned from another world. Then they were turned."

"That's what I thought you meant. That is rather unfortunate."

"Am I missing something here?" Anthony said.

"You have to understand that gods choosing to summon Heroes like yourself is a rare thing. I would never expect to see more than one or two. To see fourteen of you in the same spot means that something has gone terribly wrong. Now that I know that four chosen have been turned, that makes it so much worse."

Anthony gave him a heaping helping of side eye. "I know we're talking about the same thing. But I don't feel that much stronger than you are."

"It's not just about how strong you are. It's also about how fast you can advance. With your abilities the way they are, you can progress much faster in your skills."

"Alright. Tell us about the potential threats," Anthony said. "Are any of the quests you mentioned helpful in that regard?"

"Let me dig into the titles. Alright, the supply one seems like an anomaly. The other four mention the chosen zombies—death knights—but little else, though one is apparently in the Irumian Kingdom. The others are in the human alliance lands, the elvish kingdom, and the orcish meritocracy?"

Bob looked confused.

"They got the orcs as well?" Finley folded in on himself, "That's... how deep does this go? I'm going to need a minute."

Of all the things that elves feared, a working orc populace had been at the top of the list. Though elves lived long and wanted to enjoy the fruits of their labor, they all had one enemy that fought hard against that. For hundreds of years, the orcs of Noveria all fought in bloody wars against anyone that would fight them. That was until they started to get smart and began to fight economically.

The orcs began to create highly sought after artisanal goods, flooding the markets with the items. Over time, the coffers of the common elf and human flowed more and more to the orcish meritocracy as they amassed wealth. This put anyone who traded with the orcs at a disadvantage as they didn't accept gold coins from outsiders, only cards and card pieces. As such, cards made their way out of elvish hands and into orc hands. Then the orcs opened a series of casinos in foreign lands, under the pretense of reparations for years of being invaded by the human alliance or the elvish kingdom.

This continued the drain of capital from elves to orcs. Orc accountants became all the rage as they let elves keep more of their money, though no tinker would ever accept or solicit such help.

There was nothing that a tinker elf feared more than an orc accountant. And if what his new companions were all saying was correct, then now Finley had a new fear: zombie orc accountants.

"When the gods summoned us here," Anthony said, "some of us got more information than others. That probably goes double for you Bob. If you think that we need to do a smash and grab, we'll head down to Plainsmount next."

"I think we can start off with a recon of the town from a distance. I would say myself and the monks could slip in, grab whatever cards we can get our hands on and then slip out the opposite way, drawing attention," Bob said.

"Or we could just not draw any attention?" Anthony said, kneeling next to Finley, "Hey, are you alright?"

"I'm—I hadn't—before you told me that the orcs were affected, I guess I didn't get the whole scope of what's going on. How did this even happen?"

"Well fuck," Bob said.

"What's that?" Anthony turned awkwardly from his kneeling position.

"Another quest."

"We're going to need to bring the girls in for this," Bob said. "It's questing time."

***

Bella and Sophie were going through the food supplies and taking notes.

121

"It looks like, with fifteen people, assuming that the elf and dwarf eat about as much as we do, we'll have enough for a week? Does that jibe with what you're thinking? There's a lot of potatoes here," Bella said.

"That's good. I don't know how this is going to work long term, but I think that we're going to need to start planting crops somehow. If we can put a little plot of dirt on the back of the wagon, then I can make sure that it's watered. Finley probably knows more about planting, but we should be able to take some of these potatoes and make more."

"Finely said that he had a woodworking card skill. We should ask him to make us a planter. Though, dirt would be heavy, wouldn't it? It would probably be best if we put it in the center, like how the barrel of water is. Oh shit, we should fill that up before we go."

Bella set down her chalk piece. She'd been tallying up how many potatoes they had on the way stone.

"On it, boss!" Sophie said. "Can you turn the barrel upright and I'll—hmmm. I need a pitcher or something. Or a bucket. Ah there's one on back of the caravan."

Sophie walked over and grabbed the two buckets from the back of the caravan. Both were empty and needed to be cleaned a bit. She handed the other one to Bella and they walked over to the river.

"I think two trips will do it, Sophie. Then we'll be topped off." Bella leaned in close. "How are you doing?"

"Honestly, I feel more like myself today."

"I hear you," Bella said, pausing once they got to the river. "Some real rest will do that for you."

Two of the monks were taking turns jumping into the river and rating each other's dives. Blessedly, they were across the river.

"No, I mean, I feel more like myself than I ever felt on Earth."

"Right. Uh, are you okay?"

"Yeah, but I have some questions that are a bit sensitive. Something that I didn't want the boys back there to overhear."

Bella had seen that look before and embraced her. "There's no secrets between sisters. What's up?"

Sophia paused for the longest second of the day. Bella wondered what the heck the girl was thinking.

"I think that uh—do we have any paper products?" Sophie asked, her voice near a whisper.

"When you say paper products," Bella said, releasing her, "what do you mean?"

"Well, uh…" Sophie gave her the look.

"Oh! You know what, I had no idea that could even happen now. You'd think that being summoned to another world would take care of those kinds of problems, but no, I'll uh—how urgent is it?"

"Pretty urgent. Like I don't want to jump into the water, but also I do so uh, help me out."

"I got you. Us girls have got to stick together, alright?" Bella said.

Sophie blushed. "Yeah. Got it. Middle earth level tech for a woman in need."

"I'm sure I'll be going through the same thing shortly."

Sophie finished washing her bucket, then filled it with cold clean water. She exchanged it for the empty one, repeating the process.

"Anyway, I think we should work on our stealth skills today before we go anywhere, Sophie. What do you think?"

"Once this inventory is done, then yeah. I think we can work on that. Provided that there aren't any other big hiccups."

"Let's surprise those monks, maybe?" Bella's smile glinted.

"Hell yes."

***

"Alright, so here's the plan. We're heading to Plainsmount, which is the nearest large city en route to the capital. Finley has provided us with a good map of where the three card shops in the city are as well as the shipping warehouses. Our primary goal is to get more supplies. Our secondary goal is to find any survivors, and extract them, as well as any cards. We're going to send in a team to smash and grab anything we can from the card shops in advance. They'll meet up with us on the southern side of Plainsmount, or the northern road leading back here if something happens. We're not heading in there to fight zombies. I repeat, our purpose is not to fight them, but if we can lead them away, that would be great. It's unclear how intelligent they will be. Bob?"

Anthony handed the pole to Bob. Bella made soft attempt to grab it, causing Bob to smile.

"Mork has given me a special ability to locate all of the chosen zombies—the death knights that are responsible for taking care of the undead legions. There are four, including one that is within the borders of the Irumian Kingdom. Based on what we know, I'm going to try to see if what we do affects these chosen zombies, or if they attempt to move on us. We don't think that the zombies will be working too hard to find us out in the wilderness, and as you've already seen, we can find a way to hide ourselves out here. Not if we're followed by ten thousand of them, then we might have a problem. Though we might be able to outrun them, we need a more permanent solution."

"We're open to ideas," Anthony said, scanning the crowd. "Bella?"

"Is stabbing them all not an option? Make a wall and then funnel them through it, stab them one by one?" she said.

"That could work. It would take a ton of mana. I have a better question," Julie said. "Are there airships here?"

Though it was a general question, she looked right at Finley. For the first time, he looked unsure of himself.

"What's an airship?"

16

Before noon, the roughshod caravan and its people were finally on the road again. The compelling need to eat something eventually wore on them after an early lunch. By the time that the sun was up, their trek through the woods between Dunnamore and Plainsmount was nearly through.

They hadn't been pushing the horses as a vanguard of six people rode slightly ahead of the wagons. Behind them, the remaining horses in the herd trotted along. They had their reasons for sticking with the humans and Finley didn't blame them for it. Once he stopped pushing them to join, he was surprised how willing they were to tag along. It was an unexpected use of his handle animal skill that getting the skill to level three had afforded him. Each level felt like an evolution past the previous skill. He had never imagined controlling horses before, except for the two he had been with.

It was when they were nearly three spans away from Plainsmount when the first hint that things were amiss appeared. Unlike Dunnamore, which was largely a town meant to service the local farming population, Plainsmount was a trading town. As such, there were traders' estates and suburban sprawl. It wasn't anything that Finley hadn't seen before. Rich merchants wanted to show off by owning rich-looking estates. When the first one came onto the horizon, it was easy to tell that the doors were missing. As well, all of the windows were either smashed or open.

Bob called a halt. As he did so, Finley pushed the herd to spread out on the sides. If nothing else, they would spook easily, and in turn alert the entire party. Bob and Anthony shared a glance.

The horses moving oddly was enough to get everyone moving. Among the many side goals that Bob and Anthony set out was to get a third wagon set up. They had enough spare wheels to replace any losses. What they didn't have yet was room to transport the amount of food they were going to need.

Bella and Sophie jumped down. They hugged a large, long garden hedge as they approached the two-story building. Bob followed right behind them. Finley was tempted to follow them but knew that he had to stay by the horses. He was hoping for some more canvas material and perhaps some clothes and blankets for the humans. To find a working wagon would be a dream.

The sun was well on its way down and he considered that it was well past lunch time. He was grateful for the large breakfast—he could only take so many potatoes.

While the rogues and rangers did their thing, he took stock of the horses. He felt like it was time to swap some of them out. Whenever he did that, it would be a time when they were exposed. The least he could do was to make sure that they were drinking water, but that too seemed like too much for the time.

Really, it was the uncertainty that made him feel ill at ease. There was no telling if the people of this mansion were still there or if they had moved on. Bella and Sophie could run right out screaming with Bob on their tail. Or they could find that there was nothing useful inside.

Finley waited patiently. He didn't have much of a choice. They were close enough, within spitting distance of the outskirts of town. The amount of packed dirt roads that connected to cobblestone walking pathways made it clear that dwarves lived here.

Bob ducked into the building and almost immediately ran back towards the caravan. Behind him Bella and Sophie sprinted all out. Behind them, three zombies ambled slowly.

Finley tapped into his class powers, readying a skill.

***

Bob, chosen ranger of Mork and Olympic-level sprinter, ran like hell. With each step, his crossbow slapped against his back. He got far enough away that he could brandish the weapon, waiting for Bella to get behind him.

"Ice magic ready?" he said, placing a bolt into the crossbow.

Bella's hands crackled.

"You're up," she said.

Bob sighted down the lead zombie of the three. He loosed the bolt and it nearly knocked the zombie into the two behind it. He had to aim slightly down to hit the dwarf zombies.

Its head lolled to the side as it continued to move.

Bella blasted the ground ahead of the zombies with a thick layer of ice. Once again, Bob was facing zombies sliding on ice. The ice was only two meters long, just enough for them to fall. The rear zombies fell on their fronts, tangling up the mostly headless one.

"Get the heads!" Sophie said, a long green dagger in each hand.

"Bob! Watch our backs!" Bella shouted, pulling out an ice dagger.

Both women took out a face-down dwarven zombie, then in sync plunged daggers into the third's head.

"Ah! Freaking sweet!" Bob yelled.

All three of them caught their breath. Finley and Julie came up behind them. For a long moment, everyone stayed tense. Finley clapped Bob on the shoulder, scanning around for more threats.

"Bob, are you going to extract their cards? I want to do their last rites. It hurt me that I wasn't able to do so for the horde that we lost."

"Of course. Let me summon her."

Bob concentrated on the eldritch being known as Ca'at. A small silver summoning circle appeared in front of him, as loopy runes rose up from the ground.

"Well, that's new," Bella said.

The black beast appeared in front of him. It quickly assessed the situation and Bob could feel the idea of a question forming in the back of his mind.

"Take their cards and card shards," he directed the housecat-sized beast.

Ca'at purred.

"I hope that we don't have another hairball incident," Bella said, coming to stand next to Bob.

Bob's heart rate sped up as she linked arms with him. They watched as the summoned creature eviscerated the zombies, removing their cards and card pieces.

It only had to go skin deep to get the cards. Its butchery looked like a lost practical art that had been banned by several religions before being forgotten and excised. The creature moved with surgical precision, every movement exacting. Each cut with its tiny claws had a purpose.

Bob stood transfixed, until Bella snapped him out of it. He realized that he had been staring.

"Oh, what's going on?" he said.

"Your cat just sliced and diced these bodies like it was a custom-made machine. You don't have any problems with that?" Bella said.

"No, not really. Nothing here makes sense."

"That seems about right."

Finley walked up beside them.

"Do you sense any more of them inside?" he said.

"I don't. And something tells me that Ca'at will not kill them for us. Maybe I can get her to run through the mansion?"

"That would be a good use of a summon. Now if you'll excuse me, I don't want to have a cat throw up on my good boots."

"What did you mean Finley—aww—"

The eldritch being below him was retching card pieces onto his feet. He was glad to have the card pieces; he was far less enthusiastic about the hair and vomit. Bob could do without those. Bella, for her part, squatted down to give it the requisite head pats. Someone had to do it.

"Where did it get so much hair?" she mused.

Bob turned back to the entrance to the mansion. He had hoped for a quest to raid the house, but he got no such luck. Perhaps it was his intent? They hadn't set out to raid this particular mansion.

He checked his class card. The emblem of a bow flashed in front of a copse of trees, gold glinting off it.

Rare Class Card: Ranger Level 2

Skills:

Divine Spellcasting Level 1

Animal Handling Level 2

Favored Enemy Level 1 (Zombies)

Field Craft Level 2

Weapon Proficiency Level 3

This card grants mana.

As a ranger you may pick another favored enemy at each level.

This is a soul card and cannot be removed.

It was a combination of his Field Craft skill, favored enemy, and his pathfinder card that let him track so well.

He felt a bit lost in the suburban area. Perhaps there was a suburban ranger subclass? He smiled at Weapon Proficiency reaching level three. At least one thing was working for him.

"Bella, you want to take the lead? Sophie, right behind her ready to blast them with magic? I'll pull rear guard."

"Only the best boyfriends let their girls lead the expedition," Bella said, squeezing his arm. She released it and drew her daggers.

"I know you both have an evasion or dodge skill." He smiled, loading another bolt.

Bella walked to the front entrance, Sophie right behind her. At the wide-open door, they paused. Bella checked the door, then stepped into the large room.

Bella pointed to the closest door and they made a beeline for it. Seeing nothing in the small room, she moved on to the next room on her left.

"Clear," she said.

Bob gave her a look.

"What? It sounded cool in my head. If I'm going to be clearing dwarven mansions, then—"

Sophie sighed. "I don't hear anything and I got my perception skill up to level two. Let's clear a few more rooms," she said, pushing Bella to move forward.

They continued on, every so often whispering to each other.

***

Anthony set up what he was calling a stage left. All it meant was the caravan was pointed in a direction to quickly depart. After seeing how long it took to change directions, he appreciated how large the roads were. Rather than pointing towards the interior of Plainsmount, the caravans were pointed away. If they were clearly about to be overrun, they would head back and try to kill as many as they could.

Next to him, Julie was casting a complicated spell to build a wall. Once that was done, he would post a guard on top. The horses had been swapped around and all were eating as much as they could. The grass around here was perfectly dry and crunchy, just what the horses seemed to want.

The wall wouldn't stop anything dedicated, it was cover for the caravans. No one could tell him if zombies had good perception or not. Perhaps they would smell them. It was more than likely that dwarven zombies used their vision as their primary sense. Anthony was just trying to figure it out. If they couldn't see the caravan, would they still be drawn to it?

It took Bob's team five minutes to declare the mansion clear and ready for a raid. Anthony nearly smiled. It was a piece of good news in a week of horrors. Zan took the warriors in to do a more thorough search.

"Hey. We can go house to house for a bit," Bob said upon returning, "Or we can go right for the recon now. Bella and Sophie both have their stealth skill at level two. It can't be more than two miles from here to the nearest card shop. Oh, and I found this."

Bob held up what looked like a picture frame without a picture. It took Anthony a minute to figure out what the thing was that he was holding. When he figured it out, he grinned.

"This is good. Finley was worried that if his broke we would have to do things the hard way—in his words—though whatever that means, I have not the foggiest."

"I know, right? I told Bella to raid what passes for their freezer and then we'll see what we do next."

"I was thinking hit another mansion if possible. The closest one is what, half a mile down the road?"

They walked over to the dirt wall. It was taller than both of them, but stopped by the road. More than anything it was just obfuscation by obstruction.

Bob gestured forwards. "That's about half a mile. I can see where the town starts."

True to his words, Anthony—if he squinted—could see multiple buildings, increasing in density.

"It's a long walk while you're exposed," Anthony said. "I think the rest of us will try to get everything we can from here, and then if you're not done then, try that next one."

Anthony thought about the multiple contingency plans that they had in place. If anything happened, he could trust Bob to follow Bella to the right place.

17

"Check for survivors," Finley told Andrew. "Then take anything useful. Take Julie with you. If there are magical items, she might be able to help. I know that Bob and his team cleared the mansion, but they don't have time to do a deep search. We need them to head off to grab as many cards as possible from the shops."

"You and Anthony are going to make sure that nothing sneaks up on us, right?" Andrew said.

The dwarf should have had to look up to them. He'd found that it was easier to sit on the back of the wagon to talk eye to eye.

"We've got that part covered," Anthony said, tugging on his beard.

There was enough tension in the yard that Finley wanted the dwarf to get moving. While they were in, he was going to shore up Julie's earth working project. Two monks had been recruited to be the guards and Zan was trying to recreate the spell with her own powers. Everyone else was in conference and eating before the next step. Bella had cursed that they once again couldn't have a roaring fire, and had wanted to use the oven inside of the mansion. That had been summarily shot down as it would be a big red flag.

So once again they had slightly warmed potatoes, as Sophie used her elemental magic to warm them up one by one. Bella applied a bit of salt and butter to each before passing them out. More than one person went back for seconds, and Finley himself was impressed by how many different ways that she could make them.

"The next one looks similar in size to this one. I'm not certain why this one had three people in it. Oh, and here are the cards from the zombies," Bob said, looking up from his third potato. "One common speed skill, one uncommon accountant class card, and one uncommon that is about storage?"

"Can I see the storage one?" Finley said.

"Sure." Bob passed the card over. "That plus the frame we found means that you're going to have to teach someone how to make a card soon, Finley."

The iron card had the image of a packed wagon, with an elf attempting to load one more item.

Uncommon Card: One More!

The wielder of this card will gain the ability to increase their storage capacity, or the storage capacity of one item beyond what should be physically possible.

"I think I need this one," Finley said. "If no one objects, this should make me able to store more in the caravan."

Bob waved a hand as if to say "take it."

Anthony shrugged. "If it helps us, then take it. I want to know more about this accountant class though. Why is it uncommon, when our class cards are all rare?"

"May I?"

Uncommon Class Card: Accountant Level 3

Skills:

Writing Level 5

Books Level 4

Mathematics Level 6

Eidetic Memory Level 9

As an accountant, you can store complex mathematical matrices in your head and perform functions on them.

"Oh, someone was leveling this card. This is a good find, if questionable. It's not directly helpful, but we might get some use out of it."

"People can level cards and then, what, trade them?" Anthony said.

"There used to be a thriving market for highly leveled class cards. Orcs in particular were after those. You can imagine that they get really good after someone who knows what they're doing works on the skill," Finley said. "What? You guys didn't have skill cards like this on Earth?"

"Not really," Bob said. "We didn't even have magic, per se. But doesn't it hurt to level up a card and lose it?"

"It depends on the strength of the cards in your soul deck. For non-human races, you can't take your soul card out. You'll die. Humans aren't born with a card in their soul decks. Families have to build cards for their kids, or at least they did. Elves, we… tend to do what we are good at. I got my bartering and appraisal skill to level three and I thought that was good for me."

"My class card tells me that it's a soul card," Bob said, getting up and testing his crossbow.

"Well shit, Bob, mine does too," Anthony said. "Or at least that's what I thought it said. How do I check?"

"I—well theoretically, you could pull them out, but in a practical sense, you would die after a short amount of time. Can you visualize your card so I can see, either one of you? Like this?"

Finley held out his left hand, palm up. He took his right hand and mimed taking a card from a deck that didn't exist in his left.

He showed everyone his tinker card. The dark obsidian outline glinted around the card. He then enlarged it so that the others could see. He made the decision to not show his spore druid card as that might bring up some questions that he didn't want to answer.

"Why is it black? Oh, epic? What the hell!" Anthony said.

"It happened right before I found you Anthony," he replied. "I never thought through the implication. It was gold before—before all of my people died."

Around him a few other people attempted to do the same thing with their own cards. There were a few smiles and hoots. Once they calmed down, Anthony brought his own up and checked it out.

The mood soured on him. He knew why. Where the Goat Lord was all about being in the moment, humans were constantly thinking about things. It felt inefficient. It would have been far better if they instead stuck to a script or something.

"How many tinkers were there before all of this?" Anthony said quietly.

The only sound was that of Bob putting his bolts into a quiver. Bella sent him a glare, above her soul card's image.

"I estimate nearly ten thousand, all told," he said, "though it's hard to tell. We moved around a lot."

Suddenly, everyone was looking at him. Finley didn't get it. This was probably another human eccentricity.

"I'm so sorry, hey bring it in buddy," Anthony said, moving to embrace him. "We're here for you."

Finley didn't know why all of the sudden his eyes began to leak. He returned the embrace.

"And we will get vengeance," Anthony whispered.

Finley didn't know what to say. He just let it happen. If the human wanted a hug, he would return a hug.

"Thanks," he said.

Feelings would have to wait. He'd gotten a new card and he wanted to try it out. Best to let these humans have their moment and move on to some productive work.

***

Julie had found a suspicious barrel inside of the mansion and had brought it out. She had thought about the contents after seeing that it had a tap on one side. Her mouth watered. She had been dry for a while, but one drink couldn't hurt, could it? Andrew was a dwarf and he'd understand.

When she brought it out to the caravan, she hadn't expected the muted cheers. Nobody was going to be too loud when it was quite possible that there were zombies a quarter mile away. She'd expected to be lauded as the fun mom. Anthony shot her down about opening the tap for everyone. They needed her sober right now, they said. This brew would be for if they survived.

Julie realized that she was going to have to wait and snapped back to it. If they could wait, so could she. She'd never been able to be a social drinker, but if there was only so much to drink, there would be a hard cutoff. So why would she need to hold herself back?

"Julie," Anthony said, loading the barrel up into the back of the wagon, "thanks for this and all of the cups as well. I wanted to talk to you about what you did on Earth. You've been pretty quiet, all things considered."

"I was a social worker," she said. "I worked in a residential treatment facility."

"Ah. So you have some training then, I take it?" Anthony gave her his full attention.

"I do," she said, quietly.

"But you didn't want us to single you out? Why?"

"Maybe it's the whole warlock thing. This power just feels so—raw. Like I have to shape my will. I was only able to do those rough dirt walls because I was tapping into the raw power of it. I couldn't do—if you asked me to do some fine lines instead, I would be terrible."

"It's okay to be bad at something. You made it structurally sound. Sound enough that Finley is able to grow roots and plants inside of it. Now I'm thinking that once our recon team departs, we're going to want to take that next mansion. There are some houses further in, but I think that these two can be our bases of operations for now. With the monks helping out—"

"All three of them, yeah."

"—with their help, we can potentially spend the night here. I don't think I want to, but we can make the zombies follow us into some sort of maze trap where we can easily kill them from above. I think that we might be able to trick them into that at least."

Julie blanched. "It would be like shooting fish in a barrel. I can dig it."

"One question, though. Are you able to shift the walls?"

"If Finley doesn't put roots through them, then yes. I can, if I push now, feel that the earth is very built up. If I make the top five feet wide and then make them ten feet tall, they should be—that should be enough. It would take them time to go through a ten-foot-tall packed dirt and root wall."

"Even longer if the path underneath them is made of ice."

"See, I knew you were smart," Julie said, tugging on his beard. "Cute too."

The handsome man pulled back, his cheeks beet red.

"I—uh—there will be time for flirting later," he said, stammering.

"Sure thing," she said, "I'll get right on that."

Maybe a strong person like Anthony would be enough to keep her sober. Because the zombies were making it seem like there was no way out. And if she was going to die, she might as well die how she wanted.

***

Bella, Bob, and Sophie slunk towards the second mansion. With the road on their left, the door to the mansion would be facing the same way. They had a choice to make.

Bella stopped them next to a copse of trees.

"There are two clear entrances. I can see a path leading in the front and one path going through the back," Bob said.

"Front or back?" she asked.

"I generally prefer heading in the front door," Bob said. "But I can see the benefits of the back door. Sophie, what do you think?"

"I can see an argument for both. The back door looks a bit dirty, but could be inviting. The front door, on the other hand, has a welcoming set of steps," Sophie said. "Back on earth, I always used the back door."

"That's interesting. I would think a woman like you preferred going in the front door," Bella said. "What would you do if you were carrying groceries?"

"Well in that case, I might. But you gotta do a lot of prep work to make sure that the back door is ready," Sophie replied. "Are you ready to put in the work?"

"I can make the back door work," Bella said. "If the conditions are right."

"I think it all boils down to personal preference," Sophie said. "And who your partner is. And yeah, cleanup is a factor."

"Guys, I think you're both wonderful but is this the time?" Bob said.

"Bob, I thought you were the type of man who wouldn't rush a woman into a decision."

"Yes, I am, but—" Bob said.

Sophie was barely holding herself back.

"It's just a home invasion."

"Oh, so you want us just to enter raw?" Sophie said, snickering.

"Here we go again. Yes, I'll admit that I want to go into the house. Just pick a side or I will."

The women shared a look.

"The back," they both said, in unison.

"Great. Let's go."

18

Fear held her. The feeling that even the shadows were watching itched at her subconscious. Her heart raced, like a delivery driver looking for a tip.

Sophie methodically cleared the rooms of the second mansion, this time alternating between being the point woman with Bella. This mansion hadn't had any zombies and when they reached the open front door, they figured out why.

"If there were zombies here, they left out here," Bob said, dropping to one knee.

He was clearly doing something. It was also just as clear that he could be pretending to be doing something. Men were like that sometimes. Especially Bob because he kept trying to impress Bella. Not that he had to; Bella seemed plenty impressed by him. Sophie liked Bob enough but was a jumble of emotions since being freed.

No one expects to be caged up. Sitting there expecting to die at any time, hope was the only thing she had. She has been captured and shoved into the cage. Before she even got her bearings, or was able to fight back, she'd been hog-tied. Her captors hadn't cared if she was able to break out.

Bella had untied her.

Sophie checked the room again. It was empty. This had been a rich dwarf's house. There had to be something useful. Or at least some food. Constant low-level hunger was now normal. She wasn't thirsty, but she could eat.

Bella too was looking around for food. "Kitchen is by the back door so why don't we swing back that way? Once we clear the next floor?" she said.

"Do you think it's harder for them to climb up or climb down stairs?" Sophie asked.

There was one more floor to go. None of them had heard anything thus far. She began to walk up the large ornate wooden staircase when her evasion skill told her to move. That her rogue skill was trying to tell her to move felt entirely different than it had.

She pulled away, just avoiding a dropping zombie. Whatever intelligence governed the zombie hadn't thought about how dropping from a height would affect it. Both arms broke upon contact with the floor. The zombie dwarf had not been drinking its milk.

Standing up with two useless arms, the zombie was immediately eviscerated by three magically formed daggers.

Sophie and Bella stepped back, moving away from the second-floor balcony. Bob was halfway up the stairs before he realized something had happened.

"You girls okay back there?"

"Peachy!" Bella said.

"Just fine, boss!" Sophie said. "But you might want to dodge about now?"

Bob looked up, rather than dodging, because of course he did. Being an idiot was just a part of life. At least it looked like that for him.

A second zombie tumbled down to where he was. Bob deflected the zombie down the stairs towards them.

"Hey Bob."

Stab. Stab.

"Yeah, Bella?"

Stab. Stab.

"Fucking move."

Sophie sighed.

"Oh, yes. That would make sense," Bob said, running down the stairs.

Two more formerly living dwarves made their appearance, where Bob had been.

"You got to stop making these parties open invite Bob," Bella said, stabbing forward. "Were you on the guest list, sir? I guess not."

"I don't know if they're male or female. They still have beards!" Sophie said.

Sophie concentrated on her elemental magic, striking the second with an electric bolt. He or she stammered a bit and then fell to Bob's blows. When it fell, it was apparent that there had been a skirt of sorts, so maybe she? Sophie didn't want to misgender a dead zombie.

In their course of instruction, Finley had told her several things about his god. The Goat Lord abhorred this kind of death above all else, and commanded his followers to grow sunflowers or yellow daisies at the site where bodies were laid to rest. Once they were done, she considered dragging the corpses outside so he could say his rites. She might have taken it up herself if there was a perk associated with it.

All three of them paused, waiting for another attack. Of course, they never came when they were expected, but that was the norm. After nearly a minute of waiting, Bob took the stairs two at a time. He face-planted on the first landing where it split in two. Dwarven stairs were not designed with tall men in mind.

When he got up, he glared at the stairs as if they had done this to him personally. Sophie followed at a more sedate pace. She wasn't fully dallying but she wasn't going to be rushed. Bella waited till her partner was clear up onto the landing before moving. Bella, clearly lollygagging, could take all the time that she wanted.

The itch of the upcoming reconnaissance mission into town needed to be scratched. That speedster card sounded like it would be a good addition to her kit as well if she could get Finley to pass it over.

From the landing, they could see the broken guardrail that each of the dwarf zombies would have had to slip over. They moved. No more zombies waited for them.

Apart from a room with several cards that just sang to her heart to inspect, they cleared the final floor quickly. It helped that any of the potential zombies had decided to go skydiving. Once they were certain all the rooms were empty, Bob summoned his eldritch companion. It went to town on the dead zombies, giving them even more loot to bring back to the caravan.

The cat-shaped beast once again drew cards and card pieces out of the bodies. This time, Bob had the foresight to put a sack in front of it when it horked up the card pieces. This would have been quite tedious without Ca'at.

However, one or two cards off the top, that couldn't hurt could it? She could see Bob wrestling with the idea. All that mattered to Sophie was living to the next day and the day beyond that as well. If he offered, she might take him up on it.

"Let's get back to the guys," Bob said. "Sophie, are you okay?"

The concern in his voice snapped her out of it. She was definitely going to talk to Finley about the Goat Lord after this. Shit had begun to get weird.

***

"Alright, another base speed card and what have to have been four soul cards, all good finds. These dwarven cards seem pretty specialized in cooking the books. I haven't even seen an accountant class card before. But seeing as how it's an uncommon, I could see people using it more often," Finley said, back at the yard of their first mansion.

"Finley, I almost got hit by a zombie. One of these ten is a dodge skill. I want to take that as part of my kit for this mission and give the two speed cards to Bella and Sophie. I assume we'll be taking one of the monks with us?" Bob said, turning to Anthony.

Anthony nodded. "Brandon said that he would like to and yes he has a speed enhancement as a part of his class. He'll be your backup. He volunteered—he wasn't recruited. We'll have eleven people left here. I'm going to change the meetup spot. If you guys are good with that, this will be our primary meetup point, rather than south of town. If we need to pull out, we'll head back to the way station. For this reason, we wanted you to think about how we could communicate over long distances."

"Ah yeah. Maybe there's some magic spell? Sophie has elemental magic now, can that help?" Bob looked at them, trying to gauge if they had come up with anything.

He took a deep breath, inhaling a lung full of jerky. Anthony had several bits of jerky in his beard, but he wasn't mad. For the first time since coming to this place, he was full. He also felt like he was busy. More importantly, he was accomplishing something. Even if he wasn't the man in the arena, there was something noble about getting the entire caravan to safety. The caravan was his home now.

"Oh, and good news," Anthony said, "it looks like we'll be able to get a third wagon up and running soon. Especially if the carriage house behind that mansion unlocks anytime soon."

"You're not worried about any potential zombies behind the door?"

The carriage house itself was a good walk behind the mansion they just cleared. Bob had noted in his report that it was locked. They didn't want to approach it. After clearing the house, they tried to get this much as possible from a distance. It wasn't much.

"Not really. Julie is going to take the other two monks over with her once you're good and within the city of Plainsmount proper," Anthony said. "Also Finley, you said something about deck boxes?"

"They were pretty common. I haven't seen any on a dwarf though. I mean the dead ones. They let you slot cards that you don't want to put into your soul deck into a place where you can use them. This is mine."

Finley held up a small box. It was custom made to hold several dozen cards at the minimum. He then mimed putting a card in.

"You're limited on how many cards you can have in your soul. You can increase that limit over time. Unless you're mentally strong, that won't happen. It hurts to take out cards from your soul if they're close to the max level. It hurts but it's doable. I wouldn't."

"Someday, you're going to tell me everything there is to know about cards. That day is not today, but soon," Anthony said.

"Oh Bob? If you see a little encyclopedia about cards, do go and grab it for us," Finley said. "We're going to need something like that. And it can't hurt to have one."

Finley was already thinking about how much space it would take up. In the back of his mind, he could feel his two storage skills working together. There wasn't a lot of room for books. But he would make do. He always did.

***

Zan watched as the recon team left. And in their wake they left several dozen card pieces.

Finley had promised her that she would get the first shot at creating a card. With two frames, he could now do a side-by-side with her. Something about her class, the wizard class, made making cards better in some way. She wasn't sure how. But Finley was raving about how much easier it would be for her to do the same thing that he had done.

She just accepted it.

There was nothing you could do when the elf got enthusiastic. So when all of her busy work was done, of course she went to find him. Once they were together, they set up a working area.

Side by side, they slotted pieces into each one.

"I can see there's room for six pieces here? What do we do if we only have five pieces?

"You connect them with your mana. Watch."

The elf poured mana out of his hand. It looked like steam gathering to drop down. Then the mana condensed, forming around the five cards he'd placed there. Then he connected all five pieces. For a brief moment, the iron glinted. Zan set down her work.

As he applied his mana, the card took shape. The pieces had been iron. They stayed iron, as it became an uncommon card. Zan closed her mouth. She never wanted to make someone uncomfortable, and this extended to being shocked or surprised.

"There you go. Now go ahead, and take your turn."

Zan concentrated. She could feel pearls of mana. Andrew had explained how to do it. He had a feel for the mana of others. His whole class was built around that. She slowly and methodically placed five card pieces into her frame. Then just as she did so, she used her mana to join the pieces together.

The effect was far faster than she expected. Before she knew it she was nearly done filling out the frame. Then, she saw the first card she'd ever made.

19

Julie tried to slow her breath. She had run out of the basement. She was looking for something, anything to take her mind off what she'd found.

She found herself sitting against the mansion, looking into the yard. The hyperventilating was finally turning into regular breathing.

She saw Anthony talking to Bob and flagged him down. He nodded, then broke off and approached her. By the time he got there, she had nearly regained her cool.

"Hey Julie, you look a little flushed. Is everything alright?"

"More or less. How are the guys? We hit two houses in rapid succession. We got several good cards, are we sure that we need to send them on this mission?" Julie asked.

They were already prepping to depart. Julie didn't think that she would change anything. She just didn't like that four of them were headed off on their own. Nobody could pay her enough to wade into the possibly infested urban areas in the center of town. They didn't have enough for that.

"They're fine. If we want to make this caravan viable instead of just going it alone, then yes. I meant the whole convoy, not just the tinker wagon," Anthony said. "I'm thinking about the big picture here."

Further exploration of the first mansion had garnered enough food to stave off hunger for another day. There were some loose ends, but she was getting to them. She could see Anthony itching to do the exploration himself.

As the group's only cleric, it didn't make sense. So instead, he was compensating by working everyone else as hard as they could.

"Julie, do you think you could make it onto the roof of the mansion?" Anthony asked.

She looked up. Julie had a history with vertigo, something that hadn't bothered her in a few days. She was grateful that it had not followed her here. So long as she could keep the bottle off her brain, she would be happy.

The house would be a challenge. There was only so much dirt that could be brought out. She needed some kind of architect skill if they were going to make her do these kinds of things on the regular.

"I don't really want to, but I could if I needed to. I could do like dirt steps. But you understand that I'm taking dirt from around the house and I already took a bunch to make the wall. Also I'm thinking that we need to make four walls if we're here longer than a day. You only had me make one."

There hadn't been any zombies trying to eat them. Julie had credited that to the wall and how far they were from the center of town. They had learned a lot about how dwarves stored their food. The main thing they had learned was that the more underground they could go, the cooler it got.

As soon as she saw the barrels that had to have some dwarven brew, that was it.

"There's fucking tunnels underneath us possibly extending around the entire compound, by the way. I didn't know that until I got inside the basement and put two and two together. It's something else, it is. Reminds me of that one—tell me if you've heard this one— building in Alaska that the entire town lives in."

"Does Wes Anderson know about said building?"

"That's what I said!"

When she tapped into the earth moving spell, she could feel the open empty space beneath them. It wasn't too close, but if these formerly rich dwarves had the inkling to do so…

"Hey Anthony. Do you think that there were dwarven preppers?"

"When you say preppers, that's not some Gen Z slang for preppies, right?"

"No, daddio, I'm talking about those people who are preparing for the end times. Like stocked up for nuclear winter with a fallback plan."

"That's something. For some reason I thought of that as some quintessentially American thing. But I don't actually know where you're from. Where were you from?"

"Saskatchewan."

"That's somewhere in Canada. That's about all I could tell you."

Julie laughed. It was hard to find someone who knew anything about her home province.

"That's fine, eh. I'm not asking for much. Just a woman respectfully asking if we have someone who can pick locks, or someone strong. I think that if dwarven preppers exist, that this family might have a sealed vault or something. There's a door that I can't for the life of me open."

"That's something. You tried your magic and it failed, I take it?"

"Something along those lines." She placed a hand on his shoulder feeling the muscles through his scrubs. "Also we should consider getting more local clothes."

Anthony had probably heard about the laundry situation. Julie wanted to make sure that he didn't forget it. She didn't want to be a nag, but she would if she had to. In order to launder the clothing that her group was going to create, they would need a copious amount of soap. To say nothing for running water.

Julie had considered getting the barrel a friend. That was another thing on her to-do list.

Anthropomorphizing the wagons and some of the containers as well was on said list. It was too bad that none of the dwarves had a googly eye collection. Perhaps there was some eldritch spell that would let her make markings on the wagons.

Julie shifted a small empty jar in her hands. "Ah yeah I think when you were exploring the tunnels underneath, Andrew found their smallclothes. He thinks that he can adjust most of them for us. His won't need much adjustment. That plus the ornate short spears mean that we're going to have at least something to outfit ourselves."

"Also, Anthony, for as many smutty fantasy novels I've read, I have no fucking idea how they cleaned their clothes. I'm not going to have my bodice ripped anytime soon, but I would like to keep clean. Don't we have a cleaning card?" Julie said, eyeing him carefully.

"I mean we do, yeah, but the smell afterwards. It's like an overactive teenage boy who thinks he's about to get some."

The subtle smell had been a bit of a change from the undead smell. Upon further reflection, Julie preferred the clean teenage boy smell over the rotting flesh one. The obvious choice was pretty glaring. She didn't want to remember the cage. She shuddered, just thinking about it. They had been nose-blind to their own stench until the night prior. It was her biggest gripe after the constant threat of death and all.

"That's about right. I remember that specific time in a young man's life."

He didn't smell horrible, at least.

"Tell me you didn't pour on the sporty body spray."

"I preferred the rugged scents, especially as I was trying to cultivate my image," Anthony said, stroking his beard. "I didn't grow all of this overnight you know. Long hair takes time."

Julie considered how well put together he was for the situation. She felt like a mess, especially since she hadn't been able to find a hair tie. Then it hit her.

"Wait. Where did you get that hair tie?" she said.

"I guess I came with it?"

"How much do you want for it?" she said, grabbing his shirt. There was nothing she wanted more at that moment than to feel a modicum of normal.

"Uh what?"

She closed the distance so there were six inches apart. He gulped.

"Look at me, mountain man—"

"I'm from the Bronx."

"—we have had to figure out women's products, we are barely surviving out here and death is around every door. So the least you could do is help a sister out. What do you want for it?"

"Uh…Julie? Could you please release me?" he said.

Julie unclenched her hands from his scrub top. The situation had gotten out of her hands quickly. She stepped back.

"Sorry. Things have been a little tense," she said. She slowly counted to ten.

It wasn't that he smelled bad. In fact she kinda liked the smell. In the moment, she latched onto the one thing. She knew she was wrong.

"That's entirely understandable, bring it in."

He held his arms out. She didn't hesitate. She sunk into the arms of the bear sized man. With her head against his chest, she almost forgot that she was in a strange new world. At least she had some people with her.

Doing this alone? That would be a death sentence.

Julie stuck there for far longer than was proper. It's what you did when you didn't want people to know that tears were flowing freely.

"Hey, I know like everything in this forsaken place is against us, but I'm not going to let you down, alright?" he whispered.

"You're lying," she said.

"I'm not sure how to solve this. But together we'll do our best."

"You're a bastard, Anthony."

"Noted."

She let him go. His blue scrub top had a noticeable wet spot. She used her sleeve to clean and dry herself.

"Sorry about that," she said. She didn't really mean it. She would have preferred to continue holding him but after a minute it was getting to be a bit much. Maybe he didn't mind though?

"So uh," she said.

"Yeah."

He undid his hair, letting the wind catch it. She bit her lip. Why did he have her heart racing? He handed her the hair tie.

She held it reverently.

"Do you want to tell me how the warlock class works?"

She blinked there for a long minute. The statement had seemed like it was out of place but he was probably just trying to throw everyone off his scent. His amazing musky scent that really shouldn't have made her feel like a teenage girl.

"Let me show you." She brought up her card in her left palm, making it large enough to see. An icon of a circle glinted in a purple hue on the gold card.

Rare Class Card: Warlock Level 2

Skills:

Eldritch Spellcasting Level 3

Ritual Casting Level 2

Enchantment Level 1

Survival Level 2

Medicine Level 1

Patron Pact Level 1

This card grants mana.

As a warlock, you may have a patron.

This is a soul card and cannot be removed.

"Sure would be nice if someone else had animal handling. Your spellcasting is doing a lot of heavy lifting though. If it moved so much dirt, you oh—wow level three in the skill." Anthony's eyes were huge.

Julie smiled. At least she could impress him. With no other suitable friends around, he would be a great help. She wanted to build around her combat power in a specific way, but maybe she could stand to listen to Anthony's card theories.

"What's the pact about?" he asked. "Do you have a patron? I have a patron deity, not that I know much about them."

"I don't actually know. I mean when I got summoned, all I got was the prompt to choose a class and then a goat yelled at me?"

Anthony blinked. "Did you—you have the Goat Lord as a patron?"

"I mean, uhhh? I think her name is Cara?"

"You should probably speak with Finley then. He follows the Goat Lord. I'm tied to Yil, like I have to be for my cleric powers to work. She's the patron deity of crafters so most dwarves and some gnomes follow her teachings. I'm not even sure how this even works to be honest. Have you tried to change your patron? Is that even possible?"

"I hadn't even thought of that. That's seemingly ridiculous. Like what if I made you my patron or something?"

Or boyfriend. Were there even boyfriends in the apocalypse? It didn't really matter to Julie at the moment.

Anthony smirked. "Ah yeah. That's silly. Finley said that you have to have three or four of the five card skills to make a class card but I don't know who would agree to a pact with an otherworldly figure as a card."

"It's just the options that the god presented me with. I chose the one with magic. It beamed the abilities of the classes into my mind without saying anything. It wouldn't have been so odd if it had done anything but bleat at me."

"And then you got captured by the death knight, huh?"

"Yeah. I would prefer not to talk about that particular incident."

"Ah, yeah. Not a problem, Julie. Sorry I brought it up. I guess if you got an idea of how it works, that helped?"

"Yeah. Otherwise, I wouldn't have gotten the skill so advanced already."

"Yeah. It's a bit odd. My spell skill got to level three but Finley has been telling me that it took him ages to get his to that level."

"That's interesting," she said, flipping her hair. "So, uh, how about Bob and Bella? You think they'll do something?"

Anthony gulped.

20

Undead zombies wandered aimlessly in the center of town. If they had a direction as a group, Bob, chosen ranger of Mork, couldn't see it. The human brain was wired to see and find patterns in the wild. Bob just saw hundreds of short grey people moving around.

It was the slowest little grey man rave he had ever been to. It was his only one thus far.

Part of his survival skill made him slightly more stealthy. It helped when he used his cloak to cover most of his body. Bella and Sophie were able to hide effectively in plain sight. Brandon the monk had no such ability. However, what he didn't have in stealth, he nearly made up for in speed.

As such, rather than taking the most direct route, they had been slowly crossing from safe vantage point to point. Bella or Sophie would cross an open area when the coast was reasonably clear. Brandon would then use his monk strength to toss a brick, stone, or something loud to draw the zombies away. They would hear the sound and change the direction of their movement. As he was able to throw improvised weapons nearly half a block, the streets were emptying out more and more rapidly.

He threw the bricks further into the urban center of the town.

They had crossed three roads and had approximately two more to cross. Bob looked forwards, and then had the unfortunate idea to turn back. They would need a safe way out. Part of all of the decoy noises was to steer the horde away from their path of egress. The one to two story buildings were good enough to hide behind. If they needed to run, Bob wanted to draw zombies away from their area of safety.

He could see them ending up on top of one of the buildings without a way to get out.

Helicopters were not going to come in and save them. Airship tech wasn't quite there yet either. According to Finley, he had seen a hot air balloon, but nothing like a steerable dirigible.

Bob desperately wanted some rope to fashion bridges across the streets. Maybe shorter zombies didn't look up? He hadn't seen any of them do much more than shuffle around.

"Top of the building, let's see if we can find another way through," Bella whispered. "I'll guard the ladder."

An access ladder on the single-floor shop was positioned next to a large trash receptacle. As these were dwarves, the stench of a brewery permeated the air around it.

"I think that awful smell is helping them stay away," Bob said.

"Yeah, climb up, Bob. Meat shields first," Sophie said.

Sophie and Bella took up positions on the corner. The side they all occupied was clear but the opposite side of the building had at least five zombies. Once they were on top they could confirm the amount.

Bob climbed as quietly as he could. When he got to the top, he silently praised dwarven architecture. There was only one way up. A raised wall around the roof gave him two feet of cover, enough to stay concealed. The roof was generally level and mostly flat. He could see why.

Someone had left a child-sized lounge chair in one corner.

This had been some poor child's hideout spot. That child was probably dead and gone played on loop in Bob's mind as he made sure that the roof wasn't going to immediately drop him through to the shop below.

Once he was over, he signaled for Brandon to follow, then low-crawled to the opposite side. The two men waited for Sophie to join them.

They took turns looking over the wall.

The next two blocks raised the density of the buildings. Where there had been room between to slink, now it began to be only roads between the shops. He could see a sign for the supposed card shop and breathed a sigh of relief. Then he breathed in the dank smell of a stash and sighed. Of course someone had used the roof to smoke, leaving their equipment there.

"What do you think?" Brandon asked.

As the party leader for this mission, they had been leaning on Bob heavily. If it was just him, he might have been tempted to move for the building. The road between the front of his current building and the next was only a few yards wide. If only he had some rope, then they might be able to cross easily. Bob added that to his list of things he really wished he had easy access to: rope and a flight card.

"Do you think zombies ever look up?" Bob asked.

"Why should they?" Sophie said. "Their food is on the ground."

Bob hadn't considered that morsel of information. If nothing else, Sophie was proving to be a potent source of common-sense ideas.

"What are you thinking?" Brandon said.

The monk had gone bald and stayed bald. It reminded Bob that he was in charge of the mission but not hair care. It shone a bit like the he was a mascot for a cleaning company.

"I'm thinking I wish we had some rope and no this isn't a bondage joke," Bob said. "If Brandon could jump that far he could extend a rope back to us, but—"

He peeked his head over again.

"—there are too many of them. They would notice us if they ever looked up. Did you bring any bricks with you?"

"You know it boss." The only other notable thing about Brandon was the large sack full of "presents." Yes he looked like a cross between Santa and Krillin with it on his back, but it was a sturdy sack. At least evidenced by the seven bricks he pulled out one by one. He placed them along the wall.

"I think we need more distractions. Can you make these guys move towards the center of town?"

"That's doable. Just say when. I'll throw them one at a time."

Bob considered the other skills that Sophie and Bella had. With elemental magic, as well as a specific ice magic card, their defense was potent. Though they couldn't make a whole ice luge throughout the town they could cover a little bit. Also, if they leaned on the growth part of their magic they could make walls on either side of the road.

He brought out some of the writing implements that he had acquired from the rich dwarves and quickly drew their position relative to the northern suburbs. That was only three miles or multiple spans away. Bob counted it as one hour of walking either way, through enemy terrain.

"I have an idea. We can close this road off, using nature magic to make a wall on either side. Make a safe corridor. We would still need to jump down and over. What do you think?"

"That seems like it would take a lot of mana. I can tell you right now that one wall would take about all of my mana pool, or at least I think it would," Sophie said.

"Well, what about if we instead made a bridge? Like a covered bridge between the two buildings?" Bob said.

"You would need a support beam. These one-story buildings aren't going to bear the weight," Brandon said. "I was an engineer. Mom didn't want to pay for the conservatory."

Brandon popped his head up briefly. "That's interesting. Well, if the zombies move randomly, maybe instead what we could do is sink a trench or two down so they'll eventually wind up there and we could shoot fish in a barrel. I just want to keep them away from me and I don't have a thousand crossbow bolts on me. I don't even think that I could carry that many without some overpowered card skill."

"A trench?" Sophie asked.

Brandon waved for Bob to hand him the paper and pencil. "If we made it slightly over the average human height, then these short dwarves wouldn't stand a chance. I think the warlock Julie could do that. We would just need to make sure that we left a road for the caravan to take. These guys don't seem smart like the ones that worked with the death knight. So at least there's that—and Bob you said that there were four more death knights? I hope their influence isn't too much."

Bob was in fact tracking all four now. They showed up as little icons when he focused. He was able to tell how far away they were. Mork was nothing if not direct in how he wanted his chosen to act. Though he hadn't told Bob to go directly to kill these zombies or put a clock somewhere, he would feel a pull to complete the mission.

"There's also the other way to get them out of the way," Brandon said.

"Let me guess, you're going to have them chase you?" Bob said.

"You make the pit, I put them in."

Sophie propped herself up on her forearms. The ridiculousness of them planning this all laying down wasn't quite getting to Bob. He was getting a bit tired and it would be arguably dangerous to have his legs fall asleep.

"That could work. The setup would take more time than we have, I think," Sophie said.

"And we would get more cards and card pieces from them at least. I wonder if Ca'at can climb down a trench," Bob replied.

His summon card had very particular rules but didn't mention climbing. He tapped into its magic and got the distinct impression of a cat staring right back at him. He noped right out of that line of inquiry.

"What do you think, Bob? We do plan *M*? For 'Monk running through the streets and getting the zombies to follow?' Maybe ice some of the roads when he passes?" Sophie said. "Give me the time to make some sort of safe corridor back this way."

"I don't want to risk anything unnecessarily. How fast exactly are you?" Bob said, turning to the bald man.

Brandon drew a line over the crude map. "I could clear that distance in five or six seconds. That's about a city block. I should say that I tested this with the other monks as well this morning."

Bob rubbed his chin. They were here to recon. Anything more than that would be risking too much. "I think we have enough here to inform Anthony and make a decision."

"Then we should pack up and head back. As much as I want to get my hands on whatever cards are left there, it's too risky," Bob said. "Let's head over to Bella and let her know what's going on. Maybe she has some idea that we haven't thought of yet."

All three of them low-crawled back to the stairs. Bella was watching the ground; Bob gave her hand a squeeze. He popped up, nudging her to get down, and checked their immediate surroundings. They still had a clear pathway back.

Sophie explained the situation. Bella didn't have anything new to bring up. Brandon didn't either.

Brandon would be the first one down. He was going to use some of his bricks to distract them before running back to their previous safe spot. The overturned wagon looked very inviting at that moment. Its broken and missing wheel, much less so. Bob didn't have time to get caught up in side quests. He simply made a mental note that there was a possibility there.

The wagon would be stuck there with one wheel. Even if they picked it up, it would go in a circle. Bob's mind spun with the possibilities.

"I've got a crazy idea," he said. "Let's go back and report in."

Despite their stealth, the chaotic movements of the local zombies led three in their direction by the time they were a yard away from safety. The mansion that they had cleared second looked like it was having a yard sale with all of the junk that had been tossed on the lawn.

When Brandon ran ahead, that was when the zombies chased them in earnest.

Sophie was the last one to turn around the corner. Bob was already pointing his crossbow nervously, waiting for the zombies to pop around the corner. Just a yard away, Julie lowered a ladder down for them.

As the first one lurched around the corner, Bob loosed a bolt. At once, the zombie slipped on the ice, its feet heading over its head. The next two faced the same fate in quick succession. Sophie peeked around the corner. That had been about as quiet as they could do it.

None of the rest of the zombies seemed to follow the three. She felt in the clear, and she left Bob to take care of the harvesting.

21

"So that's about all we know. I think that we should consider making a safe passageway to the shop. I also think that from the three we killed that we could use our monks as bait to farm some more cards," Bob said.

The yard had gone from a suburban dwarf's dream to a muddy mess from all the loading and staging. Anthony, Finley, and Bob were discussing the next steps. Bob had helpfully sketched a much higher fidelity map in the dirt for the group.

The entire section was its own walled-off fortress on the outskirts of the city. Julie had smoothed over the interior several times due to how much dirt the caravan kicked up regularly.

Internal walkways were well established. Dead bodies littered the south side of the fort.

"Speaking on behalf of the monks," Brandon said, "I would greatly prefer not that."

"We got four common cards and nine common card pieces from the zombies we killed. I have a theory about the infection that I want to go after," Bob said. "Also what's up with the hair, Anthony?"

The thick hair that had been in a man bun now lay down, extending past his shoulders.

"Oh this? I wanted a bit of a change."

"This has nothing to do with Julie's new hairstyle?"

"Not at all. Can we get back to what you found?"

"Also, what happened to your top? You were wearing scrubs?"

Anthony narrowed his eyes at the remark. "Let's get back on the schedule, Bob."

Bob briefly explained how he wanted to create a safe corridor to the card shop. His intent to use natural barriers made by magical spells sounded like it would take time.

It would be like digging a tunnel through the city but above ground.

"The longer we stay here, the higher the chance that we have to face the horde at night," Anthony said. "Does anyone feel particularly like fighting hundreds of zombies at night?"

There was a general mutter of agreement. No one wanted to stay in harm's way any longer than was necessary. Half of the caravan was arranged in a horseshoe shape; the rest were on watch or resting nearby.

"I didn't think so. We can shore up here for the night or make our way back into the woods. We would just need to exercise light discipline. And the horses—well they are not really that quiet. Does anyone have a card that has any effect on noise?"

That was greeted by silence. Anthony thought about the merits of heading out into the dark unknown.

"Julie and Finley. Honest question, can you two fully encircle us with walls about that high before dark? We would need the horses to stay calm and in the center of this yard. I hadn't intended on staying in this location for too long."

Julie stood up, clearly sizing up the area. Her eyes glowed an eldritch purple. Then they resumed their original hue. His scrub top was clearly visible underneath her new dwarven coat.

"It would be an ordeal. I wouldn't be able to do much else," she said.

"I could do more, but with the horses—" Finley said, gesturing north to where they were all resting. "My two are not war horses. The rest are."

The unspoken part about how two of the horses could sink their entire mission gave Anthony pause.

"Is there a way station any closer to us?" Julie said.

"Hmm. I know of one a bit further east of here, but we would need to go through town a bit. At the very least we would skirt the beltway."

Three blocks south was a road that Finley had claimed made a belt around the entire suburb. It had connections to the north, east and south toward the capital.

"Did you see any manors with a defensible wall?"

"Unfortunately no," Bob said. "Far too many places we passed by had their doors opened or windows broken."

Julie held up a hand. "If it was just us, we could go into the tunnels and easily defend ourselves. Having good working horses with us has already saved us once. The trip only took us two hours. I know we would be going back, but I feel like it's safer, Anthony."

The herd was so valuable that Anthony would do just about anything to keep them safe. If they had to pull back before night, then they had to pull back.

"Alright. I wish I had some leader card skill, but I don't. We've made a day of it here, so why don't we go back to the way station for the night, fortify it some more and then plan out our next mission? Does anyone else have any compelling reason for us to stay?"

Anthony looked around. He didn't know what time it was. Based on the sun's position, they were in the late afternoon.

"I would like the raid the house two doors down before we go, or at the very least try to draw whatever zombies are there out. And if we could do something to board up this mansion, to keep new zombies from getting in—they probably won't be heading there on purpose. Although the wall is great, thank you Julie and Finley," Bob said.

Julie gave him a thumbs up.

"Alright. Break everything we need down and let's get going," Anthony said. "We will return in the morning."

***

The otherworldly cat once again returned with common cards and card pieces. Bob cursed his luck. At least this time there were more pieces. His only consolation was that Finley would be up all night making new cards.

The last harvest had garnered a few more pieces. It wasn't enough for him to feel satisfied. Had he been able to get into the card shop, he might have been. There was too much in between him and where he wanted to be. Mork knew that he would become a great ranger; the pathway to that was through these trials.

He was going to prove to himself that he could do it. Tomorrow, they would really hit the shop. They had enough supplies for another week. The entire group was depending on him to deliver even more food. They couldn't grow food fast enough. Maybe, If they went south enough to where the climate stayed warm all year, they could make a stand.

The wind whipped, chilling him to the bone.

He looked around for Bella. She had seemed a bit interested in him. He didn't want to mix business and pleasure but there wasn't much else going on. Their fun, back and forth banter hadn't led anywhere yet.

Then the cat threw up a hairball on his feet. He thanked it with head pats. It was too bad that it couldn't kill the zombies on its own. That, of course would be too easy.

Cards and card pieces in hand, Bob went to help Bella.

***

Bella was loading everything for the kitchen. As they would be traveling again, they should be sure to pack things in an order. A specific order for how everything would come out. She didn't need her pans to be the last thing pulled out.

What she needed was the ingredients to be available and not buried under things. Bob approached. Of course he looked freshly clean and smelled slightly like bad decisions. He looked like he was a month past a life-changing divorce.

"Hey Bob."

"Bella. Did you want some help?"

"I could always use a practiced hand. Didn't you say you used to be like a cake lord or something?"

Bob smiled at her with his mischievous grin. Bella melted. It took everything she had not to swoon. They had been through a lot in the last two days. It looked like they had a chance to make it.

"I had a semi-successful business. I wouldn't dream to take over your position though."

"Help is help."

"What about you? Bella, what did you do before?"

Bob helped load a box into the caravan. Then she stepped up and past him to move it to where she wanted. Bob had never felt so unnecessary in his life. It was clear that she didn't need him. But did she want him there anyway?

Bella grinned sheepishly. "I was a student. I was going back to school as an adult, just doing general education classes before I picked a major. I wasn't anything special."

"I don't think I've ever met someone who wasn't special. Besides, school is just one part of who you are."

Bella smiled. The smell wafted through her nose again. It was something special to be sure. It reminded her of the one guy in her expository writing class that always wanted to talk to her after class. He had been a decade her junior. She appreciated his candor. He was a bit too insistent for her.

"I mean, what else do you want to know? I was into anime and manga, but what girl isn't? I chose rogue because I thought that it would be helpful to be a trickster. I mean it's nice to learn new skills and all, but I thought that I would have a bit more combat power."

"You got the ice magic. That has been pretty great."

Bella handed him another box to pack in.

"You might have saved us entirely that night. So, yeah. I might have too many powerful cards to warrant Anthony and Finley giving me more," Bob said. He placed the box perfectly. There was no give to it. He had packed it expertly.

"Have you played any Tetris before, Bob?" Bella said, admiring his work. The man was good with his hands.

"I mean, I can't always be baking cakes. That would be absurd. A man has to have hobbies."

Bella nodded. She looked down for any more boxes. The expected half hour to sort and pack everything had taken a lot less with his help.

"Once we get settled tonight, I think we can finally crack into this barrel," Bob said. "Julie has been pretty insistent that we bring this one. We need some more mugs though. I was thinking that we could set up some hooks for cups on the side of the wagon this way we can make it feel more like home."

After two days, the wagons felt like home. With all of the textiles, they would even be warm.

Bella showed him a particular design that she admired. It was soft and cuddly with a mountain range. "Hey Bob, have you ever sewn anything before? We found a linen closet and I grabbed everything so make us some bedrolls. While we're waiting on everyone else, we can get set up."

Bob gave her the thumbs up before pulling her up. The wagon that had felt so empty yesterday was now full of things that the scavenging team thought would be useful. The large wooden box with linens was in the center next to the water barrel. Bob had arranged corridors where they could lay down around the supplies.

They were definitely going to need another wagon if this kept up.

***

The final horse was fully rested. Finley spurred them to move towards the northern highway. The outriders had already begun ahead of them,

166

checking that the road was clear. Anthony had called them his scouts. The hairy human sat next to him as they began to move. While they were moving, Finley gave Anthony the reins.

He was working on his storage skill.

The interaction between his two cards had caused his tinker skill to advance. He felt that he was right on the precipice of something significant. It was just out of reach. The thing that they needed more of was supplies. The next thing that they needed was a way to move them.

Finley would be fine with foraging for himself. There was enough in the woods to keep him happy. More than once he had been hungry enough to stop his horses at a berry bush. He could go for a while on his own. With fourteen more mouths to feed, they had to dedicate more time to catching food or foraging.

The reality of the undead breathed down his neck. He wasn't in a position to do anything. The idea of an airship tickled his fancy. Every tinker he ever knew lived their lives on the same continent. With the airship idea, they could potentially travel to the next continent. He'd heard tales of the high seas. Every tinker did. He'd even seen a sea once.

It had made his decision to stay on dirt an easy one. He wouldn't want to swim ever. It wasn't that he was afraid of swimming, but things lurked in the water. Things that were worse than he was. Powerful beings that no land lover wanted to mess with.

He pushed with his card power a little harder, thinking about the relationship between space and weight. Then he felt a little tear in reality as his storage power advanced again.

"Oh!"

22

There was a ritual to putting the horses to rest at the end of the day. Now that several of his companions had the animal handling skill, it was a group ritual. The shared movement would make sure that the horses would hold up for the long term.

Making sure that the herd was ready, Finley turned to the people. As the only person who had been able to create cards from pieces, he welcomed training another. The real worth of the cards lay in their potential. That being their magical ability and the ability to trade them.

The accountant card could do wonders for him if he wanted to cook books for a gnome. He didn't and didn't see the need for an accountant without an economy, or for that matter taxes. As he was setting up his frame, he realized the absence of taxes and levies by local lords would make his life so much easier. But also, without the local lords, he wouldn't be protected from wild beasts.

Bob sat at his side while he prepared the slate, moving it into the frame configuration he needed. Then he sniffed. "What?"

The card pieces were all in good condition, minus a few hairballs. It wasn't really a thing that they could avoid. Finley hadn't ever been someone who hunted beasts for their cards and thus hadn't dealt with the visceral reality. Bob was getting an easy way out with his summon power.

That smell hit hard. The cross between acid, wet cat, and copper made a potent mix. They had chosen to do this nearby the creek, mostly for that reason. Finley extended the frame to hit the right position for the six rectangular pieces, slotting them around.

"Is there anything we can do to affect what kind of card is made?" Bob said. His breath caught for a second, then he began to have a coughing fit.

"The mana that the card maker has can change things a bit. Andrew's ability to take mana for his artificer projects is similar to how we use mana here. It's hard to visualize it without a bit of pressure. You have to imagine the mana dropping out of your hand. As if you're squeezing a fruit for its juice."

Finley demonstrated the hand motion. "Nice and easy. Let the mana flow through you. Stop it at your fist. Now gather more, like you are creating a puddle in your fist. And try to form it into a sphere. Good. Once the sphere is solid, give it a little squeeze."

Bobs face was a mask of concentration. Then a terrible scent rose up from his nether regions.

"Silent but deadly," he whispered. "I'm so sorry."

Finley had to take several steps back. He had never expected such a sneak attack from someone that he was teaching. The combination of eldritch hairball and Bob's terrible diet overpowered his senses. It was a scent that would haunt his dreams.

That was when his own lunch decided to make a surprise cameo.

***

Bella and Sophie watched the pair from the middle of the river. Finley was ralphing into the stream, thankfully further down the way. The current would move that particular problem away.

"I told him that he needs some more fiber in his diet," Bella said. "Serves him right for skipping the roughage."

"He really didn't think about the consequences of his actions, did he?" Sophie said.

With only their heads and shoulders above the water, it wasn't clear to outside observers how deep the water was. This was of course by design.

Sophie grabbed her drink from the floating block of ice, subtly guiding it back up stream. She took a deep sip of the dwarven ale. She would need a clear head for her watch shift tonight, but for the time being?

She clinked glasses with Bella.

The minuscule head of foam moved ever so slightly.

"To Bob, may he eat broccoli," Bella said, raising her glass.

"To Bob!"

***

Julie was drinking her third mug of ale. She'd expected the alcohol content to be higher. It was closer to a mean IPA than the stout that her body craved. Her hands had stopped shaking after the second one. Something about using her mana so much had made her feel drained. It was like someone had sucked the life out of her with a bendy straw.

She was grateful to Anthony for not putting her on watch duty until the morning. Though she could see in the dark, that took mana. There was something going on with her skills.

She felt the urge to perform a ritual. She had no idea what it was but it felt aligned to her pact skill. There had to be some source to her power, something that, like Ca'at, was an outsider. She wasn't entirely sure if she should be calling them up right now. She wasn't even sure that she could.

Whatever it was didn't cost mana.

That wasn't the only reason that she had considered it. Anthony was still busy going over the next day's plans. She'd absented herself from the deliberations when the ale was broken out.

There were more important things to do. She'd held back long enough, hadn't she? She deserved this little treat. She looked over to Anthony.

And that big treat.

***

Anthony wrapped up his planning. The last person he spoke with was Andrew. The dwarf had given him some information about the specifics of what he wanted for some of his projects. They had sorted through what salvage had been taken. There were far too many ornamental weapons that held no value in actual combat.

Now they both had a good understanding of the specific things that Andrew could make. Anthony was excited by the potential for skill-powered muskets. It wouldn't be the same as his holy bolt finger guns. It might be better though.

Someone wearing his scrub top had been making eyes at him for long enough. He finished off his mug and made his way over to her.

"You alright, lady?"

"I would be more alright with some company," she said.

"Ah. I can get Sophie if you want company," he said, settling down next to her.

She had been sitting against the way stone. Once he spread out his legs, she made her way over to him.

"That won't be necessary."

He wrapped his arms around her. She relaxed into him. They hadn't really talked about what this was. That was probably for the best. Anthony didn't know what was going to happen the next day.

There wasn't anything special about how she felt. The slight feel of her warm skin warred with the cool night air.

"Are you alright?" he said.

"I'm pretty fucking far from alright," she replied, snuggling in closer. "But you're going to keep us safe, right?"

He could feel her breath catch. Just for the slightest moment, then it resumed. "I'm going to keep you safe."

"Good. Now tell me about being a midwife. I need to hear something normal."

Anthony leaned back against the cool stone. "The first thing you need to know is that every mom has a birth plan…"

***

Finley and Brandon were on watch far after the sun had fallen. The other three on watch were doing slow laps around the way station.

"You want to know about the tinkers? I'll tell you about them. But first, what are your thoughts about violence? Because there is a code that all tinkers follow."

For the first time, Finley got a prompt to add someone to the family.

***

"Alright. I don't want to steamroll anyone, but the consensus is that we start before dawn," Anthony said. "Those of you that want to ride in the wagon and sleep, there's enough room in there as well as in the caravan. Also, we have to figure out a naming convention if we're going to expand to four wagons like I hope we can tonight."

The rousing speech was given the floor by virtue of half of the people napping. The watch shift had been making sure that no trace was left behind. All of the junk from salvage had been meticulously picked through and sorted for anything useful. The rest had been buried in a far corner.

Anthony hadn't said anything about the why for it.

They all knew.

Linens that could be converted to usable bedding had been. Though some of the people went without sleep by choice, Anthony had given them some time to rest. With about an hour until dawn, they began the trek back.

***

Julie wasn't the first to throw up from the back of the caravan. After she woke up in the front of the caravan next to Finley and Anthony, she was the last.

The moving wagon felt like home. It was the plate of food that churned her stomach. Empty only for the brew that it had spent all night with, it rebelled at the first contact. The three men attempting to sleep in the caravan did not appreciate the noise.

They were all quite thankful that the smell wouldn't stay for long.

***

The monks had gotten significantly faster. As the mansion became a dot on the horizon south of them, the two scouts returned with a report. Their blistering speed reminded Anthony of those marathon runners that kept a solid pace for miles. It was close to inhumanly fast, and according to Brandon one of their skills.

If he got a chance for a monk class card, he damn well was going to take it. Finley had worked out some complicated system of how he was going to give out the cards that they salvaged and he respected that. He had requested specific items from the card store called deck boxes.

They had found two at the first mansion. A third was half destroyed but usable. Something about the boxes allowed people to use them without putting cards into their soul deck.

Removing cards from one's soul could be painful. Class cards doubly so. The problem, as Finley explained, was that there was a limit to how many cards one could slot in their soul. After a certain point, one had to use a side deck if they wanted to increase the number of cards they had in regular usage.

He held out the card that he was considering slotting into his soul deck. The image of a sprinter, poised to run, dominated the copper card.

Common Skill Card: Speed Enhancement
The wielder's base speed is increased by a third.

This card was one of the five that he would need to create a monk class card. If he saved up his part of the haul, he might have it soon. For now, though, it would go into his soul deck. He needed the speed and there didn't appear to be any drawbacks to the card. Some of the common cards were just very particular.

Finley had decided on a system where everyone would get a certain amount of card pieces each day. Right now, he set it at one common piece a day. This would get everyone a new card every six days.

They could trade them up for rare or uncommon pieces at some rate. Bob and whoever killed the zombies were responsible to turn in pieces so that they could be given out equitably. It wasn't enough to survive out here. They had to do more. Part of that was going to be making sure that they didn't give one person all of the cards.

Finley would also hold the pieces for everyone in his new magically enhanced drawer. The subtle card magic of the pieces helped his power somehow. Anyone was welcome to cash out whenever they were ready. Finley, Zan, and Bob would help create the cards with the pieces they got. Bob because he thought that his quest powers might ping as a part of card creation; Finley because he knew what he was doing, and Zan because she'd actually learned how to do it.

Anthony trusted the elf. He'd have been dead otherwise. But he also liked that he would be getting an allotment of cards. Everyone else seemed to like the idea as well. It was a little something to look forward to.

There hadn't been a lot of that recently.

23

"The yard is clear. Do you want us to establish a perimeter?" Brandon asked.

Somehow the monks had all gotten the same idea of sleeveless robes. They all had spent their time comparing their guns with they waited on Anthony to tell them what to do next. Next to him, Julie cackled.

"Do you feel confident that you can attempt to lure some of them away?" he asked.

"Me and the boys can handle this," Brandon said.

"Can you quit hopping around?"

"Apologies."

The monk walked alongside the horses.

"Can you draw all the zombies in a three-block radius?" Anthony leaned back. "Hey Bob are you good with shooting fish in a barrel?"

"What?"

"I said, fish in a—never mind. Brandon take your crew and see if you can draw them away from the three-block radius. Bob's team will then try to clear some out. I'm sending in the heavy artillery today."

Anthony patted Julie on the shoulder. She was the heavy artillery. His holy bolts could devastate a single zombie at a time. She had the area of effect spells that could take out a bunch. With Zan backing her up, the two would be able to extend the safe zone a bit further.

"Well at least I'm helping," Julie said. She leaned against Anthony. "I slept the sleep of the dead. Whatever I said last night, I claim the fifth."

"There are no fifth amendment rights here. We're not even in America. You were never even an American."

"Blame it on American television, eh?"

"You guys have such strange words," Finley said from behind them.

"Yeah, I agree," Julie said. "Why couldn't you guys have a queen or a parliament or some normal government? Heck we have a king back there."

"And a queen up here," Anthony said.

"You what—"

***

While the monks did their work. Bob, chosen ranger of Mork, had a mission.

He needed to clear a pathway to the closest card shop. He didn't need to clear one. He just needed access. And a hammer, which had been provided by Finley. Card stores apparently loved glass cases and had great locking doors. He also had Sophie and Bella to use magic on the roof so they could cut their way in.

The first thing he noticed upon getting back to where things had gotten busy was how few zombies remained. The monks were really taking their jobs seriously. This time, they carried lots of rope. The rope bridge across the main road was going to be his baby if they could get it up.

Andrew the dwarf had given them enough sharp implements to nail the rope down on one side. Then they would have to find a way across the street. Ten meters of rope would be enough for what he intended. He would tie down a grappling hook on the far side to climb up to the next roof and fasten it there. Then it would be a tightrope walk until they got more rope attached.

One of the monks ran by, drawing a pack of zombies slowly southward. He waited for them to pass, checking alongside the major north–south route.

Then he fastened one end to the building, using Sophie's help. Something felt right as he rappelled down the single story. He held on to the slack, picking up the pace as he jogged across. Then he climbed up as fast as he could, praising Mork for dwarves who had left a stack of crates in just the right place to jump from.

The rope became significantly less slack as he pulled it up to him. This roof was close to the previous design, with enough of a tilt to let the snow drop towards one of the roads. He couldn't see a clear best place to place the anchor. He grumbled, pulling out another rope that he then ran to the far corners. There he tapped two large bolts into each corner. He tied the rope off, connecting it with a series of sailor's knots when Bella arrived.

She saw what he was doing and wordlessly checked his knots. Then she checked all four sides of the roof. Bella gave him a thumbs up before placing one more bolt in a far corner. She took off some of her own rope, tossing it to the next building. It was only about five feet away. She jumped the distance easily.

When she nodded to him, he went back to provide cover for Sophie.

Sophie made everything that was difficult about his parkour look effortless. Bob really wanted to tell her to stop showing off, but now wasn't exactly the time. Perhaps that evening, he would.

Bob wiped the sweat off his brow and steeled himself for the next part.

***

"If we just dig a big trench," Zan said, gesturing at the map they'd scratched out in the dirt, "right here, at the outer perimeter of our three-block radius, we can lure them in. I understand that you're really wanting this to farm some card pieces. We want that too. I think that a lot of this hinges on how we extract the cards and card pieces."

"Right. If we use Bob's summoned creature, then it will do a lot of the work for us. And I have a ritual that acts as a magnet to card pieces. I have to stay still for about a minute though. So I would need to be protected," Julie said. "My idea is to use one of the roofs of these reinforced buildings. The only problem is if they start trying to destroy the building or something."

Zan nodded. Both women were trying to figure out how to get spells into Zan's spell book. Zan had started with three spells. Julie had instinctively known a whole branch of magic. Through trial and error they figured out a lot of the things that didn't work. Julie wanted to say that they were ready to move on to the things that did work, but knew that you never said those sorts of things aloud.

"Do you want to try the earth moving spell again?" Zan said.

"Might as well. We're covered on three sides now. The zombies will have to go all the way around. The horses might not like it but this works as a defense from a mindless enemy."

"Yeah. Noted. Do you want to do the land bridge thing?"

Julie nodded. The original wall between them and the town had been fortified by eldritch and druidic magic. At her current level, Julie could feel her magic getting closer to the next skill up, no matter how far away it had initially seemed.

Rare Class Card: Warlock Level 4

Skills:

Eldritch Spellcasting Level 4

Ritual Casting Level 2

Enchantment Level 1

Survival Level 2

Medicine Level 1

Patron Pact Level 1

This card grants mana.

As a warlock, you may have a patron.

This is a soul card and cannot be removed.

It had gained a level as well. She felt slightly more competent. Two days of being fed properly had helped immensely. Being low on mana felt like being low on blood sugar. She didn't want to deal with either problem.

"The problem with moving dirt around is that it has to come from somewhere," Julie said. "If I pull the dirt in from both sides then I'm robbing either side."

"No, the problem with moving dirt around is the mana it takes. I have an idea. Make the ground next to the wall lower. Use that dirt. Then we call green Legolas over here to shore it up." Zan gestured back to the wagons.

"You noticed too, right? I'm not the only one?" Julie said from the top of the wall. The next lot was thankfully empty, except for the patch of sunflowers that had grown prodigiously. There was something different about that area. She moved to create the raised dirt bridge so it wouldn't intersect.

Finley had been growing lots of sunflowers and yellow mushrooms. They would spring up around the bodies after he said a very loud prayer. It was probably a prayer at least. Otherwise, it had to be some terrible cosmic joke.

It was in not language that she could parse. All heavy breathing and bleating, it made her feel like she was looking at a toddler melting down. Of course this wasn't completely true. It was some offering to the Goat Lord, he'd told her later.

Half party, half animal, the Goat Lord asked his followers to mindfully send off the dead. She got a sense that this was something that Finley wanted to talk about; a special interest that he knew to hold back from telling people. He had been nothing but nice to her. Their magic worked together. She would ask him later.

"Have you ever talked to Finley about the flowers thing?" Julie asked.

"Honestly, it seems like something that he doesn't want to talk about. I mean his entire family died. He hasn't really—hey wait—you said that you were a social worker?" Zan did the classic Wonder Woman pose.

"I was."

"Aren't social workers like investigators?" Zan narrowed her eyes.

"You're thinking of detectives," Julie said. The raised pathway was now wide enough to walk on. She considered leaving a gap. "Do you think that dwarves can jump? Or rather undead dwarves?"

"I think that is a bit of a useless distinction."

"Well, it's only useless if we don't consider how they might make it in. There's a good chance that we might stay here tonight if we can fortify it enough. I think that we need to really stock up here if we're going to make the caravan a viable long-term thing."

"I hadn't thought about that. I barely am thinking beyond today." Zan fortified part of a wall with a bit of mana.

"There's got to be more than just survival on your mind though, Zan."

"Honestly? No."

Julie stopped casting, letting her mana free. "We were summoned here for a reason. It might have been a fucked-up reason, and we might be too late, but we have a chance here. We can do some good."

"The only good I see is killing zombies," Zan said quietly. "Everything else? I don't know what you want from me. You got Anthony if you want him. I'm just helping out how I can."

"Not everybody can be a hero. Not everybody should be charging into battle."

Cara, god of drug deals and overland transportation, smiled at her. In that moment, Julie could sense the pact between them. She called for a break and returned to the caravan, making sure that Zan was headed to eat something.

***

"Chin up, Julie. You've got to look your best for the end of the world," Anthony said.

Anthony readily accepted her hug. Behind him a large map of the town was taking shape in ink on what had to have been someone's stretched out drapes.

"Thanks. I see we've upgraded from the dirt model," Julie said. "Fancy."

She silently thanked Bella's card powers for making him smell like he was in a Taylor Swift music video.

Anthony beamed. "Did you ever watch any horror movies?"

"No, not really. I got too scared. I liked Evil Dead though. A bit of horror comedy seemed to be fine."

"You know that thing that they do where someone gets bitten and then they don't tell anyone?"

She pushed him back. The yard had grown more and more to look like the interior of a castle. There were many clean circles where the ground was flat as a board, a side effect of the cleaning power.

"You didn't get bitten, did you?"

"No. I just thought that you might want to check. I was going to take a break." He gestured with his eyes to the mansion. In particular the top floor.

"And you wanted to check me for bites?"

"You could check me as well. It would require one or both of us to disrobe," he said, smiling with only his eyes.

"Ah. It couldn't hurt, I guess. Then we can get some food after, eh?"

"That sounds lovely."

24

Bella and Sophie took turns carving the thick stone roof. The monks had done a great job keeping the zombies moving in a different direction. The infrequent loud sounds of bricks being tossed to draw the attention of zombies punctuated their work.

Having never cut stone, neither woman was ready for the reality of the situation. Magic could only do so much. According to Finley, card shops took their security quite seriously. There was a roll-up door that was made of some metal that Finley didn't know the name of offhand. The monks had said that it looked impressive when they passed by.

Anthony's words stirred in Bella's mind.

"Get in. Get out. Don't fail."

She edged over to the side to peek out over. There had to be a window somewhere, right?

"A fire skill would have been useful about now," Sophie said. "We would be killing it with something like a fire dagger. Wait, stone doesn't burn. Maybe we need to hit some of the bricks?"

The roof was solid. The craftsmanship that it must have taken was a credit to whoever was responsible. Unfortunately, that wasn't great for her team.

"Ideas?" Bella asked.

"A wall of fire around the door, someone slips in the front entrance," Sophie said.

"That would be mana intensive. If we had a sledgehammer, then I would say yes," Bob said.

Bella brought out a hand-sized hammer.

"Where were you hiding that—nevermind don't tell me," Bob said, groaning. "I'll provide overwatch with my bow. Sophie, you have the elemental magic for fire spells. Bella?"

"Yes, meat shield?"

"Smash."

"With pleasure."

Bella anchored the shortest rope they had to the roof.

Bob took over a position, as if he were brandishing a machine gun. Sophie was on his left. Bella checked and her infiltration skill had advanced.

Rare Class Card: Rogue Level 3

Skills:

Sneak Attack Level 3

Skill Mastery Level 2

Weapon Expertise Level 1

Infiltration Level 3

Evasion Level 2

Stealth Level 2

As a rogue, you may learn one extra class skill per level. New skills start at the average of your other class skills.

This is a soul card and cannot be removed.

She swung down, rappelling the two meters to the ground. The monks had done their work well; the block was empty. She could see several zombies that were further away. She was about to make a ton of noise.

The sledgehammer crashed against the glass storefront. Bella told herself that she wasn't going to look, but several zombies from far off reacted. It didn't change what she was going to do, just increased her speed.

She slammed against the glass several times before it cracked. Then she shot a load of ice magic right at the center of the classic glass door. The next hit took the door down. Behind the glass door was a roll-up metal door.

One quick look saw the zombies heading her way with a purpose. She might have a minute or two before they arrived at most. She got to work on opening the door, brushing away frozen shards of glass as she did so.

Above her, she heard the sound of a bolt being loosed.

At the bottom of the roll-up steel door was a lock. Her infiltration skill pinged and she realized that she didn't have any small thieves' tools. What she did have was one dwarves' tool, though. She iced the lock, pouring mana until frost rose from the floor.

Then she pounded the lock with the sledgehammer. It broke into hundreds of tiny shards. The steady *twip* of the bow increased as more zombies were taken down by Bob. She lifted the heavy door, taking one look to determine if any zombies were inside.

"I don't see another way out, Bob!" she yelled.

"Take as much as you can carry!"

He had affixed a rope to a large dwarven rucksack. He tossed it down next to her. She grabbed it and made her way under the roll-up door, allowing it to return.

The room was dark except for a few high and tiny windows.

"Jackpot."

Regular glass cases lined waist-high displays. Orange custom-grown wood bookshelves covered each wall. Several large boxes of copper cards lay ready for inspection. For about two seconds, she marveled at the display. Then she remembered that she had a job to do.

Bella smashed the glass cases as quickly and efficiently as she could. She tossed every case of copper cards into the sack until it was nearly full. She gave the line a tug, then pulled the door up enough to let it pass. The sack quickly made its way up, either via meat shield or muscle mommy.

Having the door open gave her a chance to ice part of the road. She took it.

She waited for the second sack to be lowered, then grabbed it. Checking the tie, Bella then pulled the bag into the shop. Like a madwoman, she began to unload iron cards into the second one as fast as she could.

There were precious few gold cards in the back, behind what had to be a tempered glass case. Those could wait. Volume would help a lot, according to Finley. Copper commons and iron uncommons were going to help them survive. Rare gold cards? Felt like overkill.

It felt like she was robbing a gaming store, an experience that she had never had back on Earth. It wasn't anything that she expected.

The bolts continued to fly.

Bella had to make a choice. The box with the rares was highly valuable, but she didn't know how much time that Bob and Sophie could give her. If she could find a way to open the hatch to the ceiling, she could be upstairs easily and this problem might not exist. She allowed herself a glance at the cards behind there. A few caught her eye.

Rare Ability Card: "Never tell me the odds."

Succeed on any class skill, usable once per day. Skill cannot involve combat.

"Bet you thought that looked cool, right?"

Two others looked interesting at first glance: "Suspiciously Convenient Alibi" and a gambler class card. That was when Bob started yelling, the sign that they were overstaying their welcome.

It was classic Bob behavior.

She could handle herself. She just didn't need to.

She filled up the sack, tugged on it, and raised the roll-up door just enough to let someone pull the second bag up. It wasn't heavy, just awkward like a second cousin you've only met twice.

She didn't wait for anything else. She had a small pouch for very important cards. The rares would make it in there.

She froze the tempered glass box and then smashed it with her sledgehammer. She immediately took the "Never tell me the odds" card into her soul deck.

She looked over to the hatch and activated the card on her infiltration skill. She was trying to infiltrate the roof. The card lit up something in her vision. There was a latch up there. She just needed to follow her brand-new instincts.

"Well shit."

Bella made her way up the short ladder and hit the latch with just the right amount of force. She could hear a catch release and the hatch popped up. The sky had never looked so good. Bella popped her head over, then got her entire body onto the roof.

Bob was reloading when he saw her. He briefly turned her way then nodded.

On the opposite corner, Sophie was laying down covering fire. Her particular mix of magic was sending equal parts fire and lightning down. A girl could appreciate options.

Now she needed to get all of their loot back to base.

"I'm going to get as much as I can," Bella said.

The sounds of continued attacks met her. A quick peek showed at least twenty downed zombies within what she would call a reasonable distance. For her, that meant at least three houses. They were close enough to be family, and that was a problem.

She just needed one more trip down.

They had talked about how they would deal with being cut off. She realized with a pang of guilt that she was going to be stupid if she went back. There was far too much heat on them now. The monks would only be able to do so much.

A few blocks back was safety. She could see Julie on top of a mansion, eyeing them. At least it looked like her. If she had binoculars she would be certain; there were only so many blue scrub tops.

"Bob! Let's cut out," Bella said, affixing a simple dummy trap over the hatch. It wouldn't do anything, except look imposing. She still wanted all of the books in there too. They seemed like they had some value. Also there was no good smut on Noveria, and she had more than one itch to scratch.

"I couldn't agree with you more," he said, slinging his crossbow onto his back.

Bob made a beeline for one rucksack, quickly stringing it up onto his shoulders. He looked down for about five seconds before he waved to Brandon. The monk paused to catch the first rucksack, slung it onto his back and then ran north.

"That one is on him now. I hope our caravan team has set up some sort of defensive screen," Bob said. Bella was right behind him when he summoned his companion. "Ca'at, there's a bunch of targets on the ground. More of the same—undead dwarf suburbanites. Do your best work."

The black cat disappeared as fast as it had come.

"Now, onto the next part," Bob said, grabbing Sophie's forearm. "We run."

They made their way as fast as they could over the rooftops. Before she knew it, Bella was standing next to their two-rope crossing. It was a half mile at most to safety. There were no zombies readily apparent, having all been drawn to their smash-and-grab operation. Some of them were trying to track the team as they moved over the roofs.

They had a slight advantage, having set this up in advance. Bella crossed followed by Sophie, then Bob. They made their way over the major road this way, then descended the ladder on the far side. As soon as Bob hit the ground, they ran all out.

Instead of holding his bow on his back, Bob held it in a half-ready position. Brandon had inexplicably dropped his rucksack and returned to them. That could be a problem.

Bob aimed, keeping one hand on his crossbow, even as they ran. Bob moved like an Olympic sprinter who had never been told to slow down in his entire life. Bella admired his commitment to duty, but mostly his speed.

It took nearly five minutes to return to the yard where they would be safe.

Julie had been busy. Waving at them from the third floor, she smiled.

"Did you bring a ladder?" Bob said. "This wall is new."

"There's an entrance there? A break in the wall?" Bella said. "I think that they're going to get us a ladder. Otherwise, we'll climb or go around."

True to form, by the time they reached the wall, a ladder had been dropped.

They didn't stop to catch their breath until they stood on top of the wide wall. Bella took off her gear and nearly jumped with joy. She thought better of it and instead waited patiently for Bob to remove his equipment.

Behind them about six zombies had followed them this far and they had just reached Julie's range. She began to fire purple-tinged magic beams at them.

Sophie sat down. Anthony pulled the ladder back up.

Bella felt the rush of surviving well up. Bob was looking pretty damn good at the moment.

"Bob?" She said, turning to him.

"Yeah?"

"Get the fuck over here. That was a fucking trip."

Bob smiled. He walked over to her. Placing his hands on her hips, he pulled her into him. A tear dropped down her face.

He cupped her chin and locked eyes with her. And in that moment, she let the tension evaporate. Impossibly, he somehow drew her in closer. Then he kissed her and she immediately forgot about the mission.

25

When, after lunch the Monks told him that they had found a potential fourth wagon to add to the caravan he finally knew that it was time. There weren't many things that could disturb Bob, chosen ranger of Mork.

The smell and feel of a cat throwing up a hairball at his feet, however, was at the top of the list. The two-meter fall, by contrast, didn't bother him.

"We should make a stand here," he whispered.

"Fuck that noise," Bella said. "Unless you got a quest. Did you get a quest?"

"No, but look—" He gathered the pieces, placing them into another bag that Bella had handed him. She had hidden so many bags, and he didn't even know where.

"No, you listen. I understand that we are stronger than them. We are vastly outnumbered. Theirs is a war of attrition. We're fighting to survive. We wouldn't stand a chance long term, especially if a death knight appeared on the field," Bella said with a shudder She never wanted to experience that again.

"But I killed that death knight—" Bob said.

"Yes. You did. Call that a fluke. Just because your God is telling you to hunt them down, doesn't mean just this minute. We can't re-alive those dwarves, right?"

"That is a good question. Let's go clean off and get down from here. Finley might know."

They followed the land bridge back to their growing safe zone. Finley waved to them. The two rucksacks that they had filled were already there, and the elf was sorting them.

It would have been nice to get the first pick.

***

"This pile is utility cards that are situational," Finley said. "They are the most useful. Some of them are part of a set. The pile here—the shortest one—is five class cards. None are combat classes. They have some good if questionable skills. Next to that are skill cards that I could potentially combine into another class card. Those are half common and uncommon. Then there are all of these less than useful cards…"

The largest stack was the copper stack that Finley had deemed of little to no use. That comprised about one hundred cards.

There was an established ratio of common to uncommon cards from most classes. It nearly always gave the expected result. He didn't know the particulars.

The card shop should have had a specialized series of books by one C. Ard Sharq that spelled out the particulars. He never kept one.

It was an exceedingly dry read.

"As soon as the monks get back from their diversion, we can do the blind auction. If you agree, Anthony, we can give everyone ten or so card pieces; they can bid using those."

"This is really going to help you with your skills?"

"And it's the only fair way. If we let people choose the card powers that benefit them the most in what they want to do for the caravan, instead of telling them what to do, then they'll be more motivated. I'm thinking of giving another two pieces to the ones that took on the mission. Think of it like an incentive."

On the third day since the caravan formed, they held a blind auction at lunch. The three people on watch had to be switched out twice, giving enough consideration to everyone. Finley had added the accountant card to the lot and was surprised that his was the only bid for it.

None of these humans apparently understood the importance of managing the books. He said a quick prayer to Cara, goddess of drug deals, for his fortune. The entire process felt like it had really solidified that they were in it for the long run. There was no one coming to save him, no favors to call in. Of course, he had added his accountant class to his deck by that time. He felt like his barter skill was on the precipice of what had to be another level up.

"So, Anthony, I wanted to talk to you about getting another wagon. The monks were telling me that there's one nearby. And it might have been a tinker wagon? That would be a find."

"Yeah. They're going to see if they can move it into the road, then potentially pull it partway here. One of them chose a horse power card so they're going to be able to move it a little bit. If we had some tough rope then it would be easier. They could pull it like sled dogs."

"Sled dogs?"

"It's a thing back on Earth. You know what, forget it. The point is that it's facing the right direction to pull it to a north-south road. All they have to do is get it moving over here. How long does it take to harness up the horses? I should know this."

"Too long to be out in the open like that."

"Yeah I was worried you would say that. Our next option is to have them push it as well. We're going to spend a lot of effort getting this thing here that we don't even know is viable yet."

"I want that wagon, Anthony."

"I got it—"

"No, you don't understand. If this was a tinker wagon, I want it."

"I was going to say, how badly—"

"I saved your life. I'm officially calling in the favor."

"That seems reasonable. I'll have to check with Julie and Zan who are making this maze defense thing to increase their skills, but yes."

The elf and the human clasped hands. Finley could feel his tinker skill advance. He smiled. It had been the right choice. Now he had to decide if he wanted to add anybody to the family. And what that would look like if he did.

***

Julie could see the monks running back and forth. Every so often, Bob would pop up. His summoned creature would then make its way towards the corpses. Each and every time, it would eviscerate the corpse, take the shiny card pieces, and then return to Bob.

Then Finley cast a spell that created a half-mushroom, half-daisy growth over what remained. The elf grew more green by the day. Each time he used his magic, he turned a slightly darker shade.

No one had said a word.

She had begun to wonder if she was hallucinating it.

In the back of her mind, it looked like his deity was using him as a conduit. That connection was a thing that was turning him green. Because that was what they were for.

While Finley did his magic with setting up the blind auction, Julie was hard at work. There had to be a way to unlock her card powers that seemed stuck.

Julie instinctively knew that she had to do some sort of ritual. There had to be privacy somewhere, so she found an unoccupied attic space.

The card power took over as she poured mana out into a thick chalk bar. The chalk proved to be the perfect tool to mark the floor; she crafted a large circle, big enough to house a tree.

In a haze, she added runes that she'd never seen before. The circle looked like a cross between Arabic and Korean. She knew neither. Her Canadian upbringing had taught her French and English. Three minutes after she was done, the haze lifted.

Julie blinked several times. Then she looked again with a clear eye. If someone had told her that she was going to create a demonic summoning circle, she could have done worse than this. Interspersed between the runes were nondescript bags and drawings of wagons. There were eight of each.

There was some command that she knew in her soul that would let her force the circle to start working. It took her a second to figure out. Then she sighed and said it.

"I know a guy…"

In one moment, the room went deathly silent. It had been quiet before. Now she couldn't hear outside. The horses always made a little bit of noise. Anthony and the monks had been steadily chipping away the zombie numbers when they lured them in. Now she could only hear her own heartbeat. It was fast.

"Finally!" In the center of the circle, a young woman of what had to be primary school age sat in one of those chairs that you only see in the classroom. She had a perfect tie-dye shirt that just screamed "My mother is an almond mother." Her pants looked like they had been made by someone who frequented farmers' markets, but had never been to a farm. She didn't wear shoes.

"Uh hello?"

"As you might imagine, I am Cara."

"I did no such thing. Am I supposed to kneel or bow or something?"

"The normal thing that my warlocks do is offer me a token. As I understand the situation that is not necessary. I would accept a card piece."

Julie shuffled through her pockets and grabbed a single copper card piece.

"This is all I have, is it okay?"

The goddess held it out, sniffed it, and then briefly bit it before putting it into her own pocket. "It is acceptable. As it is the most expensive thing you have which is not inexorably tied to your soul. Now let's get down to business. As you're well aware, I am the goddess of drug deals and overland travel. You can imagine that I'm not exactly thrilled about the current situation on this continent. As such, I summon to you here to be my man on the ground. Or shall I say woman on the ground."

"You want something?" Julie said. "I assume that is what this is about."

The goddess pulled out a pad of paper and a pencil from somewhere. She began furiously scribbling. "Ah. Right to business. I see the type. No, I completely understand."

"Yeah, well there's like hundreds of zombies outside that want to eat me, so I can't just have a long social call. Even if I am on rest."

"Understood. That is part of the reason that I called you to this world. We need some heroes to take down the threat."

"You want me to kill thousands of zombies?"

"Well not personally, no. There's really only four that I want you to kill in particular."

"Let me guess. You want me to kill the death knights? Mork already gave Bob a quest for that."

Cara tapped her pencil on her paper and began drawing a large stylized *S*. "Ah yes. Mork and I are having a little competition. Mork wants Bob to kill the death knights. I want you to kill them first if possible."

"What? Why can't you kill them?"

"Despite how things seem here, there are other continents on this planet that haven't been affected by this scourge. The longer the death knights are around, the more this place will turn blighted. That's bad for business."

"Business?" Julie said. She was doing her best not to roll her eyes. "What business? Everyone here is dead."

"You're getting it. Good. Alright here's what I'm going to do, should you accept. I'm going to strengthen your pact with me, which will make you stronger. In exchange, all I ask is an offering of one copper piece a week. More if you're going to try to draw more power. Also if you come across any dank nuggets that the dwarves or elves made, I'm going to need you to toke up in my honor. And that third wagon? You get that up and running and I'll increase your warlock class level. How is that for an incentive?"

"Those are all so random. You want me to toke up and take a trip?"

"I would like you to mark up the third wagon with a small shrine to me. Your ritual skill will show you how. That's how you can send me your patronage."

"I have questions."

"Go ahead."

The deity continued to write in her notepad as Julie thought. "Would it be possible to get the things we need to make an airship?"

"It's possible. Overland travel I guess could include the skies," Cara said. She applied a small stick of pink lip gloss. "Do you want that to be a part of this?"

"This what?"

"I'm drawing up a contract for you. You do these things, I give you the things you want."

"Yes. Add that to the contract. If there's a ritual to turn the raw ingredients into what I need, I want that added."

"Excellent. I feel like this will be a very profitable partnership."

26

"So this death knight, the one that you killed, what do you remember about it?" Finley said.

It was just after lunch. Everyone was getting used to their new cards. Finley and Anthony were holding counsel with Bob.

"Besides it being intelligent? Mork told me that I would probably get something special from defeating it. And I did. But the big difference between Dunnamore and here is how the zombies were organized. They're all their own here. Back there? They had the horses readied to go on the offensive. Now, I'm not sure what that means but as far as what I got from Mork, it could not have been good."

"So the death knights are intelligent and they had some kind of plan. Do you think that they were going to go after the other chosen?" Anthony said.

The herbal tea that had been found in the mansion steamed up between them. The table they were using was an ornate one. It had been dragged slowly out of the house. The chairs were rocks. Still, they were the most comfortable thing that Bob had sat on in a while.

"The more that I think about it, they were probably preparing to go capture more chosen. Something probably tipped them off about either you and Finley or me. It's what they had been doing with everyone else."

"Did you find anything? When you went back there?" Finley said.

"Nothing useful. The death knight had some stationery and was clearly going to use it but everything was blank. Perhaps he was a new addition?"

The group took a second to ponder this. Only Bob had direct combat experience against a death knight. Everyone else had been captured by other controlled undead.

"Would it be easy to kill another one? Or should I say simple?" Anthony asked, before putting his teacup to his lips. He breathed in the vapors, closing his eyes as he did so.

"If it was alone, yes. But I think they're going to have too much time to prepare. If they expect us coming, then it doesn't matter what card powers we have. We don't have the numbers."

"Are you saying that we need to go on the offensive?" Anthony said.

"I don't know the answer to that. All I know is what Mork told me. I can always see them. This little icon in my view. It tells me their direction but not how far they are. We could go after them. We could die. We could win."

This little detail did not pass Finley's notice. Bob could always see them. Finley only had the vaguest sense of how that would work.

"Well that's not part of my plans." Anthony lowered his teacup down. "Our plans."

"Once we have enough to last a few weeks, it's time for us to start moving south. If the zombies don't kill us, the cold will. We won't be able to grow anything in the cold. And even if we can hunt, most of the food here will spoil," Finley said. He liked to think that he would be going south no matter what they said. Being in a group had changed things.

"The grain will be good though, right? Oh we have to feed the horses don't we?" Anthony said. "All right. We need to get to that supply warehouse. Then we need enough time while we are there to pack everything we need and load it up."

The three of them all sighed at the same time. Horses needed to eat and this was a simple thing when the sun was warm and there was a stream nearby. When the sun played its disappearing game for more of the day, it became trickier.

"If we are able to clear out more zombies then this will be easier. We could even consider continuing this wall to entirely encircle the city. I wonder if zombies can live indefinitely?" Bob said. "There isn't that long until winter. Anthony, we can't stay here for the week that it would take. We've killed maybe a hundred zombies here, if that. The monks said that further in it's very packed."

"We're not going to win this city. Even if we did, the cleanup alone would be astronomical. My one and only goal is to survive for long enough that it will be possible to win the war. One more day here, two at most and we will move on. If anyone has a better idea, I would love to hear it, "Anthony said.

The two men and the elf waited for a long moment.

Finley shrugged. "Well enough about the big picture stuff. Tell me what we need to know about this wagon and the warehouse."

***

Finley had done the last rites for another tinker twice. Once for an elf he trusted with his life; someone that molded him into who he was today. The other time was for an elder who had passed away.

Somewhere in Plainsmount, there was another tinker. That person, whoever they were, had died here. He ached to put them to rest. One day, when all of this was over, he wanted to return.

He might not be able to bury them all himself. He would bring friends. He would give their last rites. The Goat Lord would see him through.

Moving the other reclaimed wagon was his first priority. Chances were that he would find the body nearby. Then he would be able to cook two root vegetables with one pot. Lacking the time to cook a soup, he had to let Bella take that duty.

He had the best animal control of everyone. If they found that the wagon needed animals, he would usher them there.

He expected the wagon to have a spot for one horse, rather than the two that his had. He had inherited the vendor caravan. Regular tinker wagons all had similar smaller sizes. If so, he had a horse in mind. The main reason that he hadn't gone on a mission with Bob was that nobody knew what would happen if he left. If the horses were no longer in the range of his animal handling skill, would they stay?

They might run away. Then the caravan would need to dig in.

That they had stayed so long baffled him, but what other choice did the horses have? They were little more than targets out in the wild. Monsters would be sure to make a comeback following the lack of adventurers.

It was still possible for them to survive.

It was still possible for them to make it through.

There would never be another tinker he would meet in the wild. It was still possible for him to honor the dead. Survival without change would not be sufficient.

So, using his newfound accounting card for the first time ever, he planned out his return trip. He would take his time going through every little town to find every tinker and their wagon. If he survived, that meant that there would be no zombies left. His entire continent, the place he had lived his entire life on, was vast. He began to write down how many months of supplies he would need to start that journey.

It was a welcome distraction from his current problem.

***

"The more that you move them around, the more chaotic they end up. It's like herding cats but the cats want to eat you," Brandon said.

"So exactly the same. I never really liked cats. I always thought that given a chance they would eat their owners. Plus, all that disease and shit," Julie said.

They were on top of the wall as far as they could get from the staging area. With her enhanced bond now working far better than she ever expected, Julie was able to finish off some of the details of the maze. She had played a few tower defense games before, so had a working knowledge of how to defend a fixed point. She'd never expected to actually use it. And it would have been very useful to be able to see the maze from the top down.

Fortunately, Anthony was able to recreate it on another large piece of parchment.

They were looking it over from the roof of the second mansion. As they were visible, they were able to answer one of Anthony's main questions. That being "Do zombies look up?"

The answer, through trial and deliberation, was that zombies were far more likely to go after something that was on the ground. Brandon and his monks had been trying to prove it by bringing zombies to run the maze. In so doing, they would thin out the zombies next to the warehouse they were looking for. The warehouse was only five blocks away. Three blocks south, and two blocks west.

Julie was supremely grateful that the dwarven city planners had made their blocks about what she had expected. It wasn't exactly the same as Regina, but similar enough. It made her wish that there was some sort of book about dwarven urban planning. She would take that book and curl up with it and a good drink and wait out the apocalypse. That was not an option for her.

"I really appreciate what the dwarves did here with Plainsmount. It's so well laid out. If we ever make it to the human kingdom, I expect it to be way more chaotic," she found herself saying. "Do you think that we can use some ramps?"

"When you say ramps are you talking about like, zombie skateboarding or something? Because that would be sick." Brandon mimed doing a kick flip.

Julie snickered. "They are made of flesh and bone right? There's only so much damage they can take from falling before their bones break. This is why a pitfall would be effective."

"If you just want to do that, we could just make a big hole somewhere. Then I guess we could like run across a bridge? Or push them in? You run the risk of one of us falling in. But if we had a ramp then you're opening up a possibility that the zombies will chase us up the ramp."

"Maybe like a ramp and a zip line?"

"I think we should bring Andrew in on this. You can make a giant dirt pile. Then we can smooth it out. And what like have a zip line running down?"

"This is definitely getting too complicated."

"I completely understand. Maybe we need to speak to your boyfriend about this."

The side eye she returned to him was enough for him to back down a little bit. He had to reclaim his footing on the roof and then sat down.

"I don't think we need to put a label on that right now," Julie said. "Maybe we should just focus on the mission."

"Right. Right. I can see the warehouse from here. It's large enough. If you start raising dirt walls going southward then we can cut the zombies moving east to west out. Then we can go another block south of that and start going west. Then we'll have only a reduced number of zombies to deal with, specifically the ones that got cut off. But if my monks do what they're supposed to do, then we'll have led them all south by that time."

"That will make it a hell of a lot easier, eh?"

"The ones that remain? They will be fish in a barrel."

"I always hated that metaphor. How about we just call it what it is. Zombies in a tower defense."

"Zombies in a tower defense? I can dig it."

Julie mentally modeled out how she was going to do that. Moving south, she would raise a wall to cut off the zombies moving east to west. Then she would take a long rest, conserving her mana. That would give the monks a chance to lure these zombies away.

Then she would continue, encircling a safe zone that would extend to the warehouse. She couldn't fully circle around it because they would need a way to leave. That seemed to be one of the key problems as well. If there was a way for them to leave with their wagons, there was a way for zombies to enter. Of course for this, she had Anthony and the watch.

All of the people that had not been tasked to specifically do this would be on standby.

"This had better be worth the trouble," she grumbled.

27

Sophie was fully rested. More than that, she felt itchy being on standby. She wanted to do something productive. That wasn't happening while they had such a big operation going on.

Bella and Bob had to stand watch after lunch. Bella because she wanted to cook and clean up afterwards. Bob because he had been dragged inexorably into her orbit.

She didn't say as much but had told him that it would be frowned upon for him to not do his "himbo duties." Sophie had laughed at that.

Because Sophie had the caster class on top of her rogue class, she had taken up a position as far from the wagons as they could safely get her to. Then, every time Julie extended the raised dirt bridge, she moved to grow plants through it.

Something about her card powers told her that she would be able to do this for more than five minutes at a time when she leveled up her skill again. It felt like a self-fulfilling prophecy, that her earth movement spell would help itself. Sophie's wasn't nearly as strong as Julie's, but they were on the way.

In that, she was quite happy that she didn't have to do something like extract the cards from each zombie she killed.

Ca'at was being put through its paces. Remotely, Bob was having it tear down the zombies that entered her tower defense area. Once they got deep enough in, the warriors would take spears and stab the fuckers.

At the end of the maze, Zan or whoever would put a ladder down for the monks to exit. Then, once they were up, she quickly pulled the ladder up.

The cat didn't look haggard, but its controller did. After having Anthony work him half to death, Bob probably felt it too.

One of the monks came up the ladder. Zan quickly pulled the ladder up. Sophie sighed, brandishing her spear. She had named her spear Bob. He was getting as much use as Bella was getting out of human Bob. Or at least the same amount of action.

From her vantage point, the target was easy. She cleanly pierced another zombie's head. Bob's shaft felt strong in her hands. This Bob was a product of good craftsmanship.

"Thank God for that cat. This would be so much messier without it," she said.

"Good shot. I think that more spears would make this job a lot easier," Zan said. "Not that I'm complaining or anything."

"Oh girl, go ahead. We're all a little tense here and we need to let the steam out."

"I hear that," Zan said. "It's like the damn zombies just keep coming. Like, you're spending your death doing chores? I would just lay the fuck down. There's no good reason for these guys to even be here. Ah, here comes another monk."

"He has two zombies. Ladder down, Zan. Brandon over here!" Sophie yelled.

The monk saw the spear and took the turn to make it to the ladder. He was up and over it in a flash. Zan and Sophie lined up on top of the maze, waiting for the right time.

"I knew he was fast, but damn I thought these zombies would have been faster. We're going to have to work harder and dig a hole or something. Where is that cat?"

"He doesn't remove the corpses. He just extracts the parts that we need," Sophie said.

"Damn. Well, that is very useful. And we're considering burning them?"

"Only because Finley wants to do last rites—and possibly because they could be diseased. Here comes the next batch. Spears ready."

In sync, both women dropped into a stable wide stance. Then they both speared the undead dwarves through their heads.

"Good shit, ladies," the monk said before disappearing behind them. He would run around the entire compound and then draw some more in.

"Hey hot stuff. You literally look like you're overheating," the monk said, popping back up over the ladder.

The monk paused looking first at Sophie, then Zan.

"You—you're serious?" he said.

Sophie tried to remember his name. It wasn't Brandon. She was pretty sure that his name was Juan. But it wouldn't be right to just ask him right now.

"Settle down rabbit."

Juan flexed his calf muscles. Sophie had never been a calf girl, but she could appreciate some good definition. Also, somehow, he had a mustache? She had never really appreciated mustaches before. All the other men had taken to shaving their beards or letting them grow fully out.

"I don't even know what to say to that. Were you some snarky internet commentator back on Earth?" Juan asked.

"Hardly."

"Well, whatever's been going on has helped reduce their numbers. I'm having to go further and further to bring them back. This is doing wonders for my running skill."

"Ooh! Maybe I need to pick up the monk class," Sophie said, punching the air.

"Don't wait on that. Even Anthony is looking for one of these cards. The trade value for a monk card that Isn't attached to someone's soul just skyrocketed. Meanwhile, I would love to have some of your casting power. I would use it to"—he mimed hitting something with a frying pan—"cast iron!"

"I don't think that you understand what magic is."

"Listen here, muscle mommy. I left a good job at the postal service. I left my past life behind. I didn't have any kids, but I left my dog. Just because some goddess needed me here."

"Muscle mommy? Is that what everyone's calling me?" Sophie said. She was keeping a straight face for his sake.

Juan pushed his lips together, frowning with his entire face. He raised his hands and what could only be deemed surrender. "A guy can hear something so many times, until it becomes second nature. Plus, you have all these muscles."

He was cute when he was flustered. She finally broke a smile. "I want to thank you for the compliment. I got you."

Sophie did the classic bodybuilder pose. She lifted her left arm and curled it pointing the other arm out straight towards the sky. She had never felt so comfortable in her skin back on Earth to do something like this. She wasn't sure why she didn't feel exposed. Maybe it was the world she was in. Maybe it was that she finally felt like she was wearing Sophie. Even if she was just pretending to be the best version of herself.

Today, she was.

***

Finley was sorting through all of the salvaged goods. On his left was a pile of things that would go into his caravan. Every so often one of the warriors would come and grab something and pack it in from this pile. They had been given quite specific instructions on how to pack the thing up. On his right was a pile of things that would go into a hypothetical fourth wagon. That wagon, if the pile indicated anything at all, was already full.

The problem was that there was only so much room one could make for large objects. There wasn't room for everyone to have a bunk bed. There was room, if they worked hard at it, for everyone to have a bedroll. If they took things out of the caravan, there would be room for people to sleep in there. However, there were only so many times that he would want to load and unload.

Behind him were things that might be useful but were not currently worth the space. Those items would be heading to the carriage house.

Finley sorted for a long time. At least it felt like a long enough time.

He needed a break from sorting.

He got up and stretched. It was time to check on the horses. Anthony would be making the decision to move on or not shortly. There were a cluster of horses grazing. A few lay down and he approached. He gave each one a touch to feel their internal state.

They felt satisfied, but jittery. He tried to radiate calm. Four were hooked up to the caravan. They'd been there since the morning. He led four of the most well-rested horses to replace them. Four hours in the harness was enough. He took care to inspect the four that had been standing by. One by one, he moved them out. They ran about the yard.

"I wish we had more space to range in, but we have to stay safe."

The horses couldn't nod or do anything to confirm that they understood him. All they could do was give him the impression that things were not terrible. It was enough for him. He'd heard stories of dragon riders able to speak with their dragons, though it seemed more like a children's tale. So too, he'd heard stories about wyverns, attached to their riders through some card magic.

These mythical beasts were probably only children's tales. These horses were real and right in front of him. And they were thirsty.

Finley moved to take the barrel that they had filled with water out. It hadn't been opened. He cursed. He rolled it to the center of the yard and several horses approached. He was going to need to get the horses from the caravan.

What he really needed to know was what the horses would do if things got difficult. That would really tell him everything.

***

Anthony drank his mid-afternoon tea as Finley wrangled the horses. Dwarves liked a stiff brew. He was going to have some difficulty going to sleep tonight, if the hairs on the back of his neck were any indication. He didn't mind. He had been wired since they got their new stash of cards and pieces.

With three wagons moving, they would need three drivers. Sophie was a driver, Finley was a driver, and three others had animal handling skills. Six horses would be on the caravans. That didn't leave any room for people to ride along, if every person with animal handling was tasked out. Among the salvage materials, he had about thirty-six dwarven card pieces of various sizes. Many duplicates meant he was able to really pretend that he had an actual caravan.

He hadn't gone as far as to ask Andrew to make him little figurines, but he was getting close. The itch to ask him for that kind of help grew every hour. It would be a great way to represent the battlefield, but totally unnecessary.

"Andrew, what are you working on right now?" he asked the dwarf.

"Oh, a little bit of this and that. I'm trying to salvage some of what we got. It's going to be hard for me to get boards and nails when we're moving again. Also, there was a request for some very strong industrial strength needles? And some fabric thread? Do you know anything about that?"

"Oh yeah. That's the crazy idea that we're going to build an airship. I don't know how realistic it is because I've never built one. It doesn't seem impossible. We just need the right materials for the balloon."

"Now you say the word airship like it should mean something. I know what a ship is. It's the thing that floats in water. I know what air is. Or at least I thought I did until now. When you put those two concepts together, I am drawing a blank."

Andrew put down what he was working on to give Anthony his full attention.

"It's like a bag filled with hot air? The air is hotter than the air around it, so it rises."

"Okay. But what about the ship part?"

"Obviously we would attach the ship to the bottom of the balloon."

"You say obviously but nothing about this is obvious. This whole idea is ridiculous but hey. Zombies. Do you think we'll be safe if we are observing them from above?"

"I'm kind of counting on it. Everything we learned so far indicates that they don't really look up. It might be different if we're dealing with a death knight."

28

"You see, if we retrofit an actual ship, most of the work will be already done for us," Anthony said.

"Uh huh." Finley was a bit preoccupied with changing the horses over again. He could bring the horses to water, but they were being divas.

Anthony wasn't being a diva, but he was asking for a lot. Even Andrew shook his head at the odd requests. Finley knew that they were piling up. He rather preferred to stay on ground where there was no risk of going splat.

"So, what I'm trying to say is, where can we find a ship?" Andrew said.

"Ah. Well, that's a question," Finley said. He turned back to the stout man with the gorgeous beard and long hair. "There is an inland sea southeast of here. It's quite large. Freshwater too. The only problem is that it's close to the Irumian capital."

"Ah. How far is that?" Anthony said, already hoping for some mapping powers.

"If we keep moving, pushing it hard? A week," the elf said.

"A week?" Andrew said. "I could get a lot of projects done in that time. If you need me to prep canvas, then it's possible. I would need almost a whole wagon just dedicated to storage. And this is assuming optimal conditions. Don't you have a card power related to storage?"

"I do indeed."

"Care to expand on how it works for an old dwarf?"

Finley smiled. "I have a storage power as part of my tinker class," he said, displaying one card above his left hand.

On his opposite hand, he showed his other card.

<table>
<tr><td>

Epic Class Card: Tinker Level 3

Skills:

Barter and Appraisal Level 4

Identify Level 3

Animal Handling Level 3

Storage Level 3

King Level 1

As the last remaining Tinker, you have the ability to induct new people into the family.

This is a soul card and cannot be removed.

</td></tr>
<tr><td>

Uncommon Card: One More!

The wielder of this card will gain the ability to increase their storage capacity, or the storage capacity of one item beyond what should be physically possible.

</td></tr>
</table>

"The way it was explained to me was at the fourth level of the storage skill, I would be able to create a little pocket place to store things. Right now, I'm able to store a bit more than should be possible in one of my storage bins. It's a large bin to be certain. I can feel the storage skill trying to make something with this card." Finley let the cards disappear.

"It's a card skill, modified by a card. How does it being uncommon factor in?" Anthony rubbed his forehead.

"All things being equal, uncommon cards are stronger by an order of magnitude than commons. Rare, similarly an order higher. Epic, which is the level above, is more powerful than rare, easily."

"These rare soul cards that we have, are they good? How rare is rare?"

"It wasn't unheard of to meet someone with an epic card. Rares were often sold and traded as well. My new accountant class card is an uncommon one."

Andrew blinked. "Didn't you have some rant earlier about orc accountants?"

"He was a bit drunk when he made the comments," Anthony said, smirking.

"Orcs are savage in a deal. They'll sell you the shirt off your back and make you think that you have made the deal of a lifetime."

"That's oddly specific. Did you get jilted by an orc or something?" Andrew said, leaning in.

"No. It's just something that traders say. We don't generally go into orc territory unless we have a compelling reason to do so. They are always trying to out compete us. Or they were."

"I'm wondering how this works. You find an orc boyfriend and then he tries to make you join his multi-level marketing campaign that somehow is making money, but oh no! The orc is some star performer and you're only holding him back and—"

Anthony had gotten more and more heated as he talked. When he stopped short, he blinked several times. Finley's jaw was working its way back up. Humans were weird.

"Anthony, if you want to talk about this kind of thing; I may not be the best conversationalist," Andrew said, "but I'm here and I'm on your side."

"Old girlfriends die hard."

They stood there in companionable silence for a bit. Finley understood his meaning, but couldn't relate to the girlfriend thing. Maybe one day he would take a traveling companion. He looked over the people working in the yard. A different kind of companion than this would be nice.

"I think that I'm going to take a break. Bella and Bob are ready to clean up the cookware. Maybe I can help them a bit. We'll reconvene on this later, alright?" Anthony said.

He wandered off to the middle of the staging area. Finley and Andrew let the moment pass.

"It's a tough thing out here. A new world for all of us beginning, and for you? The old one ending," Andrew said.

"Were you a poet on your world?"

"No. Just a dwarf trying to make his way through life. Sometimes you stumble, sometimes you fall, but you always got to pick yourself up. That's how you're able to pick others up as well."

"I can pick you up if needed. You don't appear to be too heavy," Finley said, sizing up his companion. He gestured as if fitting the dwarf for a suit.

"I think that I'll pass. Let me go clean up my gear, and we'll see if we can design something around your growing storage capacity, alright?"

Finley nodded. The eccentric dwarf wasn't the same as any of the Irumian citizens he'd worked with. He was warm just the same and willing to work with them when push came to shove. He idly wondered how it would be if a single person in the caravan had been born in this world.

That would have been awfully convenient.

***

"Hey do you want to hang out and distract each other from how terrible of a situation we're in?" Bella asked.

"Do I ever!" Anthony replied.

"Great! There's a crate of potatoes for you to skin. Here's a knife that seems like it has only been used as a set piece," Bella said, handing him a large ornate white knife. It felt like it would break without much fuss and not complain too hard.

"So how are you holding up?" Bella asked. "You've only got the weight of our survival on your shoulders and all, right? Not too much."

"Not too much. That sounds about right. Just a little thing called making it to the next day. I know Bob told me about your mission to the card shop and I appreciate all that you're doing."

"We appreciate you taking the leadership role. I sure as heck don't want it. I thought I'd be able to bluff my way through this or trick my way out of it. It's hard when the fantasy smashes into the reality of it."

Anthony began to slowly peel the potatoes, one at a time. It had seemed tempting. When Yil had spoken to him about a noble purpose, he agreed in principle. This stark reality was far different than anything he could have ever imagined.

"Ah, I'm sorry. Maybe we should talk about something else?"

"No, you're good. I want to feel normal again. I'm sure we all do but what even does that mean? There is no normal for any of us. Even for Finley who was born here. Everyone he knows is dead. This whole situation is fucked."

"And?"

"And—"

"This whole situation is fucked and I have a trumpet," she said, miming playing a brass instrument.

He couldn't help but giggle a little bit about the absurdity at all. He went to adjust his hair. Wearing it down was new and reminded him that someone had stolen his hair tie from him, at the same time that they stole his attention.

"You don't actually have a trumpet do you?" he said. "Because I wouldn't put it past the dwarves here to have created such an instrument."

"I did in fact find one. Apparently one of the monks knows how to play?"

Anthony's brow creased. The monks were doing so much work for them right now. The heavy lifting of being the bait while Julie played tower defense had not gone unnoted. He had all the warriors as points on the wall as well. They were trying to level skills, the only tangible way to progress in this world. Well besides the salvage operations.

Anthony leaned in. "I would hate to hear that he is some sort of accordion guy as well. There's nothing that the end of the world needs less than a bard with an accordion."

"No comment."

Bella completed whatever she was doing with the pots she had ready for the stew. She began to take from his pile of potatoes. Then she handed him a sack of onions. He didn't miss her smirk. He wondered if the onions here would have the same effect. It didn't really matter in the end for him, as he began to really let them have it.

"You're letting those onions know who's boss, I see. So have you given any thoughts to what kind of second class card you would want?"

"I was thinking monk. I would be far less useless. All I have really is my holy finger gun spells and two variations of healing. I spent four years in nursing school, then two years learning to be a midwife and now all of my magic is automatic. If I had these powers back home, I could do so much good. I might even be able to cure cancer or something."

"Well that's an ethical dilemma that I never want to have to think about. How was delivering babies?"

"It was wonderful. It's such an experience. I would take them through a home birth and it was just so satisfying to hand a healthy baby to mom. And I had Anthony Junior working with me—did you know that there were only about thirty working midwives in Brooklyn? Thirty that did house calls that is. All the others were strictly in hospitals or birthing centers. And we were the only father-son duo."

Bella blinked. "I have to admit that I never thought about it. I never intended to have kids so this is all new to me. The family definitely pressured me to, but I just got so worked up about it. There were so many problems that seemed intractable; problems that just giving people money would solve. I couldn't imagine bringing a kid into the world."

"Ah yeah. I get that. Most of my moms had enough money to pay me out of pocket or through their insurance so I had a far different experience than you I wager."

"That makes them sound like sugar mommies."

"I was a working man, being paid a professional rate. What's a little sugar between friends, eh?"

Tears trickled down his face as he finished cutting the onions. There was no difference here, onions were assholes on every world.

"Indeed. Well, there won't be any sugar in the soup, at least." Bella slid a tray of carrots over to him.

He went after them after wiping his tears away. "I think that I want to head back to the way station just for the stream. Also for the distance."

"Have you been thinking about where we are going tonight? We can hole up here. It might spook the horses to be inside of an earthen castle, but we can keep them safe."

"I think my biggest problem is water. There's so many of us that keeping fresh water is going to be a problem. Plus there's always the possibility of cholera or something else worse in the water, the longer we go on. One of my spells deals with diseases so I'm less worried but—" He gave her a look.

"It's tough to talk about diarrhea in mixed company, huh? You're worried about cholera then?"

"I can't just go and sanitize everything. I mean, we can boil some water but that's about all. It's a good thing we got that beer. That will also help."

"Yeah, about that," she said. "Are you sure that we should be keeping it around?"

"It'll be just fine," he said.

Julie popped up, from behind. She placed both arms around him and he let himself relax.

"What will be fine?" Julie said.

"The amount of beer?" he said. He could feel her tense up.

"Yeah. So long as it keeps coming. We will be fine," she said, still holding onto him.

If it was important to her, it had become important to him. He made a mental note to bring any beer barrels to be inspected.

"Are you going to go head to the front?" Anthony said. "Bob's nap is almost done."

"How can you tell?" Julie asked, turning to see where Bella was. Bella had made no secret of her designs on the bald man.

"Because he is about to meet with his mid-afternoon snack. If I'm not wrong, Bella has made him something to wake up."

Bella took that exact moment to depart, a smirk evident on her face.

"When you say made something, did you mean a giant mallet?"

"I said that she made something. I didn't say what she made."

Thankfully for Bob, the mallet was not nearly as tough as Anthony expected.

Bob, mortal instrument of Mork, winced. Rubbing at his stomach, he wasn't mad that he'd gotten woken up from his nap. He had asked for that. He hadn't specified how he wanted to be woken up. It seemed like his new special friend had a streak of malicious compliance.

He wasn't against pranks. He just didn't want to cry out and notify all the zombies around. Even with this group of unruly warriors, he didn't want to chance it.

Bob was just glad that he was walking on the top of the maze without a limp. Julie was behind him.

While he'd been doing all the prep work required for dinner, Sophie had been hard at work. The raised bridge extended another block and a half. She was actively trying to extend it to the card shop they had raided earlier.

"What in the world is that contraption?" Julie said, gesturing at his rope course.

"We needed a way in and out. I wanted to make it a cakewalk as much as possible. Hence, ropes to ascend to the block we needed to get to. Believe it or not this road up here was full of zombies."

"I bet you have a ton of cake puns."

"I've got a few in the oven. That one was free."

Julie cringed. "That felt a bit like psychic damage. Bella definitely needs to know about these terrible jokes."

"She knows. She loves them," Bob said, sighing. She probably liked them too much.

Julie gestured to one of the monks that was running on their right. He jogged over, the zombies chasing him still a healthy distance behind them. It was probably a twenty-to-one ratio.

"I want to close off this way," she yelled. Julie gestured east and west, towards the depot. Two blocks away, she could make out a tinker wagon in the center of the street.

The monk gave her a thumbs up before continuing on. She surprised Bob by continuing to walk towards the beltway.

"Uh, Julie?"

She stepped off the single-story building. Bob ran to intercept her, but her foot found solid ground. Bob watched as a bridge of earth rose to meet her.

She split the road, walking across the rapidly forming wall without a care in the world. Bob just stood there watching as the earth solidified. Once across the road, she turned to face him. Her eyes shone purple.

"You coming, Bob?"

He gulped and then followed after her. As she moved towards the sun, Julie continued to create ridiculously strong earthen walls.

The closer he got, the more he felt like this was a new development. True, he hadn't been there when she had formed the core of the walls around the first mansion, but this? This had been so unexpected. He was beginning to wonder if he could make a warlock class card. He had to be careful or he might turn as green as Finley.

It took her only a few minutes to get to the block and road in front of the warehouse that they were looking for. Large signs showed the painted image of a dark brown potato over a grey melon and several other smaller vegetables. Most of them were root vegetables, he realized. He was not ready for Bella's lectures about eating veggies, but it definitely looked like a large part of his diet would be dedicated to what they found inside.

"I really hope that we find some sort of shipping wagon that we can use," he said. "That would be great. Something with a lot of storage. Do you sense anything out there?"

"Sorry. I'm not really able to do much from here. I can sense the earth around the building, but it seems like the interior is worked cobblestone or something. At least the floor is. Why don't you send out your cat to scout?"

"Ca'at is currently working to slice and dice every zombie that they catch in the maze."

"Ah yeah. Well, he is a useful little fluffer."

"How far can you extend this wall?" Bob looked south. The monks had cleared out so much of the vicinity that he was having trouble finding any zombies.

"I'm nearly tapped out, Bob. This might look impressive, but I'm not going to be able to keep it up."

"Magical dysfunction? I hear that there's a topical cream for that."

Julie leveled a look at him. The raised earthen wall he stood upon jiggled underneath him.

"Sorry! It'll be our secret!"

"I swear to Cara, Bob. If you make this a running gag, I'm going to develop a cabbage cannon or something."

"Noted. Also Cara?"

"Cara is the god of overlord travel and drug deals. And my patron." Julie crossed her arms.

"So, like drug smuggling or something? I would say that that is oddly specific, but Mork is similar to that. Maybe this place allows that. Is this patronage a new thing?"

"Best guess? I was on the free trial before. Now I'm paying the price of admission."

"So long as your god's goals and mine aren't divergent, I think we can work together. I think we can be adults."

Julie nodded, before continuing her work.

Bob wasn't certain what Mork's long term plans were besides him slaying a bunch of death knights. After that? Maybe he would retire. Or open up a bakery. Another bakery, not focusing on cakes. Maybe a coffee business? Sell some lattes and baked goods? He smiled; he could give it a good name. He would have to think on it.

***

The last remaining contingent of zombies from the cutoff quadrant had been dispatched. Sophie received the signal, a green flag waving from two blocks north. She returned a wave. It would have been nice to have a set of signal flags for this kind of thing. Sophie made a mental note to look into it later.

Her team headed in. Sophie took point this time, with Bella in the back. They crept through the roofs to the cordoned-off area surrounding the warehouse. Two ladders near the warehouse gave them easy access to Plainsmount.

Moving as a unit, they approached the two-story warehouse. The design was one of worked iron around a brick facade. It felt just right to Sophie. To her, it appeared that dwarves valued form over function, and would have appreciated a good plaid shirt.

A single door stood next to a large imposing iron roll-up door.

When choosing between two options, Sophie had to consider which suited her more. Did she want to tempt fate by opening up the dwarf-sized door? Would the roll-up even work?

She spied a lock on the ground, clearly doing the Goat Lord's work of keeping it closed.

Sophie smashed the lock.

The door flew up. The clean dwarvish design had a failsafe, stopping it at right above her head. Of course, since the designer clearly hated workers leaving the job on time, it was incredible at keeping people where they wanted them to be. It just so turned out that the warehouse owners wanted people to stay at work. Dozens of dwarves had been stuck indoors. They, in the intervening time since the outbreak, had turned into zombies.

"Biscuits," Sophie cursed.

Sophie jumped back, putting more distance between herself and the staring horde as they turned one by one. She pulled on her mana reserves. While Sophie cast a spell, Bob shot a crossbow over her shoulder into the first zombie. The dwarf stumbled backwards from the headshot.

Sophie unleashed a focused gale of wind, attempting to knock back the dwarves. Rebuffed, several of the zombies fell backwards, knocking still more down. The zombie domino cascade effect resulted in most of them learning the meaning of floor time.

"Let's move! Backwards!" Bob shouted. He moved up next to her, reloading his crossbow. Bella came in between them, putting her hand on both of their shoulders. Still facing the threat, they started moving backwards, trying to get out of range.

"Now would be a *great* time for some artillery!" Bella said, in what could be called the world's worst stage whisper.

As they stepped back, Bella breathed out a cold icy breath. They kept moving back at an even pace, facing the zombies. Several of the zombies lurched towards them doing the zombie shuffle, a close second cousin to the Naruto run. They were greeted by the best and only bobsled team on the continent.

"All right now, run!" Bella said.

Sophie's mind drifted to the maxim about good guys and never looking at explosions. Once she thought it was a cool thing to do, but it hadn't made much sense. As a near supernova took out zombies behind her, she realized that it was something entirely mundane. Heroes didn't want to have to deal with bad vision or shrapnel.

The artillery woman herself, Julie, smiled at them as they ran towards her. Her purple eyes oozed with raw power.

The group had come up with two ladders, putting both side by side against the earthen wall. Sophie wasted no time in ascending. She knew that if given a chance, Bob and Bella would have a small argument that could set them back. Bob would say "women first please." And then Bella would be insulted.

Hence, Sophie had decided to take matters into her own hands and had two ladders brought. Also, since she was faster than both of them, she wasn't going to wait on either. Chivalry was a truly dead and beaten horse, but girls couldn't run the world if they were dead.

Thus, without any discussion, Bella and Bob both climbed a separate-but-equal ladder. Bob looked a little peeved at the situation. It was hard to make a chivalrous dedication to one's boo thing in the middle of a heated fight.

Bob sighted down his crossbow and hit the first undead dwarf that shambled through the smoke.

Sophie sent a dirt bolt to the next. She waited a second then fired a second one. She settled into a rhythm with Bella and Bob. One would attack then the next, each in turn.

Sophie could smell the smoke from her elemental magic. It would have been a good party trick. It really was too bad that there weren't any other parties going on in Plainsmount. She was the only show in town, and she would give them the best performance of her life.

***

Bella had shown up for the earth works but stayed for the fire show. As her mana waned with every shot, she took more and more time between shots. It had to have been more than a minute before she was spent. Bella brandished her spear, ready to back up whatever passed through the smoke.

After threatening to leave for what had to have been an eternity, the smoke finally dissipated. They were able to clearly see the pile of half-destroyed bodies and loot. Bella pulled her scarf up over her mouth. The others did the same.

"That was pretty great, Sophie. You really got into it there."

"Thanks. You weren't too bad yourself," Sophie said. She lifted her scarf up briefly to take a swig of water.

"I felt like a bit of a one trick pony. I won't be able to cast any ice spells for a bit," Bella said. "Bob, are you alright?"

"I am. Thanks to both of you." Bob got up from his kneeling position, taking a hand from Bella. It was obvious to all parties that Bob didn't need the help.

She quite enjoyed the little thrill of touching his forearm, lingering for the longest time. Sophie for her part was preoccupied by casting a wind spell to move the smoke out.

"Let's give them a minute to—" She exhaled, pushing out a continuous gust from her hands. "Come out if there are any more. Then, we head in?"

"Just say when," Bob said. He prepared to sling his crossbow, then moved it to his back. He pulled a spear out from where he had stored it and placed it tip down.

They gave it another good minute where no more zombies appeared. Then, they moved down the ladders to find that the warehouse had been cleared out of zombies.

Sophie double and triple checked the warehouse with meat shields one and two. They scoured it for more zombies. Finding none, they returned outside. Sophie waved to Julie, giving her a thumbs up. Julie then pulled out a flag and signaled back to the staging area.

Before long, two figures on horseback approached and they set out to do their salvage work.

30

It took Finley half an hour to get the newest addition to the caravan checked out. It would roll. It wasn't even in disuse. The previous owner had to have been moving through the area with a purpose.

They had left enough items inside the new tinker wagon that Finley had a good idea of what they were looking for. This person had been trying to trade commodities, if the amount of empty barrels was any indication, whereas Finley had been a generalist, selling and trading staples that most travelers would want.

The warehouse was full of root vegetables. It was also full of three varieties of potatoes. As fast as they could, they grabbed crates of each, placing them in the tinker wagon. It wasn't as heavy as it was awkward. When the twentieth case arrived, Finley checked his tinker card to see that his storage skill had finally gotten to level four. This small change gave him an insight that he had not had before. Every nook and cranny of the wagon seemed to expand inside of his mind. He looked inside the wagon seeing it expand, then stepped backwards.

Such an expansion would have been reflected on the outside. No such thing appeared as the wagon was no larger than it had been. He went back in to recheck his measurements. Something about the accountant skill gave him an easy measurement tool. Perhaps it was the eidetic memory, reminding him of what it looked like before. It was definitely larger on the inside than it was on the outside.

"Hey Finley, what's going on?" Anthony said.

"Something very strange is going on inside of this wagon. As we loaded it up, it got bigger."

"It's the same size as it was."

"Look inside. The interior is larger than it should be."

"You have got to be kidding me. I don't think we have time for jokes right now."

"This is serious, Anthony. My storage ability just went to level four. I think that storing all these crates of food in here has changed it. Also look," he said spreading his arms wide. He did the same thing on the inside before stepping into the outside.

Anthony tilted his head. He nodded, and then turned on his heels and walked away.

"Hey wait a second! Where you going?"

"I think I need a minute."

The salvage crew continued to hand Finley vegetables in neat stackable crates. Using Bella and Sophie, nearly every inch was covered before Anthony returned. Only a narrow passageway through the center of the wagon was left. Thankfully the crates were all set up in such a way that they easily stayed put, loaded one on top of the other.

"Anthony, I think we need to bring the rest of the caravan over here," Finley said. "There's more food and this is packed to the brim."

"I'll get them moving. It's about time to determine if we're going to stay here for the night or move onwards. Do you have any thoughts on the matter?"

Finley scratched his nose. He looked at how long the shadows were around them. "Either way we need to mount up."

"Makes sense."

***

Anthony raised a yellow flag towards the staging area they had been using. Someone on top of the mansion returned a wave with the same color flag. He then returned to the large map that had been just out in the open in the warehouse. He had affixed it to the back of the newest caravan for review.

"Anthony, what are we doing? Bob wants to know!" Julie said from atop the earthen wall. "I see you flagging down the rest of the caravan."

"We're concentrating here, and getting ready. We need to pack more of the food in."

"Alright thanks," she said before disappearing to provide overwatch. She was still on the wall, just a bit out of their line of sight.

"I wonder if we can do anything to keep this place in cold storage," Anthony said, looking to Sophie. She had been helping the salvage team once the warehouse had been deemed empty.

"You would have to ask our resident cryomancer. She would have that answer. Elemental water is separate from all those specific ice powers. She explained it to me at great length this morning. Also don't call her cold-hearted, ice queen, or the ice bitch, please."

Anthony nodded. He had never considered it. "I feel like I just want to know what she can do. She is so attached to the hip to Bob that I don't really want to separate them."

"Oh," Sophie said, smiling. "I would be too happy to do that for you."

"Oh wait," he said, his hands outstretched.

Sophie deftly pushed against the air, lifting herself up and over the earthen wall.

"Did she just bend the air around her?" He said, looking at the swirl next to him. "Nah."

He turned to greet the rest of the caravan. Zan and Andrew both drove the other wagons in. It took them a minute to get to the spot where he wanted them to be loading. Once there, they got to work. Andrew and Zan came to speak to him. The herd of horses followed closely behind, with the remaining men and women riding.

"We're going to load up everything we can. Finley has some new power to store more things inside of the wagons. With all the horses, I want everything we can grab. There's no telling what's going to happen next," he said, patting the dwarf on the shoulder.

"I'm going to go and help," Zan said. "Then I'll see if there's something about the storage magic that I can work with."

"Thanks, Zan."

"Well, I could always lend a hand loading everything," Andrew said. "No harm in doing the work that needs doing."

"Let's get going. I want to convene the council in about ten minutes. There are enough of us here to pack these wagons. There wasn't a lot of room before. Now, we have four."

The man and the dwarf went to work.

***

Bob, Mork's zombie slayer, watched as the last couple of crates got loaded in. He really wanted to help out but as Bella kept telling him, being on watch was helping. His eldritch beast was working overtime on the zombies that Julie was killing. He was conserving ammunition. He hated conserving ammunition but it wasn't like there were crates of crossbow bolts hiding around everywhere. Even the one musket they found wasn't in serviceable condition.

Bob had grabbed the musket from the warehouse as a souvenir. If nothing else, in their downtime he would ask Andrew to try to replicate the instrumentation. A guy had to have dreams after all. Dreams beyond the beautiful woman that did not want to be known by her ice powers. He had so many ice and icing jokes that he wanted to use, simmering below the surface.

Bob sighed, closing his eyes to concentrate. Even with his eyes closed, he could still see the five markers that indicated the quests. The only time they weren't readily apparent was when he was sleeping. It had taken him a while to get used to it. He had noted as much as he could about them but the icons were small. Their size was a function of how distant they were, or at least that was his best guess.

For a long moment, he concentrated on each icon. It would have been nice for one of them to bring up something about each target. Some kind of information. Bob had no such luck. He noted in passing that nothing really seemed to have changed since last time he thought about their distance and size.

Bob went through his slow box breathing process. He took a four-second inhale, paused, holding his breath for four seconds. He then exhaled for four seconds and once again held it for four seconds. It had been one of the things that his father had taught him to control his emotions. When he was an adult, he realized that it was as much for his father as it was for him. His heart rate slowed as he continued to cycle through that for five minutes.

Truly relaxed, he once again checked the icons. For the first time he recalled, one of the icons had moved. For someone so far away to move in such a way for him to notice it was a bad thing. Bob checked again, opening his eyes and then closing them. Surely, he was wrong? But as sure as a pilot who didn't want to be called Shirley, one of the death knights was on the move.

"Bella, get Anthony. We have a problem."

***

"So, one of the death knights is on the move? So what?" Anthony said.

"It is moving towards us," Bob said. "It might be slow but—"

For the second time in their council meeting, Bob closed his eyes and the entire council stayed quiet. All but two of the Caravan sat with them. Julie had opted out and kept up the watch with Brandon. They were still visible from the back of the warehouse.

"Anthony, it's taking gates."

There was a murmur in the crowd. Everyone looked to Finley.

"There are many gates in the dwarven lands. They are mostly there to facilitate trade with the elves. As one elvish company has the monopoly on gate travel, it's expensive but something that is more and more common. Or it was getting common."

"We're talking about large portals here right?" Zan said. "That's what we're talking about, correct?"

"A gate spell is tied to two specific locations and a runed stone doorway. It takes a lot of effort and some very powerful casters to create. They are relics, powerful magical items that are not intrinsically tied to cards, though they are created by card powers."

"Well that's just great," Anthony said. "I suppose that since everyone on this continent was turned into a zombie, that every gate is now open and no one is stopping the undead legions from marching through and coming right after us, correct?"

"With no guards, they would just be open portals between locations. The gates themselves only require the ambient mana to continue running. So long as the mana is there, the gates can run," Finley said. "Each gate should have a fail-safe switch that closes it."

"Finley, have you traveled through a gate before?" Zan said.

"They were just building several large enough to transport a tinker caravan through. I was going to try the one that goes from the Irumian Capital on my return trip if the fee wasn't too much."

"If the death knight is on the move, then they probably have an objective in mind. Do you think that we are big enough fish for them to try and catch us?" Anthony said.

"Fourteen chosen?" Finley said. "And myself for good measure?"

"Fourteen chosen who could be turned into death knights," Bob said, shuddering.

The council was silent for a long minute. Most thought about their time at Dunnamore. Even Bob and Anthony were not excited about the prospect of fighting a death knight.

"Twelve of the people here could have been turned into death knights. That we were able to help you is something that I'll never forget. There is no world in which I want to fight a fair fight against a death knight," Bob said. "If one is headed for us, we need to get out of its way. I will figure out a way to kill it when the time comes."

"Thank you," Anthony said. "Folks, I think it is time for us to get away from a populated area. I'm glad that we stole this large map from the warehouse. This, according to Finley, is a very current and accurate map. We are heading south around the capital. I hope we can find some other survivors along the way, but if not, we have months of supplies."

The group murmured assent.

"Let's do any final preparations, then mount up!"

31

"That's a lot of potatoes. But, better to have food and I presume that we can hunt for wild game on the way," Bella said. "It would be poetic if the gods brought us here to just watch us starve."

She paused, using her fingers to count.

"How many potatoes, exactly?" Bella said from the front of the wagon.

"Let's put it this way. You will be sick of potatoes like you have been stranded on Mars for over four hundred days and it's all you got," Sophie said.

Their wagon, the newest addition to the fleet, was in the middle one in the convoy. Ahead of them, Anthony and Finley were driving them ever southward. The beltway around the city of Plainsmount was a great place for them to get a good deal of cards. It wasn't close to the center of town and the packed gnomish and dwarven tenements. As a result, many of the undead had for one reason or another, not made it that far out.

It had taken ten minutes for them to gain a good number of followers. Bob was behind them, using the uncovered wagon to direct Zan and Julie's shots.

The ground shook briefly and their horse whinnied. The caravan continued onwards.

"Keep going old boy, we're not out of the metaphorical woods yet," Sophie said, attempting to soothe it. Her animal handling was nothing to write home about, but she could feel it getting steadily better.

Cold sweat ran down her brow as Sophie gripped the reins. She forced her unease down. The now-familiar scent of dead dwarves filled her nose as they finally turned away from the circular highway. Driving through a town packed with undead might have been someone's idea of a good time, but it sure as hell wasn't hers. The only one that was in their element was Bob's summon.

"You think it would be poetic, if the gods shat on us? Yeah, no it would be fucked," Sophie said. "But yeah, I'm right there with you. If we could get rid of this damn smell, I would be happy."

"The smell is a problem. I thought that everyone liked the aftermath of the cleanse card."

"Bella. If I was trying to date a high school boy I would be overjoyed with that card. But I am a new woman out here in this world. I'm not back working at the hospital, where all of my male patients used to make eyes at me."

"Male psych patients? They used to hit on you?"

"When I was out socially, yeah. There's a strong hard ethical line between anyone working in there and the patients."

"When you were out? I didn't know that you were gay."

"When I started dressing like a woman?" Sophie said.

"Oooh. Yeah, it's easier to forget how you used to be. I never knew you before," Bella said, putting an arm around her shoulders

"I had this joke with the theater crew. When we were meeting new people, they would introduce me like, 'I've known her since—' and I would say to myself… 'please don't say since she was a man.' And then they would say something like '—since she was into Creed.' And it was so much worse. It was always so much worse," Sophie said.

"That's just—you were into Creed?" Bella said. "Is it too late for me to switch to a different bestie?"

"Nah, you're in it now. Girl power!" she said, pumping her fist weakly.

They continued on for some time as the horses all around them moved with a purpose. Sophie noted that there were at least six people riding horses now. With their one horse pulling their wagon, as well as the other four pulling the lead caravan and the wagon, only about nine ran freely on the side. At least Sophie had counted nine several times.

The men and women were all now armed with spears and several had crossbows. Sophie had knives galore in all sizes of pockets.

"So how does it feel now then?" Bella said.

"It's just—you want something your entire life and then you get it in a way that you'd never expect. I never thought that I would have had to have the conversation about products with you, but I did and it was helpful. Everything just feels right. I can't really—" Sophie said. "There's so much else going on that it's hard to parse the girl parts from the rest of this."

"I hear that. With salvage operations and raiding the card store, this has been a uniquely one-off experience that I wouldn't care to repeat. I did like seeing all those cards though. I especially liked working with you and Bob. That was something special."

"Aww, Bella, thanks!"

They rode on for a bit without saying anything.

"Are you going to say that you liked working with me too? Or do I have to do open auditions for my next bestie?" Bella said.

"Did I tell you what I named my spear?"

***

Anthony heard a hearty laugh from the caravan behind them.

"At least someone can find the humor in this dark place," he grumbled, pulling out his sketchbook. The tiny book was clearly made for dwarven specifications, but he didn't mind. He brought it out and flipped to the page with his version of the map.

He looked for the point that he was trying to make and then put a finger over it, drawing a line from where he thought they were to where they were going.

"So the next way station is about here?" Anthony asked. He showed the map briefly to Finley, trying not to draw the elf's attention away from the road.

"The roads are correct. Since this one leads between the dwarven and human lands, both groups decided to spend their time fighting a war by proxy through it. What I mean to say is that these are some of the best-made roads. You can always tell when you're entering dwarven lands, no matter which border it is you're crossing. They take great pride in a distinct and separate road."

Anthony didn't want to correct his tour guide. Every time that Finley talked about dwarves in the present tense, he felt a little twinge of regret. Neither of them had started this war.

Anthony only had the foggiest clue as to how it had happened so fast. His guesses were at the "bad infomercial level" level of accuracy at best. Sure he knew that they were selling the smash chop, but did it actually solve all of his kitchen problems and his colon cancer? Anthony was skeptical. Whatever had caused the collapse had a far reach. Whoever had done it had done a thorough job.

"I'm just really glad that all of the undead seem to have stayed local to the cities. It would be much more difficult if they spread out. It would be more difficult still if they massed like a field army somewhere. We would not be able to take that down in any way. The best that we can do is take guerilla action."

Anthony put his papers away. Half the book was his campaign notes, with far too many question marks for his tastes. The death of actionable information felt like a feature, not a bug.

"Gorilla action? Is that a human thing?"

Anthony explained the difference from what he knew. There was no way that they could take all the zombies in a full-frontal assault. If they were fighting them, they would have to use hit and run tactics. Potentially, turn the populace to their cause. Without an actual populace, their situation would become increasingly untenable. Either everyone was turned, or they were eaten. There had been no in between, thus far.

Anthony had expected to find a few roving adventuring bands, but aside from the people summoned around Dunnamore, none had turned up. He was beginning to wonder if there was anything to rebuild, or if this entire continent would be turned into a large walking mausoleum.

"That's why we need to figure out if this has affected people outside of this continent. If we can find that out then we can find a safe haven," Anthony said.

"That would mean giving up Noveria. This is my home."

"Finley, if we want to win, we have to survive. Whether that is through killing all the undead or through raising an army across the sea, we have to survive."

The sun threatened to drop off.

"We are getting very close. Perhaps another ten minutes?" Finley said. "We should check with Bob if that death knight has been on the move again."

Neither of them wanted to hear the news, though it would be necessary. Bob had about the only good intelligence that they could acquire. Mork made him uniquely suited to his current task.

"Hey Finley, do you think that this way station has a stream next to it? The last one was pretty great because of that." The near-pleading tone in his voice struck a chord with Finley. He hadn't had to beg for anything in quite some time. Though they had been winning as a group, he really wanted the win of some time in real cool water.

"I'm reasonably certain that it does, but I haven't been that way in years. I was spending a lot of time in elvish lands, up until recently. This way station is on the far side of the Alliance. I would not have had a reason to go there except for the current situation," Finley said, raising one arm to the sky. "The Goat Lord is not happy. None of the gods are, I'm certain."

"I've been meaning to ask you about that actually. The god that summoned me here—she also has something to do with my magic?" Anthony briefly showed Finley his class card.

"Yil is the one that your powers are linked to. The way that I've heard it before is that clerics have a flavor to their magic depending on their deity. Your associated magic is about building things up. It's more favored for healing because of that."

"That is good."

They drove on without talking for a while. One of the few things that they both didn't mind was some time for contemplation. Anthony remembered those long rides in the city getting to his appointments. There were always traffic problems. Anthony liked the freedom of the open road. He would work out the flow rates for his saline solutions several times to just make sure that he had it. He did the same thing right now, thinking about the steps he would do to set up a saline lock for a delivery.

"The next major town—" Anthony began before the sound of hoofbeats grew louder next to them. Without cell phones, they had to rely on in-person communication and signal flags. As they were the lead element of the convoy, messages would have to come up from the back if something had changed.

"Message from the back," Andrew said. From the back of one of the bay mares, the dwarf looked like he hadn't been sized right for the job. He assumed their speed, after he overshot them quite a bit. "Bob says that the death knight has moved again. And it's much closer now. He expects that it took a gate to somewhere near Plainsmount."

Anthony waited to see if there was more. Bob's card powers were something else. Mork had really favored the ranger.

"This doesn't change anything for now. If they start moving towards us, then we can change course. He didn't get a new quest, did he?"

"No. I'm certain he would have said something."

"Then tell him to make a plan to fight an army of undead, I guess. Not much else to do while we are on the road. If we need to do another card inventory, then we'll do it, but I don't think we found any war-winning card powers, right?"

Finley shook his head.

"Also," Andrew said, holding a cloth sack out, "here is the latest haul. Ca'at is napping and we have dispatched all of our less desirable followers."

"Thanks," Anthony said, catching the smelly cloth sack. "Next time we need to cleanse it first."

"If you have nothing else, I'll head back to Bob."

"Thanks, Andrew. Stay alert out there."

32

"We're still heading away from the death knight and whatever they brought with them. This makes me think that there was a gate in Plainsmount. If so, it probably connects a long distance," Zan said. "That would be a wicked spell to put into my spell book."

"Yeah. I think I'll ask Cara for something like that, though it kind of goes against the travel part," Julie said.

"Does it though? Travel is movement from place to place. It's not like she is the god of extended metaphors about destinations and movement."

"Do you really think that there is a god of extended metaphors? Not only extended metaphors, but like specific travel-related metaphors?"

"We could go on a quest to determine if they exist?"

"But what if we never arrived at the destination?"

"Then the true gods were the ones we met along the way."

Julie giggled. They were trying to get a rise out of Bob, but he wasn't feeling it. Zan had swapped in driving for him several times just to keep things fresh, but everyone was running on fumes.

"I sure hope that we finally end up stopping for dinner, and that we can make a damn fire," Bob said from his space behind the driver's seat. He had taken a lounge position, doing his best impression of a hammock.

"Bob, what did we say about playing with fire?" Julie chided.

"That it's fun?" he said.

"Exactly. In fact, it's too much fun. You would do well to not have so much fun. We need you working."

Julie had so many questions that she wanted him to answer about his previous life. She'd seen him on television. She hadn't thought it was particularly noteworthy at the time. Bella had also not really told her anything. That she was so close to Bob meant that perhaps he would tell her, but that might not be the case.

Perhaps a question or two wouldn't hurt? Julie focused on the man behind them.

"Bob, you were on a reality TV show?"

Bob made a show of slowly cracking one eye open, looking at her, and then closing his eye. He then took both arms and placed them behind his head.

"I suppose I was," he said.

"I would love to hear about it. I feel like in a few days, maybe weeks, we will probably all be familiar. But Bob, I just met you the other day. If it helps, I can talk about my life? Though, I think it might be a little bit boring for you."

She wondered if he was going to take the bait. She thought that he was the kind of guy that wanted to talk about himself. She might have been wrong. She was probably right. It took a certain amount of audacity to open the bakery in Hoboken, and also probably some nepo baby money. Bob had one or both of those things in spades.

There was a long, drawn-out moment before Bob exhaled bodily and sat up.

"I guess we don't have anything else to do. What do you want to know about it?" He leaned forward.

"Tell me everything. I want to know about the crew, how filming worked, why you did what you did on camera, everything."

"Well, some of the things that happened, I'm not too proud of. They came in and filmed for a week. We had the bad luck to be right after the episode with the one bakery that got shut down for health code violations. So many people came in asking if we'd been shut down because they confused the two episodes. Honestly, I was just so happy that one of my employees put out a sign explaining the whole debacle that I gave her a raise. Cake and Bake was a whole thing. They were one of the lesser-known baking shows, so they were really trying to ramp up the drama."

"But then you launched that line of designer cakes?" Julie said.

"There was demand. Especially in October when it's wedding season? All those New York City wedding companies decided they wanted to have one of our featured cakes and we had so many requests for that one pirate ship cake that it got to be a bit overwhelming. Did you know that there was a piece in the New York Post where they counted how many celebrities had a pirate ship wedding cake? Then they calculated that two thirds of the couples broke up after that? Like we were known for this. Have a pirate wedding cake, get divorced in six months or less."

"That's a little bit more than I was expecting. There was a hit piece on you? I missed that."

"It kind of felt like a hit piece, but I understand that they were just trying to sell newspapers. I try not to judge people who are trying to stay afloat in this economy. Or that economy. Did you know that I'm less worried here about anything? I don't have to worry about my employees getting fed or their families or even like the normal upkeep of a business. That was stressful."

"I did not know any of that. It would have been nice to have more money, but I did not own a business. I got that salary. I clocked in and out. It wasn't much but it was enough for me and my golden retriever, Charlie."

"I miss dogs," Zan said.

They all fell silent for a little bit listening to the horses move.

"Horses aren't bad though. I was never a horse girl," Zan said. "I'm also not sure how horse girls grow up to be horse women or if the two are even related."

"I don't think horse girls grow up to become horse women. It's a special kind of person who dedicates their life to spending thousands of dollars on a free horse," Julie said.

"It's too bad that these horses aren't more golden retriever-like," Bob said. "Though we do owe our lives to them."

Julie shuddered. She didn't want to think about what life would be without the caravan and the horses. Her short life would have been really bleak. She might have become one of the death knights.

"Guys, do you think that the death knights have free will? Or do you think that they are just carrying out orders?" Julie said.

Zan's tenuous grip on the reins suddenly became tighter. "Why would you say such a thing? What's the difference?"

"They have to have enough free will to do the work, right?" Bob said. "They posted up guards. I know because I had to kill them. This whole mindless versus intelligent undead question—are we going to try to reason with them?"

"I don't think that they wanted to reason with us," Julie said. "I think that they wanted to turn us into death knights."

The air was a lot warmer than the hair on her arms indicated.

"Maybe we should go back to speaking about reality TV," Julie said.

"That sounds a great idea," Bob said. "This is a depressing world, and I wouldn't have wished what you went through on anyone."

***

There was a lot to do when setting up camp at a new way station. First, Finley took the lay of the land, extending his normal circle out a bit further than before. Sophie followed him, setting out an initial batch of tripwires. Their walk turned up a steam that only reached midway to his calves.

Sophie was overjoyed to see that it was clean and clear. Finley called for someone to bring the water barrels. There were more than enough people happy to help when there was the possibility of washing hands. The cleanse card was great, but sometimes humans wanted to scrub their hands a bit more than was necessary.

Once the perimeter was trip-wired, the two moved on to check the road. There was no reason to think that undead would stick to roads, even less if they were on the march. Neither one wanted to leave a gap large enough for a bee to pass through.

"Do you think that we need to raise some earth walls?" Finley asked.

"It can't hurt. Though Julie, Zan, and I are tired. Maybe a nap or something?" Sophie said.

Finley crossed his arms. "Or take it in shifts. Probably in groups of three or more. I don't know how an earth wall would do against an assault by a horde. Or rather, we don't know how a smart horde would do it."

They continued on towards the center of camp. Chef Bob and his sous chef Bella were actively cooking a variety of things that smelled like just the right amount of spice. Finley breathed in strong earthy tones with an undercurrent of salt and pepper. His mouth, betraying him, began to water.

He still had work to do. He told Sophie to take some rest and returned to the caravan. He took his time walking up to inspect every horse. By the second horse he had gotten a few helpers. It got a lot easier then. Everyone was supremely thankful for the majestic beasts and the way that they carried the caravan away from danger. He was just concerned that they were getting enough to eat and drinking and resting.

For the first time in a long time, he considered letting all of them be free. The herd would stay nearby but they all needed to rest. By his count, it had been three days since this band had formed together and he felt like he knew most of them well enough. The horses were generally easy to understand. It was the people that he was still warming up to.

Finley patted last horse before turning back to his wagon. He grabbed the frame from the back. The nice-smelling bag of cards and pieces was sitting there for him to sift through. He grabbed the small steel crate that housed all the cards that had not been picked up previously.

His next task would take all his focus again, so he looked around to see if anyone was lurking around trying to get a word in. No one was lingering on the periphery of his work area.

No one was waiting. Several people were talking quietly, and a few were still patting the horses and encouraging them to drink water. Four people were clearly on watch duty. One person was passed out drunk. Finley considered how long they had been there and how exactly they might be able to imbibe enough to fully be on their ass. They would have to be dedicated to drinking. Anthony had probably let them have the last watch shift to thank them.

Finley stood up from his frame. He walked over to check if the person—a woman—was on her side. He realized that it was Julie and checked her breathing. She was fine, just out of it. There wasn't much to do about it. He grabbed a blanket and put it around her, propping her head on the only pillow that they had, keeping her on her side.

He wondered if this was a common thing for her. He had known several members of the family who took their drinking to excess. It was always far away from towns, on the road between two places. He recalled that the parties at the way stations were particularly wet.

Instead of moving away, he brought his work closer to her. His medicine skill hadn't pinged, like he had expected it to if she was in danger. Better to be near the unconscious woman with beer breath, than not.

Finley got to work crafting a few more cards out of the day's haul. He really wanted several more animal handling cards. He set up the expectation in his mind. If there was a way to manifest those cards, he would do it. The ability had paid off so many times for him. How could he not want everyone else to have it?

He didn't think about the drunk woman in front of him. He just saw her as something else in the background. He pushed into a meditative flow state and was absorbed his work. It felt like it had been ages before he looked up. The savory smell of food had arrived far too close for him to deny his hunger.

A bowl of the soup floated in front of him. He accepted it gracefully with both hands, thanking Bella for her hard work. He hadn't even noticed that it was Bob who had been holding the bowl until it was halfway down his gullet. He nodded in Bob's direction. The ranger returned the gesture, red flames glinting off his bald head.

It was more delicious than it had any right to be. Tears dripped down his face. He remembered the first time that one of the tinkers had fed him. He remembered those first few times with fondness.

They hadn't known what he would eat. He ate with abandon. Before long he was getting up and presenting the bowl to Bob for seconds.

He remembered doing that ages ago, returning and asking for more because how could one not? The food was delicious, and he was young, restless, and hungry.

Now he had the ability to induct people into the family. It gave him a measure of hope. Hope that he would be able to rebuild everything that they had lost. Hope that he might one day encounter a tinker that he never met before. Perhaps now he would be one of the people serving up hot meals to stragglers who tagged along their caravan. He returned to sit next to Julie. He slowly wafted some of the smell towards her in an attempt to rouse her, but she was dead to the world. She might have overdone it with her mana but she deserved to eat.

He chuckled, bringing his spoon out again.

"I wonder if you want to be a tinker. It's not too difficult. As far as you're concerned, it's just a little bit of paperwork. But seeing as how you're down for the count right now," Finley said, "I feel like we can talk about this when you wake up. And maybe you should try some of this delicious potato soup."

33

Bob, sexiest ranger of Mork, couldn't sleep. There was a time in his life when he had a social media following that he watched religiously. Not just the following but specifically his number of followers. The amount of people that were hungry for cake thirst traps overwhelmed him from the start, causing him to get more digital to market his cakes. It had spiraled, as things he got obsessed with often did. He had spent a lot of time in therapy working on his obsession with getting more and more followers.

The unhealthiness of checking every day to see how many people had watched his reels had gotten to him. He would spend hours baking and then at least a half an hour a day staging cakes and slices of cakes to show his loyal followers. At first he was excited, then he became obsessed, then he needed help. It took a long time for him to admit that to himself, but in the end he found it. It just turned into another part of the job that he grew to have to do even though he didn't like it.

He felt that same twinge of the fear of missing out every time that he checked if the undead legion was on the move. No one else had that special ability, which really meant that he needed to keep watch on his new followers. There was a big difference between being chased by a zombie and having to keep one's business afloat. In both cases, he was worried about his next meal. In only one was he worried about being someone else's next meal.

The fact that he had a real-time view of where they were but only in a certain amount of detail irked him. If it had just been a matter of the quest telling him the radius or something else simpler he would have felt much better about it, but there was nothing like watching a predator closing on you. He didn't want to be eaten. Even more than that, he didn't want Bella or Sophie to be eaten. He couldn't say the same about the entire caravan, but it would be highly inconvenient for someone to be turned into a fifth death knight. If there was one thing that Bob hated more than anything, it was inefficiency and being inconvenienced.

He had spent many mornings working on his craft. In culinary command school, he learned about mise en place. It began as the technique to start working with every implement in the correct place, so there was no extraneous movement. Or at least that was his version of it. Before he started working, he always took five minutes to set up and make sure that all of his knives were correctly placed and all of his baking implements were where they needed to be. He had a specific way that he stacked his bowls and cups and where he put the milk, sugar, and flour. He was able to be meticulous there in a way that he wasn't in any other place in his life.

Those five minutes were always some of the best of his day. Looking back, he realized how much he appreciated that little bit before the chaos began.

Bob took that same preparatory spirit as he cleaned his weapons, checked his crossbow, and inspected his clothing. The subtle scent of what had to be male body spray wafted off his crossbow when he was done. When the cleanse card was used, it affected everything in radius. He didn't know for certain, but he really thought that it killed things at the bacterial level. There was no other explanation for how clean it felt.

He was beginning to have a problem where he would start to need new crossbow bolts. There were only so many times that he could fire and reclaim the ones that he had. Eventually, he would need to replace them. He had never considered this to be something he would have to do. Otherwise, he probably would have looked up a YouTube video on it or some explanatory podcast talking about it.

Bob had taken several short sticks from nearby trees and placed them around where he and Bella were sleeping. They hadn't gotten their own tent yet but they did have bedrolls. What he had done was to place each of the similarly sized sticks in the direction that each of the death knights were. Three of them were south. The other was north of him, where he imagined Plainsmount was.

He lined off all them up, taking care to really put them in a distinct location. They were all at least a meter from where he was sleeping but no more than three.

Eventually tired met wired and won the battle.

When he woke, one of the icons no longer lined up.

***

"Who here is good at math?" Anthony asked. "I'm only good at calculating drip rates."

There were two shiny rocks and one stick in formation. Anthony was trying to triangulate the distance that the death knight had traveled. He had assembled the small council of people who had volunteered to be leaders in their caravan.

"If we traveled, how many leagues is it?" Andrew said.

"About ten leagues, based on the time it took," Finley said.

"Alright. If we assume that Plainsmount is ten leagues away, and that the death knight moved, and this is his new direction, how fast did he move?" Anthony asked, drawing a triangle in the sand. "We know the angle between before we went to bed and now."

The angle that all three points made indicated that it was nearly a full ninety-degree change. As such they had some idea.

"We can't assume that it is heading directly to us from Plainsmount," Bob said.

"Let's assume the worst-case scenario."

It was like finding a full bag of chips in the garbage. Anywhere else it would have been a welcome sight.

"Worst case? If both sides are ten leagues long then the death knight moved fourteen or so leagues while we were asleep. It's around the square root of two hundred. What? Don't look at me like that. Ten squared plus ten squared is two hundred," Bella said.

"How long is night here, Finley?"

"Right now? Approximately nine hours, but when did he set the first marker?" Finley turned to the bald man who was fussing with his cloak.

"An hour after we arrived. But it was already dark for a bit then." Anthony grimaced.

"So they can move about fourteen or more leagues in seven to eight hours. It took us an hour to go that distance on the horses." Anthony looked down, trying to focus.

"We need to move on," Bob said. "Figuratively and literally. I can do this trick again at the next way station. Maybe there is a range finding card?"

"There might be one," Finley said. Anthony could see that he wanted to go check right this moment, but was holding back.

"I guess we have to move," Anthony said, putting on his best stoic face. "Then we can see if they do the same. Finley, I know I ask a lot of you but are we near any towns? Especially ones that we can defend. Or even if we can't, use against them."

"Mount up?" Bob said, standing. Bella stood with him.

"Mount up."

***

"So Bob thinks that they are following us. Is that what I'm hearing? I don't think that we're that interesting. Maybe they're just lonely. Did you ever think of that? Bob?" Bella said, putting her gambeson on for the second time, now correctly. The black fabric reflected a bit of the sunlight, but was otherwise unremarkable.

"I love how you talk about me when I'm right here," Bob said. "It's quite nice to be noticed."

Unfortunately for Bob, his gambeson was gray. They matched except for the colors.

250

"Hey. You wanted into this situationship. Sophie warned you," she said, "Right Soph?"

A full head of brown hair popped out from beneath the caravan's canvas flap door. It eyed both of them suspiciously before disappearing.

"If you're going to have a 'define the relationship' conversation right now, I would appreciate it if you didn't call me in to be the referee," the muffled voice said.

Bella lifted the flap up, glaring at her friend. "Do we have everything ready to go? Bob is just hooking up the horses now."

"I double-checked that everything was secured correctly. Do you think that Finley is going to give out some cards before we move on? It would be great for morale."

"He said something about once all the horses are readied up, but I didn't get any of the specifics. He asked to do his own thing with all the horses as well," Bella said. "He's got a lot of shit to do. And until somebody else gets their animal handling card to level three, he will continue to have a lot of shit to do."

"That's what happens when you shit hot fire. Also, that seems broken as an ability."

Bella held the flap open while Sophie dismounted. "One of us literally has the powers of Elsa from Frozen and the other one is a badass elemental druid."

Sophie took a second to pat herself down. She was satisfied that all of her bits were in the right place. Both women walked around the caravan twice.

Their main objective was to see if there were any problems that they could fix while they were stationary. While they were moving, whatever it was became out of the question. Now, at the rapidly disappearing camp, they had a chance to stave off long-term problems. When they got back to the horse, Sophia held out her hands and playfully brushed it, top to bottom.

The horse whinnied, responding to her touch by stamping one hoof. She lingered there long enough for Bella to check over everything that kept the horse attached to the caravan.

She knew that it wanted to continue to receive attention, but Bella couldn't let them go down that path. They had a time that they needed to leave by and it was drawing dangerously close.

They heard a whistle from the front and most of the band walked to meet up with Finley in the center.

***

"I worked all night on this when I wasn't resting. I think that if anyone has been asking their god for help that it is working."

Finley held out several packs of cards, each set held together via twine.

"The biggest thing is that everyone that didn't have animal handling as a class skill or card, now has the opportunity to put it in their decks. I have several more in case we find some more survivors," he said. "So at least there is that. I don't have that monk class card but I do have most of the pieces that I need to make a few other classes."

Finley didn't take his time handing out the packs. He knew which one was for which person. He just had to pass them out. When the last person had their pack of cards, he turned to address the group again.

"Most of these cards have synergy with what you already have. Everyone has three cards more now. I also have a card library of cards that are less useful. When Anthony's ready we can take some downtime and you guys can each have a turn looking for something. But each one of those are going to be pretty useless in combat."

There was a general murmur as people put cards into their soul decks.

"Hey guys, take a few minutes to get familiar with your new cards because let's mount up in five minutes. I won't be comfortable until we put more space between ourselves and whatever is on the march,"

Anthony said. "Also, any last-minute shuffles between people who really want to sit next to each other, this is the time, Bob and Bella."

The red faces of his companions warmed Finley's heart. Bella and Sophie had a quick conversation off to the side. Half the eyes were on them, the other half were inspecting their new cards.

Andrew came up to him and shook his hand. "I thought that that woodsman card was great but this combination? I really appreciate the thought you put in this."

Finley had found or made three cards that dealt with measurement, enchantment, and one meta crafting skill card. He had no use for it himself and they had a legitimate artificer with them; it made sense to give him all the options. Hopefully, with that he would be able to make the floating ship that all the humans decided was their best option.

Bob had probably gotten the worst hand of the lot. Finley had understood how powerful the cards were that Bob had and was working to figure out a way to complement his powers. The only thing that Bob didn't have was a strong spellcasting skill or card. His ranger class gave him a divine spellcasting ability, but as Bob had explained earlier that day it was more geared towards survival, simple rituals, and healing.

That was why Bob had gotten a special common card that gave him one particular spell to use.

Common Spell Card: "Did I do that?"

The wielder can cast Magical Missile unerringly to a long distance. Distance is determined by line of sight. This card has a cooldown of ten seconds, or the wielder can use mana to cast it again in quick succession.

34

"I thought that I wouldn't be able to make a difference here. You know? It looks like that is not the case. Maybe at this point in time it would be easier to just send me back home," Anthony said, over the sound of the horse's hooves.

It was just loud enough that Anthony had been able to talk the elf's ear off. Finley had been letting him vent for some time, acting as the midwife's therapist.

Up ahead, a flash of brown fur and antlers darted across the road. A full family of the creatures took the time to survey the oncoming caravan.

The sight of a few deer moving alongside of the road in a pack gave him some much-needed respite. It had been some time since he had seen anything except for horses and zombies. The fact that it looked like an entire family of them made him smile. Maybe things weren't going to be so bad after all.

Anthony wondered if it would be possible to secure anything approaching victory. Anything beyond survival had been a pipe dream up until the day that they were getting further away from the horde. Anthony had assumed that any zombies would be able to march all day and all night and would not require rest. Therefore, they would only be limited by their marching speed.

Finley's off the cuff calculations told him that the horses needed to rest for at least five hours a day. That didn't include the time that they needed to spend eating or drinking. If they had some way to get air superiority, they could just cast spells from up on high to kill as many zombies as possible. They might rain down destruction without fear of being turned.

That was part of the reason that everyone had zeroed in on the airship idea. Despite their ragtag appearance, things were beginning to look up. Finally seeing some wildlife gave him the impression that things might be a little better.

His people might just be heroes summoned from his home world. They were also some of his only friends. He couldn't imagine this journey without them. It would be even worse if they fell in battle; they would turn into death knights. At least that was the current consensus.

They rode on into the mid-afternoon without stopping for lunch.

When they cleared a ridge to see a far-off lake, Anthony realized how far apart things were. It was behind them into the north where the foothills grew and grew until the mountains touched the sky. Ahead of them, the ground finally stopped sloping, opening up into a grassland. The wooded areas on the side of them would once again recede and if there was an army on the march it would be visible.

It was unfortunate then that he realized there was smoke coming up from somewhere behind them. One of the riders came up to mention it to him. Anthony asked them to talk to Bob about it. Bob confirmed that the smoke was in the same direction as the death knight.

Something that Bob was also able to confirm was that they were not within five leagues of the death knight. Based on the death knight's movements, they might not be the intended victim.

There was no room for a back and forth as the caravan moved along. It wasn't time to discuss what they would do next, but he was ready for the next town.

***

"This next town, Arva, is only notable because it's in between so many places. There are a lot of single-family homes. This is where most of the grain is grown for the kingdom. This grain is mostly for the pack animals. They used to bundle grain off and ship it from here," Finley said.

"What did they grow up by Dunnamore? If this is for feeding pack animals that is," Anthony said, wishing he had binoculars

"Dunnamore had more vegetables and had a focus on corn. Dwarves love their whiskey and all," Finley said. "Not that I cared, mind you."

The caravan had stopped at a hill overlooking the outskirts of the town. Finley had wanted to pause to feed the horses before they considered a raid on the town. North of them, the horde hadn't shown up and it was going to be late afternoon soon. They would need to make a decision about their night accommodations, sooner rather than later.

"You want to lead a raid?" Anthony asked Bob.

Bob had begun to sketch the area, doing a model of the town in the dirt. They could see the entire place from their vantage point. It wasn't difficult to represent the roughly forty buildings with rocks. By now they had a collection.

"We go down the center. We hit these houses first," Bob said gesturing with a knife as large as his forearm. "Then we take it block by block. Once we have the first block, Julie comes in and secures it just like we did with that mansion. This time we'll try to secure two buildings. That is to say we do the tower defense thing."

"I am the tower?" Anthony said.

"You along with Finley, Zan, and Andrew support Julie. Everyone else is either on the front line or guarding you," Bob said. "It's a three-phase operation. The first phase is my team going in and clearing this block. Once it's clear, the second phase is holding it. The third and final phase is the rest of it. We do this right? We'll be done before dark."

"There are only so many houses to search," Anthony said. "You're going to have Sophie and Bella with you as well as the monks?"

"That is the plan," Bob said getting up and once again looking intently at the town. "Finley, there's nothing more of the town? I'm not missing something on the other side of the hill?"

"This town exists mostly because there's only so far that a farmer wants to walk to get to a tavern. So safe to say, there are some farming estates that are farther out but none close enough to be a factor in this."

Arva was quiet. If it wasn't for the few zombies that roamed the town, it could have been a town in Nebraska.

Anthony nodded. "I think that we're ready. Are you taking the horses in?"

There was some discussion about whether they should arrive mounted or on foot. None of them had been trained as cavalry. None had a mounted combat card or a trained warhorse. That was a huge liability. Bob guessed that he could run the distance in about twenty minutes or so, but he didn't want to try that. The grass was high enough to hide in as well which was another problem, if the zombies could find them in the grass.

"I think we all move," Anthony said. "There's no purpose in us splitting up like this. We go close enough to back you up, but far enough that if we have to split, we split."

"Sounds good," Bob said. "Mount up?"

"Let's ride."

***

Bella was the lucky one who got to lead the charge. She broke off from the caravan on one of the mares, Bob and Sophie hot on her heels.

Bella had envisioned a lot of things for her future. She dreamed of one day graduating from college and getting a professional job. She never dreamed of holding out a spear and making a charge towards a very visibly zombie-affected area.

It didn't exactly align with her vision of herself as she had been. But she could totally accept this current version.

They closed in on the very first house. Though there was a lot of room to expand, the previous residents had chosen to build close to each other. It kind of looked like suburban sprawl to her again. Three zombies in the main road took notice of them. They turned in their direction and began to move with a purpose.

Bella looked over to Bob and Sophie before slowing her canter. The horse seemed a bit wary of continuing on. She tapped into her animal handling trying to soothe it.

"It's only three zombies. We can handle three. In fact, there are three of us," Bella said. "And since I'm in charge, I'm going to count you horses. So we already outnumber them."

Her horse whinnied.

"Yeah, I hear you, got it."

Bella cast an ice lance spell at the lead zombie. She was quickly followed up by a crossbow bolt taking down the second. She gave Sophie a bit of a side eye.

She was rebuffed by a bolt of blue lightning which arced straight through the third zombie. It wasn't as loud as she expected it to be. There was no thunder, just a small explosion where it contacted.

That explosion would probably draw more zombies in. Bella turned to Bob, indicating with her head which way she wanted him to move. As he wheeled around, Sophie and Bella kept their focus on the front. This explosion had the potential to draw out some of the stragglers. As the grass was at least hip height, any zombies laying down in it could be obscured easily.

Bob had some abilities to find his favored enemy easily. He had chosen zombies after a short deliberation. It was much easier for him to spot them. Bella was just doing her due diligence to make sure that they didn't move forward and get cut off.

It was true that they had three dependable horses, but there was no way that she was going to lose them. She patted her mare while checking her mana pool; so far, so good. She kept her head on a swivel, looking for any zombies to pop up in the grass.

Bob came back to her side and gave her the thumbs up; she focused on the front. About a dozen more zombies had appeared, popping up in between the houses. Most were two blocks away, but some were further. Bella hoped that this would make the next steps easier. After all, if they had freedom of movement, why would they stay in any of the houses?

"Light them up," Bob said, taking aim with his crossbow. "I'm going to hit from right to left."

He didn't wait for them, loosing a bolt as Bella prepared her favorite spell. Mist poured out of her hands as she concentrated on the packed dirt road ahead of them. She drank deep from her mana well, as ice coalesced on the ground. She would get most of them with this spell, causing them to fall down if they walked on the ice.

It was up to Sophie to make the most of it.

Bella pulled even more mana, her cup going from half full to half empty in short order. In less than a minute, she was spent. She brought out her spear.

Any zombies that broke free would be heading straight into her melee range. She would take their heads clear off once they got into range, if they even did. Bob continued to fire bolts, his aim continually surprising her. She now saw four zombies with bolts through their heads down the main road. In their haste, several of their peers had fallen over the corpses.

The closest were still at least a block away when they encountered the ice. None of them were able to walk on the ice and after skating for a short time, they all invariably began to crawl on the ice.

This made the perfect targets of opportunity for Sophie. Bella took a moment to get completely clear of the road as Sophie lit them up.

Bella checked on Bob. There was little doubt in Bob's face as to whether he would have made the same choices. He smirked, the lightning casting alternating shade and light against him. He looked delicious and Bella wondered how long they would need to slay zombies before she could relax again with him.

Another lightning bolt snapped her out of it as the explosion was a fair bit louder than the rest. She dared a look behind them and could see Julie raising the beginnings of an earth wall, leaving a gap for their retreat if needed.

"Time to get to work," Bella said, dismounting.

She waved to the monks behind them to join the fight.

35

The monks moved in as Finley and Julie got to work. The order of business was walls twice their height, to start with. Julie had said something about making a bigger wall this time. She would live up to that, if nothing else.

"We want to make it two acres at least," she said, extending her arms to encompass two city blocks worth of space. "As this will be the safe zone. Or staging area. Where I put my tent for certain."

Finley nodded, using his own hands and eyes as a crude measurement of space. "I don't grok what an acre is, but if you show me, then I'll probably understand. You humans and your varied units of measurement. Weren't you the one who told me about killer meters?"

"Kilometers. They are like leagues but different," Julie said, waving her hands. "Not better, just different. Though Anthony and his people, they will use absolutely anything except the metric system."

"Your strange words make me believe that we are not too different," Finley said, raising plant roots through the dirt wall, fixing it in place. "You should hear what the orcs do in their counting methods."

"They got a slew of zombies in the center of town now. I think I see Bella stabbing a few with a spear. She wouldn't be doing that unless they were doing the double tap."

Finley finished a section twice as wide as his arm span, and paused to inspect his work. "That is such a specific rule. I had never thought about that."

Julie sidled up next to him. "I love that. You're a good guy, Finley. It just shows that you weren't a killer before. That's normal. Did most people fight monsters in the before times?" she asked, raising up the next block of earth. "Back on earth all the guys where I was from were good but it was a bit too—"

"Too good? Is that a thing?"

"No more like, they were too passive. I wanted someone who would treat me like a lady, but I never got that. What I got were guys that treated me like a buddy and things weren't clear as to their intentions."

"That sounds rough, buddy," Finley said, unsure of the protocol. Courtship was not something that he was keen to experience at the current moment.

Julie completed another block. They found it easier to work block by block and had gotten into a rhythm. On top of the part that they had already worked, two people were on lookout, having taken the opportunity to get above the madding crowd.

"Thanks, I guess. Ah, hold up a tic," Julie said. "They're heading in now."

"Alright."

The pair paused their work. All eyes were on the first house as Sophie tried the door.

***

It was unlocked.

"Does nobody lock their doors here?" Sophie said, pulling the door all the way open. "Were you all raised in a barn or something?"

Bella held the spear at the ready in case of a zombie. Sophie backed her up, a second spearhead always good in a fight or a tea party.

"No gods, no masters," Bella whispered as she put just the tip of her spear inside the door.

They waited a tense five seconds before heading in. Bob walked in with his crossbow fully loaded and raised like his eyebrows.

The first room was empty, opening into a hallway. There were a few doors, as well as a stairway to the second floor.

Bella opened the door to the first one, letting Sophie take point next. She hiked up her grip on her spear before looking into what was obviously a disheveled living room. Bob walked through quickly before turning back to guard their rear.

Sophie motioned to hit the next door, and they continued on. Door after door opened and none of the rooms had any hidden zombies. They kept their posture up, clearing room after room as nothing came up.

They exited the back of the house, then went around it twice looking for anything else out of the place. They waved to the caravan, half a block north. Two men waved back.

"Bob, do you want to take point next?" Bella asked.

"Let's go then," he said.

The back door of the second house was entirely missing so they made their way to it. A single zombie walked out, it having the slowest reaction time that Sophie had ever seen.

Bob sighted it down, shooting it in the head. Then it jerked back, giving Sophie a chance to dispatch it up close.

She took that option.

***

"A larger lot this time? I can't say that I blame you for making this one larger than the last," Finley said, putting the last touches on the southern wall. One of the biggest changes was adding some ramps and stairs on what would be the interior of their staging area. It was something that Anthony had suggested.

"I like a bit of land to stretch out. There's only so many houses here that we can expect to find zombies in as well," Julie said.

With the newest design, there would only be an escape route to the north, though they could easily make one in the road to the south.

Julie had demonstrated that she could just as easily lower the earthen wall if needed. Finley just didn't like feeling trapped.

Bob and his crew were working their way to create a safe perimeter. Finley expected less zombies here than in Plainsmount, due to the distance from other sites. Here, nomadic dwarves and other species roamed the plains with their tribes. Or at least they had done so.

"I'm wondering if any of the nomadic people here made it. It's a long shot. I don't know why I was spared," Finley said.

"How would we know? About the nomads, I mean. Would they be visible?"

"The ones I met had yurts with them when they traveled. A few of the tribes even had orcs with them. Their green skin and the yurts were a stark contrast with the rest of the plains."

"That would be immediately noticeable. Especially in the plains like this. I'll keep my eyes peeled."

"Thanks."

Bob gave them a thumbs up. They moved up to create the side walls on the east and the west. The southern wall was thick enough to stand on top of and walk about. It was a point of pride for the resident warlock, something that Julie had worked hard to do. It took them a little bit of time to join the northern and southern walls on both sides. Satisfied that they were at least secure for now, Finley and Julie took a break.

They returned to the wagons and horses. Anthony was breaking out tenting supplies. Several hands were helping him set up a sleeping tent not far from the houses, as others brought out anything useful.

Finley wished that he could set up a fire for the camp but he had other things to do. As the elf in charge of the horses, he needed to do a cursory inspection before he ate.

Julie handed him a sandwich of indeterminate origin. The pair of them ate in silence for a little bit. He didn't want to know where it had come from, and she didn't say. It tasted in between well-cooked and overcooked.

Before too long they were back at it. A pair of warriors guarded the opening to their staging grounds. One of the monks was the lookout on the southern wall.

Only a skeleton crew remained inside of the camp. Everyone else was working salvage operations, concentrating on the two houses inside of the walls.

As soon as Bob's team cleared a house, Andrew and his crew would get in. They would take whatever was useful, then leave. If they found anything, they would take it to the staging grounds to be sorted by the skeleton crew.

***

It took two hours to identify all the remaining zombies in Arva and kill them. The rest of the team started the salvage process. There were no signs of any nomadic people, much to Anthony's chagrin.

He examined the first batch of salvage. Precious few medical supplies joined his hoard.

The salvage teams had sorted items into useful and slightly less useful piles. Aside from the food, nothing stood out as much as the gauze they found. The long, thin paper-like wraps were on point. If Anthony ever needed to wrap someone head to toe, he would be able to turn them into a mummy.

He shuddered at the thought of a powerful undead mummy, hoping that this world didn't have such horrors.

He didn't know what he didn't know. He wanted to keep it that way for as long as possible.

Anthony had burning questions about how this world worked with all the card powers that were seemingly everywhere before. If everyone had a cool superpower, did that make everyone super? Or were they all just normal, and he was just the odd man out?

That night he wanted to make a fire. Anthony took the time to dig up a large space for him to put coals and firewood. Over the half hour it took him to set everything up, Anthony focused on the calm, quiet task of preparing a working fire. The meditative task reminded him that hard work had a calming effect on his nerves.

He could build a bonfire if nothing else. Something to warm the night that he expected would be chilly.

He wasn't even sure that they had a pot to put over it that would be big enough.

To make stew? Such a pot would be need to be enormous. He decided to be a bit less ambitious with his fire pit. That just seemed about right.

Before long, Anthony was hauling in logs from one of the sides of the houses. He made a neat pile that would make a woodsman proud, splitting a few pieces out for kindling. There wasn't a question about what he was doing. He wanted the warmth.

He grabbed some flint and steel. Then he pushed with his mana to set the entire thing ablaze. He double-checked how far the edge of the fire was from the grasslands and was satisfied at his first attempt. They would be able to sit nearby the fire and not have to worry about sparks.

The kindling took.

Anthony warmed his hands on it. Then he turned them over several times. Closing his eyes, he imagined that it would become a roaring flame before too long. Yil might protect them.

He saw several people looking at him as the fire blazed. No longer just a few embers in the pile, the fire felt alive in his eyes as a flickered.

A man could get used to it. Julie and Finley joined him after a while. They sat in silence, as if waiting for something to happen. When Bella finally showed up, she had a large cookpot in tow. It looked like she was carrying it herself from the angle.

"It's all mine now," she said, "though it probably won't be traveling with us."

Bella turned slightly, showing more skin than he expected.

"Whoa."

Carrying the pot required the combined effort of Bob and Bella. The two had a long wooden pole on which the pot's unwieldy handle rested. They set it down nearby the fire pit.

It was a clear upgrade from many of the smaller dwarven equivalent that they had seen. By human standards it was up to their navel and heavy enough to give Bob and Bella a fight. They set up a stand on either side for the pot to rest on.

Finley directed them to place it over the fire using a metal pole to bridge the gap.

Bob fought for his life as they placed the cook pot right where Finley wanted it. Sweat poured down his face as they finally placed it on top of the fire pit. Bella was undisturbed, despite carrying at least the same amount of burden. Finley for his part was just glad no one got burned.

"I'm impressed that you were able to handle that so well," Julie said. "That looks like it belonged somewhere though, right?"

"No, it was in—get this—a smithy! Though good luck getting it up and running now."

"Bella, Bob looks like he needs a shower. How are you so—"

"Clean? It turns out that I can stay cool with a very specific application of ice magic. It's quite convenient," Bella said.

"She won't share those secrets with me of course," Bob said from his prone position a few feet away from the pot.

"Really, I would rather you shower, just to check to see if you have any zombie bites, then it's on you. I can't be having an undead meat shield boyfriend. You gotta be more proactive about checking for bites," Bella said, winking slow enough for everyone around to notice.

Bob continued to lay in a heap. Finley walked over to him and extended a green hand, helping him up.

"She drives a hard bargain, that one," Finley said.

"I wouldn't have it any other way." Bob took a deep drink from his water skin, draining it. He held it upside down to drain the last drops.

"We're going to need some water for this. That probably means that we're going to need to get some well water," Finley said. "There's a cart over there behind that building. I'm going to see if we have access to the well yet."

"There's a well?" Bella said.

"Yeah, should be in the center of the town," Finley said. "I don't want to use all of our water if we can help it. We need to restock."

Finley and Bob walked to the first building and grabbed the cart, moving it from where it was. the hand cart had one barrel on it. It had been left there for long enough that whatever water had been stored in it had evaporated.

"This might be good. I'll make sure to get it cleaned before we use it," Bob said, inspecting the barrel. "I think that they collected rain with it."

"Probably so. It's difficult to get water here so they would do what they could to keep it."

"They probably needed a better barrel design then," Bob said. "Andrew can fix this crack, I hope."

The side closest to the wall had a crack. Finley inspected it, feeling along the inseam.

"The wood is too old for me to grow it back. I'll take this to Andrew. We have another bucket that I can use for the well, and I'm sure that there are enough barrels in this village for us to salvage."

"There's some good wood here," Bob said. "Just not enough. There aren't enough trees here. We could use a lumber mill or something. Do you know where we could find a lumber mill?"

"That would be great but no, I have no idea."

36

"We're staying here tonight, then?" Sophie asked the small crowd. Every person warming their hands by the fire looked up. About nine pairs of eyes looked to see if she was bringing food. Darkness was clearly approaching and the first watch had been established.

Two pairs of people walked the walls, every so often waving to the people huddled around the fire. Several people had set up tents close to the first house. The small dwarven beds weren't really good for the use that half of Sophie's companions wanted to use them for, which is to say sleeping. They were fine for the things that the rest wanted to do. If Bella wasn't checking on the stew regularly, then she would have certainly disappeared for a tryst with Bob. She might have already and Sophie could have missed it.

Anthony had insisted on doing a mount-up drill. He called it a drill, but it felt like a dress rehearsal. The point of it was to make sure that everyone had a plan to get back to the caravan in case those on watch saw something.

Sophie saw that there was still enough light to do something. It was the fourth night since they had been freed and she itched. She couldn't pinpoint the location of the itch so she went through everything she could think of. She checked her deck.

Rare Class Card: Rogue Level 3

Skills:

Sneak Attack Level 2

Skill Mastery Level 3

Weapon Expertise Level 2

Infiltration Level 3

Evasion Level 2

Stealth Level 3

Open Skill Level 0

As a rogue, you may learn one extra class skill per level. New skills start at the average of your other class skills.

Rare Class Card: Wilderness Druid Level 2

Skills:

Animal Handling Level 2

Nature Control Level 2

Elemental Magic Level 2

Survival Level 1

Medicine Level 1

This card grants mana.

As a Wilderness druid you have enhanced control over the natural world and can more easily survive in a rough environment.

She realized that she had advanced to the third level of rogue. She had a new skill which she hadn't decided on from her rogue class card. When she thought about the skill, conceptually a bunch of things popped up into her mind as possibilities. None of the potential skills had anything to do with casting more magical spells though.

On the other hand, her elemental magic skill in her druid class card had advanced. Her focus was limited to fire, earth, water, air, and plant growth magic, but there seemed to be endless customization options. She wondered if the spells would change if she didn't have her nature control skill as well. That on its own felt like it was something that she could easily abuse.

Sophie racked her brain trying to remember if she had seen Finley's druid card and couldn't remember it. Perhaps he had different skills?

She would have to ask. He had a lot of information about how the world used to be. She wanted to learn as much as she could and all of the books were in a language she couldn't read. At least he was able to find a journal so she could start jotting down her notes about this trip.

On the wall she saw Zan chatting with Brandon. The man in the monk robes was walking the lady wizard around. In front of them, a large blue book floated, its ethereal blue glow extending a meter in each direction, but no further.

"Damn," Sophie said.

There were several ladders on the walls. Two lay at opposite corners and two were next to the only exit in the wall. Andrew had worked hard on a gate so they would be able to hold it while still being able to leave. Not having to worry about being immediately demolished was quite the feeling. The door would hold at least long enough for everyone to mount a defense. And if not, Julie had left a part of the wall opposite it unreinforced by plant matter. That part would be easy to remove in a short amount of time.

Sophie walked up to the wall, using the ladder closest to Zan.

The other girl waved back at her.

"Are you guys doing alright out here? It's a tough night, right?"

"We will be back by the fire before too long," Zan said. "I was just telling Brandon here about the French Revolution."

"Oh really? Were you a history buff?"

"Back on Earth, of course. I actually wrote some Marie Antoinette fan fiction with a Yu-Gi-Oh twist," Zan said.

"She has been telling me about it at great length. Oh please, be my blue eyes white dragon or some such," Brandon said, rolling his eyes. "Of course she wrote it as a romance."

"I can't even imagine how that would go. I have to hear more about this."

"Really? I would have thought that you would be put off by it," Zan said.

"There is no entertainment here except for the drama. I'm someone accustomed to a bit of drama in my work. Not that it was a good thing." Sophie indicated the wall and the immense fortifications that they had set up to keep themselves

"This is true. All the more reason why we need to tell some good stories to keep our minds off this. This campaign, it can't be healthy." Zan nodded, taking a sip from a waterskin.

Brandon took the water skin from Zan and took a long sip. "Long term, I guess you're right. I don't know where we're going though. I don't think any of us do. Maybe Anthony has an idea but Bob? He doesn't know where we're going. And that is probably for the best."

They stopped at the corner. It was then and Sophie realized that they had been looking away from her most of that time. If they looked into the staging area and saw the bonfire directly, it would probably not help. They needed to see far outside.

"Have you guys seen anything out of the ordinary yet? Not that I'm looking for anything in particular," Sophie said.

Brandon shook his head. "So far nothing. But if the death knight is close and they build a bonfire again, we will find them."

The memory of the cage rose unbidden. She remembered being trapped there. They had dragged her away, knocking her out in the process. The bruise on the back of her head was still healing.

Before she'd gotten caught? She didn't remember. Whoever had caught them all had a plan. They were going somewhere. The fact that she hadn't been killed immediately, in retrospect, was the worst part of it.

There were so many blanks that she didn't want to fill in.

Her mind was probably deciding to save her from some tough experiences but she wasn't having it. She was going to take that feeling and use it for her art.

"Hey did you notice all of the hand puppets?" Zan asked.

"I'm sorry what?" Brandon said.

"The hand puppets. There were an odd amount in several of the houses. I guess they either had children or once had them. You weren't doing a lot of salvage, right?"

"I was checking for zombies and then moving on. I didn't linger too long anywhere," Sophie said.

The group paused at another corner.

"What do they look like?" Brandon asked.

Zan pulled a bearded puppet out of a pocket. Someone had spent their time on making it with thick woolen yarn. It was a clearly a passion project.

"If they made this, then there probably is more yarn somewhere. I should be able to make some clothes with that," Sophie said.

"You can make clothes?" Zan said.

"I volunteered in children's theater when I wasn't working and we never had money for props and costumes, so how else would they get made?"

"That makes sense," Brandon said, taking the puppet back. "I wouldn't mind a new set of clothes. All of these dwarf-sized pants come up on me like they are capris. I think part of why everyone is so cold is because we're wearing what we came with, and that's not much. Some of them are a bit creepy though."

All three of them shuddered.

"Creepy puppets. Throw them into the fire," Zan said.

"But keep the others, though?" Sophie said.

There might not be an audience for puppetry. But there was supply. With all of the dwarven hand puppets, Sophie was going to drum up demand. The people were tired of running, they could use a distraction.

***

Anthony was woken in the middle of the night for his watch shift. He quietly peeled Julie off him. Each of the watch shifts slept in as close to a group as they could. It was easier to wake up a group of people if they slept in a cluster. Julie grumbled as Anthony woke up the four people to relieve the watch shift.

Brandon greeted him by the fire. Flickering light from the fire highlighted the bags under his eyes. Anthony shook his hand, bringing the man in for a hug. The rest of his watch shift moved around the fire, shaking off the sleep.

"I haven't seen anything. Everyone is sleeping soundly. Nothing else to report," he said. "We went and patrolled the walls several times."

"I got this. Thanks Brandon."

The fire was still roaring as Anthony tossed in another log. It crackled a bit.

"I'll see you in the morning," Brandon said, departing into the darkness.

Julie joined him after a few minutes. The other three were going to take their time waking up. They grumbled but assembled around the fire. Anthony took a long look at everything. Someone was going to have to draw the short straw and go patrolling in a few minutes. He would prefer a volunteer but he would take what he could get. The other watch trickled in, moving to collapse next to Brandon.

For a minute or two they all sat in silence.

Then, Anthony slowly lifted his finger and touched his nose. Julie saw it and immediately placed her pointer finger on her nose. The other three realized what was going on and followed suit.

"Nose goes first," Julie said.

There was a hearty chuckle as the other three got up. Andrew would lead them around.

"We'll do the next patrol," Anthony said. "Shout if you see anything."

"Will do!" Andrew said. "Come on you lot, let's go see what's going on."

Andrew pulled out a small gem that flickered with light. He tapped it two times and then the light turned into a focused beam of pure red light in front of him.

"Well that's fucking convenient," Julie said. "Any chance you can make us some more of those?"

Andrew grabbed a gem from his pocket, tapped it and tossed it to her. She accepted it and immediately went to inspect it.

"Thanks," Julie said.

It was exactly what they needed. Anthony stood up. With the fire at his back, he looked out into the darkness. It was easier to let his eyes adjust before he went out. Next to him, Julie played with the newest gadget from the artificer.

He could feel her glee in using it as she flicked it on several times. She had clearly gotten used to the idea of using it and before long, was somewhat of an expert. He really wanted to have a turn with it but that he would let this one slide. She could have some fun as there wasn't much for them to look forward to at the moment.

"This is really nifty. I have to hand it to Andrew, he knows what the heck he's doing. Or at least his card skills are on point. I wish I could make something like this, I feel like I'm not really doing much around here."

"Julie my dear, because of your earth affinity, we have these walls."

"Yeah but, any of you would have done the same thing."

"Nobody else has magic as strong as you. It only got stronger after you did that thing you did."

He could feel her arms wrapping around him. Anthony didn't know what the future held, but as he grabbed her hands he hoped for a little more of these kinds of moments as well as indoor plumbing. They waited like that for a while, watching as Andrew made his way around the wall.

It wasn't until they got to the ladders that she disengaged with him. He realized that she was standing so that she could get the heat from the flames as well as his body heat at the same time.

"Clever girl."

"You would do the same thing if you wanted to be warm," she said.

He had to admit that it was true. He would have done terrible things to stay warm. They needed more blankets and pillows. He made a mental note to look for those things when he went through the salvage the next day.

37

Finley held out his favorite bowl to receive a steaming breakfast. Bella had surprised the group in the morning with yet another pot of stew. The early risers looked at her with some skepticism.

"Look, it's a new recipe. I added more spices and this should taste hopefully like it isn't the same thing we just had multiple times. Dwarves were apparently bigger on alcohol than food," she said.

"It's good guys," Finley said, hungry enough that anything would taste good.

"Finley, I'm beginning to think that you don't have a sense of taste or smell," Brandon said. "That or maybe you never had one. Do elves have a different set of senses?"

"I can assure you that isn't the case. Bella made it better this time, I swear."

Finley, first to try a new take on the same food, readily ate what was available, taking his time to savor the starchy taste of the potatoes. Bella's ice powers had been fine-tuned enough for her to do real cryomancy and it showed. The potatoes tasted fresh despite him knowing that they weren't. There was something about her ability to take a frozen potato and then just remove the coldness from it prior to cooking it.

Before she had begun cooking, Bella had done a cursory inventory of their stock and handed the results to Finley. He examined the inventory list as he ate.

He was highly ambivalent about the results. His accountant class processed the inventory and spat out one hundred and twenty days of supply.

That was long. Longer than he thought it would be. He would have to think about how useful the skills were because he was unaccustomed to that immediate calculation.

They would have enough food to last four months. That was an excellent starting place. His main problem was the lack of variety. They had eaten so many potato dishes that even Finley was growing to disdain the thought of them. Once this was all over he vowed that he would abstain from potatoes. He would eat anything but potatoes. That vow warmed him almost as much as the stew.

"If you don't like the variety, we can go hunting," Bob said. "There is nothing wrong with Bella's cooking that anyone should be complaining about. Wild game would just add more to the cook time."

"It would be difficult to hunt right now, especially since we wouldn't want you to be far from the rest of us," Finley said.

"Then there is a strange and terrible possibility of zombie yaks and wolves," Bella said.

"The offer is on the table," Bob said. "There is always the possibility of zombie yaks. We just need to hedge our bets. I wonder if yaks can be turned?"

"I don't want to even know the answer to that," Bella said.

"It's possible," Finley said, rubbing his stubble.

"Well that's another fear unlocked," Bella said. She placed a ladle of stew into Bob's bowl.

Bob promised that he would float the idea to Anthony when he woke up. By an unspoken agreement they had all let him sleep in today.

Finley took that morning to really check on the horses. He spent an hour going around using a combination of his animal handling and medicine skills to make sure that each one of them was fit for duty. Horses fed, he checked on their water situation. The barrel designated for their use was centrally located and half empty.

He hadn't expected much. The horses felt well rested. They had not grown up as tinker animals, but had readily accepted the attention. His two bay mares were ecstatic to be a part of a larger herd, something that he hadn't anticipated. The horses seemed to be more social than the humans. Already he could see a few cliques beginning to form. This was especially true for Bob, Bella, and Sophie.

He watched the horses play around for a few minutes. Their joyful games encompassed most of the camp. It made him forget their dire situation for a time. They chased each other back and forth inside of the walls.

Satisfied, he returned to the cook fire. The crew had shifted around but it was clear that at least half of the camp would be taking an early lunch together.

Bella broke out the brew that they had gotten earlier. She motioned, asking for his help to tap the barrel, to which he nodded his assent. He found a row of unoccupied bedrolls on his way to grab the implements before returning.

Had most of the camp had woken up? Many of the people he expected to see sleeping were already up on the walls or out of his sight. He handed Bella the tap and went to find his mug. One beer would serve to lubricate his joints for the work that day, what little they had to do.

Finley had never drunk beer for breakfast before. It was a pleasant, completely unexpected taste. Bella knew her way around a tap suspiciously well. The remaining foam was just a thin layer on top of his mug, the mark of a good pour for dwarven beer.

"Thanks for this," he said.

"Cheers," she said, clinking her mug against his.

Finley appreciated the foresight of a woman who wanted to start the day with a cold beer.

Dwarven beer steins, unlike their clothing, were far larger than they needed to be. If it weren't for the handle, the stein would be unwieldy to the extreme. Thankfully, dwarven stein makers thought to take in the penchant for drunks to need a strong grip.

If the watch out on the wall was correct then there was no sign of the undead legion. The horde was on the march nearby them.

Anthony had asked Bob to take several measurements to try and ascertain if the death knight closest to them had continued onwards or was returning to where it started from. Bob had taken the time to draw a circle at every corner of the compound, placing approximate azimuths at each one. One circle had five rocks, one painted white.

Fortune, or perhaps the Goat Lord saw fit to give them zero help. They were all pointing in the same direction. At lunchtime Anthony would ask Bob to do the same thing again. Then they would have to fit into proof if it was moving. That is, unless it was moving directly towards them. That was one of the blind spots that they had. They could judge the direction but not the distance unless it got within range. Bob's pathfinder range skill gave them a security cushion, provided he was awake.

It felt like they had tried everything to determine the distance. Several people had volunteered to scour the cards remaining later that day to try and find anything helpful.

There didn't seem to be a way out of this without conflict. It weighed heavily on Finley. No matter what he did, at least one death knight stood between them and their next goal. Their paths would take them crashing together. What he did not want to do was to leave it up to the death knight to set up its own ambush somewhere remote.

He knew that Anthony wanted to fight the death knight at a place in time of his choosing. Stupid humans and their notions of vengeance and equity. You couldn't get revenge as a dead man. Elves took the long-term view of things.

When Bella had her second drink, Finley wanted to say something. There was only so much to go around after all. Several kegs had been found inside of the town but most were not serviceable. The small keg that they tapped would surely be enough for everyone to have one, and there would be people who would abstain.

Finley decided that he didn't want to have a second. For now at least.

After Bella had her third drink, Finley kept a closer watch on her. It wouldn't do to have his cryomancer and head cook out of the picture by the time lunch rolled about. He was no stranger to preparing his own food. He would not have minded cooking for everyone if someone else hadn't already volunteered. Finley was a busy elf and he aimed to stay that way.

"Bella, did you really just grab a fourth beer?"

"Stay out of it, Finley. It's not your problem."

"Okay, okay."

Finley raised his arms and surrendered. She was clearly a bit stubborn about this and he didn't want to push. He did want to have lunch eventually. What he was probably going to do would be to open it up and make something special. He could make something but it was hard to grok what she wanted.

Finley had known many people who had taken to the bottle after an experience. He'd known even more who had taken to it after no experience. Sometimes it hit hard no matter who you were. He wasn't going to say anything now, but maybe later. He would have to talk to Anthony. They were going to have another council meeting around noon. This one might be the one where he decided to go after the death knight.

Bob was still sleeping. Finley really considered if it was time to wake him or not. Seeing as how he did so much for them, the family wasn't going to leave him sleeping. But with his girlfriend drinking a bit more than was proper, perhaps he might be able to talk to her. So when Finley saw Bob getting up he made the decision to go talk to him.

A smiling bald man sat down next to him. Graciously, Finley passed a bowl of stew to Bob. He accepted it happily. As they sat next to each other. Bob continued to glance up at Bella.

"Bob, you know Bella best. Do you think she's doing all right?"

Bob sighed, looking over at him. He seemed ten years older at that moment. "There's no harm in what she's doing. No one is getting hurt. I have no problem with her doing whatever she needs to do to forget what just happened. And when I say that I'm not referring to myself. I'm helping her work through her issues. None of us left Dunnamore unscathed."

Finley held up his waterskin. "A toast to the fallen. May the places that they lay be covered with flowers so that we know they lived a good life." He bleated twice, the Goat Lord's traditional ending to the prayer.

"I feel like I should have a prayer for Mork, but I've never learned one. Is that a thing here? I have to be honest. By now, I thought I would know things. Honestly, I feel rather unprepared with all the special skills he gave me."

"The Goat Lord desires flowers to be placed on the graves of men and women killed. Mork probably has the same passionate hate for those made undead as the Goat Lord does, just without the partying."

"The Goat Lord likes parties?" Bob said.

"The Goat Lord is half party, half animal. We celebrate their lives, we don't mourn. I might call them the fallen but that's another thing."

Bob frowned. "How many gods are there? I feel like I should know this. Are there different pantheons?"

"I'm not entirely certain. Yil is the goddess for most dwarves and gnomes. Mork, as you know, has followers everywhere. Cara is worshiped by traders and tinkers. There are others, like there is a god that orcs worship, and one that has to do with elves and woodlands. There are probably more worshipers across the seas."

"Okay. And when you say, across the seas, how big are we talking here. Do you know how many continents there are in this world?" Bob said.

Finley shrugged. "Six? And then there's the lost continent. Noveria is the biggest one."

"Lost continent?"

"I only know a few stories. I can tell you if you wish," Finley said. "They are mostly not relevant to anything we are doing though."

"If we were to find a way off of this continent somehow, would you know which way to go? And then if so, how to steer us there?" Bob said.

"There is a continent due south that isn't so far by boat. I have honestly never considered it before. Tinkers don't do well on water and let's just say that we were not welcomed everywhere as we were here."

"That's a bit sad. The orcs and the humans occupy the land next to the sea, correct?"

"That's about right. One of the dwarves had a good map of the continent. I'll try to find it. I know you're trying to help us, but maybe you can help Bella first?"

"I'll try."

38

Bob, chosen headhunter of Mork, led the scouting mission.

"You really think that this is a good idea?" Sophie asked, entirely unconvinced of the merits of Bob's amazing plan.

Sophie, Bob, and Bella had gone out on a scouting expedition to try and figure out what the death knight was doing. They had taken three horses and promised to turn back if there was a quest or if they got close to making contact. It was Anthony's only requirement. Bob knew that he was irreplaceable. It was getting in the way of his plans.

The scouting party was close to where the plains gave way to the forest. They had been riding, trying to get a ping, but had nothing to show for their time.

"It's probably good that the death knight isn't moving. Maybe we can do the sensible thing and leaf. You know, make like a tree and all that?" Sophie said.

"We have to determine if it's a threat," Bob said, pulling up alongside her. He had asked kindly for one of the bay mares. Both were pleasantly surprised that she had chosen to come along. Sophie was her partner in crime.

The adventurous horse hadn't spent this much time away from Finley in years. He appreciated how much both mares vibed together, and hoped that Bella and he could grow to be closer. She was gripping her reins a bit tighter today, but it was to be expected. They were out ahead of the group.

"Bob, we're getting nowhere fast," Sophie said. "We have a general idea of their location, but at this point I don't think that they're tracking us at all. Otherwise—are those orcs?"

Somewhere in the sea of grass, two figures were walking along without a care in the world. Their tough green skin was visible from a far distance, even under their cloaks. They approached the three mounted scouts, keeping their distance.

Bob had an idea of the distance that they could shoot crossbows from and was fairly certain that Sophie had just stopped around there. None of them had ever met an orc before, so this was entirely unexpected.

"They don't look like zombies. They're not acting like zombies, either," Bella said.

"Let me give them a little wave and perhaps we can talk?" Sophie said.

Bob nodded. His favored enemy skill would have told him if they were zombies.

Sophie waved at the orcs, trying to convey that they meant them no harm. The orcs looked unarmed. As they got closer, it was clear that they were carrying heavy packs over traveling cloaks. They lowered their hoods to reveal tattooed faces and tall, shaped mohawks. Bob didn't know the difference between orc genders and wasn't keen to make a summary judgment. One had blue facial tattoos on both cheeks and the other had a single red face tattoo on one entire side.

"Good day to you," Bob said, lowering his cloak off his head. It was probably a good idea to appear open. "I'm Bob and these two are Sophie and Bella. We're heading away from the undead horde which has gripped most of this continent."

The two orcs looked at each other. Perhaps they hadn't heard the news? There was a lot of space in between the dwarven settlements and they weren't entirely certain how the zombification spread so quickly.

"Ah. Well met, humans. This is Song," one said, placing a hand on the other's shoulder. "I am Borgan. We are both members of Clan Green Fang. We are here to attend a clan gathering. Please tell us more about this horde."

Bob was taken aback. The orcs smelled like they had been walking for days. And the group was upwind of the orcs. He had to steel his resolve and keep his face like a mask.

"The… Where have you been? We have been to several dwarven villages that have all been overrun to a dwarf. All were turned into zombies," Bella said.

Borgan and Song crossed their arms. Their nearly two-meter-tall frames made it so that Sophie was eye level with them from atop the horse. After a short look between the two, they turned back to the scouts. The short distance felt like a giant rift between their two groups all of a sudden.

"Is this certain?" Borgan said.

"I'm sorry. Chances are that whatever gathering you are going to might be overwhelmed. Do you know which direction your gathering is?"

"Orcish gatherings are not for outsiders. Such secrets are not given to non-clan members," Borgan said. "Allow us to close this gap. We come in peace."

The horses all watched the short procession. Bob could feel his mare tense up and he gave it several head pats.

Up close, the size of the orcs was even more impressive. They looked like they ate nothing but the jerky of strong animals with a smattering of greens from time to time. Their smell was particularly strong this close and Bob regretted his many choices.

"You're saying that there is a horde of zombies?" Borgan said. "What proof do you have of such a wild claim?"

"Back at our current camp, there are dozens of dead dwarves that clearly were taken by zombification. That would be the best proof I could muster. You are welcome to return with us to Arva, though the walk will be long for you. It took us over an hour to ride here. The town is no secret though, as it is right on the road."

"You can see it from here," Bella said. "There are the walls that we put up yesterday. Only because we're a bit higher from here."

As they looked, Bob was reminded that they had left Plainsmount going directly towards the death knight's icon.

"That explains where you were," Borgan said. "If we weren't already late, then we would investigate."

Song made a complicated sign to Borgan, using both hands. This close it was clear that Borgan's blue tattoos were parts of a seascape. Song's tattoo was clearly a red hand print.

"Song wants to tell you—slow down brother—that he believes you. You're sure about that? Okay. I don't know that orcs would be so easily turned into zombies."

Song slammed his fists on his chest. Borgan nodded.

"We have been traveling to the gathering. We took our time here but strayed a little from the path. We have been going by our clan markers, and have been avoiding dwarven settlements. Song agrees that this is unusual but is willing to see your evidence."

Bob's eyebrow twitched.

"You both want to follow us back to Arva? To be honest we were looking for more undead out here. We have a strong suspicion that they are further out this way," Bob said pointing in the direction of the death knight.

It was probably enough to give them an idea that he had a tracking power. They didn't need to know all of the details. He wasn't going to volunteer much more than that and since he had the ranger class it should be sufficient.

Song slapped his hands, pointed, then did a complicated wiggling motion with three fingers of his left hand.

"Song regrets to tell me that is the direction of the gathering. Are you sure about that? One of the markers is by there?" Borgan said. "I really don't think we should—okay, okay."

The more that Borgan spoke, the more animated Song became.

"Is there a problem? Anything we can do to help?" Bob said.

"May I offer you a use of the cleanse skill in these trying times?" Bella said.

"She's really quite good at it. You'll be smelling great in no time," Sophie added.

"Ladies, I don't think this is the time for that. Maybe once we are on the same page?" Bob said, turning to look at them.

Borgan and Song were in a heated silent battle. Neither orc seemed ready to slow down anytime soon.

"So do you want to ask why the other one doesn't talk?" Sophie said. "Or do you want to ask them if they want to smell like teenage boys?"

"Nice one Sophie." Bob rolled his eyes.

The two orcs smelled awful but he had gotten accustomed to it. It was unfortunate. The dead bodies that lay strewn around where they had camped had a specific smell that he did not want to get back to. Cleanse only did so much. It wasn't like the girls didn't use it all the time; they did. There was just so much death and carnage that finding himself irritated because two people who needed a shower badly didn't even register in his top ten problems.

It was certainly Bella's top two problems. If she used a card power on them without asking them and getting their full permission, that might cause an incident. However, if he told her that she shouldn't use it on them that would also cause an incident. Bob thought about a way to distract Bella from the problem that she thought was pressing.

Borgan and Song's silent diatribe ended.

"All right, we've decided," Borgan said. "We walked all this way to meet up with the clan. We're not that far from where we're supposed to meet them. If we want to circle back, we will head to Arva. Is it possible that you could help us?"

"I feel like we can—" Bob began.

"Absolutely!" Bella said. "Bob, don't look at me like that. We always have room for more."

"Do you have any guesses as to how far this gathering is from here?" Sophie said.

"Without giving too much away, not too much further," Borgan said. "Though I don't know how far, I expect to be there by the end of the day."

Bob wondered how much he was going to have to do to entice them to come with him. He did not feel like this was a hard sale at all. Having two orcs to help them would be a massive boon. It wasn't his place to tell them what to do. He was fighting every fiber of his being to tell him to come along with them. If they wanted to throw themselves straight into danger, he wanted no part of it.

Bella had helped him to see where he could fit in. He wasn't running a bakery right now. He wasn't trying to order the girls around. He definitely wasn't going to tell the orcs, who were bigger than him, what to do. But the urge to do so was strong with him. He took the urge and crushed it in his hand, imagining it going away. He then just waited for the orcs to figure out what they wanted to do.

At least they finally smelled like two teenage boys trying to impress the popular girl. Bob briefly wondered about the size and range of the skill. He also noticed that he was clean as a whistle as well.

"Pardon me, but what are your thoughts? We were considering heading back to our people now. Right now. I understand neither of you has a horse and I'm not sure that there are any orc-sized horses out here but we wanted to make it back and report in. We can talk as much or as little about you both as you want. So long as you don't mean us harm, we have no quarrel with you," Borgan said.

He clapped Song on the shoulder. "I think we need to check it out for ourselves. If we find something out, we will tell you. We will find a way to tell you. How long is your group intending to stay here?"

"Probably for as long as the salvage lasts. We are trying to make our way south off of the continent," Bob said.

"Off of the continent?" Borgan said, sniffing himself. "Also, this smell is wonderful, thank you miss."

Bella beamed.

"There are too many undead," Bob said. "Staying here would mean a long, slow death."

For various reasons, he didn't want to mention the death knights. Different reasons made him want to tell them about how they were probably walking into a trap. He didn't know them, but he didn't want to fight them as undead.

"Would you consider coming to Arva? We have a very strong reason to believe that there is an undead legion in that direction. I can't tell you why or how but this is just something that I know. I'll be completely honest with both of you. Complete transparency? I feel like both of you will be turned into undead and you seem like good guys. I don't want to fight you."

Both of the orcs shuddered. This brought another barrage of hand talk between the two. Bob wondered if he could learn that. He would probably just use it to pass innuendos to Bella. She appreciated a fair bit of dirty talk when they weren't on the job. She just didn't want to appear like she did. And he loved that about her.

He looked Bella straight in the eye and winked. She smiled back at him.

"What would make you guys feel better if we offered you some of the best stew you have ever had?" Sophie said.

"And cold dwarven beer?" Bella said, ice swirling around her hand. "If nothing else, we understand hospitality."

The orcs looked a bit resigned.

"Guys, whatever you're thinking just give us two hours and we'll prove our point. I promise you that we'll even bring you right back here if you need us to do that."

Borgan grunted.

The first sign that something had changed was that the scouts weren't heading back at normal speed. The second sign was that they were keeping pace with, and probably talking to, two large green creatures. They weren't running, which was enough for the watch to wait until they had something to report.

"Really? Big green guys walking with them and it took you five minutes to come down and tell me what's going on?" Anthony found himself saying. He was a bit irritated. Several days of traveling together on the edge of conflict with the zombies gave them a singular purpose. It had not ironed out their differences.

"Look here, guy," Brandon said. "We didn't think it needed to be addressed but they're all heading here. We're all tired. We made a decision to observe a bit longer."

Anthony deflated. He hadn't realized how high strung he had been. Brandon was telling him something important. The bald monk in dwarven robes waited patiently for him.

"I'm sorry I snapped at you. That wasn't me. That was this whole situation."

"Julie said something to you, didn't she?" Brandon said, putting a hand on his shoulder.

"She's just exhausted and I think I pushed her too hard."

"You didn't ask for your scrub top back did you?"

Anthony shook his head. A loud clunk sounded from behind the house. Both men studiously ignored it.

"Even I'm not that stupid. She can keep it. The pants are mine though. It looks silly with a gambeson, but they're designer. Plus I'm not getting a new one out here. Maybe there's a mending card that will help in case it gets ripped."

"You guys need to work it out. You're both too important to our survival," Brandon said. He held up his water skin and drained it. "Having the glass cannon and the leader date is a pretty big conflict of interest."

"That it is. But there's pretty slim pickings on this continent and dating should be the last thing on everyone's mind."

They both let that stand there. Anthony didn't want to go too deep into the weeds. Julie's whole situation was a bit traumatic in many regards and there hadn't been any space or time in which to heal. Arva might give them the chance to actually rest instead of constantly shifting from more to less watchful. He had a dream that they might be able to actually stay somewhere for long enough that they could stop the horde, but there would be no resupply.

No one was coming to save them.

No one was coming to save *him*.

Brandon tapped him on the shoulder. "So, do you want to send out a party to meet them?"

"Brandon, three of our people are out scouting. Six are on enforced rest—" Anthony said.

"You can't make me!" Andrew said. He was clearly tinkering with something behind the house, and definitely close enough to eavesdrop.

"—three are on watch of which you are one. The other three are myself, Finley, and Zan, and we'll be taking over for you around dinnertime. Who do you want me to send?" Anthony said.

"That's an excellent point. We can just greet them at the wall."

A wall of flame extended from behind the house.

"Let's go to the wall; posthaste," Anthony said.

"I couldn't agree with you more."

They scrambled to get away from Andrew's experiments.

***

"That one is supposed to be a flame flinger. I do hope that he changes the name," Anthony said, safely from on top of the wall.

"Flame flinger? I mean it sounds unique because he has never heard of flamethrower?" Brandon replied. "Like he is scaring the horses and that's as close as we can get to a sacred rule: you don't fuck with the horses."

"Yeah, that sounds about right. They are the reason that we're not dead after all. And here they are now."

The two tall orcs reached nearly the top of the wall. It was designed to stop human and dwarven zombies from breaking it. Finley had even shown up to observe after he realized that Anthony wasn't coming down.

"You have some history with the orcs, do any of their markings on their face or their leather armor mean anything?" Anthony asked.

"That's not any configuration I have ever seen. They are far afield of where I have seen any orc. They might be part of a migrating tribe. Not every orc is part of their meritocracy," Finley said. "I have a suspicion that one or both have an epic tier card based on how strong they feel at this distance."

"You can tell that from here?" Anthony hissed. They were nearly within talking distance.

"Yes. It takes some time but if they were to unleash their power, you would certainly feel it as a sort of pressure. The situation would be a lot worse if they wanted to fight you. I suspect that whatever they have to say is going to be informative at the very least."

Anthony looked at him with new eyes. Perhaps Sophie needed to ask more questions about which questions to ask the elf. He hadn't expected such a specific detail to come up.

"We're going to have to talk about this later. But for now, treat them like our guests," Finley said, descending the ladder.

Anthony approached the group. Bob had already dismounted and was helping Bella down as well. She looked determined to do it on her own, and he was equally ready to help. Even the orcs were watching the display with a fair bit of amusement. Hopefully, their smiles meant the same thing that a human's would.

"Hey Bob, what's going on?" Anthony said, extending a hand to Bob. Bob readily shook it. If something were afoot this would be where Bob would pass the safe word or some kind of message.

"Well we met Borgan and Song out there and they have an interesting story to tell, but first we need to show them a zombie. They have been walking cross-country for the past two weeks, and they're finding it hard to believe that what we're saying is true," Bob said.

"It's a pleasure to meet anyone who is still among the living," Anthony said. "We can show you some of the corpses that have been decomposing since yesterday. Would that be sufficient?"

"That will do," the one called Borgan said. His companion nodded.

In short order, Finley walked them around to the southern side of the city. Several short, unmarked graves lay there with sunflowers peeking up. It didn't take long for the orcs to realize what had happened.

Borgan took a knee, retching at the sight of it. Next to him, Song just stared off into space for a long time. Eventually someone brought water for them and they were ushered to the staging area.

The two orcs readily ate whatever was served to them. Bella was happier than a clam to feed them after talking their ears off on their walk. By this time it was late afternoon and Anthony was still reeling from the discovery of living enlightened beings. He had fully expected to never see any until they got off the continent. The fact that two were in front of them right now gave him hope.

"What do you think they want to do now? Bella, you seem to have the best read on their situation," he said, inspecting the stew. It wasn't the worst one she had made yet. They stood back away from the orcs as they were in silence.

"They probably want to warn their clan about what's going on. Chances are that most of their clan has been turned, killed, or eaten," she whispered.

"The way that they know how to go there is something that their clan taught them? Or at best is a card skill?"

It was eerie how quiet they were.

"They didn't say and we didn't ask. Don't promise something stupid right now. There's no way that we can take down a tribe of zombie orcs. There's nothing—I mean, just look at them. Borgan is like two meters tall. He could definitely outrun one of our horses if he had to. Not for long maybe but he could. Do you really want to wade into the forest and fight a tribe of those?"

Anthony gave her the dad face. He wasn't mad, just disappointed. "We have a duty to—"

"Anthony."

"—to this world."

Anthony realized that he was brandishing a soup spoon at her and had gone far into the fight part of fight or flight for the second time that day. Bella was also holding a slotted soup spoon out like it was a knife.

This was exactly the time that Anthony realized that he was facing down a rogue.

"Fuck."

"I can assure you that we can both lose this fight. Or I can win. Your choice," she said, holding the spoon like she meant it.

"Bella, I'm so sorry. This is not my day at all," he said. He tried to unclench himself, but the threat of her even in the abstract made him hold onto the spoon even harder.

"You both need to take a chill pill," Sophie said, as the air suddenly dropped significantly in temperature.

The cold air combined with the ridiculousness of fighting his head cook and scout finally got to him.

"Bella, this whole situation is getting to me. I didn't mean anything."

Bella gave him a full body hug. Anthony let himself be held. Then he dropped the spoon.

Bella put her spoon to his neck as she stepped back.

"You're a dead man now," she said, giggling.

"I need a vacation."

From around the campfire, they heard clapping. The two orcs had apparently been watching them and were enjoying the show. Anthony took a deep breath, inhaling the odor of a teenager ready for date night. Then he exhaled the expectation that he wouldn't lash out unexpectedly. It would happen again and he would do his best in the moment. It was all he could do.

"That was an impressive show. Do you humans often fight with your cookware?" Borgan said, standing up. "If not, it would do well. There was just enough angst there for us to think that we might want you for part of our troupe."

"Your troupe?" Anthony said.

"We're traveling bards as well as members of the clan," the orc replied. "You may or may not have noticed our large weapons cases. It's not only weapons but also selected instruments as well."

Borgan went on to explain how it was part of their travels to learn more about other cultures and bring back stories. It was something they had been trained for by the clan since they were younger. They loved traveling to the Irumian Kingdom. This gathering was one of the few chances to see the entire clan gathered in one place. It was held every second year. Part of their duties was to spread the information about when the gathering would take place. That was why they had been so late; they had been trying to find some of the further-flung Green Fang.

"Guys, I have to be honest right now. There is a real chance that if you go to that gathering, not only will you die but every story about your clan will die with you. We strongly believe that the death knights have marched on this gathering for a reason. None of us are sure of how they know what they know, but we have a good feeling of where they are," Anthony said. "I will assemble my war council but I can't guarantee anything."

"Either way, we must know the fate of our clan," Borgan said.

Anthony waved Finley over. Bob had never left. Anthony explained the situation to them as best as he could. Bob added some flavor to the discussion based on his trek out. Bob called in a few more people to sit in on the discussion.

Anthony was pleased when Julie arrived.

She had been sleeping. Without saying anything, she sidled up next to him and kissed him.

It was the last thing that he was expecting. It didn't activate his fight or flight response but he did a little happy dance. Having her around made him feel so much better that he wasn't even aware that he was being watched by most of the camp at that time. Of course, when he did realize, they were all smiling and he knew that they just wanted to back him up. He smiled back.

Julie grabbed his hand and sat down next to him.

"So, I hear we're going to war?"

40

"We're already in a war," Anthony said. "We've been discussing potential battle plans. Wait, what did you hear?"

The care with which Julie approached Anthony looked genuine. Finley had seen that kind of look before. It was something shared between family members or long-time friends. Perhaps she would be able to help him with his outbursts. Although walking up and surprising him like that probably wouldn't have gotten the same reaction that she wanted.

"I heard that you got into a fight with Bella with spoons? Or was it a food fight? If you're two-timing me with that rogue then I don't even want to hear about it," Julie said.

Anthony raised a hand, blinked several times and then settle down into a seat.

"What is a food fight? Unless you are tossing potatoes at each other, I don't really want to hear about it," Finley said.

"Guys, it was nothing like that I swear," Anthony said, potentially realizing that he was the center of everyone's attention. Even the orcs were watching him. The two people standing watch on the walls had turned, facing inside.

"Right. You're going to say this in front of our new friends?" Julie said. "They just got here and you're already making up lies about me? Maybe I should join up with them instead!"

Anthony looked horrified. Julie stepped back. Finley needed them all to concentrate on the current problem. Humans, like their salvage piles, were all over the place.

"You called a meeting, do you want to begin talks with them?" Finley said. "If I might interject, I know orcs are big on hospitality and formality so let us discuss what we have to discuss with them."

Bella and Sophie brought out tables from one of the houses. As they did so, the orcs looked at the wall, examining how it was made. Every so often, Song would sign excitedly to Borgan. Borgan would sign back with far less enthusiasm, or say something low and inaudible.

They returned to sit on the ground around the fire pit. Finley watched as Bella put another pot of something on before returning to them. The tables next to them had dozens of refreshments, another human thing that Finley was beginning to understand. Elves made eating its own thing, a special time for them to be with family and guests. Humans attacked piles of jerked meats and cheeses like they were vultures. It was cute in a way, and thankfully quiet.

"Pardon me, but my brother wants to know about the walls. He has never seen such a design. Were they always like this?" Borgan said.

"This was card magic, combining the work of two different casters," Finley said. It wouldn't do to give away his trade secrets. Or rather, their trade secrets. Nothing more needed to be said unless they wanted to pay a retainer for such privileged information. Though what he would do with any money at this point in his career stumped him.

"The work is quite thorough. We appreciate fine craftsmanship, and now that we know how it was made, it has an even more interesting background. Shall we begin?" Borgan said, raising an unlit torch. He passed it to Anthony.

It was an orc thing to give the speaker the floor. To represent that the clan worked with unity, they passed around the torch one at a time. Anthony wouldn't know any of this, what with being human and from another world and all.

Anthony raised the torch.

"First, thank you for coming to see the devastation that has been happening. We understand that you wish to go find out what has become of your clan."

Anthony passed the torch back to Borgan.

"That is correct. If it is as bad as you say, we would request your help."

Finley expected somebody else would reach out for the torch but Borgan passed it back to Anthony. Anthony looked about to see if anybody else wanted to speak.

"I have to be very honest with you right now. All of us believe in our hearts that if you go there it will mean certain death. All of us, save for Finley, have a purpose here. It would do no good for any of us to be captured or killed. Most of the people you see here were either hours or days away from being turned. We have a very strong reason to believe that a death knight, an intelligent undead, is leading an attack on your clan's gathering. If it has not killed them all by now, it will have turned most of them. Any stragglers will be hard to find for us but a lot easier for the death knight and its horde."

The orcs nodded. Borgan held out his hand for the torch. It was passed back once again. He held it up high with one arm, before lowering it to the ground.

"What we were asking for is some help. We won't be able to make it on our own, if this is the case but—"

Song lowered his hand on Borgan's shoulder. The slap of the meat meeting meat made Finley shudder.

"—we have to know if this has happened. If they are under siege or dead, we need to know."

Finley felt a knot in his gut. It wasn't a familiar feeling. He raised a hand, palm up at chest height to request the speaker role. The torch made its way through two pairs of hands to get to him.

"This is too big of a problem for us to fight. Orc clans are large and we have seen so much death. The near certainty that you are walking into a trap gives me pause. Would your clan have wanted you to throw yourself away for them? If they are dead, they will still be there tomorrow and the day after that."

Song signed to Borgan. The torch was moved back quickly. Both brothers held on as Borgan spoke.

"I speak for my brother in this. Even if we have to get closer and then find out from afar what's going on, we need to know. And so, we request your help. In exchange we will do our best to help you."

Anthony leaned forward, waiting for them to send the stick his way. By now, everyone was used to this and they passed it back to him.

"If we did this, we would have to have the whole group agree. We cannot go alone and I would never break us up. So it has to be volunteers. If you want to do this, and potentially take down this death knight, this is the time," Anthony said. "We need to all be on the same page."

Julie held up a hand, then Andrew. Bob slowly raised his hand. Bella and Sophie raised theirs as well. The rest of the humans raised their hands.

"Well?" Anthony said, turning to Finley.

"What is this whole hand-raising business?"

***

"Alright, we are going to establish a bounty system," Anthony said. "One kill is one card piece. Some of you are in support roles and might not get that same opportunity, so we'll give a card piece for an assist. If we do this, then we need to think tactically. Whoever this undead chosen is, they're also newly summoned to this world, or at least we assume. They don't know that we have what we have."

Anthony wasn't going to give up their status as chosen to the orcs so easily. They would keep their secrets close to the chest. But when sharing intelligence, he had to make sure that they were on the same page.

"You both have a bard class?" Bob asked, clearly knowing the answer. "Anything we can use in a fight?"

"Song and I can perform music to increase your speed, strength, or magical control. There are also some offensive songs that we know," Borgan said.

"Alright. We go in and our worst-case scenario is that the entire clan and then some has been turned. If that happens then we do a slow retreat, trying to get the death knight to play its cards," Anthony said, sketching on the ground. "Our mages will create a corridor of death, funneling the zombies towards us. Julie, you can make strong walls, right?"

"That won't be a problem, Anthony. You want them funneling towards the monks and warriors?"

"Yes. Those we will keep as our small frontline, swapping them in and out as needed. However, and I say this because Bob and I lived it, once the death knight is dead and the undead legion becomes brainless once again, the plan changes. Once that happens, we beat a hasty retreat and play tower defense. Make them spread out coming here so we can take them out one at a time. This may require the orcs to leave faster. Can you both run?"

The orcs nodded emphatically.

"We can speed up significantly. Song is also skilled at animal husbandry if needed and can steer a caravan," Borgan said. "Weeks of traveling made us fast and strong. You won't need to worry about Clan Green Fang."

Anthony's sketch was getting more and more complicated. The funnel began to take shape.

"This is beginning to look like a pyramid scheme," Julie whispered into his ear. "How many people do I need to sign up to make double diamond rank?"

Anthony couldn't help but laugh. He considered the whole thing a tactical role playing game or real time strategy game because otherwise it would have been too real. Julie obviously considered their lives here to be a tower defense game. Meanwhile, Bob was playing Assassin's Creed, and Finley? Finley was playing Stardew Valley.

"All right, I'm going to ask the question here now. Does everyone understand the plan?" Anthony said.

A chorus of nods and yeses greeted him. His team understood what was going to happen. "All right everybody. Let's get ready. Mount up in five minutes," he said.

***

"This is going to have to be quick," she said, straightening her outfit. She wanted to be presentable. "There's no way that we have time for anything long. Maybe later. Can I give you something extra this time and you do the same next time?"

"I'm impressed that you came to me like this. I'll agree to this. A little extra sugar this time for mommy and you'll get your treat."

The coins were laid down on the desk as before.

"That is a terrible way to put it, but sure."

***

Bob, Mork's point man, was out front. The caravan, including their new orcish allies, followed closely behind. They were approaching what he generally thought of as their top speed. It was dinnertime, or at least his stomach said so. Bella had insisted on feeding everyone something, but most of them were too jittery to eat.

The pastoral scene of waving fields of tall yellow grass did nothing to calm his nerves. Andrew had continued to work away at his flame flinger the entire time and as the wagon had come up front, he had mounted the weapon on the back of it.

As they crested the last mile before the plains gave way to the evergreen forest, the wind whipped up a near storm around them. His horse for this journey was still the strong stoic bay mare from the morning. This was where the orcs had encountered them.

He checked his card, hoping for something.

Epic Skill Card: Pathfinder Level 2

Find a friend or foe within six spans unerringly. As this card advances, the range advances.

It was then that he realized that it had finally advanced to level two. This came with another problem.

Rare Class Card: Ranger Level 3

Skills:

Divine Spellcasting Level 2

Animal Handling Level 2

Favored enemy Level 2

Fieldcraft Level 3

Weapon Proficiency Level 3

This card grants mana.

As a ranger you may pick another favored enemy at each level.

This is a soul card and cannot be removed.

He had the ability to pick another favored enemy and had considered picking orc to see if they stacked. A doubly favored enemy would potentially give some bonuses. Not that he had any idea what that would change. Monkeying around with the magic of this world had seemed like something that he was not going to touch with an eleven-foot pole. He was going to take the advantages when he could take them and avoid the bad parts.

It was then that his Pathfinder skill pinged. His concentration on the death knight was pulled completely onto focus. He knew more than anything else that it was within six spans of where he was. He wasn't sure exactly how much six spans was, but he thought it was close to a kilometer. Bob generally dealt only with freedom units except when baking. As such, he figured it was about two to four miles away the most.

They had a strong debate about the logistics of how to fight the orcs and decided on several possible paths. Then they ran out of time.

The death knight was moving.

He had a lock on the direction of the death knight. His pathfinder skill worked a lot better at the expansive distance and he felt ready to rumble. It was coming towards them.

He sent up his little signal flag to let everyone know that they were finally within range.

41

"Well, that's pretty fucked," Anthony said, looking down at the scene. "Julie, you're up."

Right as they got closer to the forest, several dozen undead orcs made their appearance. They arrived in pairs and squads. They marched with a purpose.

Anthony's fears were confirmed.

Between them, the field rose and fell so the zombies would be going down into the valley first before they could approach them at the top of their small hill. It was a good place to defend or at least pretend to defend. The hope was that it would slow them down before they got to the first trench. All the zombies needed to do was to play their part.

Monks were on both sides of their formation, piles of rocks at the ready as they loaded up sling after sling of rocks. Their job was just to keep the zombies from wheeling around them and attacking from the flank.

Julie might have overdone it a bit shaping the earth around the hill, but she hadn't fully encircled them. The project was about to begin in earnest. Julie had told him that she would have the mana needed to pull out an ace.

"Julie?"

"It would be my pleasure," she said, before turning to kiss him. "Wish me luck!"

Julie had created what had to be her magnum opus. Anthony swelled with pride. For as put-together and intimidating an intelligent enemy force could be, gravity was still a bitch. Julie was going to be a badder bitch.

***

Zan and Bob took turns firing magic missiles at some of the larger targets.

She, having studied the skill extensively, had added it as a magic spell to her own arsenal. Hers didn't have the same range as him but as they were closing in, it mattered less and less.

From a few dozen, the dwarf zombies began to mass into nearly a hundred or more. They continued to pound the enemy, picking off more of them as they got closer. Even as they picked more off and got better, the horde continued to pour out of the trees.

Anthony checked out the fortifications as he got the caravan turned around. It would do no good to not have an exit plan. Then he heard the lilting melody of two guitars. He looks to see two lutes being played by the orcs. They held their lutes like they were in a rock concert. For Anthony, everything went into sharp focus.

He checked his active deck, pleased to see that his cleric card had finally reached level three. The control that the bards gave made him feel like he could really finely apply his skills.

Rare Class Card: Cleric Level 3

Skills:Divine Spellcasting Level 2

Divine Rituals Level 1

Heal Level 2

Survival Level 4

Medicine Level 4

This card grants mana.

As a cleric you must have a patron deity.

This is a soul card and cannot be removed.

He was happy with the changes and went back to check on Julie. In the short time that they had been there, she had designed an entire series of trenches and walls that would give the zombies endless problems. She had moved earth around so that there were three walls next to three trenches so the trenches were twice as deep as they would otherwise be. What she had done next was add a bit of flair, making parts of the trenches closer to a pit trap.

The walls were also twice as high where they were adjacent to the trenches. At the same time, she expanded the walls to both sides so the zombie horde couldn't just run around it. If they were the tower, it was well defended.

When she finally took a knee, the zombies were nearly at their figurative front gates. That was when Sophie began her work in earnest. Sophie and Bella took turns. From the very first of the walls, they rained down ice and lightning. The ice luge that they created began to slip up zombies as they climbed. Those that would have otherwise made it did not, falling backwards to trip others.

Anthony looked around, counting his people one by one. Then he looked down. Of the hundred zombies that had charged them running up the hill, several dozen had already fallen prey to their traps. A few had made it into the first trench and were stuck there.

It would have been a nice time for him to have an overview of the map. If there was a drone card, one where he could have an overhead flying picture of the battle, he would have chosen that card. It would have shown his battle plan in a way that he could really dig into. He had to trust the process and his people.

"I can't see the death knight anywhere. I'm going to make it their problem," he whispered.

If Bob was able to see the death knight by himself, he wasn't giving any indication. He also knew how laser-focused Bob had been on defeating the death knights before. Bob was not going to let it have the chance to escape.

There was a lull in the horde's charge. Glints of gold revealed a small black cat sorting through bodies. Two ladders extended from the first wall up to the second. Sophie headed up the ladder to the second level as the horde threatened to pile up onto the wall. Behind her, two of the monks ran up the ladders and then removed them.

Zombie dwarves swarmed up over the wall, their hands scrabbling for purchase. Sophie spent her mana like water. Next to her, the monks used slings to launch rocks over and over again. Brandon scored a hit.

For a long moment, Anthony held his breath. Finley was in the back line waiting to use refresh on whoever needed it.

"Sophie looks like she is flagging," Anthony said.

"On it," Finley said. The elf ran over to tag her with a refresh.

"Thanks!" she said. "Can you check on Bella? She's pushing as hard as she can as well."

***

Finley ran over and tagged Bella with a refresh. The jolt of the mana leaving his body made him shiver. He just needed some time to reset himself. He wasn't going to get it here though. Any more and he was going to lose more than he wanted to. The green nearly overcame him in that moment. He pushed it back.

A white firework fizzled over the horde. Instantly, Finley lay down to scope out what had happened. The music stopped as an orc appeared from the trees. Their large frame was a greyish green. His first thought was that it was a dreadful change to a terrible day. The fizzle had to have been one of the casters spotting the target.

"Orcs are coming!" he yelled at the top of his lungs. He tapped into the green, massing mana where he would need it. More wouldn't destroy him.

The flow of undead dwarves halted as orc zombies began to filter in behind them. Either there were no more left, or the orcs had been held back.

The mass of orcs smashed through the lines, moving through the dwarves like a teacher pushing aside a tour group of rowdy children. The dwarves went everywhere, pushed or kicked aside.

Of course it was orcs. Even in his wildest dreams, Finley knew that it was going to end with orcs. If it had to have been an accountant, he would have been found out in the capital. He didn't even know what crime he would have committed but the accountants would have found something.

Then they would have pinned it on him and his whole facade would have dropped. Something about their accounting practices would have revealed the truth about him.

Tinkers weren't known to be violent. Inside the tinker community, violence was not only unheard of but beyond a last resort. No one ever killed anyone. Though it might have been rumored to be otherwise and people tended to stay away because of unfounded stories. So, when he was brought in and joined the tinker community, it was something that he hadn't even considered.

Despite how he was, they took him in. Despite the green.

Finley watched in horror as another group of orcs ran around their right flank, trying to overrun Julie's walls. Zan and Julie began firing off spells rapidly.

They might be glass cannons, but they were cannons all the same.

Attacks flew with a ferocity that he had never seen before. He was proud of the human for growing so fast in such a short amount of time and hoped that she wouldn't burn out before he was able to refresh her again. She had been one of the kindest ones.

Sophia and Bella had been worked to the bone; their mana depleted. They had been slumped over on the highest wall. When the orcs showed up on the battlefield, they got themselves back up in short order. Finley wished that he had a bow to give them. And some arrows.

They got up and began throwing rocks with the monks. Every so often one of them would loose an ice bolt or a lightning bolt at the orcs. Julie even stopped attacking to raise a two-meter-tall wall to stop the attack. The tall orcs were nearly large enough to get over the walls without having to work for it. Once one of them went down though they would climb on the back of the next, stepping up.

They shouldn't be this fast, was what he thought as he tapped into the green. Five orcs charged him. If they had been any other creatures, they might not have charged immediately, but they were orcs.

Finley knew how to deal with orcs. It would have to be a hostile takeover.

Behind him, the two orc bards' tunes reached a crescendo as he extended himself out. The green flowed as he tapped into his spore powers. He stood on both feet facing the flanking horde, both hands extended.

He let it free.

Mana poured out of him. He was the green, nothing more and nothing less. He said a silent prayer to the Goat Lord. If there ever was a time for the Goat Lord to show up, this would be that time. He just hoped it wasn't too little too late. His entire body turned green. Skin hardened, turned into a hard mossy covering. The orcs slowed to a crawl and then, miraculously, stopped.

Finley took a knee, his entire flesh a distinctly different color than he remembered.

"Thank you, Finley," he said.

***

The dozens of orcs that charged, flanking from the right, had all been consumed by a wall of green plant life. Most of them were now covered in mushrooms. Anthony wasn't sure if they were going to continue moving or not.

Finley seemed to have activated some superpower that he'd never seen before for the briefest moment, Anthony remembered that he'd never taken a good look at Finley's druid card. Sure, he had complained about it, but with how strong it was, he had expected less.

Anthony was more than happy to start casting a healing spell on Finley. When he directed his healing touch towards him, though, everything felt off and jumbled. Finley didn't look like he was entirely healing so Anthony broke it off.

"Finley, are you okay?"

Anthony didn't notice the aperture opening behind him. He didn't see the death knight walking out, sword at the ready. He didn't notice a bloody fast death coming towards him. What he did notice was Finley looking beyond him in shock and horror.

Before Anthony could turn around, Finley's arm shot past him. The long green arm extended at least two or three times his body length to catch a sword.

The death knight cleaved Finley's arm into two pieces. Green ooze dripped out of the vine-like arm.

Anthony turned to face the death knight. The parts of Finley's arm that had been severed lay there quivering on the ground beyond. The rest of it had extended and tried to wrap around the death knight's sword, holding it to the ground. Finley looked like he was losing a considerable amount of the green blood. Anthony was going to have to make this time count.

"I'll kill you!" Anthony shouted, getting his first view of the death knight.

A six-foot-tall human with a bastard sword greeted him by pulling the sword up and out of Finley's grip. She looked him dead in the eyes. Aside from her graying skin, she looked like a model. Her red eyes bored into him, and Anthony remembered that he was going to have to fight for his life.

Anthony pulled out the only weapons he had. A hammer and a short sword made their appearance as he dodged a savage blow. This time the death knight wasn't going to wait for anything. Given a chance, she would kick Anthony off the wall.

Finley looked like he was moving further away, and Anthony knew that he was going to have to protect their best chance of survival.

Blade met blade as he stopped the bastard sword with his short sword and hammer together. The cross block that he made illustrated the point that the death knight was far stronger than he was. He gritted his teeth and took one step back. He was going to have to inch his way back and give his party a chance to take her down.

"Bob! Bella! Some help here!" he shouted, taking another step further back. He took a glancing blow to the shoulder and black mist poured out of the spot.

The death knight didn't even have the decency to be an ugly person. In another life he could see himself being attracted to her. He nearly dropped his weapons until he realized that she was trying to distract him.

"Oh, you're going to get it now. Daddy's here and he is going to protect all of his kids," Anthony yelled.

The death knight missed, and Anthony tried to take a stab at her. Because the bastard sword was long, he got within her guard and then smashed her right hand with his hammer while keeping his sword arm unencumbered to block. The immediate effect of the smashing was that she now held the bastard sword in one hand. He stepped back, putting some more distance between them. If it was truly so easy, then he might be able to live through this.

Of course! The death knight might have some sort of magic, but Anthony suspected that it was gate-aligned magic based on how she arrived here. That was when he saw Julie, Bella, and Bob closing in on his location. Bob fired off a magic missile, destroying the death knight's right hand.

Julie and Bob looked determined to be the first one to kill it. Anthony wanted to risk a glance at Finley as he knew that the elf was behind him. He couldn't risk it. Finley was a big elf, and he would be able to take care of himself. Anthony ducked underneath a bastard sword swing. The death knight, it seemed, was not accustomed to fighting with only one of her arms working. Then his heel touched the edge of the wall.

She charged at him.

42

Anthony was so surprised that he took the tackle head on. Unfortunately for Anthony, they had reached the end of the wall. Finley had gotten clear as the death knight pushed Anthony.

Both fell.

There was a second in which they were in free fall and Anthony questioned everything in his life. His life didn't flash before his eyes, but he did get the feeling that someone was preparing a slide show for his benefit.

"Fuck this shit!"

They fell for at least ten feet, both crunching against the ground. Anthony could feel something breaking in his back. He cursed again, crying out in pain.

She was upon him.

The death knight was now sitting on his stomach, trying to pull her unwieldy bastard sword up for another swing. Everything slowed down around Anthony as the sword went up. Somewhere during the fall, the death knight has lost her grip and only the need to adjust had given Anthony this small respite.

The little voice in Anthony's head that sounded a lot like Finley pulled at his mana reserves. It was now time for him to act like a cleric. And if there was one thing that Anthony wanted to do ever since he got into this world, ever since he went to nursing school it was to heal himself.

And if there was a way to heal the death knight?

Anthony would be the first one to figure it out.

"Heal!" he yelled, placing one hand on himself and one hand on her. Where his bare hand contacted the death knight's body, it burned. Blue flames shot up from his outstretched hand as it went deeper, sinking into her torso. She stopped short, nearly dropping her sword.

Unfortunately for him, at this time she flashed a smile. She was a predator, and he was her prey.

She punched him in the face with her broken hand, then adjusted her grip. Anthony knew that she wouldn't stop next time.

"Fuck! Take that!" he yelled.

Blue smoke poured out, obscuring her face. This was probably the only time in the recorded history of this world where someone had tried to heal a death knight. It did not go well for either the undead or the person trying to heal it. As her visage shuddered, she began to bring her bastard sword up with her one full remaining hand.

If he died right here, he could accept this trade. His friends would be along to finish it off shortly, even if his death was just a distraction. There was a nagging feeling in the back of his head that he might rise again as a death knight. That little bit kept him going, kept the spark alive. He might die, but he would be damn sure that he would take her down with him.

She breathed down upon him, icy breath that spoke of the need for regular dental checkups.

Anthony struggled against the weight of the tall, thick woman. He had a quick flashback to his night with Julie. He realized in a panic that it wasn't going to work out nearly as well for him. There wasn't much else for him to do except pour all of his mana in a final Hail Mary attack. His tunnel vision narrowed on her, mana focusing on one final push.

She raised her arm up to take a swing. For some reason Anthony remembered his days playing at the arcades. He raised his right hand to her neck. It had never felt so heavy and at the same time, so light.

"Holy Bolt!"

A white bolt of mana blew a basketball-sized hole in her shoulder. The holy bolt continued on arcing into the sky as it lit up the battlefield. Her head hung limply on the opposite side. The bastard sword did not stop moving.

Anthony embraced his death. He had always wanted to die a good death and—

He was interrupted by part of the wall coming out to grab the death knight's arm. The wall enveloped the bastard sword and then began to pull. The red eyes of the death knight opened wide with alarm. She began to scramble to get up.

"Stay away from my fucking boyfriend!" the most beautiful voice he had ever heard screamed. "I don't want to be that girl but this isn't the time to be playing 'pick me' girl. Because I just took a DNA test—"

The earth next to Anthony crunched. The death knight was far too late.

"And I'm one hundred percent that bitch!"

Anthony relaxed into the ground. He was going to have to get up, but perhaps he had a minute? Satisfied that he had done enough, his hand dropped onto the ground and came up wet.

"Oh. Yeah, I did hit the ground pretty hard," he said, slipping into unconsciousness.

***

The effect after she had crushed the death knight was immediate. Most of the zombies slowed down significantly and lost their direction. A few kept moving towards them, but without a coordinated effort, then instead began to walk around, looking for their next meal.

"Mount up!" Julie said, drawing her dagger.

"Hey! Just because uh—" Bob said peering down.

"Just fucking do it, Bob," she said. "And get Finley. I'll get Anthony. We're going to need you to heal them."

Bob went to grab the quivering green mass that had been an elf earlier that day. Bella was already getting people to the escape route. Sophie, now behind the front lines, was counting people and horses.

"Sophie! Two wounded!" Julie yelled. "Make room!"

Julie tapped into her warlock powers, feeling the well nearly dry. She would have nothing left soon, but Zan could take her place.

"Zan! Wide area defense! I'm getting our wounded out of here!" she yelled.

"On it! Zappity zap!" Zan yelled back. Electric lightning sparks raced out of her hands towards the few orcs that had remained on the walls.

Julie used the earth as an elevator, taking her magic from an eighth of a tank to nearly empty. She pulled the corpse of the death knight out of the earth using the remainder of her power. Using her dagger, she quickly cut the soul card out of the death knight. The dark black card looked ominous, and she quickly tucked it away. The black card pieces right next to it glowed, and she put them away as well.

More than anything, she wanted to make sure that the death knight really had been crushed. That she was easily able to harvest its soul card meant that it was done. If nothing else, the magic behind the death knights required the magic of a card in their soul deck.

"I know I'm a queen, I don't need no crown," she muttered, picking up Anthony. His back was dripping wet, possibly with blood. She stiffened.

Julie pulled on her warlock powers, pulling his gambeson as close as possible to his skin. It was the best she could do to shrink it, turning Anthony into a shrink-wrapped sandwich from his torso down. She lifted him up, then slung him over her shoulder.

∗∗∗

Andrew thought that everything that the humans did was odd. This whole world with it's odd magic was reason enough for him to stick with them for the long term though.

That and the ability to make his flame flinger. Only heathens would call such a beautiful instrument of destruction a flamethrower. One didn't just throw flames.

One flung them.

Flames were meant to be flung.

As the sun began to set though, he finally got his wish. Andrew, one of the first to reach the caravan, got to set up everything. There was a reason that his cart, the uncovered wagon, was the last one in the line. Sparkling brass reflected the final rays of sunshine as he came close to touching it. It was the closest thing he'd ever had to a religious experience when he created it.

And now, he would deliver hot justice.

"Mount up!" Bob yelled again. The horses began to run.

"Everyone is on board!" Sophie yelled back.

"Or mounted!" Brandon added, from atop the horse next to him. He nodded to Andrew.

"Hold on, then!" Bella said from the front of his wagon. The horses began to move in earnest. There would be time to go back for the bodies and the loot. Hundreds of mindless orcs were following them, and they needed to create space.

"Zan, are you ready lass?" he said. Zan began forming mana in her hand, passing it to him. He didn't need much, but without one of them holding it, it would quickly dissolve into motes of mana that he couldn't use. That wouldn't help much for his experimental shooter.

"Can I have the second fling?" she said.

"Lass with you," he said, letting a flame loose at the zombies, "it ain't nothing but a gee fling!"

The flames flew, arcing over the ground towards the closest enemies. It looked like a small meteor ran through the orc it impacted.

"I got next. Also that only counts for one," Zan said, passing mana to him.

"Aye, that will work," Andrew said, passing the controls to her. "Now aim with—"

She took the controls, her eyes alight. Her shot hit two orcs and a dwarf.

"Three!" she squealed.

Andrew wasn't afraid for himself. He feared what she could do with his tools. After all, he made the tool, but she supplied the ammunition.

The flames began to spark into a wildfire behind them. Andrew turned his attention to their surroundings. He didn't know how dry the tall grass was, but it wouldn't take much.

"Three!" Andrew said.

"Well, this is going to be something, Andrew. I think that this is going to save us," Zan said, swapping out with him. Neither one of them was certain how long that the gee thing would last. The testing was supposed to go on the following day, and barring some initial test runs that day, the pair had run out of time. His gee thing was getting its field test today.

"I hope that we can get Julie back to full working strength, because this might spread into a larger fire if we're not careful," Andrew said, aiming at the nearest set of orcs. He flung another volley of flame, hitting their legs. "Two!"

"We need to worry about getting out of here first. That and are we finally getting further away from them? Did the horses pick up the pace?"

"Perhaps the fire did something? I would want to trot my arse off if I saw that behind me. I know that they have a vague sense of what's going on," he said.

***

Bob, Mork's best-in-show pony, knelt in the back of the first caravan.

An unconscious Anthony was there. He was probably going to make it through. Bob had spent all of his mana, then waited two full minutes before doing it again. He knew that he was going to have to go out there. His work wasn't done, but without Anthony himself acting as the cleric, he was going to have to fill in. Their backup healer, Finley, was in the next wagon—his original wagon—laying prostrate. Bob had given the green man one look before stepping in to deal with Julie's stoic face.

She had sat next to Bob, and without saying anything, they both had an understanding of how important Anthony was to their survival. Both of them would do their damned best to destroy their enemies.

Bob began to keep pace with the rear caravan. The uncovered wagon, the group's first new set of wheels, had served them well. It now looked like it had a grenade gun mounted on the back. At least that was how the brass instrument looked to Bob.

The caravan started to put distance between themselves and the horde. The two living orcs sat huddled in the last wagon as Zan and Andrew went at it. Sophie and Bella, he had ordered to take the front, leading the caravan back to Arva.

43

"I'm just wondering what man fumbled the play so bad that you're out here running without a boyfriend?" Anthony whispered, looking up at her. Julie loomed over the wounded midwife.

Inside the first house, a makeshift infirmary housed the wounded. It was cleared out except for the cot on which Anthony lay. Finley, he had been told, was in the master bedroom.

"Aw, you're sweet, but you are a bit too old for me. You need to be resting, Anthony," Julie said.

"I thought you said that age wasn't a barrier the last two times?" he replied, holding her hand from the cot. "Just because my back was broken, doesn't mean that we can't do the thing we did at Arva that one time."

"You need to rest, alright?" Julie replied. "You've done enough for the rest of us and we need you at full strength when we determine our next route."

"How is Finley?" Anthony said.

"Much the same. Everything tells us that he is alive, but no one's medicine skill is giving any helpful hints on what to do. It's like he is in a coma."

Anthony really wanted to sit up, but the orders were to stay put for at least a day. Then they would use a full torso cast until he was recovered. It wasn't going to be something that he was excited for, but he had given enough sets of post-delivery instructions to at least listen to his medical provider and spymaster.

"You want Bob to come talk to me, don't you? Or is it Bob that wants to talk to me?"

"He wants to make sure you're okay. I don't know if he even wants to be in charge. He feels terrible about what happened to Finley and you. He has been beating himself up. Thankfully Bella is with him. She'll set him straight."

Anthony winced. "Has she been hitting the stein hard? Finley and I were worried about her before."

"She's an adult. She can do what she wants," Julie said. "That said, I think she understands."

Anthony was worried about Bella. He was worried about the whole group, but in particular Bella seemed to have been hit pretty hard. Julie had felt like the classic Canadian stoic who wouldn't say a bad thing about her neighbor.

"Alright. How are you doing?" he asked. "Has anyone asked you that yet?"

"I mean, I'm not the one with the broken back," she said.

"It's just a bone wound. Probably. If we didn't have magic, I would have already died."

"I would have died a long time ago. I might have already died," she said. "This is a really crappy afterlife if so."

Anthony gripped her hand, as she leaned in. Her touch had him focused on how good it felt that he didn't have to think about the group's safety and security, at least for the moment. The worry that they would be attacked or overrun had been a constant problem. Now that one of the death knights had been dealt with, they could rest for at least a short time.

"You know I just met you a few days ago and it's been a while since I went on a date, but uh, do you think that we might try?" he said.

"I think we can go on a date," she said, squeezing his hand. "That would be quite nice."

"It will give me something to look forward to."

Kissing his forehead, she let him know that she would also be looking forward to it.

***

Bob, current commander of Mork's last caravan, was excited at the prospect of a lighter watch schedule. Borgan and Song had volunteered to take the night shift for some time.

"Are you both certain that you're okay with that?" he said.

"Your feline creature saved us from having to carve up our relatives. That, in itself, feels blessed," Borgan said. "The night will soon be upon us and we need to repay our debts to you. Both of us have a night vision skill and Song thinks that we need time to mourn. I understand if this is strange to you."

The orc had applied black paint in between some of the cracks in his tattoo. His brother's entire face was covered in black ink.

"If you want to take your time, we understand. I think we are going to spend some time here while we figure out where to go next. I think that I speak for all of us when I say that I appreciate your help out there. You might not think that you did much, but I felt it," Bob said, extending his arm.

Borgan accepted the hand and turned the handshake into a bro hug. Bob, unused to being the little one in the hug equation, gracefully accepted it.

Borgan left him to return to his brother. The night after their victory, nearly the entire caravan stayed up the whole night. It hadn't turned into a party, as there had still been orcs that they had to kill on their way back to Arva. It had become a watch session where people were allowed to drink from time to time. Anthony, as keeper of the watch schedule, hadn't designated who would take it, so everyone volunteered.

Bob had made half of them sleep at around midnight to make sure that someone would be there to guard them during the day. The horses were only so good at early warnings.

Bob turned to watch the herd as it peacefully grazed around the house that had become an infirmary. The horses had kept their own vigil. After they had arrived, Brandon had let them all free to roam inside their staging grounds. The horses had accepted water when it was presented, but had really clung to the house where Anthony and Finley were.

He wanted to talk to them but knew that he could only go so far. They could accept simple commands when he used animal handling. All but two were trained war beasts with the exceptions being the tinker-trained mares. Julie had let him know that Anthony was getting his strength back, which was enough for him. If Finley was able to break out of his coma, then they would be in a better place.

Bob saw that Bella was setting up dinner. His stomach grumbled loudly, asking why it hadn't been satiated. He made his way over to the pot; it was time to tend to his needs. He couldn't wait to hand back the reins to Anthony. The fire pit was equidistant from the two houses, roughly in the center of their walls. It really wasn't far but he didn't want to be asked another question.

Too many questions about what the group of them would do next had risen up. With Anthony, they had a leader with a vision. With Finley, they had the best and only local guide.

Without either? It was going to be tough.

∗∗∗

"He is taking this hard, huh?" Sophie said.

Bob was working his way to them slowly. Apparently he wanted to make sure that all of the horses were still aligned. Bella and Sophie saw him talking with Julie.

"At least we will get the update from Julie," Bella said. "Anthony might be doing better, but Finley—"

Both women shuddered. Seeing the person they had trusted so much have his arm cut off after he began to attack was a visceral reminder of what they had gone through. Sophie didn't have any idea what he was going through, but she really felt for the elf.

"Do you think that he is going to be alright? Nobody really has any idea. I mean we used to see cases in the hospital where people got injured or they hurt themselves but like it was a mental hospital. If they had physical problems they would go to a normal hospital."

Bella stirred the pot a few times. Sophie had been handing her vegetables every now and then once they were done being cut up. She had really perfected her chopping. It was a shame that they didn't have any onions. The little stock they did have had been quickly eaten as it gave the potatoes flavor.

"Sophie, do you know what I would do for a fucking bottle of ketchup right now?"

"I don't know, what?"

"Terrible, terrible things," Bella said, waving her spoon in the air. "But I can't have any ketchup. And I sure as heck can't fix Anthony myself or you know I would be in there fixing him. And the same of course goes for Finley."

"You know Bella, if we had some sugar and some tomatoes, then I could probably make some ketchup. It would only have to be refrigerated," Sophie said. "I am willing to bet that your boyfriend over there knows how. So, if you don't ask him, what I'm saying is that I will."

Bob finally arrived, as if summoned.

"Well, here is the man in question. Bob. Do you think that you could make some ketchup if we had tomatoes?"

"Do we have tomatoes? Because if so then heck yes," he said, pulling his hood down. He warmed his hands on the fire. A few seconds later, Bella grabbed him around the waist from behind.

Sophie decided that that was about the time for her to go check on some of her other interests.

"I'm going to take a break," she said, stepping back. "Heading to the clubhouse."

"Stop trying to make 'clubhouse' happen," Bella said. "It's not happening."

No matter what her sidekick said, Sophie was going to call the house that wasn't the infirmary the club house. It was too bad that Bella would be the last one to call it that.

She flicked up the set of cards that had caught her eye. Without Finley to distribute the loot equitably, she took it upon herself to organize their haul. She held six cards that had the power to change the course of someone's life.

<table>
<tr><td>

Uncommon Skill Card: Eldritch Spellcasting Level 1

This card grants mana.

This card grants access to eldritch spells.

</td></tr>
<tr><td>

Uncommon Skill Card: Ritual Casting Level 2

This card grants mana.

This card gives knowledge about how to cast prepared and ritual spells.

</td></tr>
<tr><td>

Common Skill Card: Enchantment Level 1

This card allows the user to imbue objects with mana. Effects depend on the related spell.

</td></tr>
<tr><td>

Common Skill Card: Survival Level 5

The wielder is heartier and knows how to make the best of a bad situation.

</td></tr>
<tr><td>

Common Skill Card: Medicine Level 1

The wielder knows how to do basic first aid and some secondary aid.

</td></tr>
<tr><td>

Common Skill Card: Patron Pact Level 1

The wielder may arrange one pact bond through ritual magic. Benefits of the bond will be defined by the pact.

</td></tr>
</table>

With the five she had, she was certain to make a warlock card. Julie had been exceedingly strong with her warlock class and Sophie wanted to make one for herself.

She hadn't envisioned turning herself into a rogue, much less adding wilderness druid and warlock to the mix, but the group needed more firepower. Anthony had wanted a monk card, because he foolishly wanted to be on the front lines. Sophie wanted to be safe in the back with the ammunition.

She grabbed the parts that she needed and the frame. If what Finley had said was correct then she was about to add to her already large arsenal.

Sophie smiled and began to assemble her next card.

***

Bella and Bob finished cooking all of the dinner.

"Hey Bob, do you think you can do the cleanup?" Bella asked. "I think I'm going to go have a bit of a nap before my night shift. You're joining me on that one, right?"

"Oh I forgot to tell you. Borgan and Song asked if they could take the night shift. Since we helped them out so much and they wanted some time to themselves. Also they have dark vision which is something that none of us have without using magic. I figured that one of us would check on them every few hours to make sure they're all right but other than that, you are free for the night."

Bella paused, staying in place. All the energy she put into getting up disappeared into the ether. "I am free? Huh. You're still cleaning up, though?"

"Yes, I am. Now I was thinking that we could go on a little moonlit stroll tonight and celebrate," he said. "Is that something you would be interested in?"

"That sounds lovely. Let me go to the powder room and freshen up," Bella said, accepting Bob's hand to get up. "Oh Bob, did I tell you what Sophie named her spear?"

Bob looked up from the cleaning bin. "No, you didn't? What did she name her spear?"

"She named it Bob."

"Probably because Bob is a great name," Bob said, smiling back at her.

Bella went back to the clubhouse. She was not going to give Sophie the pleasure of letting her know that was what she also called it. She would hold out for as long as possible. Sophie had already vacated their team room, so Bella was alone.

It was a perfect time to look into her large dwarven made pocket.

Bella brought out her newest prize. "Aww, yeah that's the good stuff," she said. "This world is going to be mine."

"Is that the Chateau de… Bella, this smells great."

She uncorked the bottle. It was their time now.

44

"I'm going to call this meeting to order. It is come to my attention 'cuz some of you fuck-ups, and I say that in the most generous, loving way, need to have some sort of therapy in your lives. So being the experts that we are, Julie and I have decided to help you all out. We're going to call this group therapy. I want to say that it's mandatory, but you all showed up, so good on you." Sophie said, locking eyes with a dozen people at the same time. "We just went through a lot. We're going to go through some more. Now we're going to talk about what we're doing. I'm going to give this an hour, though we may take more or less time."

A chorus of groans greeted her. Julie had been good enough to give them an elevation from which to conduct this meeting. Each person had an earthen seat exactly molded to their specifications.

"Your enthusiasm is noted. This is something I did a lot in the hospital. You can share as much or as little as you want to. The point of this is that you can speak freely about this and not let it weigh you down over time. Some of the things we experienced out there, no one should ever have to experience in their life," Sophie continued, talking to the crowd.

The elevated therapy room was reachable only by ladder. Its dual purpose was to allow them to see in all directions, while they were effectively a tower in the middle of Arva.

Sophie continued, "Shit I used to have people that had PTSD just from normal activities. I had people come in because their parents had tortured them throughout their life acting as narcissists. We don't have the luxury of not being a functional team. And with that, our social worker wants to facilitate this discussion." She turned to Julie.

"What we have to do is work together and if we have to process our feelings, we need to do it away from all of the zombies," Julie said. "This isn't some tough love situation. In fact, I would like to go first. If no one has any objections? Nobody? Okay. This last week has been something of a rush for me. I feel like I never really got a break between the working and the spellcasting to make our defenses and, well, the time I spent with Anthony. We all had a lot going on. We all had very important roles, very specific roles that kept us alive."

Julie paused to drink water.

"Therapy isn't a punishment. It's a journey. You get to go to therapy precisely because you survived. You shouldn't feel guilty about surviving. But you don't need to feel relieved either. In fact, any emotion you feel about that is valid and we understand. Killing one death knight took a lot out of most of us. Though I don't know what we're going to be doing next, three more exist. Each one is a crime against humanity."

Sophie let the silence permeate the group. Having fifteen people agree on anything was difficult. Having all of them agree to be a party to this was another thing entirely. Keeping them all in tune for that entire week, that was all thanks to Anthony and Bob. Finley also played a big role in that as well. The fact that he wasn't doing so well right now really made her sad.

Bella had helped by bringing everyone's lunch out here. Or the fact that the lookout was three stories up. Felt amazing. Not having any balconies or railings though? That felt like courting death.

Sophie drank a big drink of her water. Julie was explaining her experiences to a rapt audience. Whatever happened after the first death knight had been taken down, they had all grown closer.

***

In the five days since Julie had been summoned to this world, she had learned a ton about the people she had come with. She learned a bit about the world as well, but places alone didn't make her passionate. She loved a good beach day like every girl and for how far Regina was from any beach… she missed Cancún.

The one person, besides Anthony, that had been a wealth of information, had been Finley. His comatose state would hopefully be resolved when Anthony was back to full strength. Just because someone was strong at healing others didn't mean that it came for free.

There was one person, or at least one patron who might be able to tip the scales in her favor.

She found a quiet space in the room that had either belonged to an accountant or a dwarven child who needed such services. Setting the tone of the ritual, she moved slowly and deliberately. It was the third time that she would be speaking directly to her patron and she had the insight to do it simpler.

It took two minutes to align herself. The tie-dye shirt popped with color that didn't quite align with reality as Cara popped into existence. She still looked like a teenager who had been in detention for far too long and was thinking of creative ways to get into trouble.

"Took you long enough, then?" she said. "Great work on the death knight. Mork is displeased with our meddling, but his own chosen decided to not rush in."

"Cara, apologies that I do not have anything for you to toke," Julie said, sitting down cross legged. "I'm not even sure how the dwarves did it, to be honest."

"Well now that we know each other a bit better, I was thinking: what boon you would want from me?"

"What exactly is on the table here? I know that I'm basically some mortal instrument to clean up whatever this mess is, but I don't know what I'm allowed to ask for. Can I ask for a special card? Do you know what other cards the three death knights that remain have?"

"You got the gate spell, one of the more powerful cards. The other three, they are shrouded from me. It is rather unfortunate, however none of them have a gate card so you can rest assured that you are safe, unless one of the others finds a gate card."

Julie blinked several times.

"Is—is that likely?"

"Not very. As the card itself is epic class, its use was tightly controlled. Others similar to it had drawbacks. Whoever had them in their soul decks has not joined one of the other three in any form yet. You can imagine how valuable such a card would be, and how easily stolen."

"That's good, right? Epic cards are rare but… There are others and they're not in use?"

"I would prefer that you travel by Cara-van but sometimes a little jaunt here and there can shore up your stores. That information was free, by the by. You can still choose a boon."

"Can you do anything about Finley?" Julie said, her voice lowering. She clenched her fists. She was going to ask for unspeakable cosmic powers, but would settle for getting her friend and tour guide back.

"The green?"

"The elf?"

"Oh, my dear. That being you call Finley? He was never an elf."

End Book One

ACKNOWLEDGEMENTS

This series would not have been possible without so many people but in particular the otters: Maxine, Max, Alexa, Freya, Sebastian and Tamsin.

I would like to thank my writing group partners: Machine Capybara, Delilah Waan, Ivy C. Kendall, Caitlin L. Strauss, and Dan Harris.

Additionally, I was helped by some old crusty veteran named Joe Gillespie, and my personal devil's advocate Zaq.

The biggest thanks goes to my wife Frances for putting up with this.

ABOUT THE AUTHOR

JP Weaver was born in North Jersey and finally, over many years, escaped to South Jersey and lived in the Pine Barrens. He is now in North Carolina, which is also a land of pines. Unfortunately, pine trees do not drop pineapples.

As many of you are aware one does not have to be human to be on the internet and therefore JP can neither confirm nor deny that they are an otter hive mind, nor that such a being exists. The otters love the beach, dungeons, and dragons (was it that obvious?), and dad jokes. Rumors persist that Brandon Sanderson and the otters have not been seen at the same time, but those rumors are 100% true.

Find out more about causality, paradoxes, and Xianxia at
http://www.storyweaver.quest

Sign up for JP Weavers newsletter directly at
https://storyweaver.beehiiv.com/subscribe

Follow us:

riverfolkbooks.com

Facebook /riverfolkp

Bluesky /riverfolkbooks.bsky.social

Instagram /riverfolkp

If you want to discuss our books with other readers and maybe even the author, join our discord server using the link on our website